THE SAINT PETERSBURG FILE

A JACOB HUNTER THRILLER

DAVID ARCHER

DAMIEN WILD

The characters and events portrayed in this ebook are fictitious. Any similarity to real persons, living or dead, is coincidental and not intended by the author.

ISBN-13: 978-1-63696-471-3

ISBN-10: 1-63696-471-0

Printed in the United States of America

www.righthouse.com

www.instagram.com/righthousebooks

www.facebook.com/righthousebooks

twitter.com/righthousebooks

JACOB HUNTER THRILLER

The Kyiv File (Book 1)
The Bogotá File (Book 2)
The Havana File (Book 3)
The Amsterdam File (Book 4)
The Saint Petersburg File (Book 5)

PROLOGUE

Corporal Indrek Laanoja had been on shift at the Estonian Intelligence Center's Border Surveillance Office since midnight. He was twenty-one, nearing the end of his conscription rotation, and already counting down the weeks. In another month he would be back at university, studying politics and American literature, worrying about exams instead of border lines and flickering screens.

For now, he sat alone in the dim operations room, watching the feeds do what they always did.

He leaned closer to the monitor covering the eastern edge of Lake Peipsi. The lake hadn't frozen over yet; surface skim ice had formed near the shore, but the open water was still navigable. Most nights all he could see on the screen was the occasional slow-moving patrol craft on either side of the border. Tonight, something caught his eye.

Movement.

At first he thought it was nothing more than a cluster of vehicles parked along the Russian shoreline, maybe trucks pulled in under the trees. He adjusted the image and looked again. They were lined up neatly, closer together than he was used to seeing. No headlights, no obvious activity, but the moonlight picked out straight edges and hard surfaces that didn't belong to civilian traffic.

Indrek frowned. He wasn't an expert, but he'd been staring at this stretch of border for months. He knew the usual patterns: a guard post, a slow patrol, nothing more. This didn't fit.

He switched to another feed, one with slightly better clarity. The shapes resolved enough for him to make out armored vehicles, the kind he'd seen in training videos rather than real life. He couldn't have named the models with confidence, but he knew military hardware when he saw it. Closer to the water, darker shapes were being moved toward the shoreline. Boats, larger than the fishing craft he was used to, sitting low and wide in the water.

His mouth went dry.

Indrek tapped his headset. "Major Saar? Sir, are you there?"

Static crackled, followed by a tired exhale. "Laanoja, do you know what time it is?"

"Yes, sir. Zero-three-hundred."

"That was rhetorical. If this isn't urgent, you'd better have a good reason."

"I'm seeing something odd on the Lake Peipsi feeds, sir. Southern sector. Vehicles staged near the shore and boats as well."

There was a pause, then a soft chuckle. "You're new, aren't you, Laanoja?"

"Relatively, sir."

"Us old hands know the Russians love to show off when conditions allow. They'll pack it up by morning."

Indrek swallowed. "Sir, I understand, but this doesn't look like the usual activity I've been seeing. There are multiple armored vehicles lined up, and the boats look like they could carry more than a few men."

Silence, then the scrape of a chair and the sound of keys. "Give me the coordinates."

Indrek read them off, his eyes never leaving the screen. The line stayed quiet longer this time.

"Damn it," Saar muttered. "All right, I see it. How long have they been there?"

"I noticed them about five minutes ago, sir. There's been more movement since."

"You think they're setting up for a crossing?"

"I don't know, sir," Indrek said honestly.

Another pause. "Stay on the feeds. Record everything. I'm calling the colonel."

The connection ended.

Indrek leaned back slightly, his pulse racing as he watched the silhouettes inch closer to the water. Small figures moved between the vehicles, organizing themselves in a way that made his stomach tighten. He thought about the agreement announced only days earlier, the one everyone on television had called historic. Guarantees of peace, cooperation, and stability.

It didn't feel stable now.

Three sharp knocks sounded at the door behind him.

Indrek stiffened. No one was supposed to be on this floor at this hour except the duty guards, and they had no reason to knock. He stood slowly and turned.

"Hello?"

No answer. The knock came again, louder.

"Open the door, Indrek," a familiar voice called. "The colonel wants another set of eyes. He wants to make sure you're not imagining things."

Relief washed through him as he recognized Corporal Mihkel Vares. He unlocked the door and pulled it open.

Vares stepped in fast, too fast, and the man beside him followed before Indrek could speak. He barely had time to register the stranger's scarred face before both of them slammed him back against the desk. A gun appeared in Vares's hand, aimed squarely at his chest.

"Don't move," Vares said. "Do exactly what you're told."

Indrek froze, shock rooting him in place.

The stranger struck him hard across the jaw. His glasses flew off, skittering across the floor. Hands yanked his arms behind his back, forcing him down. Tape bit into his wrists, then went around his ankles. Something rough was jammed into his mouth and sealed tight.

They left him on the floor, breath coming through his nostrils in ragged bursts. The men had failed to notice Laanoja's thumb brushing the underside of the desk as he fell. The panic button had clicked silently.

The stranger dropped into Indrek's chair and began working the keyboard with practiced speed. Files were opened, copied, and transferred to a small flash drive. Without his glasses, Indrek could only see blurred shapes.

It didn't take long.

The man pulled the drive free and stood. Vares looked down at Indrek, his expression inscrutable.

"No witnesses."

The gun went off. Pain tore through Indrek's body, stealing his breath. A second shot followed, and the world began to shimmer like a desert mirage.

Shouts echoed from the corridor. Boots thundered on the concrete floor. Voices barked commands. A burst of gunfire erupted just beyond the door.

Indrek lay still, blood spreading beneath him, his vision fading. He was terrified of approaching death, but a sense of calm lay beneath the terror. He had done his duty, raised the alarm.

He closed his eyes for the last time.

ONE

"ANOTHER APEROL SPRITZ, MY DARLING?" SAID JACOB Hunter, pushing back his opaque sunglasses to rub a speck of grit from his eye. As always with her, he spoke Russian, one of the many languages he was fluent in. He squinted in the afternoon sun for a moment before pulling the shades down again. The view from the restaurant at the top of Lisbon's famous landmark, the Santa Justa Elevador, was spectacular. Lights were beginning to twinkle among the sea of terracotta-tiled roofs.

"*Davai!* Sure!" Irina Frolova—Jacob's partner in life and sometimes in work—reached out and stroked his hand gently. He relished the glow of warmth radiating from her body.

Three minutes later, he returned clutching fresh drinks.

"Thanks for bringing me to Lisbon, *zaichik*," Irina said, reaching for her glass. "I love it. Peaceful and... somehow I feel totally safe. Like nothing can touch us."

"I feel the same."

"It's weird," said Irina thoughtfully, "but even the people peddling on the streets seem less aggressive than anywhere else. Why would that be?"

Jacob ventured a guess—the local laid-back vibe was so ingrained that no outsiders could change it.

"It's just a façade, though, isn't it, Yakov? All that happiness on display?" she said, the Russian version of his name sounding like poetry in her mouth.

"Maybe," Jacob admitted, flipping a beer coaster back and forth in his fingers.

Irina took a long sip. "You think someone can track us down here?"

He pulled his lips into a tight, pensive frown. "I doubt it. We're far enough off the radar."

Even if someone were actively looking, he and Irina were experts at keeping a low profile. They had made small physical changes, too. Behavioral shifts. Irina wore her hair in a different style each month; Jacob placed a wedge of foam in one shoe to alter his gait.

Three years had passed since Jacob's last mission, two since the Amsterdam fiasco. His identity—and Irina's—had been blown apart when Irina was kidnapped. With the Dutch cops running the case, Jacob had been powerless to stop the publicity, meaning future operations abroad became problematic. To the point of being impossible. He was still officially employed by the clandestine agency, but its boss had deemed the heat was still on, and Jacob sat on the sidelines. Despite the efforts of the newly elected US president to smooth things over, his life was still in peril, although the degree had decreased over time. By Fletcher's reckoning, next year Jacob would be back in the game.

Two years cooped up in the acreage property had seemed like an eternity. A beautiful estate on the shores of Keuka Lake in upstate New York with plenty of land to ride trail bikes and horses, the home was still a virtual prison. After the first year with new fake identities, they had gotten braver, disguising themselves and embarking on short outings of varying distance. After twelve months, they took a road trip to Vegas, partying like honeymooners. And they had absolutely loved it.

This was their first trip overseas since Amsterdam, where Jacob had been forced to steal a piece of art in exchange for

Irina's release. Their freedom was ultimately won thanks to a brilliant CIA agent, without whom both of them would surely be dead. A traumatic experience, but they were both made of stern stuff.

But after two years, they'd decided enough was enough. Time to spread their wings once again and face the world head-on. It took a lot of mental preparation, with Jacob and Irina realizing they could be "made," that word could get back to a number of ruthless enemies they had made over the years. On balance, however, they concluded that the risk was worth the benefit to their mental health.

"I wasn't entirely sure about Portugal," said Jacob, picking up the laminated menu. Irina broke out in a radiant smile, and the dimples in her cheeks deepened. "That it would meet with your approval." He held his beer to the light, observing the little bubbles rising to the top. "It's not one of Europe's most glamorous destinations."

She laughed off the comment. "Shabby chic I think is the English expression, *da?*"

"You nailed it." He nodded, taking a swig of a local beer.

"Where to after this?" said Irina, studying the ramparts of Saint George's castle in the distance, then looking across to the broad Tagus River.

"The Algarve. The water's turning chilly, maybe too cold for swimming."

She shook her head, loose brunette curls waving. "Nonsense, Yakov. I've swum in icy Russian rivers. A little cold water isn't going to stop me having fun."

"That's the spirit. One more day here in Lisbon, then a week by the seaside."

A server approached, nodding deferentially as he cleared a space on the table and put down a silver platter of assorted seafood. Grilled sardines formed a small mountain in the middle, with lobster, crab, scallops, and chunks of fried cod placed around the perimeter.

Harpooning a lightly charred piece of fish, Jacob said, "This food makes up for everything else Lisbon lacks."

Irina pressed her lips together, unable to decide where to begin. Finally, she picked up a shrimp and sucked the meat with slurps of satisfaction. Wiping juice from her mouth, she voiced her agreement. "*Ochen' vkusno!* Delicious!"

The waiter returned carrying a chilled bottle of chardonnay. He uncorked the bottle and poured a small measure for Jacob to sample. In fluent Portuguese, Jacob said, "Full glasses for both of us. I don't like this tasting charade."

The waiter burst out laughing. "If I don't do it, I get my ass kicked by the boss."

"It beats me how you can speak so many languages," said Irina through compressed lips as the waiter retreated. "I spent a month learning basic Portuguese for this trip, but I didn't catch any of the exchange between you and that man!"

"You know it's all down to the knock in the head I got playing football. Before that, I barely passed high school Spanish." It was a white lie. He'd passed easily, but his capacity for learning other languages was indeed down to a skull-crushing concussion. He'd been knocked out cold trying to score the touchdown that would have given his school its first-ever championship. Jacob's freakishly acquired savant-like talent was a blessing and a curse.

"I'm still jealous," she said. "Russian and English is all I'll ever be good at."

He caressed her hand, lingering as he lightly brushed the tops of her fingers. "There are other things you're very good at," he said with a sly grin.

"You referring to my IT skills?"

He winked. "That too."

Later, they took a leisurely evening stroll through the Praça do Comércio, a vast public square hugging the banks of the Tagus River. Next, they checked out a packed bar, shared another bottle, this time a robust red, and listened to the plaintive crooning of singers performing in the melancholic fado style. Jacob and Irina held hands under the table like new lovers as the beautiful voices rang out in the smoke-filled tavern.

At a quarter to midnight, as Jacob stood at the window of their apartment in the Alfama district, he marveled at how Irina had stayed with him after all the shit she'd been through. His heart ached with love for her.

She called out his name—as always, Yakov in the Russian way—mischief in her tone. He turned to see her naked, glistening from a shower, sliding between the sheets. Closing the shutters, he approached the bed, heart hammering with desire, a feeling that hadn't faded since they'd first made love.

A glowing light on his bedside table stopped him in his tracks.

The text came from a cell phone number he hadn't seen for years. No name came up, but he knew who it was. His boss, Grant Fletcher.

And it could only mean trouble.

Big. Fucking. Trouble.

TWO

Clanking sounds, like metal striking metal, registered in the deep recesses of his awakening consciousness. The bleeping and blipping of medical tech, echoing voices, and footsteps. Fragments of memory began to spark through the prefrontal cortex of his brain, chasing away the fading haze of anesthesia. He remembered a phone call, urgency in Fletcher's voice. Desperation verging on hysteria—unusual for the normally circumspect man. Mention of a plea for help coming directly from President McIvor.

There was panic in the White House. Grown men and women shitting their pants in the Pentagon. Urgent action was required, but all orthodox approaches were doomed to fail. Hence, McIvor had reached out to Fletcher. There was even a vague promise to alter Jacob's contract by removing Article 7, the "no get-out clause," should he succeed in his task. Other agencies and operatives had been considered, but none were deemed capable of stopping the Russians. Only Jacob Hunter was rated as having any chance of thwarting the implacable enemy.

Then came a hastily arranged charter flight from an airfield outside Lisbon to Zurich, Switzerland. An even more hastily arranged safe house for Irina, somewhere in central Portugal. She had refused to return to the United States; her offer to assist Jacob remotely from a European base was accepted by Fletcher with gratitude. The two-hour time difference between Portugal and Saint Petersburg meant she could communicate with Jacob in near real time.

He recalled the bumpy flight through stormy skies. Greeted in Switzerland by Fletcher in an armored limousine, speeding along the snow-lined motorway to a secret medical facility.

The haze cleared faster now as he drifted back into consciousness.

Jacob blinked his heavy, sticky eyelids—once, twice, three times. The light in the room forced him to squint as he adjusted to the clinical brightness. The urge to cough struck, an insane tickling that started in the chest and moved quickly into his throat—but he couldn't do it. Nor could he close his mouth. His dry lips formed a circle but could compress no more than the circumference of the hard object wedged in his mouth. *Must be a tube running down my neck.* He sensed sweat beading on his brow. Unable to swallow, his sense of helplessness soared off the scale. His head felt like it was in a vise; the only place to look was up.

A BLUE SURGICAL mask hovered into his line of sight. Above the mask were big brown eyes beneath bushy brows. A doctor—thank God. The man spoke in a reassuring, soothing voice, the Swiss accent rising and falling. "I'm going to remove the breathing tube in a moment. The swelling has gone down enough for you to breathe on your own."

He'd had surgery multiple times before but always woke up afterward without an object stuffed down his neck—the normal way it's done. In a normal freaking hospital.

As if reading his mind, the surgeon continued, using arcane medical terms Jacob only partially understood. The gist was clear: Operations to the face and neck can, rarely, cause enough swelling to warrant the intrusive air hose. The medical team had monitored him for twelve hours, constantly observing, until the tube could be removed. "Whoever your boss is wasn't happy about the delay in you waking up."

Five minutes later, Jacob was groggy but able to pull himself halfway to a sitting position and chug half a liter of tepid water before collapsing onto his back again. The urge to cough manifested, the barking sound alarming to his own ear. The doctor assured him it would pass. A female nurse secured a cuff around his upper arm, inflated it by pressing a button, then placed a plastic clip on his index finger. A minute passed in silence before she removed it. "In the normal range," she said robotically, then left him in the bare room.

The Swiss doctor stayed, peeling off his mask and sitting on the edge of the bed. He folded his hands in his lap, calm and professional.

"I understand you were briefed on the procedure pre-op. Correct?"

Jacob nodded. "Yes," he croaked. "I know you've changed my appearance."

"*Ja, genau*. Yes, precisely," said the doctor with a curt nod. "You've undergone an RIA procedure. Rapid Identity Alteration. You may have heard something about this breakthrough protocol."

He nodded. Some months back, he'd read an article about preliminary experimentation in this area. Cutting-edge technology, far superior to traditional plastic surgery.

"Today," continued the doctor, "you have the honor of being the first person to have had the full treatment." He gave a thin-lipped smile and tapped a clipboard with a ballpoint pen. "And survive to tell the tale. Congratulations."

"Forgive me for not sharing your enthusiasm," Jacob rasped. "Care to explain exactly what you did to me?"

The doctor smiled broadly, then cleared his throat. "We placed micro-ceramic scaffolds on your orbital ridge and jawline. These have shifted your bone contours enough to reduce the chance of cameras recognizing you as... yourself. Also, your facial dermis has been layered with a bioengineered graft, subtly changing pore density and texture." The smile widened. "Best of all, we've accelerated recovery time with a hormone-laden skin regeneration gel, which is why you are not horribly bruised right now. Normally, the amount of bone and skin treatment you had would require a minimum six-week recovery. But not for you. A NATO lab in Iceland has developed what we call a recombinant peptide, KAP8—a piece of magic that will have you up and about in forty-eight hours. Is that not miraculous?"

"If you say so. I still feel like I've been tackled by a 300-pound tight end."

The doctor shook his head. "I have no idea what that means, but I shall beg your indulgence and continue." He leaned closer, lowering his voice. "Moderate discomfort is expected after the operation but will soon pass." He toyed with his spectacles. "And here's another fascinating aspect. We trimmed your hair very short, then reset the follicles. Your hair growth pattern and pigmentation will begin to alter within thirty-six hours."

"I beg your pardon?" Jacob's mind spun.

"Your hairline will recede at the sides, a bald patch will form on your crown. The remaining hair will have a salt-and-pepper appearance. Very dashing."

The urge to punch this condescending asshole in the face was almost overwhelming. "You what!"

The doctor held up one hand. "Please. This part of the procedure—all of it—is reversible with drugs and more surgery. We can make you look exactly as before. Do not panic."

"Easy for you to say." Jacob felt a hard lump bulge in his throat as he gulped. "Anything else?"

"*Ja.* We've made an adjustment to your eyes." The doctor paused to pop a mint in his mouth. "Semi-permanent overlays that bond directly to the cornea—greenish-hazel instead of your natural blue. Very becoming."

Jacob grunted.

"They will last six months before melting away."

Jacob blinked slowly. "Is that it? Didn't cut my dick in half, did you?"

"Of course not," the doctor said, blushing bright pink.

"How different am I going to look from the real me?"

"You already look very different."

"Define very."

The doctor coughed into a fist. "Perhaps a fifteen to twenty percent deviation from your original baseline. That's the margin we can create in this time frame. But similarity and difference are subjective."

Jacob pressed his palms into the mattress, wondering if he could push himself all the way up. Not yet. "What if someone who's dealt with me in the past looks me in the eye?"

"I guarantee they will not recognize you." The doctor smiled tightly. "Our medical advances guarantee your anonymity."

A tingling ran through Jacob's fingers; he instinctively held them up to look.

"I was told the place they're sending you may have records of your biometric data," the doctor continued. "Therefore, a minor procedure was performed. Effect lasts about a month, maybe six weeks."

Jacob stared at his hands.

"We micro-abraded the top layer of skin and bonded biopolymer fingerprint overlays with artificial ridges. Mild tenderness for a day or two, then exactly like your own skin."

"What about voice matching?"

"Good question. Larynx surgery was considered, but it's too risky. May I suggest—"

"No, you may not." Jacob gestured toward the door. In perfect Swiss German: he added, "Fuck off, Doc. I'd like some alone time."

He dozed for a while, then awoke with burgeoning strength in his limbs. The healing hormone must have been doing its job. He swung himself off the bed and walked gingerly across the cold tiles to the small bathroom, drip-bag stand in tow.

Inside, he emptied a seemingly never-ending stream of urine into the toilet, washed his tingling hands, then turned to the mirror.

The first thing that struck him was the lack of bandages and dressings. In his teens, he'd had a small, suspicious lump removed from his left ear, after which his head had been wrapped like a Christmas present. The lump proved benign, and the wound had taken two weeks to heal. This time, the surgery had been much more serious—his face had been cut, sliced, stitched back together. Objects inserted, drugs and hormones injected. No walk in the park. Yet the only evidence of the operation was an assortment of light pink marks covered with transparent strips of biofilm. Around the temples, along the jawline, under the eyes. That was it.

But the transformation in appearance was already obvious. And the changes would accelerate over the next thirty-six to forty-eight hours. The hazel-green eyes stared back at him like a stranger. He couldn't help the faintest of smiles tugging at the wound sites. The damn doctor had been right—the new color did suit him. He wondered how Irina would react if she saw him now.

Jacob grazed his cheek softly. It was the same skin in texture and underlying color, yet somehow different. He took a deep breath, feeling a sharp twinge in his right shoulder. One second of worry, then he remembered shoulder pain was a common side-effect of general anesthesia.

Returning to the bed, a wave of fatigue washed over him. The second he got himself reasonably comfortable, he heard footsteps outside the door.

The handle turned abruptly, and a man in a glossy gray suit entered. Without a word, he placed Jacob's cell phone on the overbed table. Then he reached into the carry bag slung around his shoulder, extracted a silver laptop, and put it next to the phone.

"Not even going to introduce..." Jacob placed a fist over his mouth to cover a cough. "...yourself?" His voice sounded as thick as molasses.

"Sorry. I thought you were asleep." The man was a forty-something cookie-cutter agent with a face like an alleyway rat and the body of a gorilla. With zero emotion, he said, "William Duff. CIA station, Zurich."

"Where's..." Jacob almost said his boss's name, checked himself at the last second, and attributed the near-slip to the anesthesia. "Where's the man who brought me here?"

A shrug. "No idea. I'm just a link in a complicated chain, doing one job." He fussed with the computer, fingers clicking the mouse a couple of times. A sideways glance at Jacob. "You recovered enough to use this?"

"Don't make me laugh." Jacob shook his head. "It's a computer, not heavy machinery."

The man cast an apologetic frown. "You've just had surgery, so I thought—"

"An A-plus for your observational skills," said Jacob, loaded with sarcasm. "You'll go far in your career. Cut to the chase and tell me what the hell you're doing here."

The man explained which folder Jacob needed to open, then recited a long password of random symbols, numbers, and letters.

"Want me to write it down for you?"

"No need. I got it."

The man exited as quietly as he had arrived, leaving Jacob to figure out what the hell would happen next.

THREE

FLETCHER USUALLY DELIVERED THE NEWS FROM THE luxurious confines of his converted warehouse apartment in New York City's upscale Tribeca district. Whether it came in a manila folder or on a flash drive, in a sealed envelope or as spoken instructions he had to commit to memory, Jacob received his orders in a face-to-face meeting with Fletcher.

Not today.

Today, the Skia director's benign face, bushy brown mustache front and center, occupied the entire screen of the laptop.

Why isn't he calling me on my cell? Jacob wondered. *What's with the dumb-ass recording?*

Fletcher wiped the lenses of his glasses, cleared his throat for the third time, blinked, redonned the eyewear, and launched into his spiel.

"I'm recording this because I don't want you interrupting me and throwing me off balance. After you've digested what I have to say, if you've got any questions, call me. But not until you reach the end of the video."

Jacob paused the recording and pressed the nurse-call button. A tall woman in crisp blue scrubs arrived within a minute, head cocked, eyes bright.

"What can I do for you?" she said in a rich, modulated Indian accent. "Are you in pain? Need more morphine?"

He shook his head. "No, but I'm starving. Could you get me a cheeseburger? A side of fries and a cold beer would be good."

"Sorry, sir, but our menu is rather spartan—just boring, healthy items on offer." She left and returned with a menu showcasing the blandest foods imaginable. Jacob sighed, choosing a ham sandwich on whole wheat bread washed down with orange juice.

On with the video.

Fletcher's face assumed an expression of utmost seriousness: crow's feet accentuated, nostrils wide, lips tight. "Hopefully, the operation didn't affect your greatest asset—your photographic memory. So I assume you recall the content of our conversation en route to the medical center."

That "conversation" had been more a rant by Fletcher. Jacob had never seen his boss so stressed out: a fake smile plastered across his face, constantly tipping little white pills into his mouth, chased down by huge gulps of water.

"Pay close attention," Fletcher continued. "Everything I'm about to tell you is important."

The upshot was as follows. A soldier had been murdered in a border observation center in Tallinn. An unidentified Russian intruder was another casualty, killed by responding Estonian forces.

The dead soldier, Corporal Indrek Laanoja, had alerted his commander, Major Robin Saar, of suspicious movements on the lake border between Russia and Estonia. The soldier was sure he was witnessing preparation for an invasion in real time. Three minutes after the call to Saar, the panic button in Laanoja's bunker was pressed, and five nearby soldiers were immediately dispatched to see what was happening. They were confronted by two agitated men in Estonian military uniforms, weapons raised. A firefight ensued: one of the hostiles was killed instantly, the other, Estonian Corporal Mihkel Vares, injured and subdued.

Laanoja was found dead beside his chair, tied and gagged, with two bullet holes in his stomach. The computer systems had been tampered with, but how and to what end was still not entirely clear.

Jacob took a sip of water as Fletcher rubbed one eye before resuming.

The traitor, Vares, was subjected to interrogation—not using the enhanced techniques favored by the CIA but good enough to get some answers. Unfortunately, not about the computer systems manipulation—his ignorance on the matter was deemed genuine. Vares admitted to being paid to arrange the safe entry of the Russian hacker via the river crossing between Narva and Ivangorod, transport him to Tallinn, and admit him to the facility's hub.

A search of the latter's body found two return tickets from Ivangorod to Saint Petersburg dated November 12. A photocopy of both tickets was in a separate folder on the laptop Jacob was currently looking at. Vares had intended to flee Estonia with the Russian because remaining in the country was not an option. Now Vares faced a decade to life in prison for treason.

It turned out that what Corporal Laanoja thought was the start of an invasion was, to use a sporting term, a dummy pass. All troops and equipment had withdrawn to original positions, which made Laanoja's murder all the more strange.

Initial suspicions that a mole had signaled Vares it was time to move naturally fell on the superior officer, Major Saar. He was questioned by personnel from the Military Intelligence Center of the Estonian Defence Forces. Saar was cleared—for the moment. The major revealed that, after talking to the corporal and looking at the live-stream, he'd also believed the Russians were on the march. He made a series of official phone calls up the chain, leading to large numbers of Estonian troops being told to prepare for mobilization. Thirty minutes later, satellite images showed the Russians moving back to their previous positions. Even so, the patterns of their assembly and the movement of so many units toward the border were considered an act of provocation.

Problem was, the Estonians were too shit-scared to call the Russians out for their act. Prime Minister Karilaid had advisers in both ears. Mild diplomatic representations had been made, encountering denials of evil intent regarding the border actions, as well as a denial of any knowledge of the intruder. The Russians had even imprisoned one of their top generals, a scapegoat, to try to smooth things over.

In Estonia, a blanket media blackout had been applied. The so-called accord that had been struck to guarantee peace, at least for the foreseeable future, had been instantly disrespected by an act of brazen arrogance. At least that was the assessment of US top brass. Fletcher was inclined to agree.

The accord was on life support, and tensions were back on the boil.

Analysts in the Pentagon, apprised of what had gone down in Tallinn, as well as operatives embedded in Estonia and Russia, believed that the dummy start of an invasion was a veiled threat to the Baltic nation: Abide by the accord—to the letter—or we will crush you. One thing the security agencies who had examined the incident agreed on was this: There was a mole in the Estonian forces and/or government much higher up than Vares. Possibly more.

Of course there are more! thought Jacob. *There are always more.*

The second conclusion they'd reached was extra alarming. The ease with which the anonymous Russian hacker—or whatever he was—had breached Estonian security pointed to something a lot more sinister.

The consensus was that hardline fanatics—a small group of outliers or perhaps even conspirators at the heart of the Kremlin—were plotting a coup in Estonia. Regime change. President Karilaid would be arrested and imprisoned and a Kremlin puppet installed in his place. After that, NATO would have to tread carefully if its members wanted to avoid a hot war with Putin.

Long story short, President McIvor, a staunch supporter of the NATO alliance, wanted Jacob back in the ring, whatever it took.

Jacob rubbed his eyes gently with the heels of his palms as Fletcher stopped his monologue to light a cigar and pour himself a glass of Hennessy XO cognac. The next thing he said had Jacob wishing he also had a bottle at hand containing something stronger than tepid water.

"You're going to Saint Petersburg in three days. I wanted two days, but it's been agreed an extra day of rest for you will make a big difference. I only pray you'll be there in time to defuse the time-bomb. The doctor tells me you'll be fit enough to travel in seventy-two hours and, more importantly, to work. Now let's talk about your legend," he said pointedly, scraping the wheel of his Zippo and relighting the stub of his smoldering stogie. "You are a Russia-sympathizing Estonian businessman. Thanks to the accord, which officially still exists, there are direct flights between Tallinn and Saint Petersburg. You'll fly from Zurich to Tallinn and from there to Pulkovo Airport. Your itinerary and full bio will be sent to you in an email, along with the names of contacts in Saint Petersburg."

Jacob sipped water, dreading this impending "business trip."

"You'll need to study a bunch of profiles. These are people we've identified as being those most likely to be orchestrating the destabilization campaign, which we believe is codenamed *Severnaya Volna*—in English, Northern Wave. I'm forwarding more detailed dossiers on these people and a bunch of background information."

Jacob paused the video, summoned the nurse, and demanded a notepad and pen. He wanted to test his memory. He was confident it would work as per normal, but after experimental surgery, such confidence could be misplaced. If by tomorrow he could recall what was on the paper, he'd destroy any notes he made.

"Finally," said Fletcher, "in addition to wishing you good luck and godspeed, I suggest you spend the next three days brushing up on your Estonian." A deep inhale. "That's it for now. Please delete this video file."

Jacob shook his head. Of all the Baltic languages, he had to get lumbered with the hardest. A smattering of Finnish—Estonian's closest relative—picked up on a mission in Helsinki four years ago would be his launch pad. He'd only required a handful of phrases in Finland; this was going to be next-level intensive study. Even with his own savant-like language skills, passing himself off as an Estonian would be close to impossible.

He deleted the MP4 file, confident Irina could track it down for him on Skia's cloud maze if needed. His email inbox contained the promised attachments from Fletcher. He opened and read them all over the next couple of minutes. He scooped up his cell and punched in Fletcher's number.

"Work?" Jacob's voice rose a semi-octave. "You have the audacity to call throwing me back into the fucking lion's den of Russia work?"

An uncomfortable laugh came down the line. "I make no apologies for that. You are my operative. You work for me." Another laugh, this one lightly tinged with sarcasm. "You've had a very long vacation on the American taxpayer's dime, Hunter. Now it's time to earn your keep. You get paid more than Taylor Swift, for Chrissake."

A massive exaggeration, even though he had no cause to complain about his hefty pay packet. "I needed that vacation, as you put it, because my identity was basically obliterated. Irina's, too. We needed to reconnect with the world."

"Give me a break, Hunter. That was pure indulgence. Your upstate mansion is like a freakin' resort. No need to travel anywhere."

"You might find it hard to believe, but you can still get cabin fever in a mansion with acres around you. Especially when you're someone like me, used to traveling, blowing off the cobwebs."

"I feel for you, I really do." A short pause while he sipped something then smacked his lips. "Your task is going to be difficult, but the goal is straightforward. If you succeed in stopping the predicted coup, you could be—at the president's discretion—a free man forever."

"I'm gonna need that in writing."

"I'll see if McIvor will sign off on it."

Jacob knew there would be nothing in writing from the White House. That's not how these things worked. Still, he now had a mountain of motivation. He took a deep breath, then aired his concerns about being able to pass as a real Estonian.

"I won't be able to pull that off, Fletch. Not even if I spent the next three days doing nothing but taking Estonian lessons."

"We took that into account. Your name for this mission is Robert Tamm. Born in Narva, on the Estonian border, where the Russian demographic makes up more than ninety-five percent of the population. This makes your being stronger in Russian than Estonian credible."

"You don't have to tell me where Narva is," Jacob hissed under his breath. "It's a well-known fact."

"I didn't know until recently!" protested Fletcher.

"Geography's never been your strong suit, has it?"

Fletcher plowed on without replying to the slight. "Your mother is an ethnic Russian, a Soviet nostalgist who yearns for the good old days of the USSR. I won't bore you with the rest of the legend right now. I've sent you all the material you need in an encrypted email."

"I've read it all."

"Already? No, don't answer that. I forgot that you're a fucking cyborg." He paused for a moment. Jacob heard Fletcher softly scolding someone—he guessed it was his personal assistant and rumored paramour, Susan Stonehouse. Fletcher coughed twice, then returned his attention to Jacob. "Anyway, we figured that if you were at least half-Russian, the locals would be more inclined to open up to you. Especially if you share your mother's ideals."

"You figured right. One more thing?"

"What?"

"Who are the conspirators?"

"In the list you got."

"Yeah, but it's a long list. What do our analysts think? Who are they leaning toward?"

"There are conflicting theories on our side, mainly because a lot of the information on the suspects isn't objective. Your Saint Petersburg contacts will probably have their own theories, better than ours."

"Anyone at home been able to do anything with the train tickets?" The details of the tickets flashed in Jacob's mind as he visualized the photocopy Fletcher had emailed. Purchased for cash on 9 November from Window 12, Finland Station, at 10:16 a.m. Train: 412 IVANGOROD → PETERSBURG. Departure: IVANGOROD 07:18, 11 November. Arrival: SAINT PETERSBURG 10:43. Carriage: 03. Seat: — (standing/no assigned seat). Ticket No.: PL-GT-74-9921 / PL-GT-74-9922.

A pity the tickets weren't bought with a card, he mused. Online would have been even better. A digital footprint offered a pathway to track down the purchaser, whereas with cash that task was almost impossible. A tricky one to pull off, but he wouldn't rule out trying to track down and grill the cashier who'd manned window 12 on November 9.

"No. I've sent a copy to Irina, plus a photo of the dead guy, but she's yet to get back to me about it." A pause, then Fletcher said, as if he'd discovered the theory of relativity, "If our analysts had all the answers, there'd be no need to send you into the field, now would there?"

"I guess not."

"Damn straight. In truth, the list is a guide. Like I said, your contacts in Saint Petersburg will have quality local knowledge. You can't beat that."

"I guess so," said Jacob with a sigh.

"Could it be Putin himself behind it?" said Fletcher. "I wouldn't put it past him to set up scapegoats."

Jacob chewed a plastic straw he'd been drinking orange juice through. "My gut says no. He's losing ground in ongoing skirmishes—why start another?"

"We've got what we've got," said Fletcher phlegmatically. "Which ain't much, apart from a list of names and chatter about Severnaya Volna."

"What went down in Tallinn proves it's not just chatter. Something's brewing."

"I'll leave you in peace now, Hunter." The words were sweet relief to Jacob's ears. There was nothing more the boss had to say that would make his task any easier. Besides, there was someone else he was desperate to reconnect with.

Jacob rolled over in his bed, grabbed his laptop, and logged onto Skia's encrypted communications network.

Irina answered breathlessly in less than ten seconds. "*Zaichik! Vsye v poryadke?* Is everything OK?"

"Brilliant," he said flatly, pressing the phone hard to his ear, as if that would bring her closer to him. "The surgeries went well. Just a couple of nagging aches. How are you holding up in Castelo Branco?"

"Fine. Except I'm nowhere near the town. It's like a hacienda out in the sticks. Pool, jacuzzi, gym, massive wine cellar—the works."

"Fazenda."

"What?"

"In Portuguese, a property like that is called a fazenda."

"Not everyone's a damned polyglot like you, Yakov," she laughed.

"Either way, it sounds like a pleasant extension of our vacation."

"It's not like that at all! None of these luxuries mean anything to me. I've been worried sick. Not hearing from you for more than a day when we haven't been out of each other's sight for two years. I can't bear it."

"I'm sorry, Irochka."

"I'm sorry, too. I know it's not your fault."

A silence ensued for a few moments, but silences between them were never awkward.

"Fletcher tells me he sent you a task," Jacob prompted.

"Not one I can complete. How can I trace a cash sale? And I've searched every database known to man, but that dead Russian isn't showing up anywhere. A regular John Doe."

"Worth a try, though."

"Always." She paused a short beat, then said, "I've got a bunch of burly security guards looking out for me, maids—you name it. Maybe they're Portuguese secret agents, I don't know." She inhaled so deeply, he felt like she'd sucked half the air out of the hospital room. "Yakov. I need to see you. Turn your camera on, please."

He groaned. Not in pain, but in embarrassment. "I don't think you wanna—"

"Show me your face!"

He relented, clicked the mouse, and saw his own, new face appear in the top left corner of the screen.

"*Bozhe moi!* Oh, my God!" she cried. "What have they done to you?"

"The doctor says it's all reversible."

"I hope so, *zaichik*. Because right now, you are one ugly *sukin syn.*"

Jacob shook his head, dismissing the insult with a fatalistic laugh. Even when she called him a son of a bitch, he couldn't help but love her with all his being.

FOUR

JACOB LOOKED DOWN AND SLIGHTLY TO THE LEFT, TO where his heart was pounding a military tattoo under his designer business shirt. Respiration was still normal, but getting that rapid heart rate under control was a priority.

A deep breath to refocus.

Stay in your role. You have every right to be here and be treated properly. Nothing bad is going to happen to you. Don't panic. Don't act weird. Don't say anything stupid to give yourself away.

Amid the faint sounds of announcements being made in Russian and English over the loudspeakers, a crack in a floor tile caught his attention. As he stared at the crack, the floor vibrated with the low rumble of a jet taking off outside.

The reality of lining up to be processed by the border guard at Pulkovo Airport in a country where scores of people—including the president himself—wanted Jacob dead almost canceled out the calm state he'd attained on the airplane. A state induced by deep meditation, breathing techniques, and a couple of stiff vodka sodas.

He took another deep breath and shuffled forward two steps, his feet feeling like his Oxford brogues were lined with lead. He dragged his virtually empty carry-on case behind him, which also felt heavy, as if it were full of bricks instead of a laptop and papers.

Up ahead, a male-female couple at one of the passport control booths exchanged glances of confusion. The bespectacled official frowned deeply, shook his head, held up a hand, and made a phone call. Straining his ear, Jacob caught the words *visa irregularities*, *detention*, and *deportation*, spoken loudly enough for everyone in the line to hear. Moments later, two men sporting bristly number-one haircuts and decked out in cobalt suits arrived, placed handcuffs on each of the inbound passengers, and led them away. The captives' heads were bowed, shoulders slumped, not a word of protest uttered.

Jacob's heart thundered, which pissed him off because he'd only just reined in his heart rate again, back to a respectable seventy-five BPM according to his Breitling smartwatch. This was the Russia he feared. Authoritarian and bureaucratic, quick to jump on any indiscretion and punish harshly for non-compliance.

The line inched forward again. Three more individual travelers were processed, this time with a minimum of fuss. Border guards stared intently at the arrivals, flicked their eyes to passports, computer monitors, then back to the faces before them. The clunk of a stamp, the snapping closed of passports, a green light, and they scurried away toward the baggage carousels.

At 23:47 hours, November 16, it was Jacob's turn to cross swords with the regime and, God willing, sneak under the fence in one piece. His mouth felt as if wadded-up cotton balls were stuffed in his cheeks, sucking out every molecule of moisture.

He'd expected to be faced by a grim, granite-faced soldier with the IQ and charm of a roof tile. Instead, he struck a rather attractive woman who couldn't have been twenty-five, thick mascara coating long lashes, strawberry-blond hair tied back in a ponytail. She made the uniform of dark green jacket, matching cravat, and crisp white blouse look like high fashion.

Instead of the anticipated border guard's snarl, she greeted him with an affable smile. He fought the instinct to be a gentleman and meet her smile with one of his own, keeping his lips in a straight line. Normal expression, normal words, normal behavior that didn't draw attention. *Just get in the door; your experience and skills will carry the day.*

"Is this your first trip to Russia, Mr. Tamm?" she asked in perfect English. Not too many years ago, when Estonia was a republic of the USSR, a citizen of that country would have been able to communicate easily in Russian. Nowadays, English was everybody's second language in the Baltic countries; young people barely knew any Russian at all.

"Yes," replied Jacob, unblinking. He decided to switch to Russian. "It's my first visit to Russia. I've wanted to come for many years, and now with this new accord, I get to live out my wish."

"You speak Russian very well." She studied his passport again. "Born in 1990 in Estonia, I see. Not many of your generation are so well versed in our tongue."

He allowed himself the faintest of grins. "It's my first language, as it happens." His words came out deliberately in a soporific monotone. "I've got a Russian mother. I grew up in Narva, right on the border, but never got to cross it. Ironic that I had to backtrack to Tallinn to fly here when the bridge between Narva and Ivangorod is only 160 meters long. Have you ever been to Estonia?"

The tactic was working. The woman's eyes were half-shut as she stifled a yawn. Jacob knew what she was thinking: at close to midnight, the sooner she processed this boring jerk, the better.

"State the purpose of your visit."

Commands now instead of questions. Much better.

The details of his legend rolled across his mind's eye like teletext on the morning news. "Business."

"State the nature of your business, Mr. Tamm. And don't be so long-winded about it." She nodded over his shoulder toward the line behind him. Her voice was now as firm as a school principal's, eyelids compressed and forehead wrinkled. The embodiment of soulless Russian bureaucracy. "We've still got half of your flight left to process, and some of us want to go home."

He suppressed the urge to bust out a smart-ass comment. Play it straight, according to the script. "I'm here to liaise with the Russian Ministry of Industry and Trade, looking to forge lasting partnerships with public and private companies. My sponsor is the Estonian Chamber of Commerce and Industry." He added that he ran a logistics consultancy with strong ties to Finland, but with the advent of the new accord, Russian partners wanted to reopen some of the old sea routes to the Baltic states and beyond, with Estonia as the bridge.

The rambling reply caused the woman's eyes to glaze over.

"I can show you the official documents if you like?" Jacob leaned down toward his case.

She shook her head firmly, ponytail swishing. "*Nye nado. Prokhodite.* No need. Please proceed." She stamped an entry in his fake passport with a flurry. The green light came on, Jacob's heart flooding with relief, as if an oncologist had just told him the stage-four cancer prognosis was all a big mistake.

As a parting gesture, she said, "Do not overstay your visa, Mr. Tamm. Penalties apply."

As if I would, Jacob said to himself. *The sooner I'm out of here, the better*. He replied, deadpan: "*Khoroshego Vam dnya*. Have a nice day."

FIVE

Suitcase collected, Jacob spotted his contact among the handful of solemn-faced greeters. A young man, early thirties, with a combover someone as young as him would regard as a genetic curse. He held a mini whiteboard to his chest bearing the name Robert Tamm. Not in Cyrillic but Latin script.

Jacob donned a pair of non-prescription glasses with thick black rims, loosened his tie, and held out a hand. "Vyacheslav Gabulov, I presume?" His nostrils flared for a split second, sensing the aroma of cigarette smoke infiltrating the arrivals hall as the automatic doors opened and closed. Nicotine-addicted taxi drivers waiting outside, desperate for a fare, Jacob guessed. "You can speak to me in Russian, *druzhok*. I'm fluent."

"That's obvious," said the smiling man. Clearly, calling him the Russian equivalent of "pal" hadn't ruffled his feathers in the slightest. Gabulov was a high-ranking bureaucrat in the Russian Ministry of Industry and Trade's brand-new Saint Petersburg office. The file stated his position as director, Protocol and External Relations Office. The perfect foot-in-the-door man for a dozen scenarios.

Gabulov took hold of Jacob's extended hand with surprisingly firm fingers. He ran his eyes up and down him, perhaps checking that the arrival matched the description and photographs he'd been given of undercover Estonian businessman Robert Tamm. Satisfied, he said, "I don't like hanging about airports." He lowered his tone to a half-whisper. "Too many ugly men in uniform. Makes me jumpy." He beckoned with a slight roll of the head, which sat upon a neck too thick for his slim body. "Follow me."

The echoing footsteps of the exiting passengers and those who'd come to meet them seemed amplified at this late hour. Like dozens of grandfather clocks ticking away. Jacob's mouth turned tacky-dry as he observed racks of T-shirts at a souvenir shop, portraits of the country's eternal president emblazoned on them. On mugs and towels, too. Smiling benevolently at the passing parade. He wouldn't be smiling if he knew who had just crossed the border at Pulkovo.

As they reached the exit to the outside world—to Mother Russia—Gabulov apologized for the freezing weather. Jacob smiled through gritted teeth and said that he'd experienced much worse. Seconds later, a blast of wind across the asphalt made his skin ache at the wound sites. As the doctor had promised, no outward signs remained of Jacob's operation, but the cold's interaction with his body was a stark physical reminder. Gabulov said conditions would deteriorate, with the mercury dropping another couple of degrees over the next week. A big system blowing in from Siberia, bringing more snow and bitter temperatures.

Perfect, Jacob thought, closing his eyes. Just like the last nightmare in the Netherlands and Belgium. He addressed his personal God in silent prayer: *Help me endure what lies ahead and get me out of here soon.*

In the parking lot, dirty snow was pushed into piles around the perimeter, overhead streetlamps reflecting in puddles. Gabulov led Jacob to a sleek armored BMW 7 Series. The license plates told Jacob the vehicle was registered to a federal government body. The driver's window was halfway down. Pungent smoke from a cheap, strong local cigarette poured out into the frigid air. Even at a distance it smelled like a burning rubbish dump. Little clouds of condensation followed the words out of Jacob's mouth. "Your ministry's got lots of money to splash on cars, Vyacheslav."

"It certainly has. And please, call me Slava." The man nodded deferentially, holding open the rear door.

A minute later, they were on their way. Inside, the driver stared intently at the red taillights of cars leaving the confines of the airport and heading for the ring road toward the city center. Jacob nodded at the back of his head and mouthed to Slava, *Can we talk freely in front of him?*

A nod before he said, "Dima's solid. He's my second cousin. I helped get him the job with the ministry. He hates the regime as much as I do." A little louder: "Don't you, Dima?"

Without turning his head, the reply came. "Even more, I'd say." The square head then turned around. An honest face, the hooded eyelids and network of wrinkles testament to a life of disappointment and pain. "My son had just turned eighteen when he was conscripted into the army, sent to the front. Killed in Mariupol on his third day on duty. And for what?" He pretended to spit out of the window. "For fucking nothing except the bloodthirsty ambitions of a few men."

The car glided along Pulkovskoe Shosse, the main artery leading into the city that locals call simply "Peter." Traffic on the road at this hour was light, snowplows with flashing orange lights clearing the way, occasional delivery trucks grinding their way to supermarkets, restocking for morning shoppers.

Jacob's eyes closed involuntarily, exhausted after enduring monumental stress over a short period. This mission was a big step into the unknown, as if he were an astronaut taking his first spacewalk. It wasn't his first time in this part of space, which should have ameliorated the anxiety. No chance.

Sleep beckoned. Jacob was one of those rare humans in which feelings of anxiety can induce tiredness instead of wide-eyed insomnia.

He felt a pointy elbow nudge him in the side.

"Sorry?" he stuttered.

"You nodded off mid-conversation. Is everything all right, Gospodin Tamm?"

Through a drowsy fog, he shook his head, registering the word *gospodin*, meaning "mister" in English. Saint Petersburg, the mission, everything flooded back in a second. He sat up straight in the soft leather seat. "What?"

"Are you OK?" Louder this time. "I was briefing you on what we know. Ideas on where we can start our search for the conspirators."

"You don't even know if the conspiracy is real," said Jacob. "I could end up chasing my own shadow here."

Slava shook his head firmly, loose strands of his combover flapping before he smoothed them back into place. Watching him made Jacob think about his own medically induced receding hairline and monk's circle.

"It is real. I can pinpoint a number of men looking to destroy the new accord with Estonia. We have the intelligence. We just have to confirm firsthand, get a confession or other physical proof, and make it public. If we do not, the plotters will oust the democratically elected government of Estonia and install a puppet president loyal to the Kremlin. This must not happen."

Jacob sighed. "Yes, I know. Regime change." He gave the slightest head shake and turned to look Slava in the eyes. "And how has that tactic worked for Russia in the past?" He recalled campaigns orchestrated by Russia and its predecessor, the Soviet Union, that had ended in disaster. If not immediately, then in the long term. On his fingers, he counted off: "Afghanistan, Prague Spring, South Ossetia and Abkhazia, and as recently as 2016 with a botched coup in Montenegro. All monumental fucking failures. Why would someone want to mess with Estonia? This is a modern part of Europe we're talking about now, not some Baltic outpost."

"Doesn't matter. Putin has plenty of sympathizers inside

Estonia, as you know. Even among the non-Russian-speaking majority."

"NATO won't stand for it," said Jacob, not even sure he was believing his own words. "Even if I fail—if we fail—they won't let Russia destabilize the Baltics."

"Bullshit. The European public won't agree to its soldiers being killed to save little Estonia. The ruling parties will listen to that because they are first and foremost interested in clinging to power, not doing what is right. Most of them couldn't even find Estonia on a map if the name was in bold and highlighted. And I'm not even talking about the attitude of the Americans."

A sigh worked its way from Jacob's diaphragm and out of his yawning mouth.

"Sorry if this is boring for you," grizzled Slava said. "I thought… we thought they were sending us the best agent."

Jacob pressed his face right into Slava's, like in a close-up scene from an Italian mobster movie. "I've been to hell and back for the cause. Now I'm back in the hell I believed I'd never set foot in again. I'm drowsy because I'm having reactions to treatment I underwent only days ago. Do not question my motivation, Slava, or I'll find a way to disappear, and you'll be on your own. You understand me?"

From his recoiled position, pressed hard up against the car door, all Slava could do was nod frantically. "I… ah… apologize."

"Come on," said Dima. "Ease up, Slava. You can tell the guy's exhausted. It's nearly one in the morning, goddam it. We have to trust him; we've got no other choice. Let's get him to the hotel, he can get some rest, and you can pick this up in the morning."

"Your cousin's too smart to be driving bureaucrats around," said Jacob. "How long before we get to the Pribaltiyskaya?"

"At this time of night with no traffic, around five minutes," said Dima.

Jacob hunched into his coat and drifted off again.

Five minutes later, the car pulled up at the entrance of the

Soviet-era brutalist hotel, an H-shaped concrete and anodized behemoth.

From the rear seat, Jacob looked up at his new temporary home, lights glowing in the windows of about a dozen of the 1,200 rooms spread across sixteen floors. His eyes scanned the façade, trying to find something warm and welcoming. Nothing. Just coldness.

Before stepping out of the vehicle, Slava slipped Jacob a burner cell phone and a small handheld electronic radio frequency scanner. "The details of our group members are stored in the phone should you need to call any of us. Plus a few extras I thought could come in handy."

"*Spasibo.* Thanks." A Skia smart satellite phone lay in Jacob's suitcase, to be used when the burner was insufficient, foreseeably for navigating the labyrinthine city's intricate network of canal bridges and side streets. He'd committed the major thoroughfares to memory, but there were limits even to his powers. He casually scrolled through the burner's pre-loaded contacts, memorized the names and numbers, and trashed the list. He'd dial the numbers manually when he made calls. "What about weapons?"

Slava blinked rapidly. "Excuse me?"

"A pistol of some kind would be nice, considering the danger I'm going to be in. Russian models are fine if you can't rustle up a Glock or an H&K. I've used Makarovs and Udavs before. But I'm pretty comfortable with most handguns. SMGs, too."

The Russian shook his head slowly. "That's way out of my purview, I'm afraid. Another of our group might be able to assist you." He paused, then scratched his nose. "The thought of giving you an illegal weapon worries me."

"Why?" Jacob patted him on the shoulder. "Simply talking with me—if the watchers figured out who I really was—could get you into a shitload of trouble. I'm afraid it's too late to worry about that kind of thing, *druzhok.*"

Slava sighed and raised his eyes to the heavens. "I guess you're right."

"You know I am."

After entering through automatic glass doors, Jacob and Slava traversed a vast lobby with marble everywhere, vaulted ceilings, and dim lighting. A speedy check-in ensued, facilitated by a surprisingly friendly receptionist. Upon seeing Jacob's passport, she said in rapid-fire Estonian:

"*Tere tulemast. Kas olete meie juures varem peatunud?* Welcome. Have you stayed with us before?"

In a far-flung recess of his mind, he translated the greeting, then latched on to the Estonian words for "Thank you. No, I haven't" before switching to Russian. "But from what I hear, it's a wonderful hotel."

The woman beamed. Much to Jacob's relief, she carried out the rest of the registration procedure in Russian. His fake company credit card swiped with no alarming bleeps, the deposit for his short stay transacted via an intricate network of untraceable offshore accounts.

The pair headed for the lobby's spacious seating area and occupied a maroon chesterfield lounge. In low voices, they discussed tomorrow's program, agreeing to meet in the hotel for a breakfast meeting at 8:30 a.m.

"There could be bugs in your room," said Slava. "In fact, you should assume there are. Use the device I gave you to sweep the room."

"This isn't my first rodeo," said Jacob with a shake of the head. "I even assume you are wearing a wire." He lunged at Slava, sneaking a hand under his shirt in a fraction of a second before retracting it and showing an empty palm. He grinned as Slava's face turned pale. "Good boy."

"*Blyad*. Holy shit," Slava spluttered. "You nearly gave me a heart attack. I thought you were going to stab me!"

"If I were going to do that, you'd already be dead." He paused. "Look, I'm sorry. But you have to stop doubting me. Full trust on your part is required." *But no full trust on my part. Never on my part.*

Someone else would be there tomorrow. A woman called Marfa Petko. Jacob recalled Fletcher's account of her and what her role would be. An accredited journalist, Petko could smooth Jacob's access to government ministries, media offices, and top-level *siloviki*. She outwardly supported the current regime—you'd have no media career otherwise—but inwardly despised it. At great risk, she was working hard in secretive underground circles to create a credible and strong opposition.

It was also Petko, Slava said, who'd know about weapons and such. She had made hundreds of contacts in the criminal underworld thanks to her thirty-year career as a reporter. And as far as criminal underworlds went, Saint Petersburg's was up there with the best of them. Moreover, she possessed a list of bribable police and other informers as long as your arm.

The photos of Marfa Petko that Jacob had seen were cause for concern. Even aged forty-nine, she was one of the most drop-dead gorgeous women he had ever clapped eyes on.

Bidding Slava good night, he took the elevator to his suite on the thirteenth floor. The corridor was empty, eerily so.

Punching his pillow, the image of Marfa Petko's sultry face pushed its way to the front of his mind.

He recited the Lord's Prayer, laying emphasis on one line in particular:

Lead me not into temptation.

SIX

Vasilevsky Island, one of the most prestigious enclaves of Saint Petersburg, was the ideal base: close to everything yet discretely tucked away from the hubbub of Nevsky Prospekt and the central business district. He'd scored a room with panoramic views over the Gulf of Finland. It was comfortable without being luxurious, with drab décor in a minimalist Scandinavian style and a fully stocked minibar.

A discreet visual and electronic scan of the room for bugs came up empty. Still, you couldn't put anything past the FSB or private firms operating on the margins, including the use of listening and filming equipment that defied detection. The only phone calls he'd be making would be internal ones to order room service or outside calls on the burner Slava had given him.

Showered, shaved, and dressed, with twenty minutes to kill before meeting the mysterious Petko, he unzipped his laptop bag and pulled out the Lenovo. Accessing any hotel's Wi-Fi service or commercial VPN in Russia was a bad idea if you had issues about privacy. Jacob had issues the size of Jupiter. Logging on to Skia's low Earth orbit satellite network, Jacob sat at a polished walnut desk to write an encrypted email to Irina. He hadn't contacted her

—on Fletcher's orders—since their FaceTime call at the Zurich clinic.

I miss you so much. So, that's the romantic stuff out of the way. Please do me a favor and look into a couple of people for me. Vyacheslav Gabulov, from the Ministry of Industry and Trade, and Marfa Petko, a journalist. I've done research, but I know you can go further than I can.

As he typed the woman's name, he felt sweat on the back of his neck. Irina would take one look at Petko and be consumed by, if not jealousy, then an emotion very close to it.

I'll be working shoulder to shoulder with them, so I need you to dig deep. I'll supply you with more names later. If you don't hear from me for a while, don't panic. It won't necessarily mean anything's wrong. Tseluyu. *Kisses.*

Around the breakfast table in the far corner of the dining hall sat Jacob, Slava, the beautiful and confident Marfa Petko, and another man not mentioned by Slava yesterday. Some basic details about him were known to Jacob courtesy of Fletcher's brief.

The new man, Ivan "Vanya" Beglov, sat with his arms crossed over his chest, an untouched croissant and steaming coffee set before him. His eyes couldn't stay still for a moment. A nervous smile passed over his face as Slava enthusiastically outlined what Ivan was bringing to the team.

First, penetration of a number of key government and private databases. Not all firewalls could be breached, of course, but Ivan had cracked a few.

Second, deep research and analysis.

Third, an absolute bonus: an isolated dacha-farm in the village of Shepelevo, about eighty-five kilometers from the center of Saint Petersburg. Beglov had inherited the ten-acre property from his parents. Located in a forest that ran along the edge of the Gulf of Finland, the dacha comprised old pasture and outbuildings his folks had worked until they got too old; the cows were sold off and the fields taken over by reed, nettle, and pine needles blown in from the shores of the Gulf. The place had been set up as a safe house, boasting a complex security system installed by Ivan himself.

Despite the praise showered on the man, Jacob subconsciously identified Ivan as a weak link. As if in confirmation, Ivan's shaking hands grasped his coffee cup, which he dropped from a height of a quarter inch above the table. The others winced as the cup clanked. He apologized, regripped the cup, took a noisy slurp, and set it down again, gently this time, but his fingers were still trembling. His entire body seemed to twitch under his shiny leather jacket.

"Is this the entire team?" said Jacob, breaking the awkward silence. "Seems kind of small to be going up against high-level conspirators." He had to bring up the obvious. "In regards to Vanya—and I don't mean to offend—he seems a little edgy to me. I don't need frightened people around. Fear can be contagious."

The sound of raised voices speaking in Arabic drew nearer. Jacob turned and recognized the traditional garb of well-heeled Emiratis: a mom and dad and their young kids. They sat at the next table, the loud volume of their conversation making a good cover for the rebel group as other guests began to filter into the breakfast room.

"Firstly, yes. As far as members you'll meet, this is the entire team. We call ourselves Gruppa krovi B+, or simply B+. The name comes from—"

"From a song called '*Gruppa krovi*,'" Jacob completed. The words meant *blood type*.

Slava nodded. "Ah... yes, it does. You impress with your knowledge of Russian music from the 1980s."

"I'm a huge fan of the group Kino." It wasn't a lie. Jacob had all the group's albums on vinyl. "What about the B+ part?"

"Ah. It's because only eleven percent of people have that blood type," said Ivan with a wry grin. "Coincidentally, it's the same percentage of Russians who reportedly... can you guess, Gospodin Tamm?"

"It's a low number, and you're a small crew." Jacob pursed his lips into a rose knot as he thought. "Is it the percentage of Russians who actually oppose Putin?"

"Well done." Slava frowned for a second before reverting to a weak smile. "Of course, that's taken from a survey that's three years old, so the figure could be even lower now. Or higher, who the hell knows?" He poked the tip of his tongue out of the side of his mouth as he buttered a small bread roll. He looked up and added, "I am truly amazed you were able to guess the answer."

"No guessing involved, *druzhok*. I know lots of shit," said Jacob, inclining his head. "I've got the recall of a savant."

"I've got no reason to disbelieve you." Slava shook his head slightly. "Back to our numbers. Yes, we are few. In addition to the three of us here and my cousin Dima, B+ has a number of loyal agents on the inside of the government, but they will only funnel us information; we must not contact them under any circumstances. They're in sensitive positions and cannot be compromised. We may need them in the future if we fail in this endeavor. I cannot reveal their identities to you. In case you are detained and... ah... tortured."

Slava took a sip of his tea and licked his lips. He tapped a fingernail on the table. "And taking up what you said before about Vanya, I'd like to put you straight."

Jacob nodded at the man, who'd seemed to have sunk into himself as he was spoken about like he wasn't there.

"Vanya suffers from a rare condition that makes him stutter and twitch frequently as if he were nervous. Don't be fooled. He is scared of nothing. And his motivation is strong, like Dima's. Vanya's sister, only nineteen years old, attended an anti-war protest and got herself arrested. By itself, no big deal. People get arrested for things like that all the time in Russia. Natasha died in prison under mysterious circumstances. No, let me rephrase that. Under unknown circumstances." He paused to drink more tea.

"And unlike me, Vanya would not have flinched if you'd pulled that looking-for-a-wire stunt on him."

"I'd like to correct Slava on two points," said Vanya. "It's not that rare—it's called essential t-t-tremor. And it's not a disease, it's a condition, and mine is relatively mild. I can p-p-perform any task you set me with the utmost efficiency." He scratched the side of his face. "And, for the record, I would give my life to avenge Natasha's death." Vanya managed to bring his dancing eyeballs under control for a moment as he fixed them firmly on Jacob, as if daring a rejoinder. None came.

Blood rushed into Jacob's cheeks. "*Prostite*. Forgive me."

Vanya grinned. "Don't w-w-worry. The cops sometimes hassle me; they think I'm drunk or stoned when I'm n-n-not. I can handle weapons and fight hand to hand if needed. Like an artist whose stutter goes away when he opens his mouth to s-s-sing, my shakes and stuttering d-d-disappear when the adrenaline is pumping. I p-p-promise, I won't let you down."

Jacob nodded, bottom lip thrust out. The confident tone of Vanya's voice was encouraging.

Petko had been silent until now, scrolling through her phone occasionally, grimacing now and then. "Gospodin Tamm," she said, as if her long-awaited turn to speak had finally come. "Have you been briefed on our suspect list? On the men behind the plot to overthrow the Estonian government?"

"I've seen a list of names. My employer told me it was a guide and that you would know more." Jacob rested his forearms on the edge of the table. "Naturally, I did some of my own research into these guys online, but—"

"But," interrupted Petko, "most of the information you found would've been useless junk, since it's created by our own propagandist media."

"And," said Vanya, "if you were reading Western sources, the information would have been patchy and a hundred percent negative."

Jacob nodded. He wasn't dealing with idiots here. "You're both right."

Petko rolled her tongue over her bottom lip. A romance writer would call the intense look she gave Jacob "smoldering." He'd seen that look on the face of a Russian woman who'd seduced him a couple of years ago: in a car in the middle of a field with bombs going off all around them. Every fiber of his being told him that Petko wanted him, even with his craggy new face and old man's hairstyle. "I suspect the list of suspects you received was a long one," she said.

"Yes, it was," he confirmed. "Too damned long."

"With the help of our sleepers and Vanya's analytical work," she added, "we have narrowed the list of conspirators down to three men. We sometimes call them the triumvirate."

"Just three?" said Jacob.

"Yes," she continued. "Separately, they pose a great danger. Together..."

Her husky voice was making Slava's eyelids flutter. Vanya, too, seemed to be in her thrall. She handed Jacob a white Bic lighter.

"This is a USB drive with everything you need to know about the three men."

"You're not going to tell me their names?" He palmed the drive and dropped it in his jacket pocket.

She drew in a deep breath. "I know it sounds melodramatic, but not here."

Jacob shook his head. This was taking cloak-and-dagger to a ridiculous level. He opened his mouth to speak, but she cut him off.

"Not here, I said." She pulled out a flip phone and consulted the screen. "I have an interview with a very annoying TV celebrity in the next hour. The rest of the day will be spent trying to get you appointments with our top three suspects. I suggest we meet again tomorrow morning at the rendezvous point. Say 7:30 a.m.?"

The Russian men nodded their agreement. Jacob said, "Fine."

"Slava will take you there."

"What about the tickets found on the dead guy in Tallinn who—"

Petko held a finger to her lips. "Again, not a topic for here."

Jacob screwed up his face. They had already discussed matters that any eavesdroppers nearby could construe as treasonous. Quietly, yes, but the words were potential dynamite that could blow up in all their faces. When he stated the fact, Petko had an answer. Not words, but a head gesture—to her right and then up, with raised eyebrows for emphasis. Two tables away, immediately to Jacob's left, sat a fat, bald man staring at his cell phone screen. Jacob directed his gaze to the ceiling, where a patchwork of mirrored tiles reflected what was under them.

The man was scrolling a blank screen. Had he been sent to watch over them?

"I'm still going to check it out," said Jacob in a whisper. "The lead is a physical one that could lead us to—"

Petko's hand went up. No come-on look on her face anymore, just a corrugated brow of annoyance.

"*Khvatit!* Enough."

She stood, gathered her things, and sashayed her way to the exit.

Dammit, thought Jacob. *I didn't get the chance to ask her about a gun.*

SEVEN

BEFORE JACOB COULD GET HIS BEARINGS, DIMA PULLED up outside Vanya's official place of employment in Lviny Pereulok. The jewelry, watch, and shoe repair business sat around the corner from the Bridge of Four Lions, which crossed the Griboyedov Canal. The façade of the building, where icicles dangled precariously from bent guttering that barely clung to the wall, was so nondescript it was almost invisible. The most basic of signs, no windows, and a gray steel door reinforced by an iron grate.

Curiously, in addition to being an IT expert, Vanya possessed the skills of a master jeweler and was a tolerably good cobbler into the bargain. Trade was always slow because Vanya, who owned the business, deliberately charged way too much for his services, opening up a lot of free time to work for B+. Vanya had proudly declared to Jacob that he always paid his rent and taxes on time, never caused trouble, and flew so low under the radar that the authorities had no reason to be interested in him. Jacob didn't share his confidence. The fact that he often met up with Slava and Petko, who worked high-profile jobs and for sure had eyes on them, put him in the crosshairs. But Jacob said nothing: B+

didn't strike him as a foolhardy bunch; they would be taking the appropriate precautions to avoid scrutiny.

Slava exited the car, cast his eyes about, and dived back in. The coast declared clear, Vanya alighted from the rear passenger side and, in a flash, had disappeared into his shop.

Curtains of snow bounced off the BMW's windshield as they drove through western Saint Petersburg, the wipers working overtime to deflect the tumbling flakes. Dima chose a complex route, taking them on a serpentine ride through the city. The car remained quiet inside, its cutting-edge technologies blocking out all but the loudest honking horns on the busier thoroughfares. They crossed bridges over frozen canals and passed bustling storefronts and packed trams; for a change of scenery, they ducked into the city's maze of narrow streets so deserted and quiet you wouldn't believe you were in the metropolis of Saint Petersburg. The ornate onion domes of the Church of the Savior on Spilled Blood drew Jacob's eye like a magnet before they made a sharp left onto Konyushennaya Square.

With Vanya out of the way, the next item on the agenda was a stop at the branch office of the Ministry of Industry and Trade. Here, Slava would introduce Jacob to the local head honcho, further cementing the legitimate presence of Robert Tamm in Saint Petersburg. Real meetings with real people were essential in order to satisfy the FSB and other potential watchers that the Estonian visitor wasn't here to play games.

"Change of plan," said Jacob as they glided past the ornate façade of the Passazh shopping mall. He leaned forward and spoke directly into Dima's right ear. "Take me to Finland Station first."

"Please," said Slava. "Let's not get distracted from—"

"I need to ask the ticket sellers a few questions," interrupted Jacob. "I wanna know about the guy who got himself a one-way trip to Estonia when he was expecting to come home."

"No problem," said Dima, turning down the volume of the radio and turning up the heater. "It's not a long journey. Maybe thirty minutes, twenty-five if we're lucky."

"They're expecting us at the Ministry," said Slava briskly. "It's your first official meeting. You can't miss it."

Perhaps sensing an argument brewing, Dima did the diplomatic thing: pulled over to the side of the road. Let the bulls fight it out. The car idled in the freezing morning, shrouding the vehicle in a cloud of exhaust fumes.

"For God's sake, relax," said Jacob, drawing out the last word. "We've got over two hours before that meeting."

"But the office is quite far from Finland Station." Slava's voice shook. "The other end of the city. It's better to arrive extra early and bide our time in the car. We can't afford to be late, or he'll refuse to see us. Word will spread quickly, and no one will want to speak with you."

Jacob blew out his cheeks. Slava's nerves were understandable, but this was verging on panic; he needed reassurance. "Don't stress, *druzhok*. We can always blame the traffic, car trouble, the weather. I'll think of something if Mr. Saburenkov makes a fuss."

Perspiration beaded on Slava's oily brow as he poked a finger under his collar and wiggled it around. "That's the thing. He's known for making a fuss."

"And I'm known for shutting down people who make a fuss. Like you right now." He snapped his head around and tapped Dima hard on the shoulder. "Finland Station. Go."

Dima made no effort to drive off, merely grunting, obviously waiting for the OK from his boss cousin.

"Are you absolutely sure about this?" said Slava. "We've already got our list of suspects. I've secured a meeting with one of them for this afternoon."

"Is my entire time here going to be spent in goddam meetings?" Jacob was being disingenuous; he knew the real world of humint espionage was dominated by them.

"Of course not. However, some are totally necessary if we are to have any hope of preventing Severnaya Volna. That means getting you an audience with my Industry and Trade boss and then with our three suspects. Unfortunately, only Colonel-

General Denis Kolodin has agreed at this stage. You have an appointment with him tomorrow afternoon, 4:00 p.m. Marfa and I are working hard to snag the others." Slava's tone grew a fraction more animated. "Kolodin's champing at the bit to wedge military concerns into the accord with Estonia. We believe he's coordinating with the—"

"Look, of course I'll meet with Kolodin. And if you or Petko can't convince the others to talk to me, I'll approach them myself." He wasn't sure how that would work, but he'd find a way.

"Marfa's sure she'll get them over the line today or tomorrow. I don't think you should—"

"Let me use the small window of time I have now to look at your files, OK? Drive me to the station and I'll read the documents on the way." Jacob could feel the frustration creeping into his voice. More calmly, he added, "I've brought my laptop for that very reason."

"It's a ton of material," said Dima, pessimistically shaking his head. "You'll need a day to digest it all. Maybe two."

"Indeed." Slava shook his head. "Marfa was right. We already have the short-list, whittled down from a very long one. That's where to concentrate our efforts. Asking questions of people working in a public area will draw attention. Train stations are crawling with FSB, looking out for suspicious activity."

"Listen," said Jacob through a clenched jaw, irritation returning with renewed vigor. "Marfa Petko might be your leader, but she's not mine. I don't have a leader; I need free rein to do as I please. It's the way I operate, the way I've always operated." After a short beat, he added, "I've dealt with plenty of hostile agents before, FSB included. I can spot them, elude them, and eliminate them all in the space of one morning."

Slava frowned. "I'm sure that's an exaggeration. However, we've been told you're our best hope, so I'll take you on your word."

"Smart move."

"You are mistaken about Marfa, though. She's not our leader. She's an alpha female, I'll grant you that, but we have no leader. Decisions are taken on a consensus basis."

Jacob failed to stifle a laugh. "Oh, boy. That's a recipe for disaster."

"Why? I thought Westerners were the champions of democracy."

"Sure we are." He'd say no more on his personal definition of democracy. "I need some think time. Tell me when we're there."

"Dima. Take the gentleman to Finland Station," said Slava, leaning back in his seat and resting his chin between thumb and forefinger. For a moment, Jacob looked past him at the shuffling citizens, treading carefully on ice-covered sidewalks, swaddled in parkas and greatcoats, beanies and ushanka fur hats. Scarves wrapped high, covering noses in the rising wind. How he missed Lisbon already.

With approximately sixteen minutes before they pulled up at Lenin Square opposite the station, Jacob inserted the USB and busied himself with the three profiles. Speed reading was a skill he'd honed while cooped up in his estate on Keuka Lake. The key was to build up your reticular activating system, which allows the brain to focus on certain stimuli—such as words on a page—and block out everything else. After two years' practice, he had attained a phenomenal speed of 18,000 words per minute with a ninety-eight percent comprehension level. To get through these files, sixteen minutes was enough.

He yanked out the flash drive and turned to Slava, the combover falling over his pate like threads unraveling from a cheap bathrobe. Jacob let out a weighty sigh. "I compliment Vanya on the way he's put these dossiers together. And like Vanya, I agree with his conclusion: the three of them are working together. But I disagree that Kolodin's the one pulling the strings. My money's on that being Sergei Semak."

Slava's eyes widened. "You can't have read all the material. It took me over a week." His thin eyebrows knitted. "The dossier on Semak alone is two hundred and fifty pages long."

"That's why I started with him. The Deputy Governor of the Leningrad Oblast is one of the dirtiest and most corrupt politicians ever to come to power in this country. And that's saying something, considering the lineup of the rogues' gallery, past and present."

"But how...?"

Jacob tapped the side of his head. "Self-improvement, Slava. I'll send you links to YouTube videos on how to level up your reading skills."

"We're here," said Dima. "What now?"

"Come with me. I need you to be my lookout. Slava, you wait in the car. Call Dima if you sense something's wrong."

"Why would anything be wrong?" The quaver was back in his voice. "Surely we weren't followed."

"I'm sure we weren't," he soothed, hand resting on the door handle. "But that man scrolling his switched-off cell phone back at the hotel was off."

"Don't worry. I remember what that fatty looked like." Slava flicked his finger like he was shooing away an annoying child. "Just hurry up, for God's sake. After airports, train stations are my least favorite places to loiter."

"I won't take more time than I have to." He looked at Dima. "Let's go rattle some windows."

EIGHT

Vending machines dispensed tickets at various points around the station's massive hall. Only a handful of people lined up at the row of ticket windows. Window 12, thankfully, was customer-free.

"How are you going to get the ticket seller to talk?" Dima said, slapping his hands together. A digital thermometer on the wall told them it was only a degree warmer inside than on the street.

"I've got a couple of ideas bouncing around in my head." He pointed at an empty bench seat with a good view of the floor space, people coming and going through the main entrance and moving toward the platforms. "Meanwhile, you take up position over there. If anything catches your eye, call me. I take it you have the number of the burner phone Slava gave me?"

"*Da.* Of course." Dima chewed his bottom lip. "Please be as quick as you can. Slava's gonna be shitting bricks back in the car."

"I'll take as much time as I need. Hopefully, it won't be long."

As he approached window 12, an idea occurred to him. He walked back to where Dima sat, face half-buried in a newspaper. Jacob grinned. Props to the man; he actually appeared to be reading it. Jacob slid into an adjacent seat and whispered over his shoulder, "Leave your Ministry ID on the seat, get up, walk away slowly, and take a position by the information kiosk. No questions."

Dima took a deep breath, folded the newspaper, and laid it on the seat. He surreptitiously retrieved his ID from his wallet, stood, and melted into the crowd scurrying about the hall. Jacob saw him reemerge by a drink vending machine next to the information kiosk, where he bounced on his toes, casting his eyes about as if waiting to greet someone off a train.

Jacob placed his shoulder bag on the seat Dima had vacated, covering the ID, slid a hand under the bag, and palmed the plastic card. The flimsy document, a real government-issued ID, lifted his confidence more than any fake identification could. Never mind that Dima looked nothing like him in the photo.

On the other side of the glass, a young woman with purple-tinged hair shaved close on one side and a discreet nose stud looked up from her terminal. She chewed gum the way someone keeps a nervous hand occupied, jaw working while her eyes evaluated him. She wore the RZD Russian Railways uniform precisely; professionalism masked whatever private irritation she felt. Jacob cleared his throat and said, "Dmitry Sechkin. RZD's Auditing and Oversight Committee has sent me here to look into an urgent matter."

"What matter?" she said out of the side of her mouth.

"The matter of money not reconciling with the number of tickets sold." He tilted his head and flashed a sarcastic grin. "Your name, Gospozha Kuznetsova, has arisen in our random computer checks." He had to call her *gospozha*, the Russian equivalent of Ms.; the badge pinned to her blouse showed her last name and first initial, Z. Not knowing her first name was unfortunate, but he knew a way around it.

"I've never heard of such a committee," she said. "We get all kinds of weirdos here. Mind if I make a phone call?"

He pressed the plastic ID hard against the glass, glanced at her name badge, and fixed her with a glare that could strip paint. "I've got no time for insolence. Aside from defrauding the state, I'm going to have a word with the station's site manager about your hair and choice of jewelry."

Her finger lightly touched the nose adornment.

"Remove it at once," Jacob barked.

The chewing stopped, the wad of gum folded into her left cheek. Her throat tightened as she swallowed. An unsteady hand twisted the stud free and tucked it out of sight under the counter. Jacob allowed himself the faintest of grins; she was putty in his hands.

"Put up your closed sign. Open the back door to your booth. I'll be with you in a few moments. Do not touch anything until I get there."

Half a minute later, after negotiating a narrow passage behind the bricked-in ticket windows, he stood shoulder to shoulder with the agitated woman. Powerful heating from a radiator negated the need for her to wear warm clothes inside the cramped space of the booth. A look through the window across the concourse confirmed that Dima was still in position, discreetly scanning the hall for trouble. Eye contact established and nods exchanged, Jacob turned his attention back to the woman. He could smell the fear coming off her.

"I need to see your passport and make a note of its number. A formality, you understand."

She grumbled under her breath, retrieving a well-worn yellow leather handbag from beside her stool and passing him the reddish-brown ID. In Russia, passports came in two flavors: international and internal. The latter were introduced after the abolition of serfdom to control the movement of newly liberated citizens. The method was so effective that successive regimes used it with no intention of ever giving it up.

Jacob quickly flipped through the pages of the woman's passport, laid it on the counter, and tapped information into a note-taking app on his burner. "Thank you, Zinaida."

"Zina," she said.

"As you please." He gave her the soulless stare of a government functionary. "Your cooperation has been duly noted." He waited a couple of seconds. "Tell me, Zina, before I go through your electronic data, am I going to find evidence of petty pilfering?"

She couldn't look him directly in the eye. "If you do, it won't have been by me. I don't steal."

"That's what they all say."

"I'm not the only one who works this window, you know." Her eyes blinked rapidly, and her lips twitched. "We work in shifts."

"If you have suspicions, tell me what they are. Naming the guilty party could save your job." His head tilted slightly as he adjusted his glasses and squinted. "The RZD has a zero-tolerance policy when it comes to thieving."

"My job? What are you even—" Her eyes rounded as she spluttered, turning her attention to the floor. "I… ah… I've got no information about other employees. Sorry."

Jacob made a calming hand gesture. "It's OK. I'm not asking you to rat on anyone. Only if you physically saw someone stealing money. Covering up for someone else can be construed as being as bad as the crime itself." He shook his head and tut-tutted softly. Time to take a gamble. "Zina, I'm gonna be totally frank with you. The system flagged an irregularity from November 9. At 10:16 a.m. on that day, two tickets were purchased from this window. They were from Ivangorod back to Saint Petersburg, not the other way around. And they weren't return tickets either. Odd, to say the least."

She mumbled a string of incoherent words.

"I know you were working that shift," he lied, stabbing a finger at her. "Worst of all, the takings don't reconcile; exactly that amount has gone missing. What's going on, Zina?"

"What do you mean, what's going on? I didn't steal anything, I swear to God. As for what's odd and what isn't, I just sell the tickets." She shrugged melodramatically. "I don't question the whys and wherefores. I'm not the fucking police."

"Language, Zina."

"Sorry." Her chest heaved under her blouse, breaths coming short and sharp.

Ease back on the pressure, Hunter. Don't make her pass out. "OK," he said, relenting for a moment. "We can get to the bottom of this. Let's assume there's a glitch somewhere. Did you ask the customer for photo ID?"

Zina nodded, lips pressed tightly together. "I always ask, and it's always given." Her cheeks reddened. "I... ah... don't always record it, though. Like if the train's about to leave and the customer is in a hurry."

"Zina, Zina, Zina," said Jacob in a drawl. "No one was rushing for a train. The tickets in question were for the next day. From another town."

"Oh yeah..." She stared at her scuffed shoes, then looked up. "OK, so sometimes I forget to demand the ID. Is that a crime?"

He shook his head. "Not technically. But it could be grounds for dismissal." He tapped a finger on the counter. "Show me the logs for your shift on November 9."

As Zina clicked a mouse, staring at the lines of data on her computer screen, the rapid blinking returned. She groaned and pointed at an entry. "Oh, shit. The customer bought the tickets with cash, so there's no way of knowing who it was." She gave an uneasy titter. "In case you wanted to know that for any reason." She cursed under her breath, then looked pleadingly at Jacob. "Please, I need this job to pay my rent."

"Bullshit," challenged Jacob. "You could get another job."

She shook her head. "My cousin works for the railway, pretty high up. I was desperate for a job, and she introduced me to one of the bigwig managers. I... oh, fuck, this is embarrassing."

Jacob quirked an eyebrow, waiting for her to incriminate herself. "I did him a special favor, if you know what I mean, and he agreed to hire me. If I can't pay the rent on my studio—which I'm behind on—I'll be thrown out onto the streets with nowhere to go. I was stupid renting such an expensive place." A heavy sigh with the beginnings of tears. "Please, if there's money missing, I'll give it to you, even though I've done nothing wrong."

"The thing is," said Jacob urgently, "the identity of the person who purchased the tickets is, as you hinted at before, important."

"Why?" Suspicion crept into her voice, fine furrows lining her brow.

"I'm afraid that information is confidential." He gave her a conspiratorial wink. "Part of an ongoing investigation."

A bleep from the computer interrupted their conversation. "Look," said Zina, taking a half-step away. "Here are the entries for all my shifts for this month. As you can see, I've got nothing to hide."

Jacob pretended to take great interest in the monitor before turning his gaze back to Zina. More in desperation than hope, he said, "Describe the person who bought the two tickets from Ivangorod. There's a chance I can convince the RZD to drop the investigation into pilfering."

"How would I remember that? Lots of people buy tickets from me."

Jacob gestured at the ticket-vending machines with people crowding around them. "Really?"

"Enough. When the machines break down—which is often—what do you think happens then?"

Jacob offered no comment on the reliability of RZD's technology, instead folding his arms high across his chest.

Zina scratched the shaved side of her head and screwed up her eyes. "Wait a minute, let me go pull up all the entries for November 9 again."

As a spark of hope ignited in Jacob's brain, he observed a uniformed cop approaching Dima on the other side of the concourse, hope now battling for supremacy with mild panic. The panic evaporated as Dima and the officer exchanged a laugh and the latter strode away, hands in his pockets.

"Look!" Zina pointed at notes corresponding to the purchase

transaction for the two tickets. "There's an extra piece of information here I didn't notice before. *Goszakaz*. Government order."

This was where Jacob could have come unstuck. If he really was the official he was claiming to be, this was a detail—not printed on the tickets themselves—that he should have been forearmed with. He had no choice but to bluff it out. "Of course I know it's a government order. That's why this thing is so messy and complicated."

She beamed like she'd just been given a Green Card and a free plane trip to America.

"What's so amusing?"

"That word, *goszakaz*, has helped me remember."

Promising.

"Go on."

Relief softened the harsh lines around her eyes, the pupils of which were dilated. Jacob wouldn't be surprised if Zina took substances to get her through the day. "Government orders are usually made and paid for online with a credit card," she said, voice amplified with eagerness. "But this time a guy came in person to collect. He paid for them in a great wad of cash."

"So this guy's only been here on that one occasion?"

"No. He came once before. Some months back."

"Who employs him?"

"No idea."

"Know his name?"

She looked up to the ceiling to divine the answer. "I think it was Oleg."

"Last name?"

A shake of the head, which slowly stopped and turned into a nod. "Actually, I do remember." She grinned. "He was so rude to me the first time that I demanded to see ID. His last name—God, this is awful—I can't remember it."

"Please try. Your future could depend on it."

She twisted her face with the effort of recollection. "Pretty sure it started with a K." Her eyes sprang open in a lightbulb moment. "It's the same name as that big ugly boxer Putin hates."

"The man who became the mayor of Kyiv?"

Her head jutted forward like a pigeon. "*Da.*"

"Klitschko?"

"*Tochno.* Exactly."

"Can you describe this Klitschko for me?"

Zina tilted her head to the side. "Isn't the name enough?"

Smart woman.

"It's an essential piece of the puzzle, true, but I like to have all bases covered. In case he's on the run and we need to alert the police to be on the lookout."

The explanation must have seemed reasonable to Zina. "OK. Let me think. This is very rough, OK? Mid to late thirties, shorter than you, maybe 180 cm tall, solid build, 85 to 90 kilos." Jacob did a quick mental conversion. Around five-nine, 185 to 200 pounds. "Brown eyes. He wore a black beanie, so I can't be sure about his hair. Quite good-looking, no scars or anything like his namesake, the boxer. Slightly upturned nose." She shrugged. "That's all I've got." She clasped her hands together in mock prayer. "Please tell me that's enough."

Jacob was already turning the handle of the door. "I hope so, Zina."

She blew out a puff of breath. "What about the missing money?"

"Don't worry about that now."

"So... I'm in the clear?"

He nodded. "For now. I'll make sure your record isn't impacted. Don't ruin the chance I've just given you."

She smiled weakly. "*Spasibo.* Thank you."

Taking long strides toward the exit, he made an almost imperceptible gesture toward Dima, who pocketed his cell and fell into step a couple of meters behind.

NINE

THE SQUARE WAS BUSIER THAN WHEN THEY'D FIRST arrived. The BMW sat exactly where they'd left it, a dark smudge among yellow taxis and trudging commuters. Exhaust fumes from idling engines clouded the air; street vendors shouted through woolen scarves covering their mouths against the bitter cold; an arguing couple wrestled a suitcase over an icy puddle.

Jacob's mind swam with thoughts—trace Klitschko, use him as an avenue to get to his master, whoever that was. Perhaps Vanya or Irina could hack into the system that created the goszakaz, determine which arm of government it came from. Cozy up to Colonel-General Kolodin tomorrow, see if he could incriminate himself or funnel Jacob toward the more likely master puppeteer, Deputy Governor Sergei Semak. Jacob's gut gnawed with the name Semak. Find the dirt on him, find the crux of the Severnaya Volna conspiracy.

He had to shut these thoughts down, focus on the here and now. Like a chess player, thinking four moves ahead is easy when you can see your opponent's pieces out in the open. In this game, he wasn't even sure who was moving the pieces on the other side of the board. First thing: get to the meeting with Saburenkov.

Jacob swung open the rear door, tossed in his carry bag, and slid in beside the waiting Slava. The scene of brutality to his left snapped into clear focus.

Slava lay slumped over the seat, his bent fingers clutching at a neck bisected by the straight red line of a garrote. At a glance, Jacob knew this was the handiwork of an expert assassin. From a small cut above the eye, blood dripped slowly onto his collar. Another patch matted the fringe of his combover. A spot marked the leather seat next to the seatbelt buckle. White eyeballs bulged, his last brief moments spent in sheer terror. Two fingers to the neck confirmed it—no pulse. Thankfully, death would have been swift, thanks to the killer's skill. Slava had tried to put up a fight—the traces of blood left behind made that clear. But surprise and a garrote win every time.

Dima's hand rested on the roof of the car, his head poking inside. Horror drew his eyebrows together, his lips disappearing behind his gums. A hand shot to his mouth, stifling a scream.

Jacob glared a warning at him. "Don't make a fuss."

"Are you kidding!" Dima hissed, tears welling, the color draining from his face. "We have to get him some help."

"There's nothing we can do. He's dead."

"No!"

"Yes."

"Are you sure?"

"A hundred percent." Jacob stared at Dima. "I've seen more dead bodies than you can imagine."

"Try CPR, anything!"

"It's pointless. I already checked his pulse. He's gone."

Dima's shoulders slumped as the reality hit him hard.

"Don't just stand there," Jacob spat. "Get in the car, quick."

Dima obeyed, slamming the door behind him with a loud thunk. He thumped his hands against the steering wheel. "I knew this was going to happen, dammit." He twisted in his seat, the horror on his face replaced by dawning, red-eyed sadness—he'd just lost a relative—and the onset of a jittery panic. "What do we do? Call the police?"

"No chance." He recalled the restriction on his movements when the Dutch police got involved after Irina was snatched. It had hampered him worse than a pair of leg irons. They had to keep flying under the radar right to the end.

"We drive away then," Dima suggested. He bashed the steering wheel again. "*Blyad'*. Fuck. I'm not sure I'm in a fit state to drive a car." He held trembling hands out as evidence.

"I'll drive if you're not up to it."

"No, it's fine. I can..." Two deep breaths. "...drive." Dima's head shook from side to side before locking eyes with Jacob as a thought dawned on him. "Have we been made? How did they find us? Are we in danger? What happens to B+ now?" There was a two-second pause that seemed like two minutes. In a voice of forced calm, he said through clenched teeth, "What do we do?"

Jacob's mind raced. Dima's panic-induced laundry list of questions had merit and deserved answers. There was no time to get into a conversation about all of them, but one required an immediate answer. What *was* the right thing to do here?

Think, Hunter, think.

He glanced out both sides of the car.

The square and the streets surrounding the station were heavily trafficked—by pedestrians and vehicles. Someone must have seen something. If not, and the killer had evaded the attention of the public, evidence of the crime must have been caught on security cameras dotted around the area.

People walked inches from the car, oblivious. The heavily tinted windows were a blessing. Jacob watched a pregnant woman with a heavily distended stomach lumber past, headphones on, perhaps listening to something to drown out the cries of a baby she was pushing in a stroller. A teenage boy laughed maniacally, cell phone pressed to his ear. Life trundled by, side by side with death.

A woman screamed, and Jacob's heart stopped. His head swiveled around, but no one was near the car now.

"What was that?" he said. "Can you see from the front?"

Dima edged forward in his seat, face almost pressing the windshield. "About a hundred meters away, near the entrance to the station. A woman arguing with a man. A crowd's forming. People coming from all directions."

Jacob pressed the button to lower his window a fraction, shielding Slava's body with his own. "I can see it. A couple of cops are attending now. One's calling on his radio."

"Should we go now?" said Dima. "While no one's looking our way?"

"*Da.*" He raised the window again. "We need to get far away, collect our thoughts, regroup. How long to get to Vanya's dacha?"

"Hour and three-quarters in this weather."

"Let's go then."

Dima pressed the start button, the engine catching with a soft rumble. The BMW eased from the curb, exited the square, and merged into the flow of morning traffic.

"Don't take the northern embankment," said Jacob.

Dima jerked his head around, grimacing at the sight of the dead man, then looking to the front again. "You're kidding. It's the fastest way. It could add thirty minutes to the journey if we backtrack."

"Fastest isn't always smartest. Go via the city center."

A head shake in the mirror. "I don't think that's a—"

"Don't think anything. Just do as I say."

"Whatever."

Jacob felt his muscles tense. Slava's death was down to him. He'd insisted on driving to the train station, not listening, pursuing his own avenue of investigation. B+ already had the shortlist. They'd done years' worth of digging, and perhaps that should have been enough. He'd not push in that direction now: Vanya, Irina, or both of them could do that—try and isolate the goszakaz, see where it led.

Jacob clenched his jaw. *He* was responsible for leaving Slava on his own and unprotected. *He* had to make things right.

The car made slow progress along the low and broad Liteyny Bridge. Glances behind and in front didn't reveal obvious tails. He sighed deeply, mentally cursing the lack of a weapon. He should have pushed Petko when he had the chance. Unless...

"Dima."

"Uh-huh."

"I don't suppose you've got a Makarov and a couple of clips tucked away in the glove box, do you?"

"Sorry, no." He tilted his head but kept his eyes forward, concentrating on the road as vehicles slowed in front of them. "B+ is an intelligence-gathering team, Gospodin Tamm."

"Drop the formalities, for God's sake. Robert will do."

"Of course. Look, we simply don't carry guns. Never have."

"Your policy needs a rethink."

"Perhaps."

More thoughts arose. In addition to the lifeless passenger, in and of itself a liability, there were other worries. Like the looming meeting with Pavel Saburenkov. Should he attend? He felt around in Slava's pockets, praying the assassin had been in too much of a hurry to get the job done to worry about taking his cell. Luckily, they had been.

"Your cousin's cell is PIN-protected," Jacob grumbled. "Any ideas what it might be?"

"Yes, we all know each other's PINs. Just in case. 0101."

He punched in the number, and the Samsung sprang to life. "I'm putting this on loudspeaker."

"One second," said Dima, a note of alarm in his voice. "Who are you calling?"

"The guy from the ministry I'm supposed to be meeting. Slava said if I was going to be late, all doors would be slammed shut. I'm going to tell Saburenkov I'll be a little bit late, but that he should see me anyway."

"You aren't thinking of going there by yourself, are you? He'll be expecting Slava to accompany you."

"Not if he's sick. I'll say he took a turn, we dropped him off at home, and he forgot his cell in the car. Hence me calling on his phone."

"Granted, that's plausible." Dima's tone nevertheless reflected doubt.

"Which means the escape to the countryside will have to wait. If I show at Saburenkov's office, having made an excuse for Slava's absence, that'll buy us some time before they realize the poor fellow's gone missing."

"Makes sense." This time Dima sounded more confident in Jacob's assessment. "Want me to head for the ministry?"

"No. Let's park up near the Summer Garden for now."

"Parking's not easy in that area. Plus we've got"—his voice was cracking—"Slava in the car."

"It's OK for now. At a casual glance, he looks like a man asleep."

A blank stare in the mirror was Dima's only reply.

Jacob made a squint-eyed smile. "Just find a parking spot in an out-of-the-way place. A side street, behind a dumpster. Use your damned initiative. You were sharp at the train station; I know you've got it in you."

Without commenting further, he dialed from memory, the number having been included in the contacts on his burner phone. It was a cell number, not a landline, so probably Saburenkov's personal phone. The number rang out; no option to leave a message.

"What now?" said Dima.

"Let me think for a minute."

"You gonna call Petko and Vanya? They need to know about Slava."

"Agreed. I'll give it a couple minutes; let's see if Saburenkov calls back."

Above the road lay a spiderweb of wires supplying power to trams and trolleybuses. Jacob's eyes were drawn to the frozen Neva River below, the vast expanse of white ice spreading east and west. In summer, the bridge sometimes yawned open at night, two sections rising into the sky, stopping traffic to allow vessels to pass through the gap. Jacob was grateful it was winter and daytime. Getting stuck on this bridge with a cadaver on board didn't bear thinking about; bluffing only gets you so far.

Slava's body sat unnaturally stiff beside him, the head listing slightly, the fine line at his throat already darkening. Jacob had pulled the scarf from his own neck and tucked it over the wound, out of a sense of decency and respect as much as anything else. He regarded the benign face of the dead man for a moment. He'd given his life for a cause greater than himself. Let his death not be in vain. Slava had been a fussbudget and a worrier, but Jacob knew he'd been a decent human being—one who didn't deserve to be executed for the crime of trying to save his country. He said a silent prayer and turned his attention to the road ahead. The speedometer was creeping over the limit.

"Slow down," said Jacob. "No breaking speed limits, no traffic violations of any kind when we're on the major arteries."

"Sorry. I'm used to getting away with anything." He flashed a watery grin in the rearview mirror. "Ministry plates."

"I don't care if you've got Putin's personal tags on the car. Just take it easy."

"I will, I will," he said with multiple sharp nods. The speed-tracking digits on the dash dropped to 55 kph, five under the limit. Even at this moderate speed, Dima's knuckles were white on the wheel. "You think someone's following us?"

"I've observed nothing suspicious. To be on the safe side, take a couple of side streets, then double back onto the Palace Embankment."

Dima nodded. The wiper blades scythed rhythmically across the windshield as the falling snow thickened. He made a left after the Troitsky Bridge down Mramorny Pereulok, drove briefly along Millionnaya Street, then executed a tight U-turn at Aptekarsky Pereulok. Baroque and neoclassical styles of architecture dominated this part of the city. As Jacob stared at the elegant three-story buildings that could have been in Venice or Rome, Slava's phone burst to life in his lap, making him jump a half inch in his seat.

"Pull in here," said Jacob, nodding at a vacant curbside space. A delivery van and a small sedan had left a convenient gap, big enough for the BMW to fit in—just.

"I thought you wanted to stop at the Summer Garden?" Dima shook his head, possibly not used to plans changing on the fly. He'd better get used to it, Jacob mused.

"Here's fine." Jacob placed a finger to his lips as Dima turned in his seat to add something. Dima nodded understandingly.

"Hello," said Jacob, swiping across the screen and tapping the loudspeaker icon. "Robert Tamm speaking."

"What?"

"Robert Tamm. From Estonia. I have a meeting scheduled with you in"—a glance at his Breitling wristwatch—"twenty minutes. I'm afraid I'm going to be late. My apologies."

A ragged cough came down the line. "I'm sorry. I don't understand. This is Vyacheslav Gabulov's phone, is it not?"

"Indeed it is." Jacob informed Saburenkov that his employee had taken ill and they'd dropped him at his apartment. He was so distracted by his aching stomach that he'd forgotten his cell in the car.

"In a nutshell, some other things have come up, and I'd like to request that we postpone our meeting until tomorrow."

"I've got a full diary." Saburenkov's commanding voice suggested a man who doesn't like to make concessions. Jacob pictured a disheveled man with two days' stubble, a crumpled jacket slung over the back of his chair, a bottle of vodka in the bottom drawer, and a string of mistresses scattered around the city.

The answer was perfect obfuscation, thought Jacob. Not a yes or a no, but a classic dismissal. Slava's assessment of the man had been dead-on.

"What a shame," said Jacob. "Because I've just had a call from my country's president. Mr. Karilaid wished me the best of luck liaising with your ministry and expressed the hope that new bonds could be forged."

He caught a glimpse of Dima in the mirror, nodding, realizing Jacob wasn't someone to be taken lightly.

"Just one minute." There was the sound of a chair scraping, mumbled conversation with three or four voices, and random scratching noises. "OK. With a bit of juggling, I've managed to push another appointment back. Come to my office at midday tomorrow. I'll organize a lunch, some drinks."

"That sounds like a plan. See you then."

At the end of the call, three cars slowly passed them on the right, slush spraying in their wake. One of them touched something in Jacob's passive memory. He rubbed his chin and said, "Did you see that silver Toyota just now?"

"You mean the one with the broken side mirror?"

"Yeah, that one."

"Look familiar?"

"Ah... I... Now that you mention it, I think I saw it back at the train station, parked a couple of spots away from us." Dima exhaled deliberately. "It's slowing down up ahead, letting the other two cars go around it. Now it's stopped. Jesus Christ, what should we do?"

"Did the license plates mean anything to you?"

A shrug. "Not government."

"Local?"

"The number ends in 78, so yes. Registered in Saint Petersburg." He paused a beat, then said, "You think it's the killers?"

"Possibly."

"It has to be." Dima's voice rose half an octave. "How much of a coincidence could it be? They were on our ass at the station, then turn up here in Aptekarsky Pereulok."

"Pop the trunk."

"What?"

"Just do as I say. I'm going to have a chat with whoever's in the car, and I need a tire iron."

"What the hell for?" Dima's eyes rounded. "You're not going to take them on, are you?"

"Insurance. I'm going to have a word, see if I can figure out what's going on."

"No tire iron, I'm afraid. No jack either. This car's designed to run on a flat until a new tire can be fitted."

Jacob swore under his breath.

"And how's a tire iron going to compete with a gun anyway?"

"They didn't shoot Slava; they garroted him."

"Doesn't mean they're not armed."

He had to concede that point to Dima.

"What's in the car that I can use as a weapon?"

"Nothing. This model's designed to protect the people inside it... except..."

"Except it didn't protect Slava," said Jacob, grasping the irony. Which meant Slava opened the door because he either knew the killer and suspected nothing, or the killer did a convincing job of appearing to be in need of assistance. He pictured the young woman with the stroller; a pregnant woman, small child in tow, tapping on the window with a look of desperation on her face may have tugged at Slava's heartstrings. Even opening the door or winding down the window a fraction would be enough for a skilled assassin to make their move. Yes, he imagined Slava would've been that gallant gentleman who opens doors to women in distress.

"No. And neither did we." The unspoken word was *you. You, Hunter. You failed to protect him.*

"Come on, think. Is there at least a toolkit in the trunk?"

A nod. "Yes, but it's basic. The only actual tool in it is a small reversible flat- and Phillips-head screwdriver."

"Great. Anything in the glove box? A Swiss Army knife?"

"No knives. Just a thermos. Hot tea with honey and lemon. I easily catch colds in the winter and—"

"I don't need a background story on your health. Is it plastic or metal?"

"Metal. And it's full." His eyebrows elevated as he began to understand Jacob's intentions. "So it'll have some heft."

"Great. Now hand me the damned thing and pop the trunk so I can get the screwdriver."

"You sure this is the right thing to do?" Dima's body was twisted at the waist like he was a human pretzel, eyes averted from Slava's body. In his hand was the steel thermos.

"We need to send a strong message. This can't be the FSB we're dealing with. My gut is screaming at me that Severnaya Volna isn't government-sanctioned; they're hired muscle working outside the system." He grinned wanly. "Much easier to deal with."

As he was about to alight, Dima stopped him. "In a compartment in the trunk you'll find a black box marked *Reflective Clothing and PPE*. Inside the box there's a bright green jacket with reflective silver strips and a matching beanie."

"*Otlichno.* Excellent." The symbols would add credence to his role-playing.

"They've got the official two-headed eagle coat of arms and ministry logo stitched into them and everything."

"Even better."

"I just remembered how I have to carry this shit in the car, just in case. Finally, I think this is a 'case' where they'll actually be useful."

Jacob nodded. Not just useful. Perfect.

"Do something for me while I'm gone, will you?"

"What?"

"Call Petko and Vanya."

"Of course. What do I say?"

"Tell them to watch their asses."

"Should I explain what happened to Slava? They're gonna have questions. Petko in particular. She's a journalist, remember."

"Journalists are used to their sources playing mind games. Tell her to leave her phone open. I'll break the news to her once I've dealt with this tail. Vanya, too."

"What if there's no answer?"

"Don't leave any messages. We try again later."

TEN

JACOB EXHALED, THIN WHITE JETS POURING THROUGH his nostrils. Then a steadying, deep inhale. He was running on instinct, not entirely convinced this was the correct action. For a man who leveraged logic, this was far from logical. His gut screamed at him: *Do it*.

He trod the icy sidewalk with purpose, the role he was about to play cementing in his mind. Each step required concentration and care. The opposite side of the laneway was boarded up for renovations, although none were happening, and it looked like the workmen wouldn't be back until spring. Windows remained shuttered; there was no foot traffic, no cameras angled at the street from on high. In fact, none were visible anywhere. But that didn't mean they weren't there: Saint Petersburg was one of the most surveilled cities in Europe—approximately eighteen cameras per one hundred people.

Thirty yards ahead, the late-model silver SUV idled, its broken mirror looking like a boxer's smashed tooth. Two large-built men sat up front, both encased in thick winter coats, heads covered in dark beanies. Jacob saw the driver watching intently through the rearview mirror as he approached, the eyes not blinking. The second guy had his eyes trained on his cell phone, head nodding.

Jacob's heart thundered, adrenaline coursing through his veins. He kept the thermos tucked under his coat and the screwdriver palmed where he could feel its molded handle. The shank was only four inches long, but it was sharp and pointy.

Jacob tugged the zipper of the reflective jacket and pulled the beanie down low over his eyes. He tapped on the window with gloved knuckles, gesturing for the driver to wind it down. From his higher viewpoint, he looked for the outlines of guns, but the men's coats covered every place a weapon could possibly be concealed. They were there, though—he had no doubt. The window crept down a fraction.

"The fuck you want?" said the driver, an objectively handsome man with a slightly upturned nose. If the description given by Zina was accurate, he was staring at the man who'd bought the train tickets: Oleg Klitschko. "We're busy."

Something about the aggressive tone told Jacob the man didn't know who he was—or who he was supposed to be. The goons must've been tailing Slava's driver, not Robert Tamm, to see where he'd take the body. Either that or they'd failed to recognize him.

Russia has its own brand of highway police, the Gosavtoinspektsiya, or GAI—the State Automobile Directorate—distinct from other branches in form and purpose. Its practitioners of law enforcement had been known for their greed and corruptibility since Soviet times. A master of vocal versatility, Jacob summoned the persona of a jaded GAI officer, one whose days were filled with the soul-sapping toil of dealing with dumb-ass members of the public. He raised his hand to his forehead, tipping them a three-finger salute and a sarcastic smile that boded bad news.

"Good morning, gentlemen."

"I said, what the fuck do you want?" The driver's lips curled into a snarl as his arms folded across his chest in the classic closed-off attitude.

Jacob coughed into his fist. "I'm an off-duty police officer," he said, adding a raspy growl. "I'm obliged to inform you that you've been driving with a broken mirror. I'm afraid I'm going to have to issue you with an infringement notice and collect a fine."

"Ha!" laughed the burly guy in the passenger seat. "Even off-duty you assholes are on the take." His hand reached into an inside jacket pocket. In an instant it reappeared, brandishing a black pistol. The driver leaned back slightly to give clear space between the muzzle and the pain in the ass wearing the fluro gear.

Jacob grimaced, waiting for the shot he prayed wouldn't come. God was listening to his prayers today. If the goon had pulled the trigger, lights out would've been quick and messy. Jacob had practiced with this very model on the private firing range of his New York estate: a 9mm P226 Sig Sauer Legion. He'd seen the weapon turn clay plant pots into dust like a laser gun in a sci-fi movie; a couple of shots from this distance would obliterate his head.

"I'm not looking for trouble, fellas." He held his hands up in mock surrender, one hand gripping his burner phone. "And I'm not even going to ask to see your licenses. In fact, I'm gonna do you a favor by giving you the chance to get off lightly. Thing is, I've already taken photos of the vehicle—your registration plates. I press the button on this phone and everything gets uploaded to the GAI server, and then you're totally screwed. Just pay the fine, and we can all go about our business. What do you say?"

"What do I say, motherfucker?" The driver unlatched his door and shoved it open. Jacob took a step back just in time to avoid a shattered tibia. He gasped as he felt one foot slip an inch on a patch of black ice.

The pissed-off driver swore under his breath, his wallet in his right hand. He thumbed it open to reveal an impressive wad of cash nestled inside the soft Italian leather. Jacob's hawk eye spotted the careless man's name printed on a driver's license behind a square of clear plastic. Oleg Klitschko.

Klitschko pulled out a sheaf and fanned the notes under Jacob's nose, taunting, before returning them to the wallet. There was enough time to clock the wide variety of currencies: dollars, euros, pounds sterling, Swiss francs, rubles. Only in Russia did people of importance—or those who thought they were important—walk around with such a kaleidoscope of cash. Foreign bills with real purchasing power to buy things that mattered and the local money for basic necessities.

"I say you can go to hell, asswipe."

Jacob tut-tutted and shook his head. "Let's not argue the point, huh? You've got more than enough coin there to cover a hundred fines every day for a year." He injected a note of respect mixed with envy. "A successful man like yourself isn't likely to miss a few bills, right?"

"OK. Just to get you out of my sight. How much do you want, *musor?*"

Jacob grinned—quite a compliment to his acting skills to be called the Russian equivalent of a filthy cop.

"I tell you what. Give me two hundred US dollars and I won't even make a record of the infringement. The photos get deleted and nothing goes on your file." He gave a lopsided grin. "Just make sure to get that defect repaired within forty-eight hours, or you could receive further penalties or have the vehicle declared unfit for road use."

"Fuck you." He sneered as he flipped the bird. "You can have rubles. And I'm not giving you more than three thousand, you fucking vulture."

The man pulled off one glove with his teeth, then the other with his free hand.

"Let's move to the sidewalk, shall we?" said Jacob, already guiding the man by the elbow.

To his surprise, the man walked without resistance, saying nothing. Deep down, even the most hardened criminals can sometimes subconsciously bend to the rule of law, even if the law's representative is a fraud.

Pulling up next to the rear corner of the car, Jacob said, "Here will do, buddy. Hand over the money and I'll be on my way."

"So you'll settle for three grand in rubles, then?"

A nod and a shrug. "I can see you're a hard man to beat in an argument."

"Didn't like being called a vulture, more like it. Truth hurts, doesn't it?"

"I've been called a lot worse. Hurry up. I want to get back in my car, out of the cold, and back to my family."

The driver separated the Russian currency from its international cousins, licked a finger, and began to count off the banknotes. Jacob looked up the pereulok, back over his shoulder—then a couple more glances at the unmanned construction site and the buildings on the side where the car was parked. Had he missed a camera somewhere? None were evident.

Out of the corner of his eye, he saw the passenger make a movement. Not to get out of the car and join his buddy—worse than that. He was bringing his cell phone to his ear. Reporting location and the interaction to his master? Had he somehow rumbled Jacob?

He couldn't take the chance. This charade had to end.

Now.

Jacob's fingers flexed around the screwdriver's short, stubby handle. He felt the muscles and tendons in his forearm fill with the life-blood of brutal, impending action.

A reptilian tongue tip poked out the side of the driver's mouth before he resumed his fast-fingered counting, working with smooth motions that a veteran bank teller would envy. He flicked the notes. "One thousand one hundred, one thousand two—"

He uttered no more words as the pointy end of the tool plunged into his larynx. The wallet fell to the sidewalk, landing in an icy puddle with a squelch. A handful of paper money fluttered earthward in pursuit like autumn leaves.

The man made indistinct gurgling sounds, the color draining from his face in seconds. He dropped to his knees, his trembling left arm supporting his body while blood gushed as if from a burst fire hydrant, crimsoning the white sidewalk. His trembling right hand pressed against the wound site, blood escaping between his ineffectual fingers.

Like a batter at home plate, Jacob wriggled his feet to gain purchase, preparing for the next stanza of violence. His left hand quickly palpated the skin at the back of the goon's neck, finding the gap between the C3 and C4 vertebrae. Satisfied he'd identified the point of greatest vulnerability, he took careful aim and thrust the screwdriver as hard as he could, deploying an overhand grip for maximum power.

The shank penetrated to its full four-inch depth, slotting precisely into the intervertebral gap and piercing the spinal cord. To finish him off, Jacob plunged again and again—six rapid jabs—each requiring effort to yank the tool free from the man's stubborn bone and flesh. With a gush of air from the hole at the front of his neck, the man let go of his throat and collapsed onto the sidewalk like a bag of cement.

Jacob placed his index and middle fingers in the soft groove beside the guy's trachea, located the carotid artery, and confirmed that the thug had expired. As with all those he felled in the field, Jacob prayed to the Lord for his lost soul.

Killing Klitschko was not the ideal scenario. Under intense pressure, Klitschko would've revealed everything he knew: who the tickets were purchased for and, more importantly, under whose orders. Too bad that option had to be ruled out. But there was still the passenger to deal with.

Still kneeling, Jacob wiped the bloodied screwdriver on the back of the dead man's jeans until it was as clean as it could get. He picked up the wallet and all the loose bills. He grunted as he lifted the body a couple of inches at the right hip, patted around, and found the holy grail: an H&K pistol.

He dropped Klitschko and regarded the gun. He pressed a button to release the magazine—fully loaded. A wry smile tugged at his lips as he tucked the piece under his belt. A rapid visual sweep of the immediate vicinity found a couple of coins that must have dislodged from the man's pants pocket. He retrieved and stashed them too.

There'd be no time to conceal a number of other clues—boot prints; hairs or skin flakes left on the victim. Jacob knew samples of his own DNA would've been collected and stored after his mission to Moscow four years ago. If those data were matched with physical evidence left behind here in Aptekarsky Pereulok, the authorities would soon figure out that Klitschko's killer was Anatoly Voronin, Jacob's identity on that mission. On the other hand, it would take a miracle to draw the correct conclusion that Voronin and Tamm were one and the same person.

But that was all theory—thoughts that distracted from the here and now.

He had to do something about thug number two. Find out if he'd summoned backup. Now armed with the perfect weapon, taking this guy alive was Jacob's priority.

Moving to the passenger side, he saw the brute chatting amiably on the phone, lips parting to reveal a broad smile with dazzling white teeth. His head tilted back as he let out a belly laugh, accompanied by the mention of a woman's name. Tanya. A glimmer of hope. Must be talking to his girlfriend, not one of his bosses.

Jacob tapped on the window, bunching his facial muscles into an expression of alarm mixed with concern. He repeated his one-finger wind-down-the-window gesture. The glass dropped two inches.

"Just one second, Tanya," the passenger said, pressing the phone to his chest. He looked up at Jacob, eyes narrowed and teeth bared in undisguised hostility. Then an oblique snap of the head. "Hey. Where's Oleg?"

"Quick, get out. You have to help me. He's had a nasty fall and hit his head. I can't get him up."

The man frowned, clearly not taken in. "Bullshit." He reached under his jacket, but Jacob already had his hand gripped around the handle of Klitschko's H&K. Jacob held the gun horizontal to the ground and racked the slide, chambering a round.

"Hang up your call without speaking to the person on the other end, put the phone on the dash, and then place your hands on either side of the weapon, palms down."

The man hesitated, not taking his eyes off the muzzle inches from his nose. Jacob thrust out his chin, gesturing to the dash with his head. "Do it, or you'll be joining Oleg in eternal rest."

"What the fuck?" he said, a shaking hand placing the phone on the dashboard. "You killed him? Who the hell are you?"

In answer to all three questions, Jacob smashed the butt of the pistol against the bridge of the man's nose. An audible crack was followed by a trickle of blood.

"What the hell, man!"

"Shut the fuck up and do exactly as I say."

Two hands moved gingerly toward the dash. The man picked up the cell and pressed to end the call. Jacob opened the door with one hand. "Give me your phone. Slowly. I'll have no hesitation in pulling the trigger if you do anything stupid."

The man complied, his fluttering eyes reflecting the growing fear that had conquered bravado.

"Have you spoken to anyone except Tanya since you pulled over?"

A frown and a shake of the head. "No. Just her."

Jacob ordered him to get out of the vehicle—no sudden movements—and walk south toward the Moyka River embankment, hands folded together in front of him. No dawdling. Once this guy was in the BMW, there was the not-so-small matter of Klitschko's body littering the sidewalk. The area was deserted now, but for how long?

As they moved, Jacob fished the man's wallet out of his back pocket and the Sig Sauer from his coat. He dropped them into the capacious right pocket of his own greatcoat, which looked like a costume from *The Matrix*. The pistol and the thermos clanged merrily as the men marched briskly.

"What's your name?" Jacob demanded.

"Andrey."

"Andrey what?"

The captive slowed a fraction to answer the last question, earning a hard dig of the gun barrel into his ribs.

"Did I say stop, asshole? Last name!"

"Kaufman."

"Who do you work for?"

"I... don't know. I just came along for the ride. To help Oleg out. Keep him company. Know what I mean?"

Jacob laughed. "Sure. And you always carry a Sig when keeping your friends company?"

Andrey shrugged.

"Never mind. You'll tell me everything eventually."

"I swear," he murmured, taking shallow breaths, "I don't know anything that could be of any use to you."

"Can it for now and keep walking."

The pace picked up again.

Thirty yards later, they reached the BMW. Dima stood a discreet distance away, leaning against a drainpipe, his head shrouded in plumes of cigarette smoke. Jacob nodded at him as he muscled Andrey into the back seat, telling him to sit in the middle and stay still.

He beckoned Dima over, handed him the captured man's weapon, and told him to guard Andrey and finish him off if he tried anything funny.

"The car's soundproofed like a recording studio, Kaufman," Jacob growled. "No one will hear the shot."

Dima snatched at the *stvol* like he handled one every day. Slide racked, chamber and ejection port checked with a glance, trigger gently pressed to confirm reset, grip panels thumbed to get a feel for the weapon. He swiveled in his seat, brought the muzzle up in one smooth motion, and rested it an inch from the captive's temple, eyes level, posture steady. "My colleague wasn't joking.

No need for suppressors in this vehicle. One false move, and your brains say goodbye to your skull."

Shaking his head in wonder at Dima's hidden talents—for handling weapons and delivering threats—Jacob jumped into the driver's seat. They glided sedately up the still-deserted lane, double-parked against the Toyota. "Andrey. Is there anything in the vehicle I should know about? Trackers, that kind of thing? Because if I later find out you lied to me, a garroting will seem like a gentle foot massage compared to what I'll do to you. Got me?"

"*Da*, I get you." He shook his head like a demoralized POW. "As far as I know, there's nothing in the car apart from the... garrote... and assorted trash. You've got our guns, wallets, and phones. There's nothing else."

"Glad to hear it. Right. Time to clean up this mess before someone gets nosy. Andrey, get out and help me."

In under a minute, with Dima standing by with the H&K pointed discreetly through his jacket, Jacob and Andrey had manhandled Klitschko's body into the cargo area of the Toyota. Jacob opened the driver's door, popped the latch for the gas tank, walked around, and unscrewed the lid. He unwound the scarf he'd removed from Klitschko's neck. Although made of flame-resistant wool, soaking it in gas by shoving it into the filler neck, then turning it around and soaking the other end, would do the trick. One spark from Dima's lighter and the scarf was burning.

Time to haul ass.

They got back into the BMW, Jacob at the wheel, Dima covering Andrey in the back seat, the prisoner wedged against Slava's body. Jacob had ruled out putting Slava's corpse in the back of the Toyota before setting it alight. His remains, even burned to a crisp, would have raised too many questions—put Jacob, aka Robert Tamm, in the spotlight for lying to Saburenkov.

They drove at a steady speed north toward the Summer Garden. No one spoke until they heard the echo of an almighty explosion that ripped through the calm of a narrow Saint Petersburg pereulok.

Andrey made the sign of the cross, eyes closed.

"A fitting cremation for your buddy," said Jacob. He drew in a deep breath. "Be honest. It was you who killed Slava, right?"

Andrey's silence told Jacob exactly what he needed to know.

"Who ordered the hit?"

More silence.

"What do you know about a guy shadowing us at the Pribaltiyskaya Hotel?"

Again, no response.

"I'll get everything I need out of you eventually, Kaufman. You might as well get it over and done with."

But Andrey was made of stern stuff. Breakable, but stern.

"Fine. Have it your way. Your reticence just makes me more determined to go hard on you later. I'm not fond of torture." He let out a sarcastic chuckle. "In fact, when I was younger I even wrote a letter to the United Nations, complaining about what the KGB was doing to dissidents, what the CIA was doing to prisoners in Guantanamo." He paused a beat. "These days, I'm not so squeamish about it. In fact..." He turned around to lock eyes with Andrey as the traffic came to a halt at a set of lights. "I wholeheartedly embrace it."

Andrey found his voice. In barely a whisper, he said, "Klitschko was the one who killed him. It wasn't me. I just waited in the car while the pregnant girl we paid a hundred dollars turned on the waterworks and got Gabulov to open the door."

A fabrication, except for the part about paying the woman. Still, Jacob nodded. "See? That wasn't so hard. I'm sure you'll remember all kinds of details—even correct ones—once we get to the dacha. For now, though, just sit back, relax, and enjoy the scenery."

Despite the outward calm he was determined to show, Jacob's nerves were jangling like a wind chime in a hurricane. With no pharmaceutical relaxants to hand, Jacob asked Dima for a cigarette.

"Sorry. No smoking allowed in ministry vehicles."

"Are you allowed to carry dead bodies in them?"

"I... ah... no." Gun unwaveringly trained on Andrey, Dima reached awkwardly into his pocket, grabbed a pack of Marlboro, and held it out across the console. His lighter followed a moment later.

"Thanks," said Jacob. The cabin filled with smoke as Dima accepted a lit cigarette. Andrey looked on like he'd kill for one. Jacob resolved that the bastard would never enjoy another cigarette for the short remainder of his life.

"Did you make those calls while I was attending to Andrey and his pal?"

"*Da*. Twice. Petko didn't answer. And neither did Vanya. Unusual, because he nearly always does."

Neither of them answering set alarm bells ringing in Jacob's mind. "OK. Change of plan. The dacha will have to wait. We swing by the jewelry shop first."

ELEVEN

Irina stared out the window of the sprawling safe house, located in a mountainous region of central Portugal. Spectacular vistas opened up across the valley. Eucalyptus had spread like weeds in the country, finding root wherever there was a bare patch of soil. She could see and smell them in the distance, crowding out stands of native pines and cork oaks. The butler, Mario, had told her the importation of the trees began in the mid-20th century to create a pulp industry. The eucalypts were completely out of control; today the species was, incredibly, the most prolific across Portugal. In dry summers, the entire country was a powder keg, the Australian blue gum trees capable of exploding in a raging conflagration that could spread across thousands of acres. She'd made a mental comparison with a computer virus introduced on one machine that could quickly infect millions of others.

For now, though, in the cool of a drizzly wet fall, there was zero chance of a forest fire. She bore no illusions that she was totally safe. The tentacles of her and Yakov's enemies had a long reach.

Sitting at the dining table in the open-plan living room, her eyes darted back to the inbox of her recently revived Skia email account. She craved words from Yakov. Nothing.

She frowned as she took the last sip of her coffee, now stone cold, prepared by one of the in-house staff. They'd been deployed with one overriding instruction: cater to Irina's every whim. When she wasn't in her sumptuous bedroom or private bathroom, they hovered about her like mosquitoes. *Would you like this, madam? Would you like that?* They took it personally if she asked them to back off. Their sad faces were enough for her kindly disposition to tolerate the fuss, at least for now.

Since her virtual incarceration in the clifftop mansion, she'd spoken with Jacob only once, on the morning following his appearance-altering procedures. Immediately after that conversation, she'd sent him an email wishing him good luck on the perilous path ahead—a lengthy message with lots of heartfelt content. Gooey stuff that women appreciate more than men.

An hour after sending that email, Fletcher had imposed a ban on her contacting him on her own initiative. Let him get settled first, find his feet in Saint Petersburg, a city he wasn't familiar with. He needed to focus, not be distracted by a loved one sending him messages, despite her good intentions. Not to mention the real possibility of him being rumbled. The Russians are experts in surveillance, he'd stressed, and they'd improved in quantum leaps since Irina was in the employ of the Ministry of Finance four years ago. The world doesn't stand still, Fletcher intoned.

Yes, she had to admit it. Giant leaps in technology had taken place since that time. AI, in particular, was so advanced that people could barely separate reality from fakes anymore.

She'd kept abreast of things as well as she could, but she was only one person working for one organization—an organization she hadn't done any real work for over the last two years. Monitoring developments in IT and cybersecurity had been reduced almost to the hobbyist level. Not being hands-on in Skia's electronics laboratory was the worst part. Theoretical knowledge could never beat practical application.

Russia, on the other hand, was a behemoth, spending billions on its arsenal of spyware, recruiting more people into its ranks. The ongoing conflict with Ukraine had been a boon to the industry. Armed conflict creates fertile soil for invention and innovation.

Even so, Irina knew Fletcher was talking out of his ass by imposing this stupid ban on her. Skia's military-grade communications service, run almost entirely through a satellite system, was as good as it gets.

She went to the kitchen and argued with the maid about making another coffee. Irina insisted on doing it herself, even though lovely, gray-haired Maria—accommodating to the point of obsequiousness—argued the point for a full two minutes. With Irina threatening to lock herself away in her bedroom, Maria finally relented, though with much wringing of hands and muttering in nasal Portuguese.

"Would you like one, too?" said Irina, pressing the button to grind the small mountain of beans in the hopper.

A firm shake of the head. "It would not be... appropriate."

"If I did make you one, how would you take it?"

"I... no understand. In a cup?"

Irina laughed. The language barrier meant a lot of extra explaining, but it wasn't a chore. It was a chance to exchange more words with a living human.

"No, I mean with milk, sugar..."

"Ah, yes." She shuffled her feet, giving an uneasy smile. "I drink it black. No milk, no sugar."

"Sit there," said Irina gently, pointing to a stool at the breakfast bar. "I'll take care of you for a change, OK?"

Maria ran her hands down the front of her apron, shrugged, and perched herself on the stool.

After making them both a fresh coffee, Maria grinning with embarrassment, Irina returned to her laptop. She read some online news, scanning the pages of *The New York Times*, a couple of propagandist Russian-language outlets, and Al Jazeera to round it off.

Relieved to read nothing about a man fitting Yakov's description being killed in Saint Petersburg, she opened Facebook and scrolled around her placeholder bot profile's feed. Assorted memes, videos, ads, and clickbaity posts about nothing. Among the endless dross, there was one profile she wanted to check on.

Her nineteen-year-old son, Vova, had posted a string of selfies of him and a couple of his pals. They were standing outside a stadium, attending the concert of a band she'd never heard of. Judging by the huge number of fans in the background of the photos, dressed in black and purple with pieces of metal through eyebrows, lips, and noses, plenty of people had heard of them.

She shook her head in wonder. Vova had come right out of his shell since moving to Florida to live with her parents. It was supposed to be a temporary thing but had dragged on longer than she'd anticipated. Vova protested at first, refused to budge from the Keuka Lake home, but after a month of being under virtual house arrest with Mom and Yakov, he'd practically begged to be released to Babushka and Dedushka.

Running the tips of her fingers along his face, she felt the gnawing ache of maternal longing for her son. Compared to Russia, living in America was so much easier for him. Irina could barely recall his biological father, a student from Kenya. She'd had a short and torrid relationship with the man before he returned to Africa, leaving her alone and pregnant. She never saw him again. When Vova was born, she knew his path in life would be difficult, with his dark skin and hair. Her parents—at the time old-school Marxist internationalists—welcomed the birth of their half-African grandchild as if he were the Messiah himself. They loved him just as much today, and so Irina had cried with joy when he relented and agreed to stay with them. At least until Skia deemed that she and Yakov could come out of hiding and Vova could return to the fold, should he choose to do so.

God, let that time come soon.

She sighed deeply amid her reminiscing, cut short as the blinking envelope icon in the corner of the screen drew her eye. Finally, a message from Yakov. She beamed wistfully as she clicked it open. She'd become so used to his physical presence. Him not being around was almost like he was dead. But now a message was like a Christmas present.

As her eyes roamed the screen, it quickly became apparent something wasn't right. The Skia email client had a default column showing the sender's local time as well as the time a message landed in the recipient's inbox—a column Irina always paid attention to. Yakov's email was sent at 07:59 a.m. Saint Petersburg time.

The message should have hit her inbox three hours earlier, before she'd even woken up. Instead, it had arrived precisely three hours late—coincidentally the time difference between Portugal and Saint Petersburg. And now, a minute later, came the dinging notification on her Skia-issued Thuraya X5-Touch satellite phone. She snatched it off the counter, thumbed open the secure client, and saw the timestamp again: 07:59 Saint Petersburg time. It was now 08:01 in Castelo Branco. Three hours had elapsed. Totally unacceptable.

She was sorely tempted to call Fletcher immediately and rip him to shreds.

No.

Yakov had to come first.

She smiled at his inability to convey romantic thoughts in words. He might be a linguistic genius, but he was no poet. She nodded to herself as she processed Yakov's request to look deeper into Gabulov and Petko. She kissed the tips of her fingers and touched them to his name, then closed the email.

Now to deal with Fletcher.

But before she did, she had to make sure she wasn't jumping the gun.

She reread the header twice, in case she'd misread something. She hadn't. Yakov's message had been sent at 07:59, encrypted through the usual band, bounced its way across the ocean, and somehow gotten stuck in a bottleneck at this end. She uttered a string of filthy Russian curse words, excused herself with a nod to Maria, and took the spiral staircase into the basement.

A tech from the Lisbon CIA station, bearing the improbable name of Ronaldo McDonald, had set up the system and given her a one-hour briefing on how everything worked. His manner had been so boring, his Southern accent so impenetrable, that it was difficult for her to follow along without her mind drifting off.

She strode to the equipment rack, a poorly assembled confusion of cabling and Portuguese-labeled routers. A lot of it was blinking in the wrong pattern. Ronaldo had wired the sat receiver completely wrong. She swore at herself for not noticing the error when McDonald was explaining the system.

She raced back upstairs and grabbed her phone. Unlike Yakov, who had photographic recall of data, she had to locate Fletcher's name in the contacts. She chose his secure office line.

"Guess when Jacob's message reached me?" she challenged before he could even say hello. "Three hours after he sent it."

"What message?"

"A personal one." Should she mention the request to dissect Gabulov and Petko? No. If Fletcher needed to know, he'd know.

"Well, the man who set it up is a clueless..." She squinted, struggling with English profanity. "... ass-butt."

Fletcher chuckled uncomfortably.

"It's not funny. Running a military-grade satellite link via domestic broadband is something only an idiot would do." She paused, realizing the mini rant had left her slightly breathless. "I could've sent a postcard faster."

Fletcher exhaled, any humor he'd found in the situation erased. "I'll see to it. The guy will drive up from Lisbon and fix it."

"No need," she snapped. "I'll do it myself."

"You sure?"

"Of course. You think I'm not capable?"

"I'm... no... I didn't mean anything. Just thought you could do without having to get your hands dirty."

"I'm not digging a fucking garden, Grant." She smiled, sure she'd hit the profanity note perfectly this time.

"I didn't mean literally, Irina. It's a figure of speech."

"Ha! I know that."

An awkward silence reigned for a few moments before Fletcher said, "Is there anything else?"

"No. Do you have any news from Yakov? Has he contacted you?"

"No." She pictured him shaking his head in his Tribeca apartment that doubled as Skia's headquarters, clipping the end off a cigar, swooshing whiskey or cognac in a balloon glass. "I figure he's got a busy day ahead of him. Boring meetings and such."

"I hope you're right, Grant."

She disconnected the call.

Her gut was a ball of worry. To take her mind off things, she resolved to find out every damned detail about Gabulov and, in particular, that journalist, Marfa Petko. Too damned attractive for her own good—there had to be a lot of skeletons in her closet.

Back up the spiral staircase, sweet Maria was in the kitchen, fussing over a couple of steaming pots and pans. The thought of a hot lunch in the middle of the day took her back to Moscow, where her own mother always made sure lunch was two courses: soup and a cooked main meal.

She smiled as she put her arm around the old woman's pudgy waist. "Thank you, Maria."

America was all well and good, but eating sandwiches for lunch was a travesty.

TWELVE

As the BMW pulled up outside the jewelry repair shop, a group of seven teenagers in Adidas tracksuit bottoms under dark puffer jackets decided this was exactly where they should stop, squat, have a smoke, chew sunflower seeds, and spit out the husks. As they chatted and made gestures with their fingers like wannabe rappers, Jacob gritted his teeth and swore under his breath.

"Just what we need," said Dima. "Street punks."

Beside him, Andrey sniggered softly. "There's probably a dozen gopniks left in this entire city, and you have to run into half of them." He shook his head and laughed again.

"I know how to send them packing," said Jacob. "Klitschko's money should encourage them to move on." He turned in his seat, glaring at Andrey. "Remember all that cash you and your dead pal had? How you were on top of the world?"

Andrey sniffed.

"Not so funny now, is it?"

The captive stared at the back of his hands, a lock of oily hair dangling over his brow. Slava's body had shifted a little, its weight falling toward the middle of the car, forcing Andrey to lean back the other way.

“Wait here,” said Jacob, glancing at Dima in the mirror. “If that asshole does anything slightly iffy, shoot him in the kneecap.”

“Gotcha.”

Jacob got out of the car and approached a thick-set male of medium height, whom the others appeared to be treating as the group’s leader. “How much to go away and continue your little party elsewhere?”

The youth stood from his squatting position and dusted sparkling crystals of snow off his gloves. He moved to meet Jacob and squared up. The fact that Jacob towered over the teen made no difference to his attitude.

“I beg your pardon, uncle?” he said, holding a cupped hand to his ear. Jacob noted the acne scars that lined his face, his mouth more gaps than teeth. A fetid stench, reminiscent of anaerobic compost, emanated from his cracked lips.

“I’d like you all to fuck off.” He pulled out Klitschko’s fat wallet. “Now.”

The punk’s eyes widened for a moment before he feigned nonchalance, offering a pouty frown. Waggling his head from side to side, he said, “There’s no need to be using that kind of language… fuck your mother.”

A burst of guffaws from his appreciative audience greeted the witless witticism. One of them called out, “Good one, Sasha!”

A bargaining card was just handed to him—the kid’s name.

“Listen, Sasha,” said Jacob, as if they’d known each other for years. “You and your buddies need to leave. I’ve got serious business to conduct here, and you can’t be around. I either pay you and you walk away, or I break your jaw. What’s it to be?”

The rest of the group had silently formed a circle around them. Aggressive energy hung in the air, pungent as the filthy air pollution that blanketed the city.

“Don’t listen to his threats,” said another voice, female this time. Under their dark tracksuits, jackets, and hats, he’d assumed they were all male.

“Give us everything you’ve got, *ublyudok*,” came a third voice behind him, using one of the foulest epithets in the Russian language. The demand was followed by the hawking up of phlegm and a loud spit. Jacob glanced down to see a white glob on the outside of his shoe. A chorus of raucous laughter followed.

Control it, Hunter.

None of the gang were older than twenty, but together they formed a real threat. Getting these punks to scram using diplomacy might've had an outside chance of working if he'd had more time to gain their trust and confidence. He had no such luxury.

A show of strength it would have to be.

The scene unfolded in a blur of motion, starting with a lightning two-fingered strike to Sasha's throat. He spun the gagging youth around and applied a wrist lock, pressing hard. As Sasha twisted his body, trying to alleviate the pain, Jacob leaned his knee forward, making the kid's legs fold up like an outdoor chair. Jacob switched to a one-armed headlock, using his other hand to press the barrel of the Sig to Sasha's temple.

None of the six in the circle had time to intervene or utter a word in protest.

"*Poshli von otsyuda!* Get out of here!" Jacob bellowed.

The gang members stood frozen as Jacob spun around, keeping a firm grip on Sasha's neck.

"Go!" he roared. He briefly pointed the gun at another of the gopniks. "Wanna die?"

Like a pack of frightened dogs, they turned on their heels and fled, slipping and sliding on the sidewalk in their haste to get away from the crazy man.

"I'm gonna let you go, and you better run as fast as your buddies. I've shot men in the back before, and I'll make no exception for you."

Jacob released the headlock. Sasha slumped to the ground. A swift kick to the ribs had him up and sprinting. He stumbled a couple of times but was soon out of sight.

Jacob returned to the driver's seat to make a quick check with

Dima. The captive was still behaving himself but getting antsier by the minute.

"I'm freaking out with this dead guy leaning against me," Andrey whined, his complexion almost as white as the snow outside.

"Then you shouldn't have killed him," said Jacob. "Should you?"

"I told you, it was Oleg."

"It was you." Jacob jabbed a finger. "It's written all over your face. Still trying to decide whether to let you live or liquidate you." He smiled as he emphasized the word, remembering that the same term in English, which also meant *to kill*, had originated from the political repressions of Stalinist Russia.

He dialed Vanya's cell. Like with Dima's two attempts, there was no answer.

"You think someone's got to him?" said Dima.

Jacob grimaced as he contemplated the possibility of having two of his team down so early in the game. "How do I get in there?"

"Um... he's supposed to let you in."

"No key?"

Dima shook his head. "I don't have one." He blinked twice, then added, "There's an intercom with a keypad. There's supposed to be two businesses sharing the one door. One's Vanya's, the other's vacant."

"Which one do I press?"

Dima grinned. "B+."

"If he doesn't respond, is there a code to open the door?"

"If there is, I don't know it."

"That's bullshit. You should all know it." Even as he said it, he realized that was an unrealistic expectation.

"Not fair," said Dima, as if reading his mind. "Do I know your hotel room number? No."

Jacob muttered an apology, got out of the car, and walked the twenty feet to the steel door. He pressed the metal button beside the faded label reading B+. The intercom crackled, a burst of static preceding Vanya's gravelly voice: "Who's there?"

Jacob breathed a sigh of relief, turned to the car, smiled, and gave a thumbs up. He leaned close to the cold speaker grille and said, "Why aren't you answering your phone?"

"I said, who is it?"

"It's Robert Tamm, fuck your mother. Let me in."

The lock gave a harsh buzz, and the door clicked open.

THIRTEEN

A FLUORESCENT TUBE LIGHT GLOWED BRIGHTLY IN THE hallway, making Jacob squint. Vanya wore an expression of mild curiosity.

"Aren't you supposed to be at a meeting with Slava's boss at the ministry?"

"Hurry, Vanya. You need to get your things together."

"Wh-wh-what things?" he said over his shoulder as Jacob gave him an encouraging nudge in the small of the back.

"Whatever you need to hunker down in your dacha for a couple of days. Toothbrush, teddy bear. Tech stuff, mostly, I imagine."

They took a left down a short corridor painted forest green. Jacob observed the large patches where the paint had peeled off, chipped and broken tiles underfoot. Next, they turned right into what Jacob assumed was the face of the business—the repair shop itself. Against the far wall, tools were spread out untidily on a solid wooden workbench: tiny screwdrivers and magnifying lenses as well as rags and bottles in a range of sizes. Abutting that was another bench, home to a cast-iron last, an anvil, hammers, and glue, plastic bottles filled with nails and tacks, some ripped and torn leather shoes. Repaired watches, gold and silver necklaces, and numerous rings lay in neat rows under a glass display cabinet, tiny labels attached to each item with the owner's name. Some of the jewelry sparkled and glinted so brightly Jacob wondered if they might be worth a lot of money. To his untrained eye, they could have been made of solid gold and silver, mounted with diamonds and rubies. Maybe the guy had some legit rich clients.

Behind a transparent PVC strip curtain, Jacob glimpsed another room. Computer towers and monitors, more precision tools, circuit boards, all framed by a Christmas-like scene of blinking green and red lights. Vanya walked through the curtain, Jacob on his heels. The contrast was stark: old-school craftsmanship at the front, modern, state-of-the-art computer lab in the back.

"Why didn't you answer your phone?" Jacob barked as Vanya went to open a humming refrigerator. "You need to be contactable at all times."

Vanya stuck his head in the fridge, pulled out a carton of milk, sniffed it, and winced. "That n-n-needs throwing out."

"You didn't answer me. Why didn't you pick up the phone? Dima and I have been trying to get hold of you."

"Sorry. The battery ran dead; it's on the ch-ch-charger." He pointed at a tangle of cords near an electric kettle.

Jacob ran a hand across his face, then waved in a gesture encompassing the small room. "You've got an array of sophisticated equipment in here. Stuff that requires your full attention to keep running properly. And yet—*and yet*—you somehow forget to charge your damned cell phone?"

"I sometimes get so engrossed in one t-t-task, I forget about regular things. Like cleaning up in the k-k-kitchenette, keeping my phone—"

A hand shot up. "I don't want to hear about it." He pushed down on Vanya's shoulders, seating him a little too firmly in his gamer's chair, which rolled back into the wall, snapping Vanya's head forward. "Bad news, I'm afraid, *druzhok*." He sucked in a long breath flavored with traces of cleaning fluid and boot polish. "Slava's dead."

The carton of milk Vanya was still holding dropped to the floor, white streams pouring in all directions.

"You're lying! This is some kind of pro-pro-provocation!"

"I'm not lying. We're getting too close to the truth. Whoever's organizing Severnaya Volna wants us to stop. If anything, his death means we cannot stop."

"Why didn't you s-s-save him? That's your j-j-job!" Vanya's face crumpled, features contorting. "How did he die?"

"He was strangled." Jacob frowned, eyes cast to the floor.

"Where?"

"In the back of the car. Dima and I left him. We thought... the vehicle is armored, he shouldn't be in danger."

"That car can withstand bombs! How did—I don't understand."

"He was tricked into opening the door to the killer. Because he has—had—a good heart."

"That's true." Vanya dug around under a fingernail with a toothpick.

"If it's any consolation, there were signs he didn't go easily. He must have fought to the end. Like a hero." He was gilding the lily, but it was what Vanya needed to hear.

"Where is he?"

Jacob coughed into his fist. "Outside in the BMW. That's why we need to get to the dacha, to hide his body until... until we decide what to do next."

Vanya's hands flew to his face. He began to sob gently, muttering *nyet, nyet, nyet*. The sobbing grew louder, his shoulders jerking in spasms. He rubbed the heels of his palms into his moist eyes, then stared at the cracks in the floor. Between ragged breaths, he muttered Slava's name over and over, each repetition softer, as if his entire world had come to an end.

Jacob stood by silently for a while, allowing the man to cry.

Slava Gabulov clearly meant more to Vanya than he did to his own cousin, the latter's reaction not even coming close to this.

The sobbing showed no signs of subsiding. Jacob blew out his cheeks and said, "That's enough, Vanya."

"What do you mean, e-e-enough? I'm fucking devastated. Slava was my mentor, a father f-f-figure."

Jacob clapped a hand on the man's shoulder. "I get it. But we have to move. Get out of the city for a while."

Vanya's face turned white. "If Slava's in the car, I'm not sure I can t-t-travel with you. Maybe I can find another way there?"

Jacob shook his head. "If you want to get out of this ordeal without having a mental breakdown, you need to do exactly as I say. Understood?"

"P-p-perfectly."

FOURTEEN

Outside, light was fading, and snow had begun to fall again. Fat flakes blanketed everything in their path, muffling the distant sounds of the city into an eerie silence.

Lviny Pereulok was only sixty-two meters long, with Vanya's shop more or less in the middle. Even through the curtain of snow, it would be easy to observe anyone coming from either the Griboyedov Canal or the Dekabristov Street end.

The gopniks were gone, but who knew who'd be next to stroll onto the scene? They had to move quickly.

Jacob waved Vanya away from the building's front door, which closed with a clang. He guided him into the front passenger side of the BMW. Vanya placed his khaki duffel bag in the footwell. Jacob handed him the H&K, then gestured with his head toward Dima in the back seat, still covering the goon with an unwavering hand.

"Vanya. You'll be taking over guard duty for a couple of minutes while Dima helps me with the body. I'd like to introduce you to our new friend, Andrey... Kaufman, wasn't it?"

Kaufman nodded, then looked up.

"This is the man who killed Slava." Jacob delivered the line deadpan, like he was reciting the dictionary.

"It wasn't me!" Kaufman's head jerked backward half an inch, his entire body shaking like he was being juiced in the electric chair. He began to blink fast, his breathing coming in shallow pants. "I fucking told you, it was Oleg!"

Vanya gripped the pistol with both hands. They shook but only slightly. He glanced at Slava's lifeless body slumped against the car door. With tears welling, he somehow managed to pull himself together and switch out of mourning mode. He took a deep, steadying breath and drilled Kaufman with a death stare, nostrils flaring. Andrey began to hyperventilate, eyelids fluttering. None of Jacob's words had had the effect of Vanya's body language.

"I know this *ublyudok*," said Vanya in a whisper. "Yeah... I know him."

"What?" Jacob wasn't prepared for this turn of events. He'd assumed Kaufman had been hired specifically to eliminate Slava.

"He came in a couple of weeks ago to get a watch repaired. Said it had given up the ghost. I checked it; it just needed a new battery. I think... maybe he did something when I turned my back on him and went to get the battery. I'd bet my last ruble he left a goddamn l-l-listening device inside."

To Jacob's shock, Vanya let fly, smashing the barrel of the pistol against Kaufman's left ear, swearing through clenched teeth. The captive's hand shot up just in time to deflect a second blow, this time aimed at the top of his head. The gun cracked against his knuckles, drawing a yelp. He flicked his hand, then shook it hard, as if that would stop the pain.

"Enough!" said Jacob. He leaned across Vanya and gripped a panicking Kaufman by the throat. "Did you leave a bug in the shop?"

A terrified shake of the head. "No way!" he rasped, his voice barely audible through Jacob's vice-like grip. "I've never seen this guy in my life."

"Tell the truth, asswipe."

"I... am... telling... the truth."

"We'll get everything we need out of you later." Jacob released his grip, and the man sagged sideways, coughing and spluttering. Kaufman's jaw locked shut, lips tucked behind his teeth. His eyes darted between Jacob and Vanya, Dima to his right all but ignored. Even though Jacob had hinted at upcoming "enhanced" interrogation, by his reticence to name names, Kaufman was clearly more afraid of whoever had given the order than of the men who held him captive.

"Dima," Jacob said evenly. "Help me get Slava into the trunk. Vanya, don't take your eyes off that bastard."

Dima and Vanya nodded in unison, obedience to Jacob now coming as second nature. Dima holstered the weapon and slapped his hands together, ready to assist with the transfer of the body. Having confirmed the coast was clear, he and Jacob hurriedly lifted Slava from the back seat. The body was heavy and awkward, limbs beginning to stiffen. Jacob took the shoulders, Dima the legs, their boots scraping against the icy pavement as they shuffled to the rear of the BMW. They eased him into the trunk, folded his knees, and covered him with a heavy tarpaulin. Jacob shut the trunk with a dull, final thud.

The snow thickened as Dima eased out of Lviny Pereulok and made a right onto Dekabristov. Nobody paid any attention to the dark BMW driving sedately along the city's famous streets, past Saint Isaac's Cathedral, the Alexander Garden, the statue of Peter the Great, and back onto the Admiralty Embankment.

Vanya sat stiffly in the rear passenger seat, facing Kaufman with the pistol jammed into his ribs. Two thin lines of dried blood looked like spider veins on Kaufman's forehead. Jacob twisted the rearview mirror and didn't like the expression on Vanya's face. The man appeared lost; Jacob could almost sense the conflicting thoughts jumbling in his head.

Jacob realized Vanya could go off at any moment. He'd attacked Kaufman already, brutally—he could do it again. His eyes were glassed over, breathing so shallow it was barely detectable. Jacob returned the mirror to its original position.

Muttering his dissatisfaction, Dima made a tiny adjustment to the mirror before focusing on the road again.

"Pull over at the first opportunity," said Jacob.

"Don't tell me you want to drive again? I've got my shit together, more than happy to—"

"Here. Stop here."

Dima slowed and turned into the curb, cars behind honking angrily.

"You swap with me," said Jacob, turning to Vanya. "I don't want you deciding to plug Kaufman before I get the chance to turn the screws on him."

Vanya grudgingly obliged, but Jacob sensed he was relieved to be away from the thug, even if the division was only a matter of a couple of feet.

Kaufman gave a wide-eyed stare as Jacob pressed the pistol into the goon's side. "Maybe put the *stvol* away?" he suggested. "Three against one. Not much I can do, is there?"

The barrel jammed harder under Kaufman's bottom rib, making him gasp. "Shut the fuck up," said Jacob. "I can knock every one of those perfect teeth out of your head with this gun. You want that?"

"No."

"Not another peep."

Out on the multilane highway, Dima drove smoothly—no speeding or reckless overtaking, total compliance with every road rule. The ministry plates should have been sufficient insurance, allowing them to deviate from the rules, but it would only take one overzealous traffic cop to throw a wrench in the works.

"I advise we go via the ring road," said Dima. "It's much quicker."

Jacob nodded, phone already in his hand. "You're the local, not me." Marfa Petko's number illuminated in his mind's eye like giant white numbers drawn on a chalkboard. The call rang out. He tried once more. Again, no answer.

After a couple more attempts, Jacob pocketed the phone. "She's not picking up, damn it."

"It's still business hours," said Dima. "Don't stress."

"Business hours don't exist when you're trying to stop a coup d'état." Jacob twisted his lips, staring at the looming Korableny Bridge. An awesome sight, the ship-fairway section of the 620-meter-long structure was bookended by two enormous pylons that mimicked the wings of the city's famous drawbridges. To the east were clusters of container cranes and dock lights.

"What she's doing is probably aligned with that goal," said Dima, somewhat defensively in Jacob's opinion. "She's got her mind on the job, I'm sure."

The car changed lanes to let a boxy police UAZ Patriot, lights flashing and siren wailing, zoom past at the approach to the bridge. They gradually blended into the dense traffic flowing along the strangely named Western High-Speed Diameter. From his seat, Jacob enjoyed a majestic view of the Neva Bay, chunks of ice dotting its surface. It would be iced over solid in a matter of weeks.

A bleep made Jacob jump in his seat. "What was that? Sounded like a toll being collected."

Dima bunched his cheeks. "Oh, yeah. Tag got zapped. I hadn't thought of that." He pondered for a moment. "Another thing I just remembered. Ministry vehicles are subject to fleet tracking."

"Correct," said Vanya. "If the GPS were to die, the mobile network would kick in. Everything leaves a trail. If somebody wanted to reconstruct our route, they could do it. Almost turn by turn."

Dima nodded. "Unfortunately, we can't just drive off into the sunset and hope the trail disappears. The fleet ops guys keep the records for up to three months." He paused. "Could pose a problem."

Vanya said, "He's right. Of course, all of it can be tracked. But it's not necessarily going to put anyone in the frame."

Jacob raised an eyebrow. "Explain."

"I can make that incriminating data go away." He smiled wistfully. "Slava had me working on a project that took a week and a half, barely any sleep, total focus. He asked me to find a back door into the ministry's systems."

"Sounds like a tough assignment."

"No shit. I like a challenge, but this was something else again. That sleepless period ended last night." He allowed himself a faint grin. "I got in."

"You're joking!" said Dima.

Jacob smiled to himself. He knew people like Vanya—and Irina—could work these kinds of miracles. Reverse Houdinis, able to get into just about anything.

"I poked at everything I could," said Vanya. "There are some places I couldn't get into—not yet. But I'm determined to crack them too. Even more so after what the bastards did to S-S-Slava." He took a couple of deep breaths. "Slava believed there was a link to Severnaya Volna in the ministry, someone who was w-w-watching him. Looks like he may have been right."

Dima shook his head. "He never shared any of that with me."

"Of course not. Nor with Marfa. He wanted to find the evidence first. Like we got on Semak, Izmailov, and K-K-Kolodin. He didn't want you two distracted from your jobs."

"Did he think it was Saburenkov watching him?" said Jacob. "The guy I'm supposed to be meeting tomorrow?"

"He didn't offer any names. Said he didn't want me to do my w-w-work with preconceptions. It's a big place with lots of employees. Could have b-b-been one of hundreds."

"Fair enough."

"Unfortunately, I couldn't crack their email system," Vanya said, frustration lending an edge to his voice. "Like in many organizations, that's the thing that gets the biggest p-p-padlocks put on it." He frowned for a moment. "I also hit a wall trying to get into the long-term archives and digital credentials. They're the keys that authenticate users and servers."

"I've got no idea what you're talking about," said Dima, shaking his head slowly.

"It's not our job to understand it," said Jacob. He reached forward and patted Vanya on the shoulder, the gun never leaving Andrey's side. "That's why you have this fella on the team."

"Thanks," said Vanya humbly.

"So what did you get into?"

Vanya shrugged. "Fleet tracking. I thought that was a priority because of how much this car gets used."

"*Molodets.* Good man." Dima nodded, appreciating the guy's smarts.

"I can see every route history, including for this v-v-very vehicle. Not only see it but edit the metadata. So if you want our BMW not to be in a certain place at a certain time, I can change that—at least in the ministry's logs. I also hacked into their m-m-mobile device management system. Employees' cell phones and tablets check in regularly. I'm now able to m-m-monitor these check-ins and some app activity. It might offer up a nugget or two."

"Can you listen in to phone calls and read texts?" said Jacob.

"No. That'd take months of work, acquisition of more hardware. And there'd be no guarantee of success. This is the Russian government we're talking about here."

"And the cameras on the streets?"

"That's right," said Dima, a note of alarm in his voice. "What if CCTV caught us at Aptekarsky Pereulok? That could fuck us badly, right?"

He had a good point, but not one worth shitting your pants over. Jacob said, "I doubt there was a camera in the part of the laneway where it all happened. I'd almost swear there were none."

"What happened at Aptekarsky?" said Vanya, curiosity raising the pitch of his voice. "You didn't mention it b-b-before, Robert."

"Kaufman here was working with another guy who sadly met with a... fiery end."

"Meaning?"

"Meaning the man Kaufman claims killed Slava got his just deserts," chimed in Dima.

"You guys killed him?"

"*Da*," said Jacob. "Unfortunate, but necessary. It's hard enough keeping this asshole"—he nodded sideways at Kaufman—"in check without having to guard two of them."

"For what it's worth," said Vanya, "you may have been recorded." He cited the statistics Jacob knew too well about the number of cameras in the city. "I'm assuming there were none visible to the naked eye?"

Jacob shook his head. "I looked hard but saw none."

"Me either," added Dima. "I can usually spot the domes and brackets quite easily." He pursed his lips. "I detected nothing in the lane."

"Excellent. There are possibly government cameras at either end of that lane—they're used to monitor traffic flow—maybe some well-disguised private ones. Apart from one small bank branch near the Moyka River, there are no businesses on that street. My gut feeling is you're in the clear."

"Gut feeling?" said Dima. "Not very scientific, is it?"

Jacob turned to look at Vanya. "You know anyone available and trustworthy who could scout the street specifically for cameras? I'd like to know if we can relax or if we need to get proactive in getting hold of footage."

"I hate to break it to you," said Vanya, "but if there's one section of the g-g-government that's got the most impenetrable f-f-firewalls, it's the MVD. Anything that looks like an attempted intrusion will set alarms off everywhere. The only w-w-way I'd have even half a chance would be to befriend a high-level IT employee with a score to settle."

"What he's saying is—"

"I know what he's saying," Jacob growled. The MVD, or Ministry of Internal Affairs—of which the police was the main branch—would be as hard to hack as the Pentagon. Going back to the scene was pointless. "Let's just assume the incident went unrecorded and proceed accordingly."

Vanya nodded. "That would be my advice."

"Radio news is up in thirty seconds." Dima's out-of-the-blue statement had the inflection of a question.

"Turn it on." Jacob could read the man's mind. Were there any recent reports of the exploding Toyota? A dead man inside it?

First up, a headline story about glorious leader Putin and the Russian army's magnificent advances in Ukraine despite the meddling of the West. The radio jock's tone was so groveling, the propaganda so obsequious, that Jacob burst out laughing.

"I'm embarrassed to be a Russian sometimes," said Dima. "Hearing all that brown-nosing."

"Do you get that b-b-bullshit in Estonia?" said Vanya. "I bet you don't."

Jacob had to think hard for a moment. "The mainstream media like to portray themselves as fact-based reporters. But you can certainly detect an anti-Russian slant, despite their best efforts to be objective. It's not a blanket bias; they have to take into account the ethnic Russian minority in the country, not piss them off too much. My mother, for example, and three hundred thousand more like her."

"Your mother's Russian?" Vanya couldn't hide his pleasure. "Nobody told me that. I assumed you were one of those rare Estonians who can speak Russian like a native."

"My heritage is part of the reason I was able to get access to Slava," he said, almost believing the words. With exaggerated reverence, he brought the tips of his thumb, index, and middle finger together, folded the other two against his palm, and traced the cross from forehead to chest, right shoulder to left—the Orthodox way.

"A believer, too," said Dima with a chuckle and a shake of the head. "We might need divine intervention to see this through."

"You can't blame them for being anti-Russian," blurted Vanya, turning hard to engage Jacob's gaze. "Look at the historical context. Your country has n-n-nothing to be grateful to Russia for. We treat our own people like shit, and other countries w-w-worse than that." He mock-spat into the glove compartment.

Kaufman wriggled uncomfortably in his seat.

"Have faith, Vanya," said Jacob. "B+ isn't the only group of pissed-off people trying to effect change. Keep doing what you're doing and one day..." As he let his voice trail off, Jacob knew his words were nothing more than trite air fillers. For centuries, Russia's people had bent the knee to the strongman—czars, despots like Lenin, Stalin, now the autocrat Putin. Rare glimmers of hope, such as those embodied by the Kerensky Provisional Government that was overthrown by the Bolsheviks in 1917, later Gorbachev with his policies of perestroika and glasnost, proved to be as ephemeral as the snow on the ground. It was going to take something extraordinary to shift that mindset—*mentalitet*, as the Russians called it. Jacob sighed. It might never happen.

Then it came.

Wedged in between the sports and weather, in a monotone, the radio announcer described a "traffic" incident in the heart of Saint Petersburg.

Emergency services confirm an incident at Aptekarsky Pereulok; a criminal investigation is under way. Police advise all motorists and pedestrians to avoid the area while the scene is processed.

"Wow, talk about understatement," said Dima, shaking his head in disbelief. "That motherfucker didn't even say serious incident."

"The MVD will not allow details of this to come out," Jacob said pensively. "No one will ever hear the name of the dead man in the burned-out car. Perhaps that's to our advantage." He was sure that if he logged on to Telegram or YouTube, some enterprising Petersburger—perhaps a tourist—would have raced to the source of the explosion, filmed it from all angles, and uploaded a video before first responders arrived. This would prompt the government to release more details, albeit vague, and claim it was an unfortunate accident or an isolated criminal act.

He'd check out the online sources once they reached the dacha.

No—why wait?

"Vanya."

"Yes?"

"See if there's any online chatter about this 'incident,' will you?"

"My phone battery died, remember?"

It would have to wait after all.

"Want me to try another news station?" inquired Dima. "One that's a bit more in-depth? You never know."

"No. It wouldn't achieve anything. The only trustworthy Russian media is run from exile, anyway." Reputable companies like Meduza and TV Rain had been forced to relocate abroad or see their employees jailed. It was time to end this topic of conversation. "How long to go?"

"To the dacha?" He glanced at the clock on the dash. "Just another thirty minutes."

Thank God.

Outside the window, night had settled in. Jacob had been so locked into the cocoon of the BMW that he'd stopped noticing anything beyond it.

As they cruised the highway, his thoughts drifted to Irina. What, if anything, would she manage to dig up on Vyacheslav Gabulov... and on Marfa Petko, assuming Marfa hadn't met the same fate?

FIFTEEN

JACOB DRUMMED HIS FINGERS ON HIS THIGH. KAUFMAN had fallen asleep, his body slumped against the car door. His lips flapped slightly as he snored. Jacob took the opportunity to remove his own necktie and tightly bind the goon's wrists. He kept the gun within easy reach. For all he knew, Kaufman could be an expert at freeing himself from restraints.

His mind began to go over recent events and how to play things from here. The toll tag record? That shouldn't be a problem with Vanya on the job. He'd access it, manipulate it, do whatever he had to do to wipe the trail. It had been several hours since the "incident" on Aptekarsky. Dima's phone had been silent the entire trip. If it didn't ring before they reached the dacha, Vanya might have time to fudge the data before any potential CCTV footage was retrieved and reviewed.

And what about Marfa Petko, the subject of conversation sidelined by the bleep of the toll tag? Dima was right about her being in high demand; her job dictated that. And Jacob understood her predicament: Being an active member of B+ while juggling the workload of a busy reporter. Still, the group had embarked on a monumental mission. She needed to be more contactable than she had been so far. It wasn't good enough. He voiced that concern aloud.

"You have to be realistic," said Dima. "Even Slava...rest his soul...struggled to get hold of her sometimes."

"I get that. But this is a different ball game. According to your own intelligence analysis, three guys in powerful positions want to overthrow the Estonian government—soon. The troop movements, the killing of the border guard, and then Slava; it all proves they aren't kidding around." He ran a hand over his face, a sheen of sweat coating his skin despite the perfect ambient temperature in the car. "Her phone's gotta be buzzing in her handbag like an out-of-control vibrator. We've tried—how many times is it now? She must sense something's wrong."

Vanya's voice came from the front. "She'd have arm muscles as big as a wrestler's if she picked up her cell every time it rang. You have any idea how many c-c-calls Marfa would get in a day?"

"Irrelevant," Jacob said. "But surprise me."

"Being a journalist in Saint Petersburg requires her to field d-d-dozens of calls a day. Maybe hundreds if there's some big event happening. I wouldn't stress. She runs her own sh-sh-show."

Traffic thinned as they left the city's glow behind, heading southwest toward Sosnovy Bor. The roads grew emptier. Nothing was visible outside except the intermittent lights of isolated farmsteads and gas stations. Jacob pictured both sides of the road bordered by dense pine forests heavy with snow. The occasional truck rumbled past, its lights cutting temporary tunnels through the falling white flakes.

In the front seat, Vanya stirred. "Slava..." he murmured. "He didn't deserve to die. He should have lived to see Russia free again. The corruption exposed."

Dima reached across and patted him on the leg. "We will avenge him. Don't worry."

Jacob stared out the windshield. He had nothing to offer. He could, of course, have told him the truth. That Russia had never been truly free. That the all-pervading corruption had been exposed before, again and again. There were zero consequences for the corrupt—only for the exposers. Good people like Slava had paid the ultimate price for bringing the darkness to light. The list of victims was as long as the different methods used to dispose of them: Anna Politkovskaya, a journalist like Marfa Petko, shot in her apartment building; Boris Nemtsov, shot dead on a bridge near the Kremlin; Aleksandr Litvinenko, poisoned with radioactive polonium-210 in London; Alexei Navalny, starved to death in a freezing, filthy gulag. On and on it went.

But what would be the point of saying all that? It could only serve to discourage.

Vanya's grief was almost palpable, filling the car like a mist. He muttered soft, incoherent words, now and then sobbing gently.

Dima kept his own counsel as he drove toward the dacha, eyes fixed on the road. Apart from Vanya's little puppy noises, the only sound in the car was the radio, playing syrupy Russian pop music.

They drove for an hour in that brooding atmosphere, down narrowing roads, the headlights picking out snow-covered birches and spruce. The forest thickened, then opened onto a faint orange glow from distant industrial stacks near the gulf.

Jacob tried Marfa again.

This time the call connected—then cut out after half a second. Weak signal. He moved the phone toward the window and redialed. Nothing.

By the time they reached the turnoff for the dacha, the horizon beyond the forest had blurred into a diffuse wash of slate gray and cast iron, the cloud-laden sky pressing down, the night crystalline-cold.

"Three more kilometers," Dima said, squinting through the windshield.

Out of the dark, the beams carved out a crooked wooden sign, half-buried in snow. They followed the zigzagging track past empty steel drums, broken wooden pallets, and the outlines of shuttered summer cottages. The road narrowed further, just wide enough for the BMW. A gust of snow swept across the track, briefly hiding it, drawing a quiet "*blyad*'" from Dima.

Jacob's cell phone buzzed. He grabbed it, index finger sliding across the screen. He put the call on loudspeaker. "Marfa?"

"*Da. Eto ya.* Yes, it's me." Her voice came through sharp, a little distorted. "Robert? I see you've tried to call me a dozen times. What's wrong?"

He inhaled deeply. "Where are you right now?"

"At my apartment. Why? There's something in the tone of your voice."

"We need to talk. In person. Not over the phone."

She hesitated. "Is this about Slava? He hasn't answered my messages all day. I'm worried about him."

Dima's eyes met Jacob's in the rearview mirror; Vanya's shoulders shot back as he sat up straight; Kaufman kept snoring. She was lying—Slava's phone was in Jacob's pocket, and she hadn't sent a single message.

Jacob looked ahead, the dark outline of the two-story wooden dacha now visible like a ghostly apparition through the trees.

"Can you travel tonight?"

She gave a sarcastic laugh. "You kidding me? I'm bushed. I need a hot bath and an early night."

"It's still early. Have you forgotten what the stakes are? You're tired? Quite frankly, I don't care."

"*Khorosho*. OK." A sigh. "Where are you?"

"Shepelevo."

"The house?"

"Yes." It was good that she was careful—didn't mention which house over the phone. A point in her favor. But she'd better have a good reason for lying about trying to contact Gabulov.

"Got it."

He heard the scrape of a cigarette lighter, the first deep drag of smoke.

"I'll grab a few things and jump in a taxi. Give me two hours, two and a half to get there."

"Good decision," he said quietly. "Just keep your phone turned on."

He ended the call before she could ask any more questions.

"She n-n-never tried to call Slava, did she?" Vanya said flatly.

"No," Jacob said. "She didn't."

SIXTEEN

MARFA STEPPED OUT OF HER COURTYARD ARCHWAY. She lived in a complex of renovated apartments in the heart of the city. People here were professionals, high earners who tended to keep to themselves, and that was exactly the way she liked it. Three other apartments shared her floor; she knew none of the occupants.

The wind chill had subtracted another ten degrees from the temperature. She shivered under her hat, thick gloves, and ankle-length fur coat. On the positive side, the snow had eased—easier to hail a cab.

She marched two blocks to get well clear of home base before stopping curbside and raising a hand. Five taxis zipped by, one spraying dirty slush that missed her boots by centimeters. She extended a middle finger to the bonehead behind the wheel and cursed him and his family, immediate and extended. The sixth taxi stopped. A well-maintained yellow-and-green cab, its driver leaning across the seat to unlock the door. She got in without hesitation, shutting the cold out behind her.

A swarthy, gold-toothed man with black stubble and a long nose glanced at her in the mirror. "*Kuda, krasivaya?* Where to, beautiful lady?"

No point calling him out on the sexism. The behavior was hardwired into many men from the Caucasus.

"Southwest. Past Lomonosov."

He pursed his lips. "Going as far as Sosnovy Bor?" His bushy eyebrows lifted a couple of millimeters.

"About that far."

"Quite a long way, lady. Six thousand rubles even, and I turn off the meter."

"Five. Cash in hand."

He grinned. "When the meter's off, you think I'm gonna take a credit card? Six thousand, or I drop you at the next tram stop."

"Fine. I'll pay the extra thousand, even though I know you're ripping me off. But I want a quiet ride, no music, and no Formula 1 antics."

"You drive a hard bargain, *krasivaya.*"

"Can we just go?"

He let out a breath through his nose and started the engine. Only once they were moving did he ask, "How far exactly? Right into the town?"

"No."

Sosnovy Bor, home to the aging Leningrad nuclear power plant, was a designated closed city which could only be entered if you were a resident or had valid authorization. "Head for the village of Shepelevo, on the Gulf of Finland." She didn't give the street address because she didn't know it. "I'll direct you by landmarks when we get closer."

He nodded slowly. "I'll take you to the point where the paved road ends. After that, if it's rough, you walk. This is no SUV."

"That's fine." The paved road ended right at the gate, where Vanya would fetch her on a Polaris UTV.

Marfa sent a short SMS to Vanya signaling her arrival: *Don't leave me waiting in the cold.* She flicked through her recent messages and smiled with the satisfaction of having pulled the wool over her enemies' eyes. Not easy, but she did it.

Colonel-General Kolodin was the first and relatively easiest, confirming he'd be free for an hour tomorrow afternoon. Then that snake, Deputy Governor Sergei Semak, promised he'd be available at 8:00 p.m. Finally, CEO of BaltEnergoTorg, Marat Izmailov, was agreeable to a chat in his plush modern office the following morning. Bang, bang, bang. All three sent polite, personal messages—not via their reception desks but directly to her cell phone.

Their respective departments had kept Petko on a long leash for a week. Two days ago, before the Estonian arrived, she had almost given up. But there was something about the man that spurred her on. Vanya had better have some champagne to celebrate this win. If not, it didn't matter. She extracted a gold hip flask from her bag, took a swig of vodka, and smacked her lips. The driver tut-tutted and gave her a disapproving stare but said nothing.

The darkness of the night rushed by outside. Gas station lights glowed like outposts in the desert, the only noise the rhythmic humming of the cab's tires on frozen asphalt.

She looked at Semak's message, shaking her head at the guy's nerve. The deputy governor was an old-school chauvinist pig—a hundred times worse than the taxi driver. The cabbie had no agenda; it was in his cultural DNA to flatter each and every woman he met. Semak was just a creep. Married for thirty years to the same woman and, it was widely rumored, an enthusiastic devotee of high-end prostitutes. *Marfa. I'd be delighted to host such a beautiful and intelligent woman as you in my private chambers at Suvorovsky Prospekt. Don't have dinner beforehand; I'll ask the chef to organize something special.* To him, she was "beautiful" first, "intelligent" second. It was a unarguable fact of life, she reflected, that looks can open doors. Thankfully, she had been genetically blessed.

Breaking through to score interviews with all of them had taken a lot of persuasive talk. Rebuffed on the phone by stern-voiced receptionists, she had swallowed her pride and gone tapping on doors, using every trick she knew to get past gatekeepers. Perhaps fed up with her annoying persistence, the gatekeepers relented. She was granted brief meetings with each man, but a few minutes was all it took to land them. She could charm the pants off a monk, her wise ex-husband used to say. Indeed, many pairs of pants had been dropped at the side of her bed over the years.

When she told the arrogant suspects she wanted their views on the new Russo-Estonian accord, their faces lit up. They'd love to talk, but it was a highly sensitive topic and, accordingly, the men made demands of her. Promises of flattering copy across all the magazines she syndicated her work to; stock photos vetted to make sure they captured their best features; no negative talk regarding the men having conflicts of interest in terms of their jobs and the success of the accord with Estonia. Of course, she promised. She would respect their every wish.

Her canyon of cleavage, revealed when she shed her jacket, hadn't hurt her efforts either. The question was, how would they react to the appearance of a surprise guest: Robert Tamm?

The driver spoke rapidly in his Georgian accent, pulling her out of her thoughts. "Just went through Pulkovo. I don't wanna overshoot any turnoffs. I do, it'll cost you more."

Marfa put her phone away, tucked her hair behind her ears, and rocked forward in her seat, anxious not to miss the landmarks. So much to tell the team. Slava, in particular, would be impressed by the colorful details she'd added to the basic texts she'd sent him. And that Estonian man—he was gruff, superior, old-mannish, controlling. But there was something sexy about him that made her heart flutter just a little.

Three minutes later, they passed a dimly illuminated signpost pointing to a scrap metal yard. Then a dilapidated concrete bus stop covered in graffiti.

"Slow down, it's tricky." Through the gloom, she made out the dry stone wall. "You'll miss the...STOP."

The car pulled over gently to the shoulder.

"Right here is fine." She handed over a wad of folded bills. He counted them quickly, nodded, gave her a broad smile, and, visibly relieved to be done with the beautiful yet pain-in-the-ass woman, demonstrably turned the volume up on his stereo. She recognized the tune as a popular Georgian folk song she'd heard a million times—twenty-six years ago, when she was a junior correspondent in Tbilisi. She smiled and said, "What a lovely song."

"Yeah, it's great," he said flatly. "Take care."

Marfa stepped out into the bitter cold, her face stinging in the lashing wind. She frowned as she shivered. No one was there to fetch her.

She plucked a cigarette from her bag, almost disappeared inside her coat to light it, and sent a plume of moist smoke into the air. She pulled out her phone and switched on the flashlight—a meager, narrow beam, but better than nothing. About to call Vanya and tear him a new one for his tardiness, the round lights of the UTV cut through the blackness. The vehicle bounced over the driveway's deep ruts as it approached the entrance to the property. A man jumped from the vehicle and opened the gate. It wasn't Vanya.

"Put the cigarette out and get on," commanded Robert Tamm in a voice that brooked no argument. The faintest of smiles played on lips barely visible between his scarf and tugged-down beanie. "You'll catch your death out here."

SEVENTEEN

"WHERE'S SLAVA?" SAID MARFA. SHE DROPPED HER BAG on the floor and pulled a wooden chair up to the table with a loud scrape. "I want a word with him."

Jacob toyed with the handle of a china teacup, inspecting the contents as if seeking inspiration from the strong, black brew. Finding nothing to inspire, he nodded at Dima, sitting at the head of the table. "I can't find the words. You ask her."

"Why did you lie about trying to contact Slava?" said Dima, a half-smoked cigarette dangling between his fingers. "Robert's had Slava's phone on him since 10:30 this morning. No calls, no messages. We know the phone's working fine because Robert used it to make a call. Tell us the truth, Marfa."

She stood, finely manicured hands gripping the edge of the table so hard her knuckles showed stark white through the thin layer of skin. "I asked you first. Where is he?"

No one spoke.

"Answer me, for God's sake." She let go of the chair, walked to a window, twitched the curtain, and spun around sharply. "Don't go twisting things, making accusations against me like this. I do not lie to the group!"

"Calm down," said Vanya, coming from an adjoining room

with a laptop cradled on his forearm. "I think you should answer Dima's question f-f-first." He took a seat next to Jacob, flipped up the lid, and switched the machine on. Jacob had asked him to chase down the *goszakaz*, a task Vanya admitted wouldn't be simple. He'd sent an email to Irina giving her the same task. "I've been with Robert for several hours, and Slava's phone has been silent the whole t-t-time."

Marfa's lips disappeared behind her teeth, eyes growing as wide as they could possibly grow. Her hands remained on the table. "For God's sake, it's gotta be a technical problem. Now for the last time before I end my association with you morons and sign a deal with my sworn enemy, Channel One, where's Slava?"

"He's d-d-dead," said Vanya, his voice cracking. "And your lying makes us w-w-wonder whether you had something to d-d-do with it."

She dropped back into the chair like a stone, face as pale as chalk.

"What do you mean, he's dead? No way! We were all at breakfast this morning. He was fine..."

"There's a guy trussed up in the cellar," said Jacob, gesturing with a flick of the head. "Name of Andrey Kaufman. Ring any bells with you?"

She shook her head, one eye narrowed. "Kaufman? Not a Russian name. Never heard of him."

"He—or his deceased colleague—killed Slava in the parking lot at Finland Station. Garroted him." Jacob quickly explained how he and Dima had left Slava alone in the BMW for twenty minutes while he questioned a woman about the mysterious train tickets. In that short space of time, the killer had struck. It later turned out that the man who bought the tickets was the same man Jacob had offed in Aptekarsky Pereulok.

"My God," said Marfa, her expression blank. "This is turning into a nightmare. Why did you kill that man? Was your life in danger?"

"It could have been," Jacob snorted. "Besides, we had to send a message to whoever ordered the hit on Slava that we're not to be trifled with."

"Couldn't you have...detained him?"

Jacob pinched the bridge of his nose and said nothing. The scene played back in his mind, the way he'd repeatedly thrust the screwdriver into Klitschko's neck. Like an enraged animal, not characteristic of him at all. Perhaps Marfa was right. Maybe he should have taken him prisoner together with Kaufman.

"Well?" said Marfa.

"It wasn't practical. They were both armed, and I had to act fast."

Dima nodded. "I was there. He's right." He flicked ash into a tin ashtray. "And from what I saw, we're damned lucky to have Robert on our side."

Jacob gave a wan smile. "Thanks for the vote of confidence." He turned to Marfa with a stern expression. "After I've decided how we should proceed now with Slava out of the picture, I'm going to extract every piece of information out of that guy that I can. If he points the finger at you, Marfa..."

She gave a bitter laugh. "That's not going to happen."

Jacob pressed her while she was on the back foot.

"What about the name Oleg Klitschko?" he barked. "Sure you don't know him?"

"Another name I'm not familiar with." She took a deep draw on the cigarette, the paper dwindling as the tip glowed bright. "But I did hear about the incident on Aptekarsky."

"How?"

"A Telegram channel. A woman posted that she heard an explosion, raced to the scene, and saw a car on fire. She uploaded a short video: people milling about, firefighters shooting foam at the flames. I'm sure there are more videos out there. People are posting comments that it's Chechen terrorists starting their shit again." She spun the packet of Camel on the table. "Jesus Christ, how wrong could they be!"

Jacob nodded, pleased. That type of misdirected speculation

was to their advantage. Maybe Vanya could help fan the flames. Drop a flood of bot comments into the threads pushing the Chechen angle.

"You tell me Slava's dead." She shot them all a suspicious stare. "What have you done with his body? Show me."

Dima gestured over her shoulder toward the back door. "He's in the barn. It's cold in there and secure. He'll be safe from the wolves, at least." He held up his cell phone, a photo of the body lying on the barn floor, eyes closed and hands by his sides. Marfa gasped, blinking rapidly.

"You just left him lying there like that? Exposed?"

"Of course not. After I took the photo, we covered him up."

"We're getting off track." Vanya slapped his hand on the table, the cracking sound making everyone jump in their seats. "She's not answering the d-d-damn question." He glared at her. "Why did you lie about the m-m-messages?"

"I'm really getting sick of you, Vanya," Marfa fumed, scrolling through her phone, thumb flicking over her list of sent messages. "Look—everything I sent to Slava. See?" She held up the phone, showing the screen to the three men in a panoramic arc.

Jacob said, "Weird. There were no alerts." He scratched the side of his nose. "Do you expect me to believe he had you blocked? A key member of the team?"

"No way he'd block my number." Marfa stiffened. "When I message him, he's usually quick to respond. And I didn't lie. I sent them. Every one, as you can see. I can't control what happens on his end."

Jacob pulled out Slava's phone and entered the PIN. He pressed a button on the side to check the volume. All sounds were set to maximum levels. A downward finger flick from the top of the screen revealed a subset of the device's core settings. His eyes caught a light-blue rectangle with prominent white text: Do Not Disturb. He tapped it off.

Immediately, the screen came to life. One notification appeared, accompanied by a loud ping: New message. Then another. And another. In a growing cascade, unread messages stacked up, sliding into view faster than Marfa's fingers could have typed them. The phone vibrated with each arrival, an unrelenting rhythm that filled the quiet room.

Marfa's shoulders eased, the tension draining from her face. "See? I told you. I wasn't lying. And there are other messages there, including from his boss. His voicemail box will have a shitload of messages, I'm sure."

Jacob allowed himself a faint, private smile, noting the small flare of satisfaction across her face. The sudden surge of messages made it feel as if the truth had finally caught up to the delay, materializing in front of them both.

"You gonna say sorry?" Jacob challenged, head tilted toward Vanya.

He shrugged. "I guess." In an insincere school-boy voice, he added, "Sorry, Marfa."

It weirdly made sense to Jacob. For all his IT smarts, Vanya carried the air of an absent-minded professor: He could just as easily forget to consider the settings that a phone's owner may use as he forgets to charge his own phone.

Marfa went to the double-door refrigerator. "Got any wine in here? I'd even settle for a beer."

Jacob was out of his chair in an instant, closing the fridge door as she tensed, trying and failing to keep it open. "I can smell booze on you already. No more."

He grabbed her by the wrist. The perfect way to sober her up lay in the barn. "Come with me." He tossed a glance that encompassed everyone. "In fact, we'll all go."

The air inside the rickety clapboard barn was thick with the smell of old horse manure and decomposing straw. Engine oil and petroleum aromas added an extra layer, creating a rural potpourri that took Jacob back to his estate on Lake Keuka. Vanya had told Jacob he'd gotten rid of the livestock on the property soon after he gained the deeds. Not because he didn't share his parents' passion for the animals; he was simply too busy to give them the care they needed. And growing vegetables? Forget about it.

Vanya flicked a switch, and the place lit up like it was broad daylight. Slava lay on a concrete slab at the far end of the barn floor where they'd set him, under a cheap construction tarp Dima had found on top of a wooden storage rack. The blue plastic gave the deceased all the dignity of an online order waiting for pickup.

Jacob crouched beside the body and lifted the corner of the tarp. Slava's eyes were closed in eternal slumber. As he pulled the sheet down to reveal the red groove on his neck, he heard Marfa's sharp intake of breath. Still crouching, he turned his head to the right and up to see her clamping a glove over her mouth. Two streams of tears poured from her eyes as if a faucet had been turned on. She gave a fatalistic nod, like she was ID'ing a relative at the county morgue. Jacob put the tarp in its previous position, stood, and took Marfa in an empathetic embrace. He felt her arms reach around his waist and pull tight, her breasts squishing into his ribcage.

They must have stood in this pose too long for Dima's liking; his forced cough echoed in the vast open space.

The pair separated, taking a step back from each other. Vanya looked on with steeply V-shaped eyebrows of prudish disapproval. Jacob didn't give a shit what Vanya or anyone else thought. When someone in your team was so obviously hurting, they needed comforting.

He regarded the blue tarp again. Leaning over, he pulled the edges tight. "Temperature in here's what—minus ten degrees?"

"About that," Vanya murmured. "The same temperature as the old produce storeroom." He took up a position half a step from Jacob.

"Let's get him in there. I don't like the thought of him lying in the middle of this big open space. Rats get hungry no matter the temperature. They'll get the scent of death sooner or later, chew through this plastic like it's candy floss."

Vanya rubbed his chin. "Hadn't thought of that."

"Where's the storeroom?"

"Close. A hundred meters away, give or take. Right next to the machinery shed."

"Makes your next job that much easier. Go fetch the UTV."

Jacob and Dima lifted the tarp by the corners. Slava's weight bent the plastic, producing a low crackle that made Marfa flinch. They carried the body to the open roller door, feet shuffling as they went, where they set him down gently.

Vanya was back with the UTV in five minutes flat, engine rumbling, exhaust pouring out of the vibrating tailpipe.

Gusts of bitter wind cutting into their faces, Jacob and Dima loaded Slava's wrapped body onto the back tray of the Polaris four-seater. They climbed into the cab, and Jacob eased the UTV across the yard to the storeroom, engine growling like an angry guard dog in the frigid air. Inside the storage building, far better insulated than the drafty barn, the two men hauled Slava onto an elevated steel bench and placed additional layers of plastic sheeting over him. Even though the chances of vermin getting in here were almost zero, they tied the body tightly with thick rope and muscled him into the cold room, closing the door reverentially.

No more words spoken, they rolled back to collect Marfa and Vanya, who climbed into the back seats without a word. Jacob gripped the wheel hard, wondering what the hell he was doing in this surreal moving tableau, and steered the Polaris across the snowy terrain toward the dacha. He pulled up at the back door and killed the engine. Like returned Arctic explorers, the four of them stamped snow from their feet and headed inside to the warmth of the wood-burning stove and to synchronize the lies they'd need to invent about the missing ministry employee, Vyacheslav Gabulov.

"LATER," Dima whispered, almost to himself. "When we finish this... we'll organize a proper burial for Slava."

"I guess so." Vanya's eyes kept flicking to the back door.

"Expecting guests?" said Marfa.

"Of course n-n-not."

"Worried someone's gonna come and discover us?" Her voice dripped with sarcasm. She'd take a long time to forgive Vanya for his accusations against her.

"No...I...I'm not. I've set up an unbreachable security system on this property. No one's going to get in here without me knowing about it."

Jacob believed him.

Upon arrival, Vanya had given him a guided tour of the dacha, pointing out the protective measures he'd put in place. The whole perimeter of the five-acre property was sealed tight. Two layers of cameras—standard optics outside, thermal inside. If there was a power failure, batteries would keep everything running for days.

Vanya had buried an array of seismic sensors around the property and hidden microwave motion detectors in old electrical boxes. Infrared trip-beams were installed low to the ground; anyone trying to crawl in would set them off. Windows had glass-break detectors. If something triggered twice, floodlights would come on like the Winter Palace.

The lack of weaponry was a problem: Should a team of hitmen storm the dacha, they would have to make do with the two stolen pistols and random farming implements. A scenario he preferred not to dwell upon. In a quiet moment, he'd hit up Marfa about her underworld contacts.

"What I am worried about," continued Vanya, "is what the f-f-fuck we do now. After Slava got killed so easily, we need to act fast. Unless we can cut the head off the hydra, I fear we're all gonna get picked off." He nodded toward Jacob. "As far as I'm concerned, we should cede leadership to R-R-Robert. He's basically giving the orders now. Let's formalize it."

"Hang on a second." Marfa's voice rose in tandem with her eyebrows. "That's not how we work."

"Sorry, Marfa," chimed in Dima. "You're outnumbered. Like

I said, I saw Robert act decisively with Klitschko. I don't advocate killing, but it had to be done. None of us would have had the balls to do what he did." He flicked ash onto the concrete floor. "We've been operating on this stupid democratic principle. That works fine at the level of a society, maybe even a large organization..."

"But it doesn't work for us," said Vanya. "I don't want to think about planning and shit. I'm sure Dima doesn't either."

Dima, leaning against the kitchen sink with his arms folded, nodded. "Correct."

"Slava made the call for outside help. Robert was sent to us for a reason. Let's not undermine him by bickering."

"I don't like being spoken about in the third-person when I'm standing right here," said Jacob, arms across his chest in a vain attempt to beat the cold. "But the men are correct, Marfa. Democracy by committee doesn't work for small teams; in fact, it's a death warrant. If four people row the boat in four different directions, you go nowhere."

"Short version," said Dima, "we need an agreed leader. And, as much as you might not like it, Marfa, Robert's it."

"Thanks for trusting me," said Jacob, giving the men a thin-lipped smile. A rag-tag bunch, if he was to be totally honest. None of them smiled back at him, although he did detect signs of grim relief: more relaxed facial muscles, even breathing. Marfa, at first indignant, also appeared to be onboard, albeit reluctantly.

"My first order is one I'm sure none of you will argue with." He nodded at Vanya. "Make us some tea."

"On it." Vanya filled the samovar, lit the element with a practiced flick, and let it rumble to life while he set out the mugs. When the steam finally hissed and the top pot was ready, he poured the dark concentrate into four cups and cut it with hot water, sliding the brews across the table without a word. Dima located packets of traditional Russian cookies—dry *sushki* and gingerbread *pryaniki*—and tipped them onto a brightly colored plate.

They spent an hour discussing tomorrow's program: Marfa to

accompany Jacob to meetings with Saburenkov and Kolodin and discretely chase up weapons dealers; Vanya to dig for details on the goszakaz and whatever he could find on Kaufman and Klitschko. Dima would do the driving.

"What about Kaufman?"

"I'll deal with him when the rest of you hit the hay."

"You gonna…" said Marfa, holding a cigarette with trembling fingers, "kill him?"

"I'd prefer not to. He could prove useful as a bargaining chip after I've wrung him out." He dunked a pryanik in his steaming tea and took a bite. "Let's see."

EIGHTEEN

SHE STOOD AT THE DOORWAY, STARING AT JACOB AND the gagged man who was tied securely to a wooden chair brought down from the kitchen.

He couldn't see her. He *smelled* her. Musky perfume, a touch of stale cigarettes and booze. And something uniquely hers that defied definition.

Sleeves rolled up to the elbows and leather belt in his hand, he coughed, took a step back, and turned to face her. She wore a dark green terry robe, hands thrust in the pockets. On her feet were a pair of tan men's slippers.

"Close the door, please, Marfa."

She took a step into the basement, turned, and shut the door.

"Aren't these rooms supposed to have water dripping from the a crack in the roof, a single naked light bulb hanging from the middle of the ceiling?" she said, hunching her shoulders as the robe slipped a little.

"In a Tarantino movie, sure."

Jacob cast his eyes around the room. Instead of the clichéd scenario Marfa had described, the basement setting was as clean and clinical as a hospital operating theater. In addition to an office desk and a couple of black-and-orange gamer-style chairs, the cellar held a metal rack with several network servers, small boxes of hard drives, and a row of switches and routers. A stainless steel double sink below overhead cupboards. A workbench along one wall carried soldering tools, spare drives, cable testers, adapters, and neatly organized diagnostic equipment. Nine cold LEDs in a tight three-by-three grid turned the basement into a bright, shadowless box, perfect for grilling Kaufman under the unforgiving light.

"This is more your intergalactic sci-fi background," said Jacob, taking a handkerchief from his pocket and wiping the lenses of his prop glasses. "Why are you here and not asleep like the other two?"

"You only assume they're asleep."

He flicked his wrist. The Breitling told him it was 02:17. "I think it's a fair assumption." He repeated his first question. "Why are you here?"

She tugged the soft belt of the robe tighter around her waist. "It's not cold, either. Almost...cozy."

She was right. A Daikin air-conditioning system regulated by a wall-mounted climate controller set to a constant ambient temperature of 71.6°F kept the environment stable and predictable.

"You're good at avoiding questions, Marfa. Perhaps I need to tie you down like this asshole to get a straight answer out of you."

"The reason I'm here is simple." She huffed like a spoiled brat and pulled a cell phone out of her pocket. "I want to take a couple pictures of this man before you...kill him." She gave a mirthless smile, barely a crescent. "Plus I want to hear what he has to say firsthand. I know you're our new dear leader and all, but I trust no one to tell me the whole truth."

Jacob saw a flash of terror in Kaufman's red-veined eyes when she said 'kill.' The man was stripped to his satin boxer shorts, surreally adorned with images of pineapples and palm trees. Sweat and grime lined his lean, muscular body. Almost too handsome to be a sacrificial goon, Jacob mused. His attractive physical attributes seemed to be having no hormonal effects on Marfa, whose face twisted into a sneer of contempt as she crept closer.

"That's near enough," said Jacob. "And off the record—to use a term you probably hear a lot—I'm not going to kill him." *Yet*, he added in silence.

Kaufman blinked at a rate that was almost a blur, his sigh of relief like a blast from an air hose. He turned his head away at the sound of Marfa's camera taking a photograph.

"No point acting all shy, Andrey," said Marfa, her voice carrying the tone of a mother berating a child. She turned the phone horizontal and snapped off another shot. "You'll go down in history as the useless piece of shit who failed to stop us from stopping your masters." The sarcastic half-smile returned for a second.

Kaufman wriggled like a worm on a hook enclosed in plastic wrap.

"But you're not totally useless," she continued, "because my Estonian friend here will coax you into spilling your guts. I was hoping for a literal version of that expression, but I guess I'll have to settle for the figurative one."

Jacob told Marfa to put the phone away and go back to bed. He needed her to be clear and aware tomorrow when she took him to see Kolodin. For the first meeting with the trade guy, he wouldn't need her, but the general was expecting her, not Robert Tamm. She'd need all her feminine wiles to explain his presence. She'd be required again at 8:00 p.m. for his surprise appearance at the deputy governor's office.

"I'm not leaving," she said with a pout and a hand on her hip.

Jacob gave a tiny nod. He walked to a workbench and opened a large black plastic tool box, selected a pair of blue rubber gloves and a boxcutter knife. He donned the gloves, then held the knife up to the light. It glinted like a Christmas ornament. No rust marks, clean as a whistle. Kaufman's body rocked from side to side as Jacob approached, holding the knife in his outstretched hand, twisting it back and forth. Jacob stopped abruptly and turned his head toward Marfa. "You really want to stay for the show?"

She nodded slowly, unsurely. "Of course I do. Make him pay for what he did to Slava!"

Jacob walked behind Kaufman, who rocked his body hard against the bonds, arms and wrists, legs and feet straining. The chair thumped against the concrete floor. A fistful of dark hair in his strong fingers, Jacob yanked hard and placed the blade against the prisoner's pulsating throat. In a hoarse whisper loud enough for Marfa to hear, he said, "Stop moving, Andrey, and I won't cut your throat."

All motion in the chair stopped, save for the rise and fall of Kaufman's chest underneath a coiled band of thick rope and the twitching of his cheek muscles. In a lightning move, Jacob grasped the lobe of the man's left ear between thumb and forefinger. The other hand, firmly gripping the yellow handle of the knife, dug the triangular blade in at the top of the ear, pushed and dragged at the same time. In seconds, the organ was separated from the body. He strode to the front of the chair, holding up the severed ear, dripping with blood, an inch from Kaufman's quivering, almost translucent face. "Not such a pretty boy now, are you?" He tossed the ear into the sink, where it landed with a plop.

Marfa's bloodcurdling screams drowned out the muffled cries under the cloth gag.

Jacob's eyes burned a hole in the space between them. "Marfa. I need you to attend to the wound. Quickly, find some antiseptic, bandages, maybe painkillers. Vanya will know where."

She froze, face draining of color, then shook her head so hard that her flailing black hair hid her eyes for a moment. "I... I can't—"

"Marfa," he barked, "you will."

Her knees buckled and her hands shook. Then, just as it looked like she was going to vomit, she spun on her heel, flung the door open and bolted, the sound of loose slippers thwapping against the floor and up the stairs.

Jacob found a rag, wiped the blood from his forearms, and tugged off the gloves. No one would be attending to Kaufman's wound. Nursing the prisoner was never his intention.

As the blood continued to drip onto Kaufman's neck and shoulders, leaving little splatter marks on the floor, Jacob reflected on how his heart had hardened so much over the last decade. Even two years ago, he never would have treated Kaufman this way. He always left the rough stuff to others, while he watched and cursed the tormentors. After constant exposure to the levels of inhumanity people were capable of, a little of that inhumanity had rubbed off. Raw cynicism had taken a firm hold, and it would take many years to lose it. And with all the emotion taken out of it, Jacob knew that playing nice with thugs like Kaufman was a waste of time and effort.

He approached the cowering man, gently patted his sweat-soaked hair, and untied the wet gag, flecked with blood. He stepped on a pedal to open a trash can and dropped the gag in it. Kaufman, back turned to Jacob, spluttered and coughed, making gurgling noises like he was about to choke. Those sounds were replaced by wheezing and sharp intakes of breath and fragments of incoherent words.

Jacob set his cell phone on a little tripod and pressed play to make sure everything was working. It was. He hit pause. The beginning of the interview would be rough; that was unavoidable. Once Kaufman was broken, the interrogation would turn civil; that's when the camera would go on. If Jacob needed to get physical again, he would turn off the camera until calm had returned.

He fetched a gamer chair, dropped into it, and scooted along until he was a foot away from Kaufman. At this distance, he could smell the ammonia of piss and the foul body odor. A shower would sort him out later. Or six feet of soil.

"Sorry I had to slice that ear off." He chuckled as he manipulated the lever under the seat to raise it a couple of inches. "It was the only way I could get her out of the room."

"Why did you...want her...out of the room?"

Jacob didn't answer. Instead, he fetched his leather belt from where he'd set it down on the walnut desk—a quality piece of furniture that must have cost Vanya a pretty penny—doubled it over, and flexed it to form a loop that made a loud snapping sound as he tugged the ends.

"Speak to me again out of turn, and I will flog you like they used to flog mutineers on pirate ships. Understood?"

A quiet nod.

Jacob shook his head, walked behind Kaufman, and let fly with the belt. With one mighty stroke, the steel buckle left a deep impression in the middle of the man's back. Kaufman screamed almost as loudly as Marfa had.

"You will answer me with words, not gestures." He resumed his seat. "I need your answers recorded: vision and sound. Don't test my patience. Do. You. Understand?"

"*Da.* Yes."

Jacob smiled as benevolently as he could, never letting go of the belt. "Much better. Let's begin." Jacob's eyes widened. "Oh, I forgot. Be right back." He walked toward the door, stopped, and turned to Kaufman. "You won't go anywhere, will you? That doesn't require an answer, by the way."

Upstairs, he first checked the bedrooms. Dima lay under a quilt, snoring like a broken drain; Vanya sat before his glowing computer screen, Kaufman's and Klitschko's cell phones beside him. He said he was chasing the elusive goszakaz, and he'd examine the phones next. Marfa appeared to be sleeping. He placed a hand on her bare shoulder, poking out from under striped flannelette sheets, and whispered her name. She groaned and rolled over. There were creases on her face left by the pillow. Sound asleep despite the ordeal she'd just witnessed. Or perhaps because of it—acute dissociation cascading into a full shutdown. Jacob recalled the term 'post-adrenal crash' mentioned early in his training, but to him it was simpler. Her mind had retreated to dreamland, somewhere safer than Slava's body and the basement and the bloody severed ear.

In the kitchen, he rinsed his hands, filled a large jug with water, and stacked two plastic cups. He also grabbed a small salt shaker. A minute later, he was pouring a glass of water down Kaufman's throat, then more genteelly sipped from his own glass. Another drink for a very thirsty Kaufman, then he dabbed stray droplets from the man's lips like a mother fussing over a toddler. "There, there, that's better."

Jacob crossed one leg over the other, resting a clipboard on the table formed by the V of his bent right leg. He took a pen and began to draw meaningless doodles.

"Did you kill Vyacheslav Gabulov."

He poured a handful of salt into the palm of his hand and rubbed it into the red mess that was once an ear. Kaufman screamed, tears flowing and snot pouring. Jacob washed his hands and returned to his seat.

"I know you're holding out, Andrey. Very brave but very stupid. Again, did you kill my colleague?"

Through a mouthful of gunky phlegm, he managed to whisper, "No, I did not."

Jacob tut-tutted and returned to the tool box. Inside was a special device, gifted to Vanya by a traveling Israeli sympathizer of Russian heritage he'd met years before on a corner of the dark web. Vanya had assured Jacob that the man was thoroughly vetted and had come up clean. The Israeli refused to say how he'd smuggled in the UZI-Pro stun baton into Russia; all Vanya knew was that it worked.

Jacob checked the charge and flicked it to high-output before testing the arc—one sharp blue snap. Compact, rubber-sleeved, and delivering roughly 800–1,000 volts in short pulses, it looked like it could break the best secret-keeper in the world.

"Once more," said Jacob calmly. "Did you kill Vyacheslav Gabulov?"

"No. I told you a hundred times already. It was Oleg."

The charged baton made solid contact with the soft triangle of flesh just below Kaufman's ribs. His muscular frame jolted, and a strangled wheeze erupted from deep in his stomach. A second brief touch—right at the inner thigh where the femoral nerve runs like a live wire—blasted him sideways, his legs thumping against the chair.

"Next one's to the balls, *druzhok*. Again, did you kill Vyacheslav Gabulov?"

Desperation and fear widened Kaufman's eyes, making every fiber in his body twitch, sweat ooze from every pore. There was confusion in those eyes, too. Jacob could read his mind: admit the truth and be executed—and who wants to die?—or keep lying and endure unbearable torture that might never end.

"I'll count to three. One, two—"

"Yes, fuck your mother! I killed him."

Jacob sighed as he closed his eyes. He stood, walked to the tripod, and pressed play. "Go on, Andrey." On the way back to his seat, he gently brushed his fingertips against the top of Kaufman's veiny right wrist. "There's a good fellow. Let's get this out of the way and you can have a nice hot shower, a meal, maybe a glass of ice-cold vodka."

He smiled briefly before the words came in a torrent, like a child telling his mom about his first day at school. "Oleg paid the woman fifty dollars to cry so Gabulov would open the door to see what was wrong, and that's when Oleg jumped in and pointed the gun at him and made him open the back door."

The floodgates were open now; Kaufman would not stop until he'd divested himself of every piece of information he possessed. He tilted his head back and sucked in several liters of air in an attempt to get his breath back. He launched straight back into his account of the assassination.

"I jumped in the back, and Oleg told him, Gabulov I mean, to keep his eyes to the front, and that's when I leaned forward and choked him with the garotte." Tears ran down his sweaty cheeks. "It wasn't easy...he struggled. I'm sorry..."

Silence reigned for a full minute, save for Kaufman's heavy breathing.

Over the next thirty-eight minutes, facts dropped. At least Jacob assumed they were facts because statistically, people who have been through what Kaufman had endured and then start to talk do not lie. There are exceptions, but Kaufman didn't fit the bill.

They were hired by a man who worked for Marat Izamailov's company, but Kaufman couldn't remember exactly what its name was. The guy was an old acquaintance of Klitschko, and he and Kaufman, who called themselves the Two K's, were eager to make some good coin. They were paid five thousand euros each to murder Slava. Oleg was the contact, Kaufman merely extra muscle. They'd met each other in Kresty-2 prison a couple of years ago and become, if not friends, then associates.

"My friend is analyzing your phone and Oleg's. If he finds anything on them incriminating you in organizing your crime... I'm afraid it's the end for you."

He gave the ghost of a smile. "You'll find nothing. Except for a lot of calls and texts to my daughter. Photos of her, too."

"Daughter?"

"Tanya." His bottom lip quivered. "She turns nine next year. Since her mother died, I've been raising her."

Grumbling under his breath, Jacob stopped the camera and used his cell to call Vanya, asking if he'd had a look at Kaufman's phone. He had. What was on the home screen? A picture of Kaufman with a smiling little girl in a dress holding a red helium balloon.

Jacob closed his eyes and looked to the ceiling, asked the Lord to forgive him for torturing Kaufman, and thanked Him for Tanya, whose very existence was enough to spare this asshole's life. He replaced the cell on the tripod.

"Just a couple more matters to discuss, Andrey. Then I'll untie you, get your ear...I mean your wound...cleaned up, and make you more comfortable."

"What matters are you talking about?"

"Some boring questions about your life that my boss will

probably want to know about." He folded his arms across his chest. "The president of the USA will be seeing this video. Bet you never imagined that, huh?"

"Jesus," muttered Kaufman. With forced black humor, he added, "I'll be a...a celebrity. And look at the state of me."

"That's fine. I'm sure she'll understand."

NINETEEN

THE STERN-FACED RECEPTIONIST ANNOUNCED THE visitor and closed the door behind her, leaving Colonel-General Kolodin standing at the threshold looking a little lost, the arrogant jutting jaw not fully disguising his angst. He smiled for a quarter of a second before his mouth returned to its normal state of resigned grimness.

"Good morning, Marat Ibragimovich," he said dully before limping his way over the floor. He crossed the expensive Bukhara rug slowly, his highly polished boots pressing into the thick woolen pile. The complex weave pattern in pomegranate reds and indigos seemed to ripple underfoot, briefly hypnotizing him with their swirling sunbursts.

"Your early arrival is appreciated." Izmailov stood, moved to Kolodin, and embraced him in a bear hug.

"At my age, it's actually getting easier to be an early riser. The bladder is nature's perfect alarm clock."

Izmailov grinned at his co-conspirator's self-deprecation. He valued the experience and wisdom of the eighty-year-old old war horse, but there were emerging signs his health was on the wane. Subtle signs but there nonetheless.

"Please." Izmailov gestured to the three-seater leather couch.

"I'll organize the refreshments while you read this." He tossed a thin stapled document onto the coffee table, called his secretary, and placed the breakfast order. He hung up the phone and said, "The report's from my mole in the Estonian Center for Defense Investments, responsible for their army's fuel procurement. I believe it warrants our close attention."

Kolodin smoothed his trousers and sat down gingerly. He grimaced, leaning slightly to the left. He still carried a piece of jagged metal deep in his left hip, a souvenir from a 1980 ambush outside Jalalabad, Afghanistan, where a mortar shell had turned a house into a cloud of flying brick, stone, steel, and glass. Surgeons had left the fragment in place—too close to nerves and major vessels to risk fishing it out—and four decades later, it had shifted just enough to grind against bone and soft tissue. It left him with a constant ache that flared whenever he walked more than a few steps.

After half a minute, Kolodin began to breathe more easily. As the general donned his gold-framed reading glasses, Izmailov took note of the liver-spotted hands. There seemed to be more black marks than even a month ago. The symptoms of aging were taking their toll and fast; hopefully, the old-timer would live to see the Severnaya Volna operation succeed.

The billionaire oligarch CEO moved to the window and looked out, not wanting to put Kolodin off by crowding him with his presence. Let him read and digest the information, see if he was as confident of success in Estonia as he was when they hatched the plan together with the wily fox, Sergei Semak. Izmailov was beginning to get nervous—he had a vast fortune to lose if it all went to shit. Kolodin and Semak, twenty years younger than the general and twenty older than Izmailov, could afford to be more phlegmatic, more gung-ho. Their interests were ideological; his was business, a chance to dominate the Baltic energy markets.

A twist of the blind revealed the sprawling city of Peter the Great below in all its winter glory. A fairytale vista of ice and snow framing green and gold cupolas, black spires, and pastel colored buildings. Such a contrast with the heat of Makhachkala, the capital of Dagestan, where he grew up.

Izmailov remembered how he had hustled around the refineries as a young man, eyes wide for opportunities in the 1990s, when lucrative state assets were sold off at fire-sale prices. Possessed with innate grit, a sharp tongue, and a hunger that could never be satiated, he'd outmaneuvered larger players while still in his twenties. Every prize he acquired, every utility he seized under the banner of BaltEnergoTorg, was a step farther away from that gritty childhood in Dagestan, toward his ultimate goals of wealth, power, and influence.

Returning to his seat opposite Kolodin, he watched the veteran's lips move as he silently read the report, eyes blinking like a rat exiting the dark of a drainpipe. He licked his index finger and flipped over the last page of the report, placing it on the low rosewood table with a frown.

"I'm optimistic we can overcome these minor obstacles. A couple of noisy politicians opposing the accord can be dealt with properly once we seize power. We pay them what they want, and your company will be supplying all the fuel for their army for the next fifty years."

"My man has identified some potential troublemakers in the armed forces' top brass."

"Same goes for them. Me getting that fool General Golytsin jailed as a scapegoat for the false-start invasion has calmed the Estonians down, convinced them it was simply a big mistake."

Kolodin leaned back as the buxom blond secretary Galina placed a silver tray on the table. She bowed to both men and scuttled away.

In a tone of absolute certainty, Kolodin continued, "Opposition in Tallinn will crumble once the land invasion—the real one—is over and we install our own government. NATO will do nothing to stop us. And Putin...well, he'll thank us in the end.

The first step toward reclaiming the lost republics will have been taken."

Izmailov tapped the top of the flimsy document, now with a couple of brown spots where the Colonel-General's shaky hands had spilled tea.

"There might be minor problems in Estonia, but we've got fucking major ones on home soil. We can't even think about land invasions until they're solved."

Kolodin blinked slowly, his sleepy, hooded eyes owl-like. "Is that the reason for this early meeting?"

"You may have heard the news of the explosion in Aptekarsky Pereulok, yes?"

"I did see something about that in my newsfeed. What of it?"

"That was a shot fired at *us*, my dear Denis Petrovich. The man lost at the border monitoring facility in Tallinn, that was factored in and expected. This is different. One of my foot soldiers got cremated in his own vehicle yesterday, barely five kilometers from where we sit. Clearly payback for what we did to Gabulov. And they're holding Kaufman hostage. Thankfully, the man is an ox who knows nothing of our plans."

"*Bozhe moi!* Good God! The arrogance of those fuckers. What about your infiltrator, Vanya Beglov? Can't he let us in the door of his own dacha? We ought to be able to crush them easily. They're a small group, after all. Tiny."

A firm nod. "Yes, that's true. There's only three of them left with Gabulov out of the picture."

"You must be counting your own mole to get that number," said Kolodin with a touch of incredulity.

"I am. He's got feet in both camps. Don't forget what happened to his sister for speaking out against the regime. Murdered."

"We're not the regime," countered Kolodin robotically.

"Doesn't matter. We're *establishment*. Which is practically the same thing to some folks." Izmailov reached for a chocolate croissant. Decadent for breakfast, but he planned on smashing out a two-hour gym session before lunch. "And because of Beglov's divided loyalties, we can't just charge in like a bull at a gate. We need to think carefully about every move we make. Use his intel but with forethought."

"What's he been telling you? You seem reluctant to share much of it, Marat."

A shake of the head. "No reluctance. I just wanted you to read the Estonian report first. Get the lesser of two worries out of the way." He drew a hand across his face, stubbly already despite shaving before he went to bed last night. "And the reason we can't simply 'crush them,' as you put it, is that this Robert Tamm—you remember that name...?"

"Sure. The mysterious Estonian envoy who just happened to cozy up to the people trying to thwart us the minute he stepped off the airplane." Kolodin reached for a pastry, changed his mind, and leaned back in his seat again. "If I recall correctly, your guy Beglov said he wants to hold talks with all three of us."

"I didn't want to do it at first, but I think we should go through the motions."

"I *still* don't want to talk to him. He's a damned spy."

"Yes, he is." Izmailov took a bite of croissant and wiped flaky crumbs off his lips with a linen napkin. "Beglov told me in a message this morning that Marfa Petko has tricked us all into meeting with *her* as a way of slipping Tamm into our midst."

Kolodin shook his head. "I should have guessed. Why not rat her out to Roskomnadzor?"

"On what basis?" Izmailov could think of nothing Petko had done as a journalist to warrant the censorship agency clamping down on her.

"Does there have to be one?" he scoffed. "I'd be happy for someone to put a bullet in her beautiful head, just like that bitch Politkovskaya."

"Steady on, old boy." Izmailov gestured for calm, palms down. "Who knows what kind of kompromat she has stashed away on us? She's smart enough to have something set up where if she dies, the mud gets released."

"Like Semak fucking Kazakh whores? The whole country knows about that and doesn't care."

"I'm thinking more along the lines of our operation."

"I know that! But if she has anything on us, why hasn't she gone public with it yet?"

A shrug. "Playing the long game, I guess. Waiting to get something incontrovertible she can pass on to the authorities or the Western media. Not sure which would be worse." He gulped down a mouthful of tea. "We need to play it smart: talk nicely to Petko and to that Tamm prick, too. We can't risk them blowing Severnaya Volna out of the water."

Kolodin muttered his hesitant agreement. "OK. Let's talk to him, spin him a bunch of bullshit, and send him on his way."

"Agreed." Finally, the old boy was starting to see sense.

He took a small sip of tea. "What does Semak have to say about this?"

Izmailov's desk phone rang. He excused himself, cleared his throat, and spoke to Galina for twenty seconds. "I guess we're about to find out. Sergei will be here in fifteen minutes."

"We were this close to finalizing a date." Kolodin illustrated the statement by making a small gap between thumb and forefinger. Then, without warning, he crashed his fist onto the table, sending shock waves through the crockery. "Dammit it all to hell, let's eliminate Tamm like we did Gabulov. The whole lot of them, and your fucking mole for insurance."

Izmailov sucked in a quart of air. Kolodin had just agreed to talk nicely to Tamm; now he'd flipped again. His instability was becoming a genuine concern.

"The challenge we face is that Robert Tamm is not only responsible for killing one of my men and torturing and maiming another. He is also, according to Beglov, in direct communication with the Estonian president. He dies on this trip, so do our hopes of taking control. They're already edgy after detecting our mini rehearsal on the border."

Despite his words to Kolodin about Vanya, his trust in the mole was low. Beglov had been turned by big money, not conviction, and he still had an ax to grind over his dead sister. When someone's whole heart wasn't in their job, you could never be sure about their ability to deliver.

Still, having Vanya Beglov reporting back intel was an asset not to be sneezed at. Izmailov remembered that summer's day eighteen months ago when he'd turned Vanya like it was yesterday.

He'd booked the appointment under a false name, asking for a 3.2-carat diamond ring to be reset, promising to pay handsomely for the service. Beglov, reputedly one of the best in the business, could barely contain his excitement. Izmailov buzzed from the street the next day, already certain who he'd find behind the counter: the overconfident IT genius who'd left a microscopic trace in the BaltEnergoTorg email server, convinced he'd wiped it clean. One of Izmailov's staff had flagged the intrusion. He watched the awkward man lean over a watch under the lens and knew he was there for the taking. An hour later—and several hundred thousand euros into the red—Izmailov had his new operative.

Kolodin waved the concern away. "I'm not so sure. If we take out Tamm and then make our move before the Estonians have time to mobilize properly, I think that's a plus for Severnaya Volna."

Izmailov gnawed a fingernail. "Let's tip-toe our way with Tamm, wait till he's out of the picture, shore up our support, and..."

Kolodin shook his head. "Semak gets the deciding vote on this."

"Of course." Would Semak be persuaded by Kolodin's confidence? Izmailov hoped not.

As they waited for the deputy governor to arrive, the men

drank more tea and spoke about mundane family matters and a topic that animated both of them: ice hockey. Izmailov sponsored one of the country's most popular teams, and Kolodin was a huge fan. The old man's tone was a lot calmer on the safe ground of these subjects, smiling and laughing as he nibbled at the pastries.

Semak arrived on the stroke of 08:30. A formidable figure at six foot two and with an athlete's build, he always professionally presented with slicked-back dark hair, razor sharp suit, and shoes so shiny you could see your reflection in them. And most remarkable, in a land where smiling for no reason is considered a mark of stupidity, his trademark, almost permanent lopsided grin. Izmailov always thought that trait made the deputy governor resemble an American politician more than a Russian one. Something must be working, though, because he'd held his position for almost eight years. Picked by two governors with totally conflicting platforms, no less. In essence, he was a cunning political survivor who knew it was best to remain an appointed official —in power—rather than risk it at the ballot box.

He shook the hands of the men already present, twisted one of his ruby cufflinks, and took a seat next to Kolodin. He nodded sagely as Izmailov brought him up to speed with the occasional gruff interruption from Kolodin.

"I share Denis Petrovich's sentiments to a degree," said Semak in a conciliatory tone. "It would be nice and simple to crush this so-called B+...I don't even know what to call them...ring?"

"Dirty asswipes," suggested Kolodin, drawing a reflexive guffaw from the other two.

"Well, that's pretty accurate," said Semak, patting the pensioner general on his bony knee. "I'll bow to your seniority." He clicked a pen repeatedly as he pondered, Izmailov and Kolodin waiting patiently for him to continue. "But in this case, Marat Ibragimovich's idea to be watchful is one I agree with. After Marat rang me yesterday and told me about this Robert Tamm..." —he nodded at Kolodin—"asswipe, I took the liberty of contacting a friend in MID. He tells me Tamm is here on a single-entry ten-day visa, and he's already been here for three. We talk to him—distract him with smoke and mirrors—until the visa expires in seven days and"—he made a dusting-off-the-hands gesture—"we're done with him. He goes back to his president with a boring report that pleases everyone."

"He's murdered a Russian citizen," said Kolodin. "We're expected to simply allow him to waltz out of the country unpunished?"

Semak coughed into his fist. "Let's be clear. We killed their man first."

"Bullshit. Klitschko did. A convicted felon. Nothing to do with us."

Izmailov nodded, then enumerated points on his fingers. "One: Klitschko was paid in untraceable cash. Two: I made sure every contact with him was in a public place. Three: I had someone frisk him for a wire." He smirked. "Not that he'd be sophisticated enough to even think of that. He won't be missed. Kaufman's even less of a worry. If they off him, all to the good."

Izmailov stood and helped himself to water from a carafe. "Opening up an investigation into Klitshko's death with the aim of fingering Tamm will blow up in our face."

Kolodin's weathered face got wrinklier as he smiled. "Not an investigation. A hitjob."

Semak compressed his lips. "Let's make a compromise. We see him off over the next seven days, treat him like a VIP, tell him we are totally invested in the accord succeeding."

"Sounds reasonable," said Izmailov.

"You, Denis Petrovich, will make preparations for a ground invasion through Narva on"—he made a quick check on his phone—"November 23rd, one day after Tamm leaves. Have all your border units and mercenaries on standby for that date." A grin flourished on his face. "And to make you happy, let's organize a hit on Tamm inside Estonia once he's been back for a month or so. Home invasion gone wrong, something like that."

Kolodin pick up his cup and saucer together, took a sip with a pinkie extended, returned the crockery to the table, and smacked his lips. "I can live with that compromise."

Izmailov looked up at the ceiling, grateful for Semak's ability to smooth things out. With him at the helm, they actually stood a good chance of seeing this thing through.

"I've got a couple more suggestions," said Semak. "A bit of housekeeping to do."

Once Semak had finished outlining the next steps they had to take, the three men toasted their future success with a glass of Armenian cognac and Cuban cigars. As his guests shuffled out the door, Izmailov placed a call to his stuttering mole.

He wouldn't like the order.

Not one bit.

TWENTY

He'd swept the house from top to bottom for bugs, the outbuildings too. He found nothing, but it didn't mean the place wasn't infected. Tamm was a sadistic freak who needed close watching. What he had done to Kaufman was messing with his mind. Tamm was some kind of James Bond crossed with a merciless Spetsnaz soldier. He could be as tech savvy as anyone out there, capable of secreting devices all over the place. Maybe his NATO pals had slipped him something powerful and undetectable.

It made no sense to be worried; it wasn't logical, yet Vanya's heart thundered as he placed the call. To eliminate any risk, he'd gone outside and wandered to the dilapidated woodshed by the iced-over duck pond in a tucked-away corner of the property. A hundred more steps and he'd be dipping his toes in the icy waters of the Gulf of Finland. The trees were thick here, blocking the light of the early morning and the blustery wind from the north. But it was still damned cold. He could barely feel his face.

"They've all gone. Headed for the city to meet up with Slava's b-b-boss."

"How's Kaufman?"

"Alive. The wound's bandaged up. Dima cleaned it all out first. No f-f-fever or signs of infection."

"What are they planning on doing with him?"

"No idea. Tamm's still m-m-mulling it over. My gut feeling is that Tamm wants to spare him, maybe use him to negotiate later. I'm on baby-sitting duty."

"You are? Sounds like you're outside. Why?"

"I don't trust Tamm. He could've planted stuff in the house. Listening devices. I'm taking no chances."

"No, I mean why are you leaving Kaufman alone if you're supposed to be guarding him?"

"It's OK. He's locked in a room, hands and feet tied. Even if he got out, where's he gonna g-g-go in his condition?" Without waiting for a reply to the question, which was anyway rhetorical, he added, "Dima's coming back after he drops the other two at Saburenkov's." He gritted his teeth and began to pace back and forth, to keep warm and to calm the nerves. "Listen, Marat. I've been giving you everything you wanted, updates several times a day. You know virtually everything that's happening in B+." He leaned against the trunk of a birch tree. "Why did you have to k-k-kill Slava! You know how hard it was for me to pretend to Tamm that I d-d-didn't know about it after you'd already called and told me?"

"But you did it, Vanya! You are capable of great things if you only set your mind to it. I knew it the day I walked into your workshop."

The flattery wasn't washing. "You could have gotten away with your stupid scheme without murdering my friend."

"A friend you took money to betray," Izmailov scoffed. He hesitated a moment, then said in a more conciliatory tone, "It was Semak's decision to liquidate him. I voted against it, but Kolodin...well, he's a bloodthirsty old prick. He sided with the deputy governor, no persuasion needed."

"I'm not sure I can go on with this assignment...it's t-t-tougher than I thought. I...Slava...was a good man." He wiped a tear from his cheek with the back of a thick glove.

A staccato laugh. "A good man? And what about his... perverted past?"

Vanya pulled his scarf up and took a deep breath through the woolen fibers to regain control. This was nothing but provocation by Izmailov. A year ago, there had been allegations in the ministry about Slava: sexual misconduct, harassment, stalking. An inquiry cleared him, declared the complainant to be a vexatious woman. Vanya believed the findings of the board of inquiry, but most of all he believed Slava. Now he was dead. "Fuck you."

Instead of a rebuke, Izmailov spoke calmly. "You have to kill Kaufman."

Vanya glanced down at the little path he'd created in the snow, stopped pacing. "You'd better repeat that," he said with a nervous laugh. "It sounded like you said you want me to kill Kaufman."

"That's exactly what I said."

"I...can't. I'm not capable of murder."

There was the sound of papers flicking on the other end. "I'm reading your military service record. Top of your class in combat sambo, jiu-jitsu, and wrestling."

He looked up at the sky, praying for a miracle that he knew wouldn't come. "That same record will tell you I avoided mobilization to Ukraine in 2023 because I inflicted an injury on myself." Having received the *povestka*, a sweat-inducing draft notice informing him of his impending trip to Mariupol, Vanya knew there was only one way to get out of it. Replacing a watch crystal, he deliberately pressed down with too much force. The glass snapped, shooting a sharp sliver into the base of his palm. The shard cut across a flexor tendon. Doctors repaired what they could, but grip strength never fully returned. "Not because I'm a coward but because I can't kill another human being."

"Oh, but you can. And you will."

"And if I refuse?"

"One of two things. I tell your violent Estonian friend that you're a fucking traitor, or I report you to the MVD for aiding and abetting in the murder of Oleg Klitschko."

"I had nothing to do with—"

"You were in the vehicle, Vanya. Which was torched. So we'll add arson to the charge sheet, shall we? All of this can be confirmed in the text you sent me yesterday at...11:45 a.m."

Vanya swore under his breath. He should never have consented to using SMS as a method of communication. Emails he could wipe, even sent ones if he... He bit his lower lip and swore again. No he couldn't. BaltEnergoTorg's email servers were even harder to crack than government ones. It was his own carelessness in leaving a crumb that had led to him being caught by Izmailov's staff member. Hence the shitty predicament he was in now.

Bluff him out.

"Send someone else to do it. I'll let them in the front gate, and they can finish him off. I don't have the stomach for it."

Three deep inhales and exhales came down the line. Almost vampiric breathing. "Sorry, Vanya. I need to test your loyalty to me. My colleagues think I made a big mistake taking you on. If you refuse my orders, they'll be mighty pissed." Izmailov paused as a phone rang insistently in the background. He barked an order, another voice said *da*, and the ringing stopped. "This place is a madhouse, Vanya. With the new accord, so many business opportunities are going to arise. This is the beginning of the end of Russia's isolation. It begins with Estonia, then the whole world will open up to us again. Don't you want that?"

"Of course I do."

"I can offer you a lot more than you've already received. Wealth you can only dream about. You'll be the one taking your expensive jewelry to be reset, not the dumbass fixing it." He laughed from a place deep in his stomach. "You'll be so rich you won't bother getting broken things repaired; you'll toss them out and buy new ones."

Vanya watched a crow hop from one branch to another, caw when the branch failed to hold its weight, and fly off toward the Gulf. To be that bird, to have that freedom. When a situation gets a bit hairy, just take off for a better place.

"Still not doing it."

"All right. I'll tell you what. I'm going to go and intercept Petko and Tamm at Saburenkov's office this morning. Let them listen to the entire conversation we're having now."

"*Blyad'!* Fuck!" He should have guessed this would happen. But what could he have done differently? Insist on face-to-face meetings every time with the oligarch? Expect Izmailov to subject himself to a body search for a wire? How could he have been so naïve! Taking the Dagestani dog's dirty money was the biggest mistake of his miserable fucking life.

Izmailov proceeded to make him feel even more like a loser.

"I'm sure that Robert Tamm, if he's the mastermind you say he is, has already worked out a way to breach your so-called fortress. He'll slice you up like a ripe tomato, my friend."

"OK. Seems I have no choice." He couldn't believe the words coming out of his mouth.

"You'll do it?"

Vanya could imagine the sick fuck getting a hard-on at the thought. The aphrodisiac of power, bending people to do whatever you want. To kill on command.

"*Da.*"

"I want you to text me when it's done. Upload a video as proof. And don't try any AI shit. I've got techs in my company who have software that can detect even the highest-quality fakes."

"How am I gonna do it? There are no guns on the property. Dima and Tamm took away the pistols they stole from your goons."

"Improvise." A loud chuckle so evil it was almost a caricature burst into his ear. "Just get the job done. I'm giving you one hour. Good-bye."

"Wait..."

"Yes?" The impatience in Izmailov's voice was almost palpable.

"What do I tell them after it's...done? When they come home and find him dead?"

"You'll think of something."

TWENTY-ONE

TRUDGING BACK TO THE MAIN HOUSE, VANYA COULD barely see for the tears pooling in his eyes. The white landscape shifted and shimmered like a mirage. He stopped walking and blinked the tears away. This wouldn't do. Where to find the motivation? It shouldn't be this hard. The job was like a mathematical formula with only one possible answer. Kaufman killed Slava, your good friend, so you kill Kaufman, the asshole. Easy.

Except it wasn't easy. He'd happily accept someone else taking Kaufman out. But to do it himself...?

Oh, dear God.

He stopped at the barn. His breath came in plumes of moisture, pale sunlight peeking through the broken wooden slats. A noticeable smell of rodents hung in the air, the lingering twenty-five-year-old scent of dairy cattle and worn leather.

There was plenty of old gear in the barn, hung up on hooks, stashed away in crates and boxes, some lying on the ground in a muddle, covered in dust and cobwebs. The farming lifestyle had never held interest for Vanya, hence the chaos and disorder. He liked the isolation of the inherited property, the fresh, clean air created by the forests and the gulf, the chance to get away now and again, but it could never quell his natural instinct to base himself in the city.

After ten minutes of searching, weighing up the pros and cons of each potential implement, some of which he didn't even know the names, he selected the pitchfork. There were sharper tools, smaller and easier to carry. But it was the length of the handle that made the decision for him. The handle would put a bit of distance between him and the victim. Vanya imagined he could stab the tied-up Kaufman with it, repeatedly if necessary, like how an enraged bull gores a trapped matador pinned to the arena wall.

Would he need to feel rage to kill?

Of course he hated Kaufman for what he did but not enough to make murder the logical function of that hate. Hell, he doubted he'd find it easy to kill the more deserving Izmailov. Perhaps the first tentative stab would produce enough blood to fire him up, revealing a savagery he didn't know he possessed.

Oh, dear God.

He ran his gloved fingers over the four tines: rusty with age but pointy enough to do serious damage with the right amount of force. With a bit of grinding, those tines could be restored to their original state. Made shiny, like a vintage piece of jewelry. The handle was worn in spots, a couple of thin cracks but still good enough to be used for another fifty years.

Balancing the pitchfork in his hand, its shape tugged his mind back to more carefree days. He remembered helping his father and uncle turn and stack the cut grass into neat hayricks, a few afternoons each season when the weather held and the work felt like exercise, not a chore. Now that same tool was on its way to execute Kaufman, and the old memory of happy times sat uneasily in his chest.

He kicked the snow from his shoes, took off his gloves, and jammed them into his coat pocket. He opened the back door, fingers trembling, heart thundering. It was all about self-preservation now. Too late to think about fight or flight. For Vanya, there were no options left.

Inside, he poured himself a tall glass of tepid water from the faucet and chugged it down in one swallow.

Tamm had put Kaufman in a room on the western side of the house. Last night, the goon had pissed, shat, and showered under Tamm's watchful eye. His bedding consisted of a single mattress, blanket, and pillow barely thicker than a slice of bread. The room was a small space—two by two meters—that had been used to store spare firewood.

The logistics of filming himself murdering Kaufman in such a small space would be difficult. He considered setting up a tripod in the hallway, opening the door, and...

No, that scenario would not do.

He had to bring Kaufman out of the room to a bigger space. There were several choices, but he figured the best was the downstairs computer room, back where Kaufman had had his ear sliced off. Two hard-wired cameras operated there, covering the entire floorspace, which negated the need to set up anything. Last night in his own bedroom, via these same cameras, he'd monitored Tamm's violent interrogation of Kaufman.

To get the hostage down there, he'd have to remove the tie around his ankle. Kaufman could shuffle along a level floor with the zip tie on, but negotiating the stairs would be impossible. A risky move. A wounded and desperate bear can be dangerous, even against a capable opponent like Vanya.

He gnawed his thumbnail for a second as he paced back and forth in the kitchen, pulse racing. Dutch courage would help to carry out this mission. He opened a cupboard, pulled out a bottle of scotch, poured a large measure, and drained it in a second. To his dismay, the alcohol only increased his heart rate. He'd need the whole bottle to get properly relaxed, but then he'd be too drunk to get the job done.

Coughing and spluttering, he made his way downstairs and

secreted the pitchfork behind a rack crammed with laminated manuals.

His phone buzzed. He ignored it, but the device buzzed again. He plucked the cell from his jeans pocket, expecting both messages to be from Izmailov.

Wrong. Only one was. Tamm had sent the second.

He read Izmailov's brief SMS in preview mode. *Get it done. You've got 26 minutes left.*

Vanya's breathing grew shallow. Time was flying, and all he'd done was procrastinate.

He thought about ignoring Tamm's message for now, but curiosity won out.

Keep an eye on Kaufman. Give him something to eat and drink, a bathroom break. Don't worry about him overpowering you. He's mentally and physically wrecked after yesterday's interview. But as added insurance, I've left Kaufman's Sig under the kitchen sink. It's fully loaded; I trust you know how to use it. I'm planning on staying at the hotel tonight. Better optics for the authorities if I do that. Marfa says she can get me a weapon today from a bent cop she knows. Any problems, call me. Keep Kaufman's spirits up. He's got a young daughter, use that as leverage to get him to cooperate with you if he gets feisty. I'll be in touch after my meeting with Saburenkov at midday.

Vanya dabbed the sweat from his brow, blinking up at the middle of the ceiling. An atheist, he did believe in the power of nature, karma, that kind of thing. Everything had gone to shit, but providence had intervened with a small gift. Killing Kaufman with a gun would be a whole lot easier to manage than stabbing him to death with a pitchfork. A squeeze of the trigger, bullet to the back of the brain—job done.

He looked to the corners of the room where the cameras were installed. He'd elected not to tell Tamm about them when he explained the basics of the security system. The computer room was Vanya's sanctuary, a place with secrets others didn't need to know about. And where a scene of Shakespearean proportions was about to unfold.

HE TAPPED on the door of the small room. Vanya shook his head, annoyed with himself. *Why am I even knocking?*

He turned the handle and pushed it open, fingers of the other hand firmly gripping the pistol under his jacket. It was dark in the room, the curtains drawn tight. He flicked on the light with a backward pat of the left hand.

Kaufman, head swathed in a white bandage, sat against the wall, knees drawn up to his stomach.

"Are...are you f-f-feeling OK?" said Vanya in a monotone.

"What do you th-th-think, mother-f-f-fucker?" mocked Kaufman. "Look at me." He held up his bound wrists and touched a cheek to his forearms, indicating the location of the missing organ the best way he could. "Tortured then disfigured by a fucking maniac!"

If only Kaufman knew how Vanya hated his stammer to be mocked. How the children at school had tormented him without mercy. Ignorant adults, too, liberal with cruel taunts. It's why he preferred to work solo and only mix with people he knew were pure of spirit, like the members of B+. Even Petko, with all her arrogance, would never mock him.

A red mist formed before his eyes. That uncalled-for jibe was the straw that broke the camel's back. The idiot had just sealed his fate.

"I know," said Vanya. "The man who abused you is an asshole." He forced a smile, feeling a strength blossoming, the beast within finally emerging.

"You gonna untie me?"

"I'd really like to make you more c-c-comfortable, but..." He gave a slight tilt of the head, pressed his lips together, and shrugged in the classic there's-nothing-I-can-do-about-it expression. "Orders are orders, know what I m-m-mean?"

"Listen, pal. Oleg slipped up, told me some stuff about the guy who hired us. Untie me, and I'll tell you all about it." The desperation in his eyes, spotlit by a flash of bright lightning outside the window, was more obvious than a bad poker player's tell. He had nothing.

"I tell you what, I'll cut the tie around your ankles, but n-n-not the wrists. Fair?"

"Thanks," Kaufman said with a nod. "You've no idea the cramps I've had."

Fuck your cramps. "I'll take you downstairs, b-b-because..." He paused as the sound of thunder resonated inside the dacha. Vanya couldn't recall a winter thunderstorm in this region for at least ten years.

"B-b-because what?" Kaufman couldn't help himself.

Vanya swallowed a profanity.

"Because I've got a coffee machine down there. And a p-p-pack of cigarettes." He forced a smile. "Thought you might like..."

Kaufman was wriggling on the carpet like a caterpillar trying to shed its cocoon. "Of course I would like. Help me up, for God's sake."

Even with the zip tie removed, Kaufman was in such bad shape that it took a minute to traverse the short distance to the top of the stairs. Vanya right behind him, he glanced down the stairwell, turning his head.

"Listen, pal. My legs have no strength in them. Can't you bring the coffee and smokes up here?" He pouted like a spoiled child. "I'll never make it down."

"Oh, I don't know about that." Vanya dipped his shoulder and rammed it into Kaufman's back, pitching him headlong down the precipitous stairs. Kaufman hit the first few risers hard—thuds, cracks, a jolting spin as his head, elbows, and knees slammed against hardwood. He tumbled the rest of the way in a messy clatter of limbs before landing on his back with a smack, the air punched out of him as he went still.

As he stared at the body below, breathless and mouth agape, another text arrived from Izmailov. *Five minutes left, Vanya. Don't chicken out.*

He stared at the screen and screamed, "Fuck you, Marat!"

At the foot of the stairs, Kaufman's twisted body blocked the way. *Rude bastard.* Vanya trotted down and stepped over him, grabbed both ankles, and dragged him into a corner. He stood back half a step and regarded the broken figure with a finger pressed to his lips. Kaufman's chest rose and fell half an inch, bubbles forming at the corners of his bloodied mouth. The man was a tough specimen, no doubt.

What to do?

The beast answered and took full control of mild-mannered Ivan Beglov. He bent down and rolled Kaufman onto his back. The pitchfork, abandoned as a bad idea, now seemed the perfect weapon. He retrieved it from behind the rack, felt the satisfying heft in his hands, and returned to the body.

He stood with his legs straddling Kaufman's torso, pitchfork gripped tightly in both hands.

Consciousness was slowly returning to the prisoner, who blinked rapidly before his spider-veined eyes stretched to maximum circumference. "What...the...hell?"

"Apologize for m-m-mocking me, asshole!" Vanya roared.

"What are you talking about?" Kaufman groaned in agony as he wriggled onto his side in a futile defensive move. The rusty tines were on his neck in a flash, pinning him like an insect.

"Roll onto your back, again, you p-p-prick." Vanya breathed in shallow bursts, adrenaline pumping. "Apologize, I said. You made f-f-fun of my s-s-stutter."

"Oh, Jesus." Kaufman obediently rolled onto his back, sighing with the effort, his body nothing more than a loose casing of broken bones. "I'm so sorry. I didn't...mean to—"

"Too late, *ublyudok.*" Vanya raised the pitchfork high and

drove it down hard, the tines penetrating halfway into Kaufman's neck. As four thin fountains of blood gushed from the holes, Vanya repeated the blow, thunder booming outside as the soundtrack to Kaufman's death. Four more holes appeared, four more little geysers. Gripped by the fury of a hundred demons, he stabbed repeatedly until Kaufman's neck had turned to pulp.

He heaved the tool across the room. It thudded into a white board covered in illegible notes, leaving a long crack in its wake, then landed on the floor with a loud clang.

Vanya marched to his work desk. Even though there was plenty of light in the room, for atmospherics he flicked on his prized banker's lamp with the green Bakelite shade. He fired up a powerful laptop that had a permanent home on this desk.

While the programs and apps were warming up, he returned to Kaufman's body. With his cell, he snapped off a photo, then one from each side. The accompanying text to Izmailov said: *Hi, Marat. Kaufman disposed of as you requested. Not a bad job, what do you think? I regret to inform you that Severnaya Volna is about to crash and burn. Please, and I mean this most sincerely, go fuck yourself!*

As extra theater, he drafted an email to Izmailov. He reviewed the video of footage from inside the computer room to make sure it showed the murder of Kaufman clearly, uploaded a file to Yandex Disk, created a link to it, and dropped it in the email. He composed some fitting body text to go with the video and scheduled the email to send in three hours.

He created a fresh cloud folder, plugged the phone into a port with a USB cable, and dragged the entire contents—minus apps and program files—across. The copying would take a while, so he used the time to compose a penitent letter to Marfa Petko, the last of the original three B+ members who'd still be alive within the next hour.

Marfa. Forgive me. By the time you get this, I'll have been slouched in my favorite gamer's chair for a while, having shot myself in the head. If I was a Japanese warrior instead of a Russian peasant, I would have gone out by falling on my sword, but the closest I could find was a pitchfork and it wasn't really suitable. Shit, I'm rambling.

Please see the mission through to the end as we swore to each other we would.

Marfa, I've been a spoke in the wheel, working on the quiet for Izmailov. He caught me trying to hack into his email servers, had proof, and was going to hand me over to the FSB if I didn't agree to turn. But now I hope I can atone for my sins. While I was dribbling intel to Izmailov, I was keeping records of all my dealings with him. Plus a few other tidbits I found in a part of BaltEnergoTorg's systems that I was *able to penetrate undetected.*

You'll find a folder in my private encrypted cloud archive containing what I believe is enough material to go public to the Western media and stop Severnaya Volna. Stuff I saved on my computer and cell phone. Send a copy to Vladimir Vladimirovich Putin, too. I'm sure the president would enjoy reading it all and calling Izmailov, Kolodin, and Semak to account. The encryption key—the key to sinking those bastards—on my private cloud is as follows: 4#553^439M6Д6Я!У.

Also, please tell Tamm I never got around to looking for the goszakaz, but if I were him I'd start looking in Izmailov's systems. He mentioned something to me about sending a man to Tallinn to manipulate the Estonians' surveillance setup. I guess it was probably the guy killed at the border monitoring facility. Find the order for the train tickets among BaltEnergoTorg's documents, add it to my material, and that should sink Severnaya Volna for sure.

Again, forgive me. Da zdravstvuyet Rossiya! *Long live Russia!*

PS. In my archive you'll also find highly detailed files of all the sleepers in the Russian government who've been dropping us intel over the last five years. Treat the information with the utmost confidentiality. Oh, and please make sure Slava gets a proper burial. Kaufman you can feed to the pigs on the neighbor's farm. I killed the bastard with a pitchfork and sent a video to Izmailov. He's also going to get a video of me checking out. I told him their scheme was on borrowed time. Perhaps it will force them to cancel Severnaya Volna without putting anyone else in danger.

Much love, Ivan Beglov

He scheduled the email to send in two hours.

One more task.

He kept it brutally simple. He wrote a tiny script that told his NVR to copy a block of time—exactly the next thirty minutes of CCTV footage—into a separate directory and upload it to a server based in Vilnius. The suicide would happen inside that window; the camera would capture everything automatically. Upload completed, the server would fire off a scheduled email to Izmailov containing a URL to the clip. He scheduled the email for thirty minutes after the one with the link to Kaufman's death, closed the terminal, and left the script running in the background. All he had to do now was make sure he was dead before the upload window ended.

With the thundersnow storm now raging outside, he made himself a coffee on the Breville machine, twice as strong as he normally took it. He sipped the hot brew, savoring the extra flavor of a double shot with three sugars. He smiled smugly as a stroke of thunder clapped somewhere over the Gulf. Even if grid power went down, his self-designed UPS would kick in, and the transfer would be successful. He remembered a beautiful word he learned in English class at college. *Prescient*. Able to think ahead. That's what he was.

He unwrapped a packet of Rothmans cigarettes that Dima had left in the kitchen and inhaled smoke from the first cigarette he'd put in his mouth in seventeen years. He coughed and gagged and took another drag.

Beautiful.

He opened a folder on his computer, picked his favorite album by the iconic '80s band Kino, and clicked on the song. Their song. "*Gruppa krovi.*" He sang in an off-key tenor—no stuttering—scooting along and spinning in his wheeled chair, puffing away between the lines, stopping to sip coffee in the instrumental parts. Eyes closed tight, he savored the genius of the late composer, Viktor Tsoi, who died in tragic circumstances and too young. In so many ways, just like Vanya.

A bleep.

The progress bar had reached the end of its journey.

The copying was done.

Next, he uploaded another folder to the cloud. A background indexing bot had been funneling emails and other files relating to Izmailov, including videos of meetings they'd had in this very room since Vanya had taken thirty pieces of silver to betray his colleagues.

Although Vanya never managed to crack BaltEnergoTorg's actual inboxes, it didn't matter. There were other ways. He'd spent long nights trawling through BaltEnrgoTorg's digital backrooms, excavating half-forgotten folders and servers until he found what he needed—files on Severnaya Volna someone had taken from the company's email system and tried to hide in an old bookkeeping directory. Whoever hid the documents had done the hard part for him. By the time he finished piecing everything together, Vanya realized he had enough missing links—evidence meant to stay buried—left in a place only someone like him would think to look. And it might have stayed buried, too, if not for Izmailov's bullshit. *Fuck you, Marat.*

The archive propagation lasted for four more loud repeats of "*Gruppa krovi.*"

Coffee drunk, cigarettes smoked and stubbed out, song sung till his throat ached, Ivan Beglov walked over to the corpse of Andrey Kaufman and delivered a swift kick to the side of its head. A deep, steadying breath before he took the pistol from under his belt, racked the slide, and fired two test bullets into Kaufman's face, turning it into a bloody Picasso portrait.

He sat back in his gamer chair and closed his eyes. As thunder rolled outside, he swallowed hard and pumped a bullet through his temple.

TWENTY-TWO

JACOB SMILED AT THE HOTEL RECEPTIONIST, exchanging some meaningless words. While Marfa and Dima waited in the parking lot, having returned en route to their respective residences for a reconnaissance run, he took the elevator upstairs. His own sweep of the room showed no signs of intrusion.

After showering and shaving off a shadow of stubble beginning to clash with his new salt-and-pepper hair, he chose his attire. Conservative all the way. A no-nonsense charcoal gray suit, tailored and with a tight weave. A white, spread-collar shirt paired with a deep navy silk tie. Over the top of that, his woolen greatcoat with deep inside pockets and a couple of external hand-warmer pockets. He opened the safe and took out the satphone. The single hair he'd placed on the screen perfectly matched the photo he'd taken of it yesterday using the burner cell. As he stuck it in his pocket, he couldn't dispel the feeling that today was going to see a quantum shift in the mission's direction.

He engaged in small talk with the same receptionist on the way out, simply to establish his presence in the hotel. Not staying there overnight wasn't great for his cover, but every little effort to ameliorate that unavoidable circumstance was worth making.

"All good," he said, taking a seat next to Marfa in the back, placing his laptop on the space between them. "No sign anyone's been in my room."

"Nor mine, more's the pity," she said with a lascivious smirk. "I prefer to see a messy bed in the morning." Jacob had seen his reflection in the mirror. The rapid identity alteration procedures had aged him ten years, the bald patterns particularly unattractive. He couldn't believe he was worthy of her flirtatiousness.

"My place was clean, too," said Dima, grinning at the exchange in the back seat.

"Very pleased to hear it." As the BMW moved across the slick asphalt, he extracted his laptop, checked the time, 09:17, and began to type.

The email to Irina was short and to the point. *Vyacheslav Gabulov is dead, turn your attention to Ivan Beglov and, as before, Petko. Keep working on the train tickets. They were collected by a man called Oleg Klitschko. Will call you soon, Yakov xxx*

Something about Vanya's circumstances bothered Jacob. Yes, there was a sizeable inheritance, his parents having made good during the privatization wave after the collapse of the Soviet Union. They never got to own any companies, according to Vanya's official file, but their positions as executives in the forestry industry presumably translated into big wages, although the figures weren't available. Mom and Dad had lived modest lifestyles, acquiring the dacha-farm for a song in 1992. In theory, it was possible they managed to save a lot of money, which Vanya inherited along with the dacha-farm.

And yet, the money required to set up the computer and surveillance systems, the heating upgrades, other improvements around the property, not to mention the array of gear at his business in the city, would have been significant. Perhaps more than Mom and Pop had left behind. Jacob had asked Petko bluntly, "Do you know where he got his money from?"

She waved the question away, said he was loyal to the core, and she wouldn't have been surprised if some of his rich clients at the jewelry repair shop had bestowed largesse upon him. She waved an emerald ring under Jacob's nose. The piece, even to his uneducated eye, was spectacular.

"This was a hand-me-down from my great-great-grandmother," she said. "Somehow it survived a couple of revolutions and several wars. Vanya restored it to its former glory. The man has talent, and I know rich businessmen and women in Saint Petersburg would be prepared to reward him greatly for his excellent work."

That also made sense.

So why was suspicion gnawing at Jacob's stomach?

The car pulled up at the tall electric gate of the ministry's fleet operations office. A uniformed guard crushed a cigarette under his boot and saluted the driver. Dima dropped the window a fraction.

"Good morning, Dmitry Pavlovich," said the guard. "You're in trouble, I hear."

"Why?"

The guard nodded at the hood of the vehicle.

Dima laughed. "I don't think it's a sacking offence to park under cover in the middle of a thundersnow storm, is it? By the time it was over, this place was shut down. There was actually big hail out where we were last night. Get any in the city?"

"None. Just a lot of lightning. Most of it early this morning." The guard shrugged into his high-collared gaberdine greatcoat. "Anyway, it's your problem to deal with." He leaned in and whispered, "Two drivers got sacked yesterday, so I'd be on my best behavior if I were you."

He stood back a step and waved them through.

Jacob and Petko waited in the idling car in the lot, heating turned up almost to maximum. Dima went inside to spin their concocted lie about Slava's absence and book the vehicle out for another day.

"He'll be OK in there, won't he?" said Jacob.

"Because of what that guard said?" she scoffed. "He's full of shit."

"I just hope they believe his story—our story—about Slava."

Dima had proven his worth in some tricky situations already, but dealing with rule-loving administrators in Russia could be harder than hand-to-hand combat with trained fighters.

Petko applied a thin layer of fire-engine red lipstick, pressed her lips together, and checked the result in a compact mirror. "Dima's a brick. Solid and dependable, able to think on his feet. He's not scared of bureaucracy like most Russians."

"He'd better not get the car taken off him. We never got around to scrubbing the damned trunk after...you know."

She nodded, a tear rolling slowly down her cheek, spoiling the just-applied makeup. "I still can't believe it. Slava! Of all people." She pointed at her bosom. "I'm the one you'd think most likely to..." She couldn't go on, wracking sobs shaking her body.

Jacob, despite his better judgment, slid over and placed an arm around her. Her understated perfume contained some ingredient that got under his skin. Or maybe it was just her pheromones. *Ignore, Hunter.* She emitted muffled sobs into his scarf for a minute before pulling back. She apologized and stepped out of the car. She lit a cigarette and sent clouds of smoke skywards.

The temperature had risen since yesterday, sitting around -4°C; there was barely enough wind to ruffle your hair. Jacob figured that made it warm enough to join her for a cigarette. He'd already smoked more on this mission than he had in the last three years.

Standing with their backs against the car, they said nothing to each other for a while, watching the gate open and close, the guard giving the same stony-faced treatment to each new arrival. A steady stream—Jacob marveled at how the post-Soviet regime hadn't shed its big-government style of running things. A driver for just about every senior official in the Ministry of Industry and Trade was a scenario that would be reflected across the board. Great for keeping the unemployment figures low.

"How did Vanya Beglov come to join B+?" said Jacob. "I mean, it can't be easy in a totalitarian state for opponents of the ruling elites to get together."

Marfa stared straight ahead. Her profile was fashion-magazine-model perfect, Jacob thought. All features straight and in classical proportion. He guessed the maturity of her years had only enhanced her physical magnetism. Irina had a thousand flaws by comparison, but he could never cheat on her, not even with the flawless journalist.

"Not eager to answer?" Jacob flicked ash into an icy puddle. "Fair enough. You don't need some interloper questioning everyone's motives."

She scraped her boot on the gritty asphalt where the heat of automobiles had depleted snow cover. Hugging herself with her right arm and smoking almost arrogantly with her left hand, she continued to stare into the void.

His cigarette, only half smoked, hissed as it fell into the puddle. He turned to get back in the car when she spoke.

"He was the one who started it."

"Excuse me?" This was the last answer Jacob expected to hear.

She nodded a couple of times, flicking her head back. "That's right. It was his baby. He was the one who found me and Slava. Convinced us we were the perfect fit." She chuckled in a deep tone.

"How?" Jacob could feel his mouth hanging open. The files he'd studied were based on the erroneous assumption that Slava was the founder.

She sighed, long and sharp, like she was letting out a week's worth of irritation. "None of us were looking for each other, like people do on dating sites. We weren't an underground cell with matching badges and a manifesto to change the world. Vanya was just... there."

Jacob said nothing, knowing she'd elaborate.

"One night three years ago, I was covering an anti-war protest in Kazanskaya Square. Trying to get a few quotes for a syndicated puff piece, paint the crowd as malcontents. Cookie cutter article, know what I mean?"

He nodded.

"I saw him standing off to the side, not shouting, just watching, hands in his pockets. He had a kind of lost look on his face. I expected him to spin the usual line. *Ya apolitichen*. I'm not into politics. Instead, he unloaded, face red as a beet. He told me his sister had been arrested at a similar rally at the start of the"—she made air quotes—"*special military operation*. You could get arrested for calling it a war or even holding up a blank piece of cardboard with tape across your mouth." She stopped to puff on her cigarette, holding it between her thumb and forefinger like a man. "He told me his sister 'fell ill' in custody and died two days later. He swore he'd dedicate the rest of his life to avenging her death. You don't forget a person telling you something powerful like that."

"What did you do with the quote?"

"Nothing. The quote was unusable under this regime."

Marfa shifted her weight, her face growing more animated as she warmed to the story. She launched three perfect, fat smoke rings into the atmosphere and watched them dissipate into nothingness.

"A few weeks later, I ran into him again. I took a watch to be repaired at a place recommended by a girlfriend. I couldn't believe my eyes when I saw Vanya, the same guy from the protest, behind the counter. Slava Gabulov was there, having a look at some second-hand jewelry, a gift for his niece. Total coincidence. They got talking, and politics slipped into the conversation. Slava dropped one sentence—just one—that you wouldn't say unless you were sure the other person was on the same wavelength. Vanya caught the vibe instantly. It was like a pair of twins meeting who were separated at birth."

She rubbed her arms, pulling her coat tighter as a chilly gust blew through the lot. "Vanya's the one who started connecting the dots. He told us we each had access to parts of the system others didn't. I had contacts in all layers of society through my work; Slava had insight into trade delegations and regional bureaucrats; Vanya was a friendly, unimposing young man swimming in private clients who were sometimes careless with their gossip. He said we didn't need to fight anything—just pay attention and gather *infa*." She laughed. "I trusted him instinctively, and so did Slava."

"How did you end up with a string of sleepers in government departments feeding you *infa*?" said Jacob, enjoying the sound of the Russian slang equivalent of intel. "The reports I read were a bit sketchy on that point."

She turned to Jacob, face open and honest as well as beautiful.

"We didn't recruit any sleepers. They kind of recruited themselves. There's a channel called TyomKam, an anonymous message board for people who despise the regime but aren't brave or stupid enough to say it out loud. Vanya lurked there for a couple of years. He'd put up feeler posts, ask questions that were more like hints, and people started contacting him more directly. Some dropped into the shop rather than communicate online. A lot of them still do this.

"One day, among the chatter about a looming accord with Estonia, someone mentioned a project called Severnaya Volna. That's when we started to get people mentioning our three guys: Izmailov, Kolodin, and Semak." She folded her arms. "He protected the informers' identities, wouldn't even tell us. That's how much integrity he has."

"I'm impressed that the three of you could build something like that from a chance meeting."

"So you should be," she said with a frisson of pride. "But you know what?"

"What?"

"I get what you were implying with your questions about Vanya. That he's possibly a mole because of things you think don't add up." She fired a steely glare. "He's no rat. I mean, he could have turned us all over to the triumvirate of evil at any time, but he hasn't, has he?"

Jacob dodged the question. "I understand your loyalty to him, especially with him being the founder. The story you just told me helps clarify why. But sometimes you've got to ask yourself some hard questions. Russia's history is full of examples of idealists betraying their own principles for pragmatism. Or because they were bribed, threatened, blackmailed, you name it. Could any of that apply to Vanya?"

"What a load of horseshit!" She ripped open the door and held it. "How about you sit up front next to Dima for the next section of the ride?"

The BMW swallowed her, the door slamming so hard the guard stuck his head out of the sentry box to see if everything was OK.

Jacob gave him a friendly wave and sedately got into the front seat.

TWENTY-THREE

DIMA CLAPPED HIS HANDS TOGETHER AS HE RESUMED his seat behind the wheel. "Great news. They bought the story. Actually, both stories. About Slava..." He closed his eyes and made the sign of the cross. "...And about the car not getting returned on time. Better news, we've got the car for the whole day. Only if I don't return it before 8:00 p.m., there could be serious employment problems."

Silence greeted his joyous announcement.

"Hey, what's the matter? Did I fart or something?"

Jacob said, trying to sound buoyant, "Marfa and I had a difference of opinion, and we're just waiting for the air to clear."

He heard Marfa laughing in the backseat. "I apologize for my harsh words, Robert. You don't know Vanya like I do—like we do—and it's only natural for you to be skeptical. Proper, in fact."

Dima said, "We've got some time to kill before the meeting with Saburenkov. I know a great little place to grab a snack on the Griboyedov Canal."

The chance to simply chill and catch their breath, if only for a short while, appealed to everyone. Dima eased the car out of the lot, waving with excess enthusiasm at the guard, who frowned as he snapped off a salute.

The clouds had vanished, no sign remaining of the surprise thundersnow storm. News on state-controlled radio mentioned that a man had been hit by a bolt of lightning and killed in Petergof, twenty-four clicks out of Saint Petersburg center, but overall damage from the freak weather event was minimal. In political news, recent wrinkles in the Russo-Estonian accord had been ironed out overnight at a hastily convened meeting between the countries' presidents and foreign affairs ministers, as well as some military top brass. A senior general on the Russian side had been fired for negligence over an incident that had upset some people on the Estonian side. Confidentiality and security implications meant no further details could be released but, rest assured, said the announcer, the accord was on solid foundations, and relations between the two countries were set to blossom like never before.

Jacob shook his head. "If we can't find the smoking gun soon, the triumvirate is going to start thinking about making a move. I've got a colleague trying to find proof of purchase for the train tickets. She's an IT specialist like Vanya, only better. MGU graduate, worked in the Russian government's darkest corners for a short while. Still, I don't like her chances of cracking the RZD's database."

Dima barked a sarcastic laugh. "Yeah, good luck with that."

"I agree that we need to make a breakthrough, only I can't see where that's going to come from," said Marfa. "If the Estonians get lazy on the Russian border with all this sickening good-will, Kolodin's gonna be itching to strike. He..." Her phone alert chimed. "Just one second, gentlemen."

"I'm about to pull up at the café," said Dima. "Want to take it inside?"

She held up a hand. "No. I need to check it now. It's from Vanya."

Jacob nodded. "Coffee and cakes can wait a minute."

"Maybe Kaufman's giving him trouble," ventured Dima, nosing the wheels into the curb and switching off the engine.

"He'd be a fool to try. Vanya's capable of kicking *my* ass if he's in the mood."

"An email instead of a text message. Odd." A loud advertisement for men's deodorant came over the radio. "Turn it down, please," said Marfa, the request more like a command no one would dare ignore.

Marfa's exhale burst from her lungs like she'd been punched in the solar plexus. She held the phone to her chest, lips trembling, almost undulating. "No. This...can't...be...real."

Jacob twisted in the front seat; Dima did the same.

"It's a fucking suicide note!" she screamed.

"Oh my God. We've gotta get there before he does something," said Dima, pressing the start button.

"No," said Marfa, her voice hollow. "It's too late. He's... already done it."

"No way," said Dima, shaking his head, lips compressed. "Not possible. He wanted to live, to avenge his sister, see the establishment pay for her death."

"Wait a minute," said Jacob. "What did he write, exactly? Maybe it's some kind of mistake." Despite his effort to calm things down, her reaction had his heart slamming against his ribs.

Marfa's chin joined in the trembling of her lips, the power of speech lost for the moment.

"Come on, Marfa!" said Dima, reaching out and shaking her knee. "Snap out of it, for God's sake."

Marfa blinked rapidly and gave a little head toss, like someone coming out of a trance.

"He said he...shot himself." Her faced was flushed, eyes growing moist, and the facial gymnastics showing no signs of abating.

"Don't be ridiculous," said Dima, sinking back into his seat but keeping his gaze firmly fixed on her. "How can he shoot himself dead, and then write an email about it? That's absurd."

"He scheduled it to send later, you dolt!" Marfa unbuckled the seatbelt and collapsed sideways, pulling her knees up into a fetal position. "Slava, now Vanya," she mumbled. "We're never going to..."

Jacob wanted answers, not defeatism. The only way to do that was to read the email himself, not wait for Marfa to divulge its contents. "Give it here." He gently pried the phone away, her fingers reluctantly letting go. His eyes narrowed as he read and understood the message in ten seconds.

"Oh my. This is bad."

"What?" said Dima, pouting.

Marfa sat bolt upright. "Bad? It's a tragedy. Two dead men, the best two. Just me and Dima left, and *he* doesn't even understand how email scheduling works. And *you*." The stare she gave Jacob could have cut steel. "You were so quick to accuse me of deceit but didn't even think to check Slava's phone settings." She shook her head and said with dripping sarcasm, "Or maybe they have different kinds of cell phones in Estonia, how would I know?"

"What?" said Dima. "Is he dead or not? You're worrying me, Robert."

Jacob sucked air through his teeth. "She's right about my failure to look at Slava's phone settings. Everyone makes mistakes, me included. But this..." He tapped the phone's screen so hard Dima winced. "This is a monumental fuck-up. Sending this stuff to Izmailov was the height of recklessness. Did Vanya think the guy would just roll over and let us bring them down?"

"What are you talking about?" Marfa's face contorted in disgust. "He's just killed himself to save the operation."

"Like Christ dying on the cross to save us all?" said Jacob, laying on the sarcasm. "Give me a break; that doesn't wash. Whether he meant to do it or not, he's sold out B+, and we have to salvage a very fucked-up situation."

"No, you are *so* wrong. And...I think Vanya was totally right about one thing. They'll probably call it off now, knowing we have the goods on them." She edged forward on her seat, face alive with hope even wet with tears. "And if they refuse to back down, we've got all the aces. Vanya's given us the incriminating evidence. We grab it from his archive, present it to the world, and...bingo... those three assholes go down. Maybe there are more maggots in their ranks, on the Estonian side, too." She forced a wan smile. "And no, he's not Jesus, but he's left us what we need to get the job done."

"Please," said Dima, his voice desperate. "Will someone tell me what the hell's going on here?"

Jacob apologized for leaving him in the dark and summarized the email's contents in a few short sentences. Dima's eyelids stretched to their limit as he took it in, shaking his head slowly. At the end of it, he said, "I may be a little slower than you two, but isn't Vanya's email a little, I dunno, vague?"

"What do you mean?" said Marfa. "He's very specific. His own Aladdin's cave contains the evidence, and all we have to do is open it up."

"I don't think it's that simple."

"Dima's right," said Jacob. "Vanya didn't say 'look in folder x and you'll find y.' No, it's one big dump of information that needs to be sifted through. Like Dima said—vague."

"The *goszakaz*, dammit!" Marfa's eyes glowed. "He said it would have come from Izmailov's company. He sponsored the hitman, and Klitschko bought the tickets. The purchase order—"

"He said *we* have to look for the goddam order," Jacob interrupted. "By getting into BaltEnergoTorg's systems. You can bet that with this heads up, they'll block every possible place a hacker could get in. We'll never find it." He pondered for a second. "It's probably been wiped completely." A thought occurred to him. "We have to go back to the dacha. Now."

"What?" said Marfa. "You've already begged off with Saburenkov. You can't do it twice."

"We're assuming this is real. Could be bogus, someone pretending to be Vanya."

"It's come from his email address."

Jacob, still clutching the cell, examined the email sender's address for obvious signs of fakery. A zero instead of an O, the digit 1 for a lower-case L. No. It looked legit. ivan.beglov@mailnet.ru.

"There's another scenario," said Jacob. "Someone's there with him, a gun to his head, making him write this stuff so we go running to save him, into a trap."

"You think that's likely?" said Dima.

"If he's really told Izmailov he left a dead-man's switch for us to trigger...maybe." He sucked in a lungful of air. "Let's try calling first."

From memory he dialed Vanya's phone number and switched on loudspeaker. It rang out, then went to voicemail. If only Jacob had the knowledge to log on to Vanya's security cameras. He hit the phone's home button and was about to hand the cell phone back when he saw it. An icon on Marfa's phone. Rostelecom's "Umny dom" or "Smart House" app. He turned it on and showed the screen to Marfa.

"Is this for remotely monitoring home cameras?"

"*Da*. It can turn also on the lights, music, some other things."

"I don't suppose this has a link to the dacha, does it?"

She laughed bitterly. "Of course not. It's for my apartment. I've become very security conscious lately. Journalists are an endangered species in this country. Even careful ones."

Dima was already throwing the car into drive. "What are we doing? Are we going to the dacha or not?" He tapped his watch. "It's an hour to the meeting with Saburenkov."

"No meeting today with Saburenkov," said Jacob. "If Vanya's email contains the truth, there'll be no meetings with any of them." He turned back to glare at Marfa, then Dima at the wheel. "And the two of you might be in a shitload more trouble than you ever imagined possible."

"What do we do now?" said Dima, calm and stoic despite Jacob's warning.

"We go back to Shepelevo." He paused a moment. "You still got the H&K?"

Dima shook his head. "I left it at my apartment. If I'd been ordered to hand the car back just now, they might've found it. And that would have been awkward, to say the least."

"The Sig's at the dacha, so we've got nothing. We can't risk going back to your apartment. Marfa's either."

"What are you saying, Robert?" said Marfa. "You're scaring me."

"I've got tom-toms sounding an alarm in my gut. We need to arm ourselves, and we have to be on guard. You told me before you knew where we can get some guns."

She said nothing, just breathed shallowly.

Jacob jutted his head forward. "Well?"

She looked up at the ceiling of the car then back to Jacob. "I was hoping it wouldn't come to this. But yes, let me make a phone call."

TWENTY-FOUR

Dima turned into a short driveway and pulled up in front of a brown tilting garage door. Cars lined one side of the narrow street, classic Soviet-era three-story buildings walling them in. The neighborhood was old and poorly maintained, tiles barely clinging to the walls of the long lines of characterless apartment blocks.

With the engine idling, Marfa sent a text to her contact. In less than a minute, the garage door opened, a dim light shining from the back of the space. Inside stood a man swaddled in dark clothing, on his head an ushanka with the flaps tied under his chin. Large build, bearded, the veteran detective stood with his legs apart and arms folded across a barrel chest. The man had been useful to Marfa over the last decade, funneling inside information about suspects and criminals, often tipping her off about investigations before they officially began.

MVD Special Investigator Boris Mladenov, Bulgarian by birth, loved the law—in the sense that he loved knowing all about it, how to avoid getting trapped by it, and the best ways to bend it without getting caught. He was not a fan of enforcing it or blindly obeying it. Still, he'd enjoyed a long and mainly trouble-free career in the Sledkom, the MVD's investigative branch. At fifty-nine, Mladenov was due to retire from the MVD in the middle of next year. The state pension promised only a modest retirement, and so, as he'd said to Marfa, he was delighted to engage in today's lucrative off-the-books transaction.

"Will you be OK?" said Jacob, eyeballing the imposing dark figure in the shadows. "He looks like a mean son of a bitch."

"Don't worry. Boris and I go back a long way." Marfa's tone left little doubt that the two of them had enjoyed more than a working relationship over the years. "Boris would do anything for me."

"Wave if you need a hand. We'll be right here, just a few meters away."

She walked across the icy pavement with slow, deliberate steps, the streets in this run-down neighborhood neglected by the city's winter maintenance crews.

"You brought friends. Who are they?" said Mladenov, tilting his head. "Can I trust them?"

"You don't need to know about them. Just that they—and you—are my best hope."

He grunted. "Are you in trouble?"

She nodded. "Yes. Gotta keep a low profile, scope a few things out, stay out of harm's way. You know, the average life of a journalist." She forced a sharp laugh.

"Anything I can do?"

"Apart from selling me the goods and wishing me luck? Nothing."

He opened his mouth, but she pressed a finger to his lips. "Shhh, Boris, my sweet. I know you're almost out of the MVD; don't spoil the rest of your life by getting involved in my crazy shit."

"What if I want to get involved?" He pouted through his beard.

She shook her head. "Please...don't push it." She smiled warmly as she craned her neck to look up at him. "You've done so much for me over the years, *zaichik*. You've got a wife and three children to worry about."

He waved the concern away. "Lidya is just someone I share a house with these days. No love there anymore. The kids are grown up and..."

Her lips tightened. She could easily get all sentimental with her old lover, but she had to be practical. She could sense the frustration of Tamm and Dima growing in the vehicle, watching the drawn-out exchange.

"The guns, please, Boris. We need to be going."

"You have the cash?"

As much as he played the worried, romantic hero, Boris had one concern above all others. Himself.

"Of course."

She handed him a large buff envelope containing nine thousand dollars. She'd gasped when Jacob opened the tote bag he'd retrieved from the Pribaltiyskaya. So much money, in so many currencies. He said it was a gamble to go back to the hotel after what Vanya had done—if he really did it—but not having protection was an even bigger gamble.

Mladenov peaked inside the envelope and whistled. "I'm not even going to ask where this came from."

"Naturally. Just as I'm not asking about the origin of the weapons. Speaking of which"—she made a winding motion with her finger—"could we perhaps...?"

"Of course." As he walked the couple of meters to the rack, he told her what she was getting. "Three submachine guns, which fell off the back of an army truck, and eighteen magazines. I'm throwing in the big duffel bag for free."

He slung the bulging sack over his shoulder and grunted. "I'm bringing this as far as the threshold." He placed it down gently when he got to the open doorway, gestured to the street with his head. "Get your people to turn the car around and back it up all the way so we can drop the stuff in the trunk. Away from prying eyes."

Marfa walked gingerly back to the car and got in. "What's wrong?" said Jacob. "Did he change his mind?"

"No. Spin around and back up. He's just being extra cautious."

With the car backed up, Jacob got out, holding his hand out to Mladenov. "Robert Tamm."

"What sort of a dumb name is that?"

"Estonian."

The detective's body tensed, his mouth morphing into a sneer. "Marfa tells me she's in trouble. Are you and your buddy behind the wheel the cause of that trouble?"

Marfa moved between them. "Let's just get this over with."

"That's my intention," said Jacob, taking a step back but never taking his eyes off Mladenov. He was like a refrigerator with clothes on. "I just wanted to get a rundown on the weapons, if you don't mind. I like to know what I'm buying, especially when it costs me nine grand."

Mladenov shook his head and chuckled. "All I can tell you is they're Vityaz PP-19s and they take standard 9 mm Luger ammo." A shrug. "Never fired one, so I can't tell you what to expect. However, the gangsters I liberated the guns from used them in a number of extremely violent holdups, resulting in the deaths of twelve people, two of them innocent bystanders. I figure these bad boys will see you through most scenarios."

Jacob knelt and unzipped the bag. He lifted back an old tartan blanket and caught a flash of matte metal. The stocks were folded, eight curved stick magazines stuffed down the sides. He'd look up the specs on line, but at face value, they looked clean and in good condition. He heaved the bag into the trunk, pushed the button to close the lid, and was about to get back in the car when Mladenov stopped him.

"I see you've got government tags. Would you like to change them?"

"To what?"

"MVD Transport Division," he said. "I've got a set that have been gathering dust for a while. They won't hold up to real scrutiny, but they could buy you some time."

"How much do you want?"

"Gratis. They're not easy to sell." He thrust his hands in his pockets.

"We'll take them."

Dima reversed the BMW almost all the way in, and Jacob quickly swapped the plates over, tossing the originals in the trunk.

The crooked detective embraced Marfa, patted her on the back, and whispered words of encouragement in her ear. He turned to Jacob, fixed him with a thin, humorless grin, and said, "Anything happens to her and I will track you down and kill you." He thrust out his jaw. "Oh, and try not to get pulled over."

"That's the best advice I've had for a long time." He extended his hand, and this time Mladenov shook it.

The detective disappeared from view as the garage door descended and closed with a crunch.

Back inside the car, Marfa exhaled sharply.

"He's a good man," she said. "Always ready to help me out of a pickle."

"He's been good to us, at least," said Dima. "So I can't argue with that."

As the false-plated BMW wound its way through Saint Petersburg's maze of narrow streets and bridges and back out onto the open highway, Jacob fired up his laptop and tethered it to the satphone.

"What are you doing now?" said Marfa.

"Learning about our new weapons."

After a few minutes, Marfa asked, "What have you learned?"

"That your friend, Mladenov, really *is* a good man."

And he also knew a good woman—one who, he hoped, could somehow breach Vanya's digital fortress and gain access to the dacha's security system.

He sent her two words over Skia's proprietary messaging app. *Call me.*

TWENTY-FIVE

THE HANDFUL OF SHORT REVIEW VIDEOS OF THE VITYAZ PP-19 submachine gun Jacob watched on YouTube were encouraging. Thumbs up from gun enthusiasts around the world. A compact weapon with low recoil, and best of all, accurate. Even an average shooter could hit a man-sized target at a hundred meters. Ideal for urban combat. Getting them was a stroke of luck among the prevailing misfortune of the mission. He prayed they wouldn't have to fire a single round.

He closed his laptop, feeling his nerves twitching with electricity. He took a deep swig of water from a plastic bottle and replaced it in the console receptacle. The shock of Vanya's apparent treachery must have hit harder than he thought, the mission now compromised in a way he could never have foreseen. A glance at Dima, his fingers gripping the steering wheel tighter than necessary, face a pattern of stress lines, told him he, too, was struggling.

And then there was Marfa, hit hardest by the two deaths in the team.

"How far to go?" she asked from the back seat, her anxiety almost palpable. "Every time we pass a big, dark car I want to scream."

Dima checked the GPS screen. "Forty-six minutes."

She muttered something unintelligible, then tapped Jacob on the shoulder. "Hey. Wise leader. What good are those weapons I scored for us if they're lying in the trunk? They should be loaded, lying within reach. On our laps."

She had an excellent point.

"We'll stop once we clear suburbia, find somewhere secluded, and familiarize ourselves with the weapons, fire off a few rounds, then keep them handy, like you say."

"I know just the place," said Dima. "Forest tracks that no one uses." He paused to allow an ambulance and a couple of cop cars, lights flashing and sirens wailing, pass on the left. A collective sigh of relief, then they were back in the traffic. Dima added, turning to Jacob, "Believe it or not, I'm looking forward to getting my eye in. It would give me great pleasure to do to Izmailov what you did to Kaufman."

"I get it," said Jacob. "We all want revenge. Now's not the time to be thinking about that. Once we confirm Vanya's either alive or dead, we proceed." His mind swam: If Vanya had done what he said he had, there'd be three bodies littering the dacha now. What a clusterfuck this was turning out to be.

In an almost whiny voice, Marfa said, "Why don't you just go to his archive via that?" She pointed a well-manicured finger at the laptop.

"That's actually a good question."

"A fucking excellent question!" said Dima, a trace of accusation in his tone. "Why not?"

"Because maybe I click on that link and some kind of tracking virus is released into my computer. Maybe someone's waiting for one of us to do just that, ready to send the troops after us."

"Shit," said Dima. "Is that even possible?"

"Even if it's not, I've got a lot of confidential stuff on here, and I *do* know clicking random links can let the bad guys in via a Trojan horse even if you have the best defenses in the world." He paused to let the scenario sink in. "By rushing to do the right thing, we could lead them right to us. I'll forward the email to my colleague in Portugal. She'll look at the URL details and the key and know whether it's safe to open or not."

THEY WERE WELL clear of urban Saint Petersburg, snowy fields opening up on the left and dense forest on the righthand side of the road. Dima had changed the route: This time they were tracking close to the coast.

"We're five minutes from the walking paths I was telling you about," said Dima as the BMW navigated a deep pothole. "Apologies. As the saying goes, Russia is famous for fools and bad roads."

The satphone set off its distinctive old-school ringtone. Jacob snatched at it, put the call on loudspeaker, and answered breathlessly. "Irochka?"

He sensed the eyes of the others on him. Calling Irina by that diminutive form of her name was a dead giveaway that they were closer than simply professional colleagues.

"I've been so worried," Irina said. "And I've missed you so much, *zaichik*."

This was getting way too personal. He took the call off loudspeaker and held the cell tightly to his ear. He toyed with a loose thread of his scarf. "Are they treating you well in Portugal?"

"Too well. It's driving me crazy."

"Any updates on the tasks I gave you?"

The sound of her clearing her throat came down the line. Her taking a sip of something. Her favorite chamomile tea, he imagined.

"I've been trying to track down the *goszakaz* for the train tickets. RZD's defenses are rock solid, same with BaltEnergoTorg, whose security shows signs of having had some serious beefing up. But I'll keep trying.

"I've also been looking into the guy who collected the tickets at Finland Station. Didn't find anything useful, but I've got an idea how I might use Klitschko to get to Izmailov via the back door."

Jacob grimaced. He hadn't told her he'd killed Klitschko. That could wait.

"Also, those profiling jobs you gave me. Vyacheslav Gabulov came up squeaky clean, from the little I could find on him. A career man, life-long bachelor, probably gay, but in Russia, you stay in the closet if you want to survive. And...ah...I'm sorry he's dead."

"So am I."

"As for that Marfa Petko, well, what a piece of work she is. Rumor has it she's slept with half the influential and powerful men in Saint Petersburg. Some of the women, too!"

Jacob rolled his eyes, knowing this was unfounded jealousy and spitefulness talking. "Apart from that, though, she seems to be on the level, and I think perhaps you can trust her, but be careful. Just don't let her seduce you, Yakov. She's very beautiful."

"I won't. I promise."

"Good. Now, Ivan Beglov. He's a mysterious one. He—"

"Vanya's not with us. There's a good chance he could be dead, too."

"No! What...?"

"We're yet to confirm. That's the main reason I asked you to call. I need you to try and breach Vanya's security system. Cameras, sensors, locked doors, alarms. Can you do that?"

A pause and a deep breath. "Yes. In the sense that I can try. Can't promise anything. You'll need to supply me with as much information as you can. I'd need an IP address at the very minimum. Better, the brand of his cameras, router, other gear."

"We don't have any of that. This is a situation no one expected."

"Oh dear. What do you have? A physical address at least?"

"I'm putting you on loudspeaker." He pressed the button and asked, "Either of you know the dacha's address?"

"No idea," said Marfa. "I can only find it using landmarks."

"Dima?"

His chest puffed out as he recited, "47A Sadovaya Street, Shepelevo village, Lomonosovsky District, Leningrad Oblast."

"Couldn't be more specific unless you had the registered lot number," said Jacob. "Well done."

"Not really." Dima grinned cheekily as he pointed at the digital cockpit display. "It's programmed in the satnav. Those damn things make drivers lazy, me included. No one knows how to use a proper map these days."

"Did you catch that?" said Jacob.

"*Da. Uslyshala.* Yes, I heard it. It's a needle-in-a-haystack thing, but with some snooping around. Don't expect anything, OK? I'll try, but you're going to have to have some alternative plans."

"Understood. Another thing I'd like you to do."

"Really? That's not enough?"

"I'm going to forward you an email from Marfa's phone. It contains a URL and an access key. This could be a cornucopia of information to sink Severnaya Volna."

"You were right to be cautious. I'll open it from this end, run a little background verification program on a sacrificial machine in case it's a booby trap."

"Don't spend forever trying to crack Vanya's security. The archive is vital, too. Maybe more so. If we don't get out of this, I'll need you to find the smoking gun in the archive."

"What do you mean, if you don't get out of this? You will get out of it, you understand me!"

"Understood."

"Once I've got inside his system, what then? Turn everything off?"

"No. Leave it all running. I'll call you when we're close to the dacha. Shouldn't be too long. Stay by your phone." He paused a second, debating whether to ask or not. She might see some horrific stuff on the feed. In the end, lives were more important than Irina's sensibilities. "If you get in, I'd like you to look at the camera live feeds for me. See if there's any sign of intruders and...if Vanya's dead or alive in there."

He heard some heavy breathing. "OK, *zaichik*."

Dima was slowing to a stop next to a signpost for a hiking track. It looked like it had been made fifty years ago. He gestured right with his head: They'd arrived at the soon-to-be weapons testing ground.

"I know you get sick of me saying this," said Irina. "But please be careful out there. Russia's a dangerous place for you."

"I've got two exceptional allies with me. Which improves my chances by an order of magnitude."

"Good to know."

As he disconnected the call, he was already thinking about storming the property, alarm systems be dammed. They would get in and out as fast as they could and run for the border. Opening the car door, he wondered how the others would take to the idea of becoming refugees in another country.

TWENTY-SIX

THE TEXT MESSAGE HAD COME NEARLY THREE AND A half hours ago. Since then, big-time CEO Marat Izmailov had been stumbling around his office in a daze. He drank espresso coffee until he couldn't stand the taste anymore, stalled a meeting with key executives that should have been all wrapped up by now, and did almost enough pacing to complete the daily-steps target programmed into his smartwatch.

He re-read the text for the umpteenth time, trying to figure out what to do about it.

Holding a shaking palm to his moist forehead, he stood by the window, not so much admiring as absorbing the winter landscape below, its stark whiteness the perfect match for the static white noise in his brain. He couldn't sit for long, but when standing, a pain jagged in his ribs, so he flopped onto the soft Berber sofa. Lying on his back, Izmailov concentrated on his breathing to restore calm and figure out a way forward. Two rapidly smoked cigarettes hadn't helped at all.

He had to admit, he'd underestimated Vanya Beglov. The disingenuous fuck, acting like he was squeamish, incapable of murder. Then...those photographs. Stomach-turning imagery that looked like a maniac had been let loose from the asylum with a meat cleaver. The last time he saw anything like that was when a gleeful Kolodin had shown him pictures of Ukrainian soldiers whose faces had been burned off by thermite drones.

The degree of savagery suggested that, perhaps, Vanya's every move had been an act. His betrayal of B+ had seemed genuine over the last six months: He'd taken the proffered money and reported on a semi-regular basis. The intel was good—timely and accurate. Knowing Slava Gabulov's movements ahead of time had certainly assisted in tailing him and, ultimately, liquidating him. Again, he tapped his temple with his forefinger. That was a stupid idea, too. *His* stupid idea, that Kolodin had leapt at and Semak had needed convincing about. That had seen Klitschko killed.

Stupid, Marat, stupid.

Until now, Vanya had been a good, well-behaved boy. He'd learned things from Izmailov that could have been used against Severnaya Volna, but he hadn't acted upon that knowledge. B+ had not made any decisive moves to thwart them.

Again, Izmailov cursed his own stupidity. Had he not painted Beglov into a corner with threats, perhaps the man might have still been useful, not promising that Severnaya Volna would "crash and burn," whatever that meant. He should have used more carrot, less stick.

The desk phone rang, jolting him out of his thoughts.

His secretary reminded him of an afternoon appointment with a Moscow businessman anxious to make a move on the re-emergent Estonian market. Russia's most ambitious entrepreneurs were ringing the phone off the hook. It was no secret that BaltEnergoTorg was going to be a big player in the new space created by the accord. The 'Balt' part of the name was kind of a giveaway.

He crushed out a quarter-smoked cigarette in a pewter ashtray with a savage twist as the realization hit.

Perhaps the photos were a double-bluff? They certainly looked real. Izmailov had told him no AI trickery. But maybe it was? He'd have to get someone in the tech department to analyze it.

His cell phone chirped. An email, sent from Beglov's special account used only for communication with Izmailov. Eyes blinking rapidly, he opened it. More brutality?

A link to a video.

His pulse thundered in his veins as he thumbed the URL open. A horrible foreboding gripped his soul. Something awful was coming. He squinted as the camera captured a body—Kaufman's body—crashing to the bottom of the stairs with a nauseating thud, like a paratrooper whose chute had failed to open. If this was AI, he'd eat his fur shapka.

The fall didn't explain what he'd already seen in the photos—the mush where Kaufman's neck should have been. Vanya must have shot him at some point.

His hands shook as the video kept rolling.

Now Beglov drags the body to a corner. He grabs something. What the fuck is that? A...pitchfork? Jesus. Now he's stabbing, over and over and over.

Izmailov turned off his phone. This was real footage of revenge-filled violence. He rubbed his chin almost hard enough to remove stubble.

Before he had time to digest the atrocity he'd just witnessed, another email from Vanya landed in his inbox.

What the fuck? How many more?

Subject line, in English—*Show time*. A single link in the body of the email. He opened it without a second thought. It couldn't be worse than Kaufman's brutal execution.

The video began innocently enough, with Vanya making coffee, opening a pack of cigarettes, and smoking one. Then loud music started playing. Kino's song "*Gruppa krovi*." Like many Russians of the right vintage, Izmailov knew every word by heart. Then bizarre scenes of Vanya scooting around on an office chair, propelling himself with his feet, smoking as he goes, and singing his lungs out. Was he drunk?

Next, Vanya sits at his desk, energetically typing away for a while, his face a mixed-bag of expressions. He gets up, retrieves a gun from somewhere, and...what the hell?...kicks Kaufman's lifeless body and fires two rounds point blank into the dead man's face. He smiles, satisfied the weapon is up to scratch, and calmly walks to his desk again. He sits, closes his eyes, and...oh, holy Jesus...shoots himself. A single shot, a collapsing body, the chair rolling back on its wheels.

Izmailov froze as the clip ended, replaying the final seconds twice, three times, as if expecting a different outcome to materialize. His pulse pounded in his ears and throat. Izmailov understood the message thoroughly: If Vanya was willing to kill himself on camera, he'd already made sure the rest of the evidence was waiting somewhere Izmailov couldn't reach.

That's what he meant by crash and burn.

Izmailov lit yet another cigarette with trembling hands that rarely trembled.

He started to experience a moment of hesitancy. A Hamlet moment. To call them or not to call them, that was the question.

Semak had to know; he was the captain of this out-of-control ship. He'd hatch a recovery plan. Not Kolodin. The general would suggest all-out nuclear attack.

He pulled up Semak in his contacts and placed the call.

TWENTY-SEVEN

A SIGN AT START OF THE NARROW FOREST SERVICE road said *Gravel, Sand & Firewood for Sale. Call Sasha*. Then an illegible phone number. Judging by the state of the rusty metal and the short length of the phone number, Sasha must have died sometime in the 1970s.

Gazing out the window, Jacob's world dissolved into a thick blanket of snow and the sagging branches of fir and birch trees extending to the very edge of the track. The BMW's winter tires handled the frozen crust with ease. The radio was turned off, reception so bad in the forest all you could hear was white noise. The trail tightened even further, the tree branches brushing the sides of the car until they emerged into a clearing bordered by a rectangular pond about the size of a small ice rink. Beyond the opaqueness of the trees, the Gulf of Finland was preparing to freeze over.

"This is where we get out," said Dima, switching off the engine. "Out here in the summer, you get eaten alive by mosquitoes. And in winter, only deer and idiots walk the trails."

"Good thing we brought two idiots along," Marfa muttered. She slid out of the back and stamped her boots on the compacted snow. "If I get shot by either of you, maybe a passing deer can carry me out of this death trap."

Jacob stepped out last, breath instantly turning into vapor. A meter to his right, a crooked signpost half-buried in a drift warned hikers to be mindful of prevailing weather conditions.

Dima was right; this was the perfect place. Secluded, no cars, no houses, no prying eyes. The steady wind moaning off the gulf would muffle the sounds of the guns. Jacob walked to the trunk, opened it, and looked down at the bag of toys.

Three Vityaz PP-19 submachine guns, eighteen loaded mags. He would have liked suppressors, but you can't have everything, especially in a rushed black-market purchase.

"Let's see what we're made of, shall we?" said Jacob.

Marfa selected the first weapon in the pile with shaking hands and a forced grin, lips drawn back. Dima handled his almost lovingly, stroking it gently with the tips of his fingers. Jacob took the last one, checked the chamber, checked the safety mechanism, checked everything twice more. He made sure Dima and Marfa knew what the main working parts did, asked them to repeat back the information, and was satisfied they could begin. They set the fire selector levers to the lowest position, semi-automatic, to fire one round at a time. No need for raking bursts.

"Targets?" Dima asked.

Jacob scanned the clearing. A fallen spruce. A battered garbage can. An assortment of discarded green and clear bottles scattered around a collapsing picnic table.

"There, there, and there." He pointed in turn at each target. "From twenty meters, then thirty."

They fanned out, leaving plenty of space between them.

"Dima first," he said. "Stand clear, Marfa."

Dima nodded, raised the weapon, stuck out his tongue, exhaled, and fired.

The bullet thudded into the middle of the fallen tree. The second drilled through the garbage can, leaving a tiny crater. The third obliterated a vodka bottle, shards flying in all directions.

"Not bad," Jacob said.

"Not bad?" Dima scoffed, lowering the gun. "That was perfect. You know, I was the best shot in my battalion when I did my two years' military service." He gave a lopsided grin. "Haven't fired a shot since then."

Jacob shrugged. "What can I say? You're a natural."

He bowed theatrically.

"Step back ten paces and do it again."

Dima fired three more shots, not as accurate this time but damned close. A touch high on the log; clipped the edge of the garbage can; missed all the bottles, striking the snowy ground between them and sending up a shower of slush. He frowned, then licked his bottom lip. "Let's hope the bad guys are no more than twenty meters away."

Jacob just managed to suppress a laugh. Dima's grounding presence might be the one thing that kept him from losing his mind.

"You're up, fearless leader," said Dima. "Let's see what you've got."

Jacob rolled his shoulders, took a stride forward, and adopted an aggressive, forward leaning stance. He raised the gun and closed his left eye. His right eye looked through the open U-notch sight, aligning it with the top of the front post.

He squeezed the trigger.

Bang! Two inches to the right of Dima's first shot into the tree trunk.

Again. Into the exact hole Dima had made in the trash can, widening it by a couple of millimeters.

The third shot sliced the neck off a bottle like it had been severed from its body by a machete.

He retreated fifteen paces and repeated the sequence, all three bullets hitting millimeters from his first-round shots.

Blinking snowflakes from his eyelashes, he realized the forest had gone silent except for the breathing of the three humans in its midst.

"Show-off," said Marfa, breaking the silence. The way she twisted her lips and shook her head failed to mask the hint of admiration in her words.

"Your turn, ma'am," said Jacob with a gentle nod. "All of us need to be ready and able to contribute, including you."

Her bravado slipped. She walked to the spot where Dima had stood, a shaky leg raking an X into the snow. She held the weapon a little too rigidly, shoulders hunched tightly, elbows tucked as though she was trying to keep out the cold. Jacob stepped over and adjusted her stance quietly: a tap to the foot, a slight rearrangement of her grip.

"Relax and breathe," he said. "Aim a fraction lower than you think you should. The recoil's light with this model, but it still rises up."

Marfa grumbled that she understood perfectly well what to do and sighted along the barrel. Her breath quivered.

She flinched at the loud crack of the shot, which went way wide of all targets, hitting nothing but air.

"*Blyad'*. Fuck it. Oh well, better than shooting one of you two in the ass," she said, manufacturing a smile that was more like a grimace.

"Try again," Jacob said flatly. "Relax. Don't overthink it."

The next shot slammed into a tree trunk—not the target, but at least a tree.

"One more. You can do it," Jacob said encouragingly.

She swung the gun to the left, aimed at the nest of bottles, and hit one. "Yes!"

"That's it," Jacob said. "You're finding your range."

Her shoulders eased as the gun dangled at her side. She began to breathe with greater ease. "Can I go again from this same distance? Further back I've got no chance of hitting anything."

"Of course," said Jacob, gesturing for her to step up. "You have to walk before you can run."

She fired again—this time striking the garbage can in the

upper third. "Yes!" she cried in triumph and gave a little hop, like she'd won a gold medal at the Olympics.

On a roll now, she swept the gun in an arc at a new target—an indistinct, dark patch on a branch three meters off the ground. She gritted her teeth and squeezed the trigger.

A sharp yelp split the air.

Something fell, tumbling on the way down.

A small animal hit the snow with a sickening, soft thud.

Marfa froze.

"Oh my God," she whispered. "No. No, no, no—"

She dropped the weapon in the snow and stumbled forward, hands shaking uncontrollably. The animal—a squirrel—lay twisted, its fur blotched with blood. Its long tail flickered once, then went still.

She knelt on the ground next to the squirrel and howled.

"Marfa, stop," said Jacob, shaking her by the shoulder. She ignored him, crying in shrill, ragged breaths.

"I murdered the poor thing," she sobbed, wiping at her tear-streaked face with the back of her glove. "He was just—just sitting there, minding his own business. Good God. I thought it was a knot in the wood. Why did it have to be there?"

"It was an accident," Jacob said, crouching beside her. "You couldn't have known."

"That doesn't change anything, does it!" she barked, grief flaring into self-loathing. "It was alive, probably happy with a little squirrel family. And I killed it, snuffed its lights out, just like that." She made a finger-snapping motion, her gloves preventing the accompanying click. "What kind of person does that?"

Jacob held her gaze. "It's not your fault."

Marfa, fragile since Slava's death and brittle since Vanya's suicide message, did not need this to happen. She wore her boldness and confidence like others wore clothes, but it was mostly a façade. Now something inside her had cracked, perhaps irreparably. He'd have to nurse her the rest of the way. The third rifle would be useless to them now.

"It's not about the squirrel," she whispered. "Although I'm devastated that it's dead. It's everything else. All of it."

Jacob placed a hand on her shoulder. "This isn't on you."

"Tell that to the squirrel," she said, her voice trembling.

Dima approached slowly, gun slung behind him. "Marfa... I'm so sorry you've been caught up in this."

"Don't," she said, turning to glare at him. "Just—don't. I'm adult enough to live with the consequences of my actions. I knew B+ wasn't going to be a fucking sewing circle."

A spark of resilience. Jacob wondered if he'd judged her too quickly.

The wind moaned through the trees again, the chill factor making them all shiver. It was time to get out of the cold, back into the BMW and crank up the heating. Jacob stood, held out a hand, and pulled Marfa to her feet.

"We're done here," Jacob said quietly. "Let's see if Irina has found us a way in. Or if he have to bash the door down and figure out how to turn off the alarms before someone nasty comes snooping."

Dima bent to collect Marfa's dropped weapon, removing snow from it with a swift brush of his hand. They moved through the forest in silence, like monks on a pilgrimage.

Jacob walked behind Marfa, Dima in front. He observed the jerky movements of her arms and legs as she trudged along, eyes fixed on her boots. Snow had started to fall thicker again, creating a curtain that blurred the tree trunks and branches into a soft wall of pearl-gray. From somewhere far in the distance came the faint rumble of a train, the hum of traffic.

Jacob matched her pace, giving her room. She hadn't uttered a word since they left the clearing, but her breathing had become more even. Perhaps the cumulative shock of extreme events was settling into resignation.

When the BMW came into view, covered in a white mantle, Jacob touched her elbow, and she turned around.

"You're in a dark place I've been in many times before," he

said. "I've lost people very close to me, people I've worked with. It will get better with time, believe me."

Marfa shook her head. "You don't know that."

"You're still here while others haven't survived," Jacob said. "That means something."

"All it means is I've been lucky—so far. You really think we're getting out of this alive?"

Jacob didn't answer right away.

"The triumvirate will hunt us down if we can't knock them out first," she said.

He nodded. "I'm glad you've grasped the reality of what's in front of us. They won't roll over knowing that we have in our possession what Vanya left for us. But we *can* take them down."

She folded her arms and took a step back. "Uh huh, so now you believe his email contained the truth?"

"It's beginning to feel that way."

They had reached the car. Jacob opened the door for her. She pulled her scarf tighter around her neck and slid in without a word.

Dima, loading their weapons back into the duffel, glanced over the roof of the car. "She okay?"

"Not really," Jacob said. "She's a liability but one we're obliged to carry."

Dima closed the trunk. "Then we move?"

"Yes," Jacob said, sliding into the passenger seat. "Let's get out of here. How much fuel do we have?"

"Nearly a full tank. Why?"

"Until we hear from Irina, we need to maintain a holding pattern, drive along random back roads. Hopefully not for too long."

As the BMW started up, every instinct in him warned the same thing: Don't drop your guard for a second.

Getting the weapons was a stroke of luck. Hitting targets took skill. Surviving the onslaught that his gut told him the triumvirate was preparing to unleash would require something greater.

He uttered a silent prayer. For their safety and for Irina's success.

TWENTY-EIGHT

IRINA TRIED THE OBVIOUS ANGLES FIRST, DIGGING INTO the services delivered to the dacha's street address—electric, gas, and water—hoping against hope that one of the utilities companies used a weak system she could sneak through.

No good.

Every doorway remained steadfastly shut: they either demanded photo ID or two-factor identification codes sent to Ivan Beglov's cell phone or some other requirement she couldn't provide. After twenty minutes of pursuing dead ends, she pushed back from the desk, muttering under her breath. An address alone couldn't buy you much these days.

She stood, flexed sore fingers, and paced the floor for a while. The moment of clarity appeared like clearing clouds on an overcast day. She prayed her hunch was right.

A tap on the door.

"Yes?" she said impatiently, wanting to get on with the job.

Maria popped her head around. "Can I get you something, dear?"

About to send her on her way, Irina changed her mind. "Got any of those delicious egg tarts?"

"Sorry?"

She wracked her brain, thought she remembered the Portuguese word but was sure she'd pronounce it horribly wrong, so instead asked for a pot of chamomile tea.

"Of course," said the maid. "You sure you donna wan' some proper lunch?" She smiled, dipped her head, and raised her eyebrows, as if she had something irresistible boiling away on the stove.

"Sure," said Irina with a sigh. Anything to get her gone.

With Maria's footsteps echoing down the corridor, she noticed her stomach grumbling. It was close to midday, and she'd eaten nothing since seven o'clock last night. An aroma of frying onions and garlic floated through the crack in the door, and she felt herself thinking seriously about food.

But not before she'd performed the hack.

She preferred to work with the curtains drawn. The 180-degree view of a clear, sparkling Portuguese winter's day, with olive and citrus groves stretching into the distance and snow-capped mountains of the Serra da Estrela range, was an unnecessary distraction. She thrived in semi-darkness, like a mushroom.

She chugged water, then set to it.

Jacob had said to get into the cameras and alarms first, Vanya's archive second. But what if the answer to the first problem was contained in the second?

On a separate basic laptop—an expendable one should a virus be introduced—she typed in the URL to Vanya's cloud archive, then entered the complex pass key. She watched the loading wheel spin. Ten seconds, twenty. Still spinning. *Come on...*

It opened.

She sighed and made a face of disappointment when she saw the vast size of the holdings. A mass of folders and individual files covering a plethora of subjects. Latin and Cyrillic fonts jumbled together. A nightmare.

She didn't leap into the detective work. For a minute, she monitored the little watchdog script she'd written—a digital tripwire—run its sweep across the sacrificial laptop. When it reported no outbound spikes, no hidden processes waking up, and no nasty surprises slipping into the hard drive, she knew the link was safe. Now she could move to her own, much more powerful machine.

Back on her trusty Lenovo ThinkPad, she pulled her top lip under her front teeth, concentrating like she was in a sudoku competition. She repeated the process of entering the URL and pass key. This time the archive opened twice as fast.

The item she desperately sought was a folder or file that, *please*, contained the necessary configurations for the security systems. Passwords would be lovely, too. Tech people always saved their own configs. She did, and so Vanya must have too. Ideally, his laptop was still plugged in at the dacha, and she could wake it up remotely.

Maybe.

It was a long shot.

But first she had to sort through the maze of material.

She exhaled through her teeth.

Let's see if you left a door ajar for me.

She searched via the browser for a number of terms she thought might contain gold. The obvious ones, like cameras, alarms, passwords, doors. In Russian and English.

Nothing.

Her heart sank. There were simply too many folders—over five hundred—to open and trawl through. Jacob would be at the dacha in thirty minutes or so, and she'd achieved precisely nothing.

For want of better ideas, she ranked the folders in alphabetical order.

None of the names seemed to make any sense; no obvious categories like Admin or Audio or Apps or anything even close to useful. Instead: Amber, Aluminum, Apples. Random words.

Her eye caught one obvious name.

B+

Why not?

She clicked the icon.

Inside were more folders, each named after a Kino song. Sadly, the band was no one-hit wonder; the list contained more than ninety song titles. At the very top was '1. Muraveinik.'

Her heart skipped a beat. The word, meaning anthill, had an extra metaphorical meaning in Russian: a network of tunnels or paths.

Surely, *surely*.

And there it all was.

The anthill contained all the Wi-Fi credentials, a password export vault, device configs, even a .txt document called *Hardware Notes*.

Maria returned, walking almost on tip-toes, poured a cup of tea, and left, Irina's gaze only leaving the monitor for a second to briefly thank her with a smile before returning to the archive.

By the time the tea had cooled to a drinkable temperature, she had found everything she needed. She shook her head with a grin, barely able to credit that she was able to seize control of the dacha and command it like the captain of a warship.

Irina didn't bother going in through Vanya's laptop, although the password for remote access was staring her in the face. Instead, with the configs and device credentials sitting neatly in the archive, she could hit every target directly from Portugal. Which was going to save a bunch of time and, hopefully, some people's lives.

One by one, she authenticated into the dacha's system—first the network video recorder that handled the internal and external cameras, then the front gate controller, then the alarm panel.

Within minutes, she had full administrative access: live feeds from every camera, the ability to download and edit recorded footage, control of the driveway gate, and toggles for every sensor in the house and on the grounds. No fancy tricks or somersaults needed—just clean entry using the keys Vanya had stored away.

Once inside the interface, she finally saw the structure of the system: eighteen cameras, all feeding into a receiver that Vanya could preview on a laptop or cell phone app. Eight external cameras, ten internal. More than a New York bank would have. There were other things she wasn't familiar with: seismic sensors, microwave motion detectors, infra-red trip-beams, glass-break detectors, motion-activated security lighting.

She leaned back, hands tucked behind her head, and took a couple of deep breaths. Satisfied with her work, but also realizing she hadn't done anything requiring a great deal of brainpower, she took a sip of tea, now stone cold. Didn't matter; she preferred it that way. More refreshing.

An insistent tapping came on the door. Not because Maria was suddenly respecting Irina's privacy. Turned out she'd been forced to kick at the closed door with her toe because she was carrying a massive tray loaded up with food. Grilled fish, a hill of steaming fries, and roasted vegetables. On a side plate, a *pastel de nata* tart. A glass of chilled white wine to wash it all down. Saliva pooled in her mouth.

Maria placed the tray on a spare table and shuffled out again, singing something folksy to herself.

Irina couldn't stop to enjoy the meal as it should be enjoyed. She grabbed a handful of fries, stuffed them in her mouth, and turned to the beckoning monitor.

She hesitated, anxious about what she might see. A mouthful of fruity chardonnay to steel the nerves.

She clicked the first live feed—exterior front gate entrance cam. Snow drifted past the lens in slow, diagonal waves. The ground was covered in fresh, undisturbed snow; no one had been in and out for several hours at least. She nodded appreciatively as she realized this camera was of the pan-tilt-zoom variety. A quick check—they *all* were.

The rest of the external cameras—driveway approach, front porch, back porch, north wall, south wall, barn and storage room exterior, also showed nothing obviously suspicious. No footprints except tiny ones left by birds. No tire tracks. Nothing but the bare branches of birch bending under the weight of snow dumps.

Nothing had been recorded by motion activation on any of the external cameras since early morning, when three people left the property. Jacob—how wonderful to see him!—and two others, presumably Dmitry 'Dima' Sechkin and, yes, it was obvious by her whorish strut, Marfa Petko. A few words were exchanged among them, some hand gestures, before they hopped into the sleek BMW and drove away sedately.

Back to live. She panned the front gate entrance camera to get an overview of what the dacha looked like. A squared-off, snow-covered hedge running on either side of the long driveway that ended in a perfect circle.

The two-story house, perhaps twenty-five meters wide, was clad in dark wooden clap-board, a stone garage connected to the house by an enclosed walkway. Three dormer windows in the attic. White trim around large windows that looked like they were European tilt-and-turn, triple-glazed to handle the coldest temperatures. In fact, although she guessed this was an old building, perhaps originally constructed in the 1950s or '60s, it was clear a lot of money had been spent on additions and renovations.

She paused to sip wine—not a usual lunch beverage for her, but when in Portugal—and then moved to observe the interior feeds.

Her screen was split into sixteen squares, ten showing the camera feeds, six blank. She tsk-tsked. Why didn't he have nine cameras? It would make the macro view so much easier. She went from feed to feed, double-clicking each tile to display on full screen.

She raised her eyebrows when she realized three of the interior feeds were actually for the interior of *external* buildings. A machinery shed, containing a bright red universal terrain vehicle; a barn—untidy would be a kind way to describe its condition; and a produce storeroom. The interiors of the outbuildings showed in a crisp, well-defined grayscale, meaning Vanya had purchased expensive high-quality infrared cameras.

Renovations, top-notch gear...she wondered who was paying

for all of this. As she understood it, B+ was a tiny outfit focused on gathering intel, not building a fortress.

Next, the kitchen.

Modern country-cottage style, like you'd see all over the American Midwest. Soft blue pastel cabinetry, an island bench with stools around it. Two-door steel fridge, induction stove top. This was *not* your typical Russian dacha. At least not the ultra-basic kind where she'd spent summer vacations as a child. The kind where you fetched water out of a well in a bucket and went to the toilet outside in a hole in the ground.

Living room cam showed black leather couches, a giant TV screen, and not much else.

The bedroom cams revealed two made beds and two unmade with clothes scattered on the floor.

There were two cameras left to check. So far, she hadn't picked up any signs of intrusion or disturbance anywhere on the property. It appeared it was safe for Jacob and the others to return to... For what purpose? she wondered. Irina had neglected to ask, and Jacob hadn't explained.

Attic next.

Cardboard boxes, cobwebs, dust. Piles of old paperbacks, some vintage kids' toys that Vanya had probably played with twenty-five years ago. With nothing to base it on, she felt a sinister vibe about this space. She dwelt on the thought for a second, then realized the entire property was giving off an evil vibe. She shook her head. Too many Stephen King novels.

One camera left.

Irina double-clicked the computer room feed.

A large, brightly lit rectangle. White paint, clinical and characterless, like a hospital. Banks of servers and towers, cables snaking across the floor. Steel racks jammed tight with all kinds of paraphernalia: CDs and DVDs, plastic ring binders, more cables, plugs, chargers, the whole nine yards.

Wait.

Something on the floor caught her eye.

She zoomed in. "*Bozhe moi.* My God..."

The chair careened backward a meter on its casters until she crunched into the wall. She stood, grabbed the glass of wine, and drank what was left. She wiped her lips with the back of her hand, sat down, and rolled the chair back to the desk.

She stared intently to make sure she wasn't imagining it.

No. It was real.

Two bodies.

One shoved up against a storage rack, face gone, the neck like raw steak. Who was this? Vanya?

She zoomed in, leaning forward and focusing with wide eyes. It was like watching a horror movie or a car crash, where you're scared shitless and your stomach churns, but you still need to see it all.

The man had a solid build, like a weight-lifter. He was wearing clothes a couple of sizes too small for him but was barefooted. Dark hair matted with blood, blood all around him, dried into cobalt shadows on the concrete floor. His limbs were splayed in all directions, like he'd fallen from the top of a building. A meter from the body lay the last thing she would ever expect to see in a computer room: a long-handled pitchfork, its tines covered in blood. *What the hell?*

Breath hitching, she panned the camera toward the second body, half-slumped over a tipped gamer chair. Another man, slighter of build, this time the clothes fitting perfectly. Dark blood pooled around his head.

Irina's pulse spiked so hard she could feel blood flowing in her lips.

She zoomed in on the dead man's face. Eyes closed, an almost peaceful expression, a large hole in the region of the right temple. There were enough of his features left intact to make an identification. She'd seen photographs of this man. There was no doubt in her mind: This was Ivan 'Vanya' Beglov.

A pistol lay inches from his right hand. She assumed he'd shot himself; however, she couldn't rule out the possibility that somebody had staged the scene to look like a suicide. She shook her head.

It's not for me to speculate.

Still, the evidence of her own observations told her it wasn't a setup.

She rubbed her face, wondering what to do next. Trawl through the five hundred folders to look for evidence against Severnaya Volna? That's what Jacob wanted, but the prospect filled her with dread.

The question was put on pause when her cell phone rang. She snatched at it.

"Irina, this is Robert." Jacob launched into his spiel so fast she knew he must be on loudspeaker. Lest she say his real name. "We're parked a hundred meters from the dacha and eager to move. Please tell me you got in."

Something in his tone told Irina he was optimistic but at the same time steeling himself for a negative response.

"I got in."

"Hallelujah."

"But not the way you were expecting."

She explained how she'd stumbled upon the folder containing Vanya's logins and configs.

"He's dead. Vanya. I saw him. It was...horrible. Looks like he shot himself, but...I guess you can make that judgment when you see for yourself."

The sound of Petko bursting into tears and howling made Irina feel guilt for her ill-will against the woman, based on nothing but jealousy.

"Any signs of intruders?"

"None that I could see. I checked all of his eighteen cameras and found nothing...apart from...you know." Her hand shot to her mouth. "There's a second dead man inside!"

"We know."

"You do? Why didn't you tell me?"

"It needed verification. We only had an email from Vanya

claiming he'd murdered the man. We weren't even sure the email itself was legit until now."

"You could have at least warned me about the possibility—which turned out to be a reality, dammit." She felt her breathing become ragged, like she'd run a hundred-meter sprint. She hated being used, but deep down, she knew Jacob had played it correctly. Having preconceived ideas of what she'd find could have frustrated her thinking processes, stopped her from finding the way in.

"What about the alarms?"

"Still on, as you requested."

"Please turn them all off. And deactivate the electronic locks."

"Give me a second...done."

"Could you also please—"

"Open the front gate?"

"It's scary how you can read my mind sometimes."

"Isn't it just," she said dryly, toggling to the doors-windows-and-gates interface and pressing a button. "Also done."

"Thank you, Irina. Really."

She nodded instinctively, though there was no one to see it.

"I'm...why are you even there? Now that I've got the archive right here in front of me, surely there's no need to put yourselves in danger by returning."

"We won't be here for long. I'd like to retrieve two of the bodies and take them away, try and arrange a decent burial for these men."

"*Two of*? You mean there's more! I didn't see any other bodies. What the hell are you talking about?"

She heard a deep swallow. "Slava Gabulov's body is stored there, inside an outbuilding. We had no other option."

"OK," she said quietly, the horror of the rising body count turning her numb. "Just... be careful in that house. The place scares me, even all the way over here in Portugal."

"It's just a house, Irochka."

"Bullshit. It's got bad juju. Do what you have to do and get out, fast." She ran a hand through her hair and pulled it away slightly damp. She must have been sweating despite the coolness of the room.

"I have no desire to linger there any longer than necessary."

"Good."

He confirmed that her next job was to find the incontrovertible evidence against the triumvirate, the needle in the haystack that lay hidden in Vanya's files.

"I don't even know where to begin, apart from the obvious search terms. It's a total mess."

"Then you'd best make a start on it."

"Keep me updated when you can, OK?" She tried to keep the desperation out of her voice and wasn't sure if she'd succeeded.

"If you need help, ask Fletcher to get some of his people to do the spade work. In fact, ask him anyway."

"Understood."

The line clicked dead.

Irina sat there for several long moments. She was mad there were other people with him and she couldn't use the words she wanted to. To tell Yakov that she loved him more than life itself. Tears welled in the corners of her eyes. There were too many deaths already on this mission. If it claimed him, too...it was unthinkable.

Jacob was the most capable person she had ever met. He had so-called allies with him, people he'd described as "exceptional." She didn't believe that for a minute. These people were amateur activists with a cause who'd just happened to stumble onto something big. Instead of Skia getting involved, the case should have been handled internally, the plotters turned over to the regime, evidence or no evidence. Russia's legal system was famous for operating in an evidence vacuum, sending people to prison based on nothing but hatred.

But none of these decisions were hers to make, and that was definitely for the best.

God help him.

She opened the curtains for a moment, soaked in the incredible beauty of the vista below, and wished her man was here to enjoy it with her.

Besides in the mountains, snow rarely fell in Portugal. Jacob was up to his knees in the stuff, freezing his ass off trying to save the world. She felt a bitter chill in her bones, suddenly remembering the obscure word "simulpathity." Jacob had used it to drop his last tiles in a game of Scrabble. And, of course, to win by a mile. Fletcher was furious, claimed Jacob had made it up. He'd rushed to the dictionary, only to find that Jacob was right, as usual. The word meant to experience the emotions, usually pain, of another person over a long distance. Exactly how she was feeling now.

Time was ticking, she knew it, but the food was there, and she was starving. She wolfed down every last morsel, then rang Maria on an extension and ordered strong coffee and cookies.

She took a cold shower while she waited for Maria. After the maid had brought the coffee and cleared away the almost licked-clean plates, she changed into a pair of soft pajamas and a fluffy robe. If she was going to bust her ass all night, she may as well be comfortable.

TWENTY-NINE

THE DACHA, AS OMINOUS AS IT LOOKED IN THE DIM winter light, somehow seemed stripped of danger after Irina had checked the place and given it the all-clear. At least as far as the cameras could pick up. Jacob knew it was a feeling best not to misinterpret as fact for two reasons: The cameras didn't see everything, and the triumvirate's henchmen could show at any time, guns blazing.

Which meant they had to move fast.

Having taken the wheel to give Dima a rest, he rolled the BMW to a crunching stop on the icy driveway, directly opposite the front door. The woods bordering the property cast their eerie shadows in the light of early afternoon. He dropped the window to listen. There were no sounds except for the low moaning of the wind and the chirping of forest birds.

He told the others to wait as he got out with the SMG. He closed the car door gently, hand firmly on the pistol grip, buttstock by his ribcage, muzzle angled slightly upward. It had only been a minute and a half since he'd disconnected the "reassuring" call with Irina, but well-trained bad guys could have made their way inside in less than that time. Out of habit, he scanned the windows, doors, and roofline and eyeballed the ground for fresh tracks. No signs of life, no movement; all was precisely as they'd left it this morning.

On the outside, at least.

He sucked in a deep breath as he contemplated the horrors awaiting them within.

Dima stepped out next, his weapon hanging low and ready. With his natural affinity for the Vityaz and his overall bullishness, he was a valuable asset, for which Jacob was grateful.

Marfa came out last, almost stumbling. Her limbs moved with stiff jerks, like she'd slept too long on a plank of wood. The color had drained from her face, only her cheeks turning rosy in the cold. She'd been silent for the last fifteen minutes, apart from wailing when Irina confirmed Vanya's death. The woman was tough, but that was in the cut and thrust of politics, dealing with arrogant public figures. Yes, she'd learned about weaponry in her military-service years, been on assignment on the fringes of war zones. But in a real-world situation where violence threatened her own life and those of her colleagues, she had crumbled.

They entered through the front door, the keypad on the wall gray and lifeless. Jacob led Marfa into the living room. Dima headed downstairs to the scene of the carnage.

"I need to see Vanya," said Marfa, exerting resistance with her legs as Jacob pressed her shoulder down. "Let me see him."

"Not happening."

"Please!" Losing the unwinnable battle of strength, she dropped onto the leather couch, a puff of air escaping her lungs. She looked pleadingly at Jacob. "Why are you doing this to me?"

"What good would it do to see him?" Jacob placed the gun down on the floor, sat beside her, and took her clammy hand in his. "Remember him alive."

She looked at the ceiling, then into Jacob's eyes, almost pleading. "I saw Slava's body, didn't I?"

"He was in a much...tidier... state than Vanya. Barely a line on his throat. Vanya...shot himself point blank." He compressed his lips hard. "Trust me. At that distance, the shot didn't leave a neat little hole. The round hit the temple and blew out a section the size of a fist. There's bone fragments everywhere. It's not something you need in your mind. Not on top of everything else going on. Have you ever seen a head that's had a big hole blown in it?"

"No..."

He stood. "Listen. I realize you're fragile, and I *will* take care of you. But we're wasting time. Grab yourself a drink of water and lie down for a spell. Dima and I will retrieve the bodies, get them into the car, then we go. No stopping till the Estonian border. Meanwhile, you *do not* move beyond this room and the kitchen, one quick bathroom break allowed. Understood?"

Lips quivering, she gave a tiny nod. "Please be quick, Robert. I don't like it here."

Jacob was downstairs in a heartbeat, glad Marfa had capitulated so easily.

Now to work.

Dima was hunched over in a corner, a patch of vomit by his feet. He turned as he heard Jacob approaching, wiping a string of snot from his nose. "I'm sorry...I—"

"Don't apologize. Normal reaction. You over it?"

Dima nodded, but Jacob knew it was a lie.

"OK, let's get him upstairs. Kaufman stays where he lies."

"How do we carry him with the guns over our shoulders?"

"Very carefully. I'll go backwards to make it easier for you. You take his feet, I'll take him by the armpits."

With the slings cinched and weapons slung over their backs, inch by inch and grunting with each step, they hauled Vanya up the stairs. They had to change their grips every few steps as the body kept slipping. Vanya's neck unfortunately took a natural dip to the right, putting the large, gaping exit hole directly in Jacob's line of sight.

They caught their breath at the top of the stairs, then quickly moved through the hallway, much easier now on a flat surface, and out to the cold air. With one of the back seats folded down for extra room, they angled Vanya into the trunk, knees tucked in, shoulders turned, body set diagonally to make the fit work.

Next, they went for Slava. A day in the cool storeroom had kept the cadaver from bloating, but his skin had turned stiff and waxy. They strapped him onto the UTV and bumped their way back to the BMW, its trunk lid yawning. They worked quicker this time, lifting and maneuvering Slava in silence.

Closing the trunk, Jacob said, "Go and look for fuel cans. If you can't find any, try and siphon some gas out of the UTV." He sighed. "Can you do that?"

"*Govno vopros*. Piece of cake." Dima tilted his head. "You gonna burn down this lovely dacha?" There was genuine disappointment in his voice, as if he had a personal stake in the property. "Seems a shame."

"Too bad." He took an instinctive 360-degree look around. No movement anywhere. Good. "I'm going to grab everything useful I can find in the computer room. You never know what could be on his hard drives. Meet me there when you've got the fuel. And don't dawdle."

"Understood."

"Then we burn the dacha to the ground."

In the computer room, Jacob was jolted by indecision. So much gear, total chaos. He called Irina on the satphone.

No time for pleasantries.

"It's me. I need help. You still connected to the cameras?"

"Wait." Ten seconds later. "I see you."

"Good. I don't know what the hell to take. I've got the laptop. Tell me what else."

"There could be valuable items in the desk and filing cabinet drawers, but I can only see what's on the surfaces."

"Right. I'll check the drawers."

He flung drawers open and rifled through them, tossing

hanging files and loose papers left and right. It was all junk to his eye. He grabbed a handful of small USB flash drives from the top desk drawer and held them up. "These?"

"Why not? They don't take up much room. Take them. Leave the rest of the small stuff."

"What else?"

"Any loose external drives? Anything labeled? Any portable units near the monitors? Anything connected by a single cable you can pull out clean?"

Jacob scanned fast, eyes darting all over the place. He grabbed what looked physically self-contained or expensive: a slim external SSD plugged to the main tower; a black drive on the side table; a small network-attached storage device with a carry handle. He held each up for her imprimatur.

"If you've got space, take them."

"Cables?" he said.

"Leave them." He heard the unspoken rebuke in her voice and cursed himself for asking such a stupid question. "Just take the devices themselves."

"Take one last look, Irochka. Anything I've missed?"

"If you can manage that mid-sized tower, take it."

"OK."

A cardboard shipping box leaned against the leg of a workstation. He opened the flaps, dumped the packing foam onto the floor, and stuffed the haul inside, tower first, then the rest. It was a tight fit. He lifted it off the floor. Heavy, but he could carry it on his own if he had to.

"That's it," Irina said. "It's probably all ballast, but you never know."

"Thank you, Irochka. I'll call you from Estonia."

"Are you planning to get the others out of Russia?"

"Yes."

"That won't be easy, Yakov."

"I'll think of something. Love you."

Jacob snapped the box shut just as Dima barreled in, arms bulging around two jerry cans.

"It's almost as if Vanya wanted us to find these," said Dima. "In clear view on a shelf in the garage."

"Put those against the wall, next to Kaufman." Jacob pointed at more empty packing boxes and the pile of papers on the floor. "You know what to do. Wait three minutes then spark up your lighter."

Jacob slowly walked upstairs with the box of gear, second jerry can balanced on top. He set the box by the front door and headed for the back of the house with the can. He went methodically from room to room, sloshing fuel on curtains, bedspreads, rugs, everywhere until the can was almost empty. The air grew sickly with fumes.

Marfa lay on the couch, an arm draped over her forehead. Jacob grabbed her—half-dazed—by the arm. "Give me your lighter and go to the car."

She sat up, fumbled in her coat pocket, and held out the lighter, blinking uncomprehendingly. He snatched at it and spun her around by the shoulders. "Go wait in the car."

He dashed to the other end of the house, setting fire to curtains in one room before moving to the next.

He cupped his hands to his mouth. "Dima! Hurry up!"

Dima appeared in the kitchen doorway, face flushed with a wild, childlike joy.

Jacob set the lighter to a fuel-soaked dishtowel, the flame engulfing it in seconds. He turned to Dima. "Come on!"

As a parting gesture, he turned on the gas stove to accelerate the process.

They rushed out through the front door into the freezing air as the dacha began to roar behind them. Two car doors slammed, seatbelts were buckled, deep breaths were taken. An almost euphoric feeling gripped the two men.

"We have to go now," said Jacob. "This life is done for you two. No turning back."

"Ah..." said Marfa from the backseat, her spirits marginally brighter now she was out of the house she hated. "Where are we going, exactly?"

"Estonia. Where else would I go?"

"What about us?" said Dima. "We've got no visas. They'll turn us away; that's if the triumvirate doesn't get us first."

"Visas won't be necessary."

"Of course they're necessary," said Marfa. "You might be an Estonian citizen, but we aren't!"

Jacob cleared his throat. Might as well tell them now. "I'm an American citizen."

The silence in the car lasted fifteen seconds before Dima's raucous laughter shattered it. "Yeah, and I'm Napoleon!"

"I'm serious." The reply was abrupt and deadpan, bringing the laughter to an immediate halt. "The only part of Estonia I've seen is inside the airport. They say Tallinn's old town is something everyone ought to see in their lifetime." He smiled warmly. "We should all look forward to it."

"Oh my God," Dima muttered, then said to himself more than to Marfa, "He *is* serious."

"Turn right at the end of the driveway and head west. If you want to get out of this in one piece and see Tallinn, listen to me and do as I say." He shrugged. "There are no other options."

Dima slammed his hand on the steering wheel. "What the fuck is going on! Since you came into our lives, two of us are dead"—he jerked his head toward the trunk—"and now we're all scrambling to stay alive. Tell me you're not working for them, damn you."

"Of course I'm not working for *them*." Jacob's voice shook. "If I were, you'd both be dead."

"It makes sense, Dima," said Marfa. "Yes, he's a duplicitous prick, but we've got Vanya's material; soon we'll find the proof in there to send Semak and his pals to prison for life."

"They deserve the death penalty," Dima growled. "Nothing less."

"It equates to the same thing in Russia." Marfa laughed sarcastically. "No one survives for long in the gulag."

"I'll explain everything on the way," said Jacob. Everything, of course, would be a highly edited version. "But I want you to believe me: Once we arrive at the Estonian border, I have the authority to demand you both get asylum in the West."

As Dima engaged the engine, Marfa gripped the headrest and pulled herself forward. "Hey. Is your name even Robert Tamm?"

"Yes," he lied, simply because it was easier.

"More bullshit," said Dima. "Listen to how he speaks Russian. Better than me!" He rolled his shoulders and sniffed. "You CIA, Tamm?"

"Something like that."

"Get me asylum and I'll forgive you for the deception. Canada's always appealed to me. Better yet, New Zealand. As far away from this shit as you can get."

"It's a deal." Jacob extended his hand, but Dima ignored the gesture.

"Are we taking Slava and Vanya to Estonia, too?" said Dima, slowing to negotiate a hairpin bend. "I'm not sure asylum is a tempting offer for them."

"No, of course not."

"Then why did we bother putting them in the car? They could have been cremated in the house, like Kaufman and Klitschko before him."

Jacob said, "Turn off at the hiking trail. We'll take them to the clearing where the squirrel died. Leave them there, say a prayer, and go."

Marfa burst into tears, nodding. "Yes! That's perfect. It's peaceful there."

Dima shook his head. "No way. Wolves will take them."

Marfa held up a finger. "Would you rather they end up on a slab in a morgue, forensics pouring over them?" She shook her head rapidly. "No. There's no dignity in that. Better the wolves take them, don't you think? It completes the cycle of nature."

Dima rolled his eyes and sighed deeply. "Fine," he said with grudging acceptance. "The clearing it is."

"Look!" Marfa pointed to the east. The jagged tips of flames were rising above tree tops in the near distance. A billowing plume of smoke, stark and black, rose into the sky. "You two are A-grade arsonists, I swear."

"By the time anyone gets there, the place will be charred ruins," said Jacob. He touched Dima on the shoulder. "Go a bit faster, will you? This will have to be the fastest memorial service in history."

Ten minutes later, damp and exhausted from carrying the bodies one at a time twenty-five meters across uneven, snowy ground into the clearing, Jacob and Dima collapsed into the car. Marfa blubbered in the back, holding a handkerchief to her face.

The service had comprised the first line of an Orthodox funeral prayer. While Dima and Marfa stood with heads bowed, Jacob recited: "O God of spirits and of all flesh, Who hast trampled down death and overthrown the Devil, and given life to Thy world, do Thou, the same Lord, give rest to the souls of Thy departed servants in a place of brightness, a place of refreshment, a place of repose, where all sickness, sighing, and sorrow have fled away. Amen."

They reached the main road without seeing anyone except a bread delivery van going in the opposite direction. Dima pushed the BMW, tires biting into frozen asphalt. The woods blurred past as they curved around Gorovaldayskoye Lake, heading for Sosnovy Bor and then south toward Estonia. Two weeks ago, the trip to the border would have taken nearly five hours due to the crossing at Ivangorod-Narva being closed. Now, thanks to the accord, that border point was open again.

Jacob looked over his shoulder to see the flames of the burning dacha higher than before, the smoke thicker. "You were right, Dima. It is a shame we had to burn down that old house."

"Fuck that," Dima said, dropping the window and lighting a

cigarette. "I'd happily trade that entire property for one bottle of Canadian maple syrup or a slab of New Zealand butter."

So would I, thought Jacob. *Any day of the week*.

He fished the satphone out of his pocket. He'd promised asylum. Now he prayed Fletcher would play ball. It was 7:00 a.m. in New York. He rehearsed the request in his head and dialed the number.

THIRTY

Irina's pulse was still racing from the exchange with Yakov. Watching him on the camera link, desperately scrambling around that computer room, breathless and confused, summoned up her protective, maternal instincts. How she wanted to hug him, tell him everything was going to be OK. That he should abandon the house, get the hell out of there, the gear wasn't worth risking his life for.

Her intuition told her the items he salvaged wouldn't contain anything useful that the cloud archive didn't. Maybe he took them to prevent others from getting their hands on them? Yes, that made sense.

Out of sheer curiosity, she turned on the camera again.

"What...the..."

She inhaled sharply, hand flying to her mouth. Smoke and flames filled the screen; she could barely see anything through the curtain of gray and orange.

Was he trapped in there?

You must not contact him of your own volition. Fletcher's clear order.

Fuck that.

She dialed the satphone.

He answered immediately. "Irochka? What is it? You've found the *goszakaz*?"

"No!" she roared. "I went back to the camera, saw the fire. Thought you might be trapped in the house. What the hell happened?"

He didn't answer right away. She heard an exchange of words in the background.

"Scorched earth policy."

"Pardon?"

"I couldn't take the risk that I'd missed something vital. A written list of the sleepers in the government, something like that. The place had to burn. And...I'm sorry I didn't warn you. I didn't think you'd be returning to the camera for another look."

Was he stifling a laugh? The asshole.

"I'm furious! Don't do something like that ever again, do you promise?"

"You know I can't promise. But I'll do my best." He stopped to say something to one of the people he was with. Then, back to her, he said. "I'll call you when we get to Estonia. Hopefully before the end of the day. Please keep digging, though. I know you can find the proof. The *goszakaz* will be the clincher."

Irina knew why without him having to say it. An official, government-issued order directly tied to the murder of the border guard was clutch. It would not only destroy the triumvirate; it would also be a bloody nose to the regime, even if it *was* rogue elements within it behind Severnaya Volna.

Call ended, she rubbed her eyes with the heels of her hands and took a sip of tepid water from a glass. A glance at the camera feed—dead.

Keep digging, he says. Her brain was fried, and her fingers ached from typing. She was sick of digging.

Fletcher had been on the phone three minutes ago, asking precisely the same thing. The president was growing impatient. She'd been expecting Yakov to perform magic and have all the answers already. Naïve woman.

Fletcher told Irina the full complement of Skia's IT staff was now focused on the case, but no one was getting anywhere. She needed to step up.

She told him the answer probably lay in one of the Russian-language folders, in a Russian-language file. And if anyone was going to crack it, it would be her.

Clicking on yet another folder, number 226 from the top, simply named *Procheye A*, or Miscellaneous A, she stared intently at the monitor.

What kind of bullshit is this?

She edged closer to make sure she wasn't hallucinating.

A box came up: *Vvedite parol'*. Enter password.

She put her head in her hands. This couldn't be happening. None of the other folders she'd checked and scanned had this secondary layer of protection. She nodded to herself, grasping the reality: The other folders contained dross; this one was the nugget.

There was every chance Skia lab staff had confronted the same folder and were wrestling to crack it open. There was a secure chat group open on a Skia version of Zoom, but no one was talking. They all must be heads down, butts up, no time for conversation.

She called Maria, ordered more coffee and egg tarts, cracked her knuckles, and set to it.

She opened an AI program she'd written herself. She'd happily shared it with the other agents, but so far, her coded magic had failed to provide anyone with the answer. Repeating the folk definition of insanity falsely attributed to Albert Einstein —doing the same thing over and over and expecting a different result—she re-ran the program. She fed in every single scrap of information gathered on Ivan Beglov, his colleagues, Semak, Kolodin and Izmailov, their connections, their favorite colors and zodiac signs, everything bar the kitchen sink.

The program ran for two minutes, coughed, spluttered, came up empty.

Maria brought the refreshments, bowed, and was gone like mist.

Irina exhaled sharply and pushed her chair back, letting it roll until it banged into the whiteboard behind her. She stared at the stucco ceiling, as if the answer might be hiding in its textured surface. There had to be a logic to this nonsense. From what she could gather, Vanya wasn't a random guy. He was messy and disorganized in his own space, but according to the profile, at the same time meticulous and a perfectionist. He was a predictable producer of quality work within the universe of his own strange rules. People like that don't choose secondary passwords on a whim.

She sat up straight again, turned her neck from side to side, took a sip of overly sweet coffee, and, for want of a better idea, typed in another Kino song title.

Nothing.

She cycled through the entire discography, growing more irritated with each rejection. When she hit *Zvezda po imeni solntse*, "A Star Called the Sun," her breath hitched for a moment. One of Viktor Tsoi's masterpieces and definitely the kind of heroic-romantic choice a Russian geek might choose.

Denied.

She tried more of their big hits: *Kukushka*, "The Cuckoo," *Mama Anarkhiya*, "Mother Anarchy," and *Videli Noch*, "We Saw the Night," each time the archive throwing up the same rectangular box, not caring a damn for her mounting frustration.

She paused at *Zakroi za mnoi dver'*, "Close the Door Behind Me," tapping the enter key with a flicker of hope. The archivist part of her brain whispered that the song title itself was a command. A door shutting or a message encoded. Something so obviously the opposite of open that it could mean, paradoxically, open.

It didn't.

She tried variations—just the first word, just the last, transliterations, Latin and Cyrillic scripts, numbers assigned to letters.

None worked. She leaned forward, rubbing her forehead. She needed help from the men who'd created the Enigma machine; sadly, they were all long dead.

"*Idiotka*," she muttered at herself. "Thinking like a fan-girl, not a decoder."

She stood abruptly and paced the length of the room. Yakov's voice echoed in her mind again—*Keep digging. Dig any more and I'll pop out in China*.

She mentally chastised herself: Yakov was out there in the freezing cold, on the run and risking his life. Meanwhile, Maria was delivering her whatever she wanted, whenever she wanted, *and* she was working in her pajamas. All the same, she was drowning in digital quicksand with no one tossing her a rope.

Her thoughts turned to Vanya, his last moments before he ended it all. The note he'd sent Marfa.

The email!

She'd been too caught up in the existing files that she'd neglected to treat his farewell note—containing the very key to get into the archive—like a piece of the puzzle.

Could it be? No...no chance.

She entered the original key and waited breathlessly.

Denied again.

Then another lightbulb.

She hadn't run the full text of the email through her AI parser program.

Irina quickly found the forwarded message, copied the text, and pasted it into the program. She hit Enter.

The screen flickered for a moment as the program worked in the background. Lines of analysis scrolled.

Then, ten seconds later, it stopped dead.

A single result appeared on the screen: *ЗЗМДЯУ*.

Irina frowned, yet something familiar was contained in those apparently random letters. "What the hell..."

She compared the extracted letters to the content of the email.

And there they were, contained in the original key, separated by numbers and other characters.

She looked again, brain buzzing. She said the names of the letters aloud phonetically in Russian.

“Ze... ze... em... de... ya...oo.”

Zakroi za mnoi dver', ya ukhozhu. “Close the Door Behind Me, I’m Leaving.”

She gave herself a mental head slap. She’d almost gotten it right, even without the AI program but had forgotten the full name of the song. Forgotten that most people left off the last bit. Not considered that Vanya would choose the *long version*, the one that spelled out his own departure from the world. *I’m leaving.*

He had hidden the password in plain sight—the first letters of each word, disguised as nonsense.

Hands shaking, she returned to the archive and typed the Cyrillic letters: *ЗЗМДЯУ*

The loading spinner appeared, an invention surely designed to torment the impatient. Five seconds. Seven. Nine. *Come on.*

The folder opened.

Rows of subfolders appeared like dominoes falling. She panicked for a moment, clicked the first, half expecting another roadblock. It opened right away. All of them did.

Vanya had named everything logically in this folder. *My meetings with Izmailov at the dacha—videos*; *My meetings with Izmailov at the jewelry shop—videos*; *Payments made to me by Izmailov—PDFs*; *Emails and text messages between me and Izmailov.*

She randomly clicked files; they all opened obediently and without fuss. She watched a couple of videos, the vision sparkling clear and the sound captured perfectly. In one clip, recorded in what appeared to be the jewelry store’s workshop, Izmailov was mildly drunk. The Dagestani billionaire was blathering on about his wife who didn’t understand him. As she was about to click out of the clip and try another, the footage jumped. Izmailov was a lot more inebriated now, slurring his words but making plenty of sense.

The conversation had shifted.

He was talking about Kolodin sending a man to Tallin, to interfere in the Estonians' border surveillance software. Vanya appeared frightened but was smart enough—*clever man*—to pour another drink for his odious guest. *In vino veritas.*

Vanya egged him on to spill more. And so Izmailov did.

Irina turned up the volume. As the two men interacted, she felt like they were fictional characters, that she was watching an old spy movie.

Izmailov: Kolodin, the old dog. He's ordered an army unit to stage a dummy invasion. Can you believe it?

Vanya: No way!

Izmailov: Well, a dummy *preparation* for an invasion. Enough for the Estonians to get in a flap.

Vanya: You're kidding!

Izmailov: No. And there's going to be another one soon. A real one, with a (he burst out laughing) full-blown coup d'état to follow on its heels. Then Kolodin will pull back his renegade forces.

Vanya: Putin will demand his head on a platter.

Izmailov: (shakes his head) No. He'll give Kolodin a fucking medal. Maybe raise a statue to him.

Vanya: Sounds like bullshit to me.

Izmailov: It's true. Semak's financing it, through his EU contact in (a pause to hiccup and take another drink) Belgium. I'm putting some of BaltEnergoTorg's cash towards it, too. (He touched the side of his nose and smiled.) Off-shore channels and all that.

Vanya: Kolodin will never get away with it, you know. NATO will—

Izmailov: Fuck NATO! They'll do nothing. And you (he stood up, staggered, helped himself to another drink), little gay man, will do nothing about it either. (He pointed a finger.) Or... you...die.

Irina looked at the time counter. The video ran for twenty more minutes. As much as she'd love to watch it all now, she had to alert Skia. Let Fletcher and the president decide the next steps. It was time to send them the secondary key and the location of Vanya's holy grail.

Fingers a blur of motion, she composed a brief email to Fletcher, CC'd it to the head of the IT lab, and tapped SEND. She leaned back in her chair and let out a loud exhale.

With Skia alerted, she could trawl through the files at her leisure.

Another folder caught her eye. Unambiguously called *Names and contact details of sleepers*. Respect for the people on that list prevented her from even opening the files. Fletcher wouldn't show the same respect, but she prayed he'd treat the information confidentially.

Irina changed her mind. She was totally done with this task.

She sagged forward, forehead resting lightly against the heel of her palm. The relief of accomplishment made her slightly dizzy. She reached toward the monitor like she needed to touch the screen to believe it.

She'd found it. Everything Yakov needed. Everything President McIvor needed to end Severnaya Volna. Everything Izmailov and his asshole colleagues feared.

"Spasibo, Vanya," she whispered to the dead man she'd never met.

A notification appeared on her side monitor: *New message from Grant Fletcher.* She didn't open it. Something else took priority.

She needed to give Yakov something.

Good news.

She sent a simple four-word text message. *Archive cracked. Fletcher notified.*

She went to shut down her machine, eager to take a nap and

maybe a stroll around the olive groves, when her phone chirped. Fletcher. She capitulated.

"You received my email?" she said.

"Yes, Irene." He called her by the anglicized version of her name, the one on her American passport. For nearly a minute he thanked her effusively, like she'd just offered to donate a kidney to save his daughter's life.

"Glad to help."

"We need more."

Her gut churned. "It's not enough? Come on, Grant!"

"It...could be. But I've just spoken with the president. She wants the gos-thingy."

Irina rubbed her brow. *This cannot be happening*. "*Goszakaz*. Government order."

"Yeah, that. And Jacob agrees with her. I've just been on the phone to him. We can really pile the pressure on the Russians if we can demonstrate that those damn train tickets were ordered by one of our three amigos, or even a department related to them. I'm giving you two hours."

"Two hours? Even in the movies it's a minimum twenty-four!"

"I know, I know." He paused, and it sounded like he drew on one of his favorite contraband Cuban cigars. "Look, the IT boys and girls this end have begun compiling the material from the folder you cracked into something digestible for the media. McIvor will push ahead with an announcement in two hours, whether you find that government order or not. But she really wants it to...be the...what's that French expression?"

"Coup de grâce?"

"Yeah, that's it." Another deep inhalation of smoke. "But just between you and me, you do this for me, and I will push as hard as I can for Jacob's release from Article 7 of his contract."

Irina blinked. She had one idea how to pursue this. One. And it wasn't even a good one. But for Jacob to be given his freedom from this life, even a shit idea was worth a try.

THIRTY-ONE

"THE LITTLE PRICK OF A JEWELER PLAYED YOU FOR A fool, Marat Ibragimovich," said Colonel-General Kolodin, regally occupying an armchair in the luxurious office of Deputy Governor of the Leningrad Oblast Sergei Semak.

Izmailov held up a decanter and raised his eyebrows at Semak, seeking permission to pour.

"Go ahead, Marat," said Semak. "Everyone's a little on edge. We could all do with a drink right now."

"We need to stay calm, keep perspective. We've got time to make things right," said Izmailov, peeling back his thin lips in a sneering grin. Despite his words, calm was the last word he'd use to describe his own state. He poured a generous measure of scotch into three cut crystal glasses, put them on a silver tray, and wiped his hands on a small towel.

"What time!" roared Kolodin. "Beglov had kompromat on us —*you in particular*—coming out of his ass. We need to crush them and pray, pray fucking hard, that he was bluffing."

Izmailov extended the tray toward Kolodin as a peace offering. He regretted it instantly as the old general took a swipe and sent all three glasses flying, some of the contents splashing on Izmailov's up-to-now immaculate trousers.

"What the hell!" exclaimed Izmailov, grabbing the towel and rubbing his legs. "Have you lost your mind?"

"No. Just my temper." He leaned back in the chair, the challenging look on his craggy face not softening. "You can afford the dry cleaning, so don't be a crybaby."

Semak stood from behind his massive eight-by-four-foot walnut desk and made a calming gesture. "Gentleman. Let's think this through logically."

"That's right," said Izmailov.

Semak sat, reached for his desk phone, and punched in a number. "I'm calling that Saburenkov buffoon. He was supposed to be meeting with the Estonian this morning." He pressed a button, and the dial tone boomed in the office. A man answered on the fourth ring. "Sergei Semyonovich! What a surprise. To what do I owe the pleasure?"

"A quick word. I've got an appointment scheduled with an Estonian envoy called Robert Tamm, organized by that delightful reporter, Marfa Petko. I wanted to clarify something, but no one's been answering my calls. According to Marfa, you were supposed to meet Tamm today. How did he seem to you?"

"He seemed invisible, Sergei Semyonovich. Stood me up like an ugly date. I've tried calling Slava Gabulov to see if he knew anything. Still sick, I guess. Also not answering. To tell you the truth, this wall of silence is worrying me."

"Hmmm," said Semak noncommittally. "I'm sure there's a genuine reason. Thanks anyway."

Calls to the Pribaltiyskaya and the Estonian embassy also came up empty. Semak contacted an underground casino operator with circumspect employees, and for the promise of a possible license to open a new venue got eyeballs on the hotel, the embassy, and Petko's apartment.

"They're obviously at the dacha," said Kolodin. "With all due respect, you're wasting your time with this surveillance."

The oligarch's phone rang. One of his security detail he'd

dispatched to the dacha twenty minutes ago. "My man," he said, pointing at his cell on the table before scooping it up.

"Loudspeaker, please, Marat," said Semak.

Izmailov rolled his eyes, answered the call, and pressed the loudspeaker button. "Yes, Kirill?"

An eager voice on the other end brought news.

"The dacha's on fire, Marat Ibragimovich."

The three men exchanged looks of alarm.

"What? How bad?" said Izmailov.

"Real fucking bad. Massive flames. I've never seen anything like it."

"Could they be inside?" said Semak in a hopeful tone.

"No way," said Kolodin. "They're too smart; they're destroying anything we could scrounge from the joint."

Izmailov rubbed his forehead like he was trying to remove a stain.

"We couldn't get near it; you can feel the heat from the end of the driveway," said the subordinate. "I can hear sirens in the distance. We shouldn't be hanging around."

"Head for Sosnovy Bor. We need to get a fix on them," chimed in Kolodin, addressing the man like he was his own employee. "They're probably heading for the Estonian border."

"Already going that way. We figured that would be their next move."

"That guy sounds like a massive improvement on those other clowns who got themselves killed," whispered Kolodin, drawing a wince from Izmailov.

"Wait a second," came Kirill's echoey voice.

"What?" said Izmailov.

"I think I can see them, three hundred meters ahead, making a left turn at a big shopping complex...Can you see the name of it, Ilya?"

"Lenta hypermarket."

"I know it," said Kolodin. "Five or so kilometers from Sosnovy Bor."

"You sure it's them?" said Izmailov. "We can't have you going on a wild-goose chase."

"It looks like a government BMW, 7 series. Ilya's looking through the binoculars. Just a second."

The three men said nothing. Semak remained in his seat, Kolodin made a face of displeasure, and Izmailov paced like a caged tiger.

"It's got MVD plates on it now, old ones that were retired a couple years ago. So yeah, I'm confident."

"Read me the plates!" hollered Kolodin, cell in his hand. As Kirill recited the number, the general tapped the information into his phone.

"That vehicle's faster than the one we're in," said Kirill. "I can't promise that—"

"Doesn't matter. A unit in Sosnovy Bor will launch drones within minutes. But keep after them."

"Thanks, Kirill," said Izmailov and disconnected the call.

"What's the point of observing them with drones?" said Semak. "At some point we're going to have to intercept them."

Kolodin smiled the way crazed killers do before they pull the trigger. "These aren't for observation. These are military drones that fire missiles. The enemy can be tracked and exterminated in under thirty minutes."

"Beglov told me the ministry cars are armored," countered Izmailov.

"So are tanks. But these drones turn them into scrap metal." He held up a hand. "Vote, please, gentlemen."

Semak nodded. Izmailov shook his head slowly but changed it to a slow, unconvincing nod.

"What if my men could catch them alive, would either of you agree to that?" said Izmailov. "The Estonian could be carrying information useful to us." He knew he only needed one of them to agree for the proposal to be carried.

Both men shook their heads gravely. Kolodin glared at Izmailov and said, "I do wonder how you made so much money, *druzhok*. If this little group of amateur sleuths had anything, they would have already passed it up the chain. And if I'm wrong"—he held his arms out to the side—"then finishing them off is our only possible option."

"I hate to admit it, but Denis is right." Semak gave a half smile. "I'm an expert in plausible deniability. If any sordid details come to light, there are a million ways to make the world believe it's bullshit."

Izmailov sighed. Sweat pooling under his shirt, he drained another scotch as Kolodin called his private unit. Outvoted, he could only hope Kolodin was right and Vanya Beglov had been bluffing.

THIRTY-TWO

DIMA UNDERSTOOD THE NEED TO CHANGE DIRECTION without being told. A left before a sprawling hypermarket took them away from the traffic moving toward Sosnovy Bor.

"GPS tells me I can drive in a U-shape around this settlement before we rejoin the highway," he said.

"Perfect," said Jacob, not really knowing if it was perfect or not but trusting the technology.

"Any objections if I smoke?" said Dima, the cigarette already in his mouth, lighter ready to spark.

"Only if you don't share with me. I'm fresh out," said Marfa.

With the two of them smoking sullenly, small cracks in the windows sucking out enough air that Jacob didn't asphyxiate, he mulled over his recent brief chat with Fletcher. The chief's agreement to talk to the president about granting asylum to the two remaining B+ members had filled him with a sense of purpose. With two tragically dead, it was paramount that Dima and Marfa got out of this not just alive but with a future.

Jacob, the barrel of the SMG pointed downward in the footwell beside him, kept half an eye on the side mirror. Every building, every tree line, every road sign felt like a potential threat. He hadn't said anything to the others yet, but a dark-blue sedan had been driving behind them for a couple of minutes. It hung back a hundred meters or so, but Jacob's instincts told him the car wasn't following them by sheer coincidence. This seemed a low-traffic road; so far they'd encountered no vehicles coming from the opposite direction, and from what he could see in the mirror, there was nothing behind the Lada.

Dima must have sensed Jacob looking in the side mirror; his eyes flicked to the rearview, cigarette twitching between his lips.

"What do you make of that, Robert?" he murmured.

Jacob nodded. "That Lada's giving me heartburn. Speed up a little."

The engine growled as Dima edged them faster. "He seems to be matching us."

Marfa twisted around in her seat. "I can see two guys. The passenger's on his phone. Got his head lowered."

"Of course he has," Jacob said. "That kind of body language screams tail." Out of the side of his mouth, he said to Dima, "Take it up to one ten."

"Limit's 90 kph here."

"You're worried about a speeding ticket at this point? There's no GAI in sight. Go!"

The BMW's engine uttered a lower note as Dima stepped on the gas.

"They're exactly the same distance behind us as before," said Marfa.

"Okay," Dima muttered, "that's official confirmation that they're bad guys."

They sped toward the end of a residential block, a line of brutal thirteen-story concrete slabs. Dense forest pressed in on the lefthand side. Ahead was a sweeping bend around more monolithic blue-and-gray apartment buildings. "This way will bring us back onto Leningradskaya Street," said Dima. "Links up with the highway toward the border at Ivangorod. I'll shake them along the way."

Then Jacob heard a stomach-churning sound: a faint buzzing that quickly rose in volume, like an angry wasp.

Dima heard it next. "What the hell is that noise? A helicopter?"

Marfa gripped the sides of the console, leaning her head toward the windshield. "Where is it?"

"Behind us, hovering over the Lada," Jacob said sharply. "But it's not a chopper. It's a drone."

The small shape came into focus in Jacob's mirror. Two feet across, maybe slightly more. Four rotors, rounded nose. Definitely no toy, this was a sophisticated machine the experts would term military-adjacent. Jacob had made a habit of devouring information on Russian military hardware. Drones, in particular, had become a recent interest. From this distance, he clocked this one as a Zala, likely a 421 series. No way to tell the specific model, but he didn't need to. All he needed to know was that it was a strike-capable surveillance drone and that it posed an immediate existential threat.

"*Blyad'*. Fuck," Marfa breathed. "We're doomed." She started waving her arms around, muttering incoherently. "Why did I trust you, you Estonian idiot!"

"Shut up!" roared Jacob, stifling the urge to deliver a slap. "Hysterics don't help. Let Dima concentrate."

His words had the desired effect. She curled up sideways on the back seat, hands over her eyes, sobbing quietly.

The drone swooped lower, trailing by a few meters at just above car height, matching their speed with unnerving precision. Jacob felt the first ripple of cold in his stomach.

"It's painting us," he said.

"What the fuck does that mean?" Dima replied, jaw tight. "Speak normal Russian."

"It means it's targeting us with radar. So floor the fucking gas; try to weave, but don't put us in a spin. Can you manage that? Oh, and pray."

Dima swore under his breath, questioning the legitimacy of

Jacob's parentage. The car zoomed ahead, gently veering left and right by fractions of degrees. He added, "*Polny pizdets.* What a fuck-up."

The much-less-powerful Lada pursued doggedly, the driver throwing caution to the wind on the icy road. He kept closing the distance, the drone now back atop the Lada, sticking above it like a devil's halo.

"I've got a better idea," Dima said. "I see a gap in the trees. A track. We have to take it." He braked suddenly before jerking the steering wheel left.

The BMW spun a perfect 360 degrees, stopping on the road's gravel shoulder and facing into the dark forest. Jacob gritted his teeth and braced in his seat, waiting for the drone to fire. Marfa let out a wail. Dima exhaled like he'd been punched in the stomach.

Jacob stared out his window, desperate to locate the twin trackers. The Lada and the drone had come to a standstill, the driver and the drone momentarily stunned by Dima's audacious maneuver.

Dima grunted, squared his shoulders, and pressed on the accelerator. The BMW shot toward the forest line, tires spitting gravel as it plowed over the rough shoulder. The drone and the Lada followed.

"Nice try," said Jacob. "They're still coming, but we've got better odds in the woods." *Who was he kidding?*

"For fuck's sake," muttered Dima, glaring at the rearview mirror like it was an ally of the hunters.

"What?" said Jacob, unable to see anything in the side mirror. Out the window, there was nothing but a wall of tree trunks and snow.

Then he heard it.

Another drone but emitting a higher pitch.

A part of the second drone appeared squarely in the middle of his mirror. He recognized the outline. An autonomous FPV. Although a kamikaze, he almost felt a sense of reassurance. This model looked relatively small compared to others of its ilk—with a modest payload—meaning the armored BMW stood a chance of surviving if it was hit. And so did its human cargo. A slim chance but still a chance.

"Do something!" cried Marfa, sitting up and looking out the back window. "It's almost upon us. Can't we use our weapons?"

Oh sweet, naïve Marfa.

"No. We stop for one second and we're all dead. These things are brutal. Just stay down."

She quickly assumed her previous position as the buzzing of the new drone rose to an almost deafening level.

For some inexplicable reason, the forest path opened up, now several meters wide. Jacob soon saw why: it was a rest stop. A couple of massive snowplows stood idle about seventy meters ahead. The machines loomed nearly ten feet high, industrial-orange monsters of flaking steel hulking against the dark forest interior.

"Get between them," barked Jacob. "If we scramble, we can jump out and crawl under."

"Like a bomb shelter?"

"Something like that."

Nothing like that.

Dima gunned the motor, the vehicle fishtailing before straightening. The BMW slid between the two snowplows, the gap just wide enough, metal scraping metal as they squeezed in.

Jacob held his breath.

Shit.

He'd miscalculated—there was no way to open the doors. They were trapped. The first drone had made its way to the other side of the snowplows. Both drones and the Lada now hemmed them in on both sides. It was just a matter of seconds.

Through the windshield, a dangling tangle of pipes and hoses obscured the first drone, almost blocking its view of the BMW. The buzzing Zala was struggling to make sense of the situation.

Good.

Behind them, the evil-looking quadcopter's whining dropped, then rose again.

Bad.

Jacob twisted and saw a tiny red dot of light pivoting in midair. "Jesus Christ. It's locking on." He began to recite the Lord's prayer in his mind.

"Everybody down," Dima whispered, head ducking under the steering wheel.

With inevitable death staring him in the face, Jacob would not look away.

He stared at the red light.

The drone dipped, then turned around and began moving away.

What the hell?

Jacob squinted as the drone approached the Lada, an ear-splitting noise rending the air as the FPV slammed into the sedan. A true kamikaze.

A dull boom rang out before orange flames engulfed the car.

Jacob shook his head: How wrong he'd been about the payload being modest.

Dima and Marfa jolted upright, turning to look behind them.

"Stay down!" said Jacob. "We've still got the first one staring at us."

They obeyed without question.

He narrowed his eyes and studied the scene on the other side of the windshield. The Zala seemed to have frozen like a deer in the headlights. An inner voice told him he could take it out.

He pressed the button to lower the window.

From his bracing position, Dima said, "What are you doing?"

"Shhh."

Jacob wedged the Vityaz against his shoulder and twisted sideways in the cramped gap between the BMW and the snowplow's steel flank. He wriggled his butt in the seat and leaned out just far enough to sight a piece of the Zala three meters in front of him.

He took a deep breath and squeezed off a short burst; the dying drone pinwheeled into the trunk of a birch tree.

Dima raised his head, grabbing the steering wheel like it was a life buoy. "How the hell did you even hit that? And why did the other one fire on the Lada?"

Jacob shrugged. "A glitch, bad firmware, operator error on the other end. These things happen more often than you'd imagine."

"I'm just glad it happened now."

Marfa's head popped up, face streaked with tears. "Are we safe?"

"No," said Jacob. "Far from it. We've got to get out of here. They'll know this attempt failed; they won't waste time launching another."

"Where to?" said Marfa.

"Estonia. That part hasn't changed. But we've got to ditch this BMW."

Jacob ordered Dima to take the fastest route back to the hypermarket, where there'd be an assortment of vehicles to choose from in the parking lot.

"On it."

THIRTY-THREE

Colonel-General Denis Kolodin preferred his own company to that of others. His advanced years meant that a lot of his peers, men he'd once enjoyed shooting the breeze with, discussing the issues of the day, playing chess, were dead or infirm. Some were still alive and able to socialize at an acceptable level, but they were stuck in the past, yearning for the Soviet Union to return.

Kolodin knew that was never going to happen. Never should happen. The model was flawed in so many ways it would take three sets of encyclopedias to document all the problems properly.

No, a new way forward was necessary. He would never admit it to anyone in this country, but the little Austrian corporal who'd led Germany had the right idea. Even the horrid Chinese today had a good game plan. Rule by a benevolent yet strict authoritarian one-party state while retaining private ownership, flourishing corporations, the Orthodox church—things the people wanted and needed. Kolodin didn't hold with the racial supremacy nonsense, of course. Despite him sometimes making silly mistakes, the Dagestani was a valuable ally in many ways.

Likewise Semak, a man of Jewish background who'd changed

his surname from Semach to make it Slavic. A brilliant organizer and a smart man, rightfully the one to head Severnaya Volna. If only nominally.

Kolodin was the true leader. Izmailov and Semak must know that in their hearts. And that's why, with the cards falling the wrong way, he now had to act unilaterally. Tamm, Petko, and their boneheaded driver would soon be wiped off the face of the earth. His units in Sosnovy Bor had more than enough strike power to destroy them. It was just a matter of time. And if Izmailov's worst fears came true, then Semak was right. They were experts in denying facts—they'd all been doing it their whole lives.

But now that the remaining B+ scumbags had somehow survived the drone attack and escaped, shown they were adversaries tougher than appearances would suggest, it was time to take the next, logical step.

Sitting in the priceless hundred-year-old carved chair his father had passed on to him, Kolodin pressed the button on his old-fashioned house phone. He waited for his subordinate in Ivangorod, Colonel Martyn Ashomka, to answer.

"Colonel-General? I haven't heard from you in a couple of days. Must be important."

"It is."

"Care to elaborate, sir?" Curiosity raised the tone of the commander's voice.

"You will initiate the land operation at first light."

"Excuse me, sir?" Incredulity instantly replaced curiosity.

"Circumstances this end necessitate an expeditious operation." He gave a wheeze. "In other words, no messing around." He paused to let the information sink in. "No wavering, no gung-ho improvisation. Everything hinges on sticking to the plan."

"Understood," said Ashomka with barely disguised enthusiasm. "I've been waiting for this moment."

"Excellent. I knew you'd stay strong. Listen up. Your group of special assault units will cross the line at precisely 0500 hours."

"Yes, Colonel-General."

"Narva must be secured within the hour," Kolodin pressed on. "Should be a smooth process. The majority of the locals will be on our side. But I don't want any drama: no displays of flags or banners, no soldiers behaving like they've just liberated Berlin."

"Sir. Discipline in the ranks is beyond question."

"Well done, Ashomka." Another wheeze rattled his old lungs. "Order of seizure: administrative buildings, police offices, railway. Secure all roads in and out. Any resisters are to be arrested immediately and locked up. No excesses, got it?"

"Absolutely. I'll put all the unit leaders on standby, inform them of your orders."

Ashomka was the perfect man for this role. Kolodin would make sure he was richly rewarded.

"I'll make a follow-up call at 0400 hours," Kolodin said. "A word of caution, Martyn. There will be strong reactions to our operation from all over the world. Be prepared for them."

"I will be, sir. You can count on it."

Kolodin dialed the next number, written in his private notebook in his assured, cursive style. It rang twice before a voice answered.

"Sir," said Colonel Viktor Andrejev, commander of the Estonian First Infantry Brigade. "Good to hear from you."

"I hope you mean that, Viktor," said Kolodin. "Once you hear me out, you might change your mind."

"I doubt that very much."

Kolodin had met the polite and businesslike Andrejev twice and held him in high esteem. He was an ethnic Russian who had to tread a very fine line professionally. Not everyone in the Estonian armed forces was welcoming of Russians in their ranks. Six years ago, one Russian officer had been arrested, tried, and sentenced to fifteen years prison for treason. Andrejev had so far kept his nose immaculately clean.

"At some point tomorrow morning, you will receive urgent NATO directives. You must ignore them. Your brigade is to remain idle. No one is to leave barracks until further notice."

"Yes, Colonel-General."

"Immediately after this call, you will deliver instructions to our mole in border surveillance, Major Robin Saar. Tell him that all systems must be taken offline at 0455 hours."

"Yes, sir."

Only one more call to make.

The First Vice President of Estonia answered with breathless excitement. "Colonel-General?"

"Tomorrow," Kolodin said, "you will assume authority under the continuity provisions. My people will drive you from your apartment directly to the parliament. Do not lose your composure. The transition of power must look...normal."

"Yes, of course. And the president—?"

"Fuck the president," Kolodin said. "You focus on your job. Don't concern yourself with anything else."

"Yes, Colonel-General. I'm ready."

Kolodin hung up and felt the silence spread through the old apartment on Liteyny Prospekt, restored to its original late-nineteenth-century luxurious grandeur with a little financial help from Izmailov.

He crossed to the sideboard and twisted the cap off a bottle of wheat vodka. He poured a single measure into a shot glass and tossed the firewater down his throat.

He climbed the stairs to the second floor, knees creaking almost as much as the old floorboards, and eased open the bedroom door. Anna, his loyal and loving wife of forty-five years, lay on her side, breathing softly, her matronly mane of gray hair spread across the pillow.

He leaned over and kissed her cool forehead. Her afternoon naps had become a daily habit, her ovarian cancer in remission. He looked at her pallid face and wondered if she might be heading for a relapse.

Kolodin stepped back, closed the door, and sat on his side of the bed, elbows on knees. He was too old to be embarking on this adventure, but if not him, then who?

The pieces were now in motion. By first light, the border would be unprotected, his units on the march, the Estonian parliament within his grasp. The NATO response would come too late, if it came at all.

He lay back, hands folded over his bony chest, rheumy eyes closing. He dozed for an hour before returning to his office.

He read over the notes he'd taken at every strategy meeting with Semak and Izmailov. They'd thought of most things, but with an operation like this, there would always be unknowns.

The invasion would go smoothly.

It was what would happen in the Kremlin in the immediate aftermath that was the biggest unknown factor.

Once it sank in, Vladimir Vladimirovich Putin would understand and approve.

He had to.

THIRTY-FOUR

Robin Saar watched television with his wife, half-focused on the Danish crime series they both followed out of habit. The detective's exaggerated quirks irritated him, but Nora enjoyed it, and he pretended to as well. While she took a bathroom break, he sipped his tea, ate a square of chocolate, and scrolled through videos on his phone. A clip of a dog baffled by a simple magic trick made him laugh, but the moment ended when his new work phone vibrated. The secure line displayed an innocuous contact name, though he knew who the number really belonged to.

"This is Colonel Viktor Andrejev," the voice said when he answered.

Nora returned, eyebrows raised. Saar covered the phone and told her he needed to take the call in the kitchen. She nodded and turned her attention to a magazine.

"I'll get straight to it, Major," Andrejev said. "Kolodin has confirmed it. The raid begins tomorrow before dawn. Your role is critical."

Saar's pulse climbed. Until this moment, the operation had felt abstract, a plan other people discussed while he executed small supporting tasks. Now the weight of it settled on him. "Understood. What do you need from me?"

"At zero four fifty-five, you will shut down the entire border surveillance grid. Cameras, towers, sensors—everything. Then you will run the diagnostics script I'm sending in encrypted mail. It will appear to command as a scheduled reboot."

"We don't run scheduled reboots," Saar said.

"You do now. My email, copied to high command, will authorize trial maintenance cycles. No one will question it before the coup. Afterward, it will be rescinded." Andrejev's tone carried the confidence of a man who expected obedience. "Your timing must be exact. The crossing begins five minutes after you pull the plug."

Saar leaned against the counter and forced himself to breathe steadily. "I understand."

"You've proven your reliability already. Allowing that Russian technician into the facility was not easy, yet you and Vares made it work. And don't worry about Vares. He will be released and cleared once the new government takes over."

A faint warmth spread through Saar's chest. Approval from the commander of Estonia's First Infantry Brigade mattered more to him than he liked to admit. "I did only what the situation required."

"And you will be compensated accordingly. There will be a position for you at the embassy in Moscow, dealing with high-ranking circles. Your wife will enjoy the social life. Consider this a step into a wider world."

Saar closed his eyes for a moment and pictured Nora smiling among diplomatic guests, far from the drab border surveillance complex. "Thank you, Colonel."

"After you trigger the shutdown, remain out of sight unless contacted by me or our Russian colleagues," Andrejev said. "I will call again at zero four thirty. Be at your post."

The line cut before Saar could reply.

He stayed still with the phone pressed to his ear, as if waiting for the voice to return and confirm he had heard correctly. Finally he opened his alarm app and set it for two in the morning. When he returned to the living room, Nora had the remote poised.

"Everything all right?" she asked, touching his knee.

"Yes. I've been called in. Someone went home sick, so they need a replacement." The lie came easily, shaped by weeks of practice.

She frowned. "They've been leaning on you ever since that awful incident. You'd think they'd let someone else cover the shift."

"Normally they would," he said, already thinking about the incoming diagnostic script. "But there's a new protocol rolling out, and the juniors haven't caught up yet."

She sighed. "At least watch the rest of the episode with me."

He put his arm around her and nodded. "We can do that."

THE OPERATIONS ROOM FELT CLAUSTROPHOBIC. Saar had ironed his uniform as Andrejev suggested, though he had no idea who might see him. The parking lot outside lay silent, the snow reflecting the lights in harsh white. He placed his forehead against the cold glass and let the chill ground him.

Corporal Laanoja's death returned uninvited, as it often did. The kid had never expected a gunfight inside the facility. Saar still saw him on the floor, bleeding through his uniform, eyes wide with confusion. He told himself the death had been a tragic but necessary cost of the operation. The justification never fully settled, and the suspicion that Vares had fired more out of impulse than fear lingered like a stain he couldn't scrub away.

Vares sat in a cell somewhere, unaware of tomorrow's promises of exoneration. According to Andrejev, the coup would rewrite the nation's story and place the loyal in positions of influence. Saar wanted to believe that. He needed to believe it, though the conviction no longer felt as solid as it once had.

He returned to his desk. The testing script lay embedded where he had placed it, invisible unless someone knew exactly what to look for. Another piece of sabotage joined it—the remnants of the earlier Russian tampering, carried out by the hacker who had died before reaching Saint Petersburg. Saar had endured the interrogations that followed, relying on rehearsed lines and a steady tone. He had remained committed, and the cause had seemed clear. Tonight it felt less so.

Before five, the grid would go dark. NATO analysts would notice eventually, but by then, the teams would be across the border. Bureaucracy would slow any response. Meetings would form, committees would discuss, and the window would hold long enough.

He brewed strong coffee and stepped outside for a cigarette, the cold biting the exposed skin of his face. Sleep was no longer possible. He would stay awake, carry out the orders precisely, and vanish into the background until summoned.

A dull ache of guilt lived beside an emerging pride. Both felt undeserved, yet neither would leave him.

The clock on the wall continued its steady march toward morning.

THIRTY-FIVE

IT TOOK FIVE MINUTES OF FRANTIC DRIVING TO LOOP back to the Lenta hypermarket. All eyes in the BMW constantly checked the skies for more drones and the road behind them for another terrestrial tail. A crow flying close to the hood of the BMW caused all three of them to jump in their seats. Apart from that scare, they arrived at the hypermarket unscathed and unfollowed.

The parking lot was almost full, cars packed closely together and barely a spare spot. Jacob scanned as Dima cruised the lot.

"You know how to steal a car?" said Dima. "I'm only good with old ones, without all the fancy locks and alarms."

"Me too. But there's a much better way." Jacob's eyes lit up when he selected the mark. A late-model black Toyota RAV4 next to a shopping cart return bay. A man was loading boxes into the cargo section.

"Pull up next to that guy, Dima. I mean, right next to his ass. Quietly." He turned to Marfa. "When I say go, we all jump out. While I'm chatting to the man, Dima gets the two other guns out of the trunk. Marfa, you help him load the stuff we took from the dacha into the back of the Toyota."

"We're taking his car from him?" she said, incredulous.

"Yes," said Jacob. "And he's coming with us."

She pursed her lips and shook her head. "*Gospodi*. Jesus," she whispered.

Dima braked, the BMW pulling up to a silent stop two meters from the slightly built man in his mid-thirties.

"Go!"

Everyone leapt from the BMW. In five seconds Jacob had the barrel of the Vityaz pressing into the man's stomach. "Do exactly as I say and you won't get hurt."

The man's cheeks began to tremble. "Please, take my money. I've got a wife and—"

Jacob pushed the barrel harder. "And you will return to her, don't worry. We just need your car. Now get in the driver's seat, nice and slow."

Dima, instinctively knowing how this had to play out, had his weapon trained on the man, allowing Jacob to get into the rear seat behind the driver. As the man gingerly took hold of the grab rail and pulled himself in, Jacob heard his colleagues tossing their own gear in behind the man's shopping.

In less than thirty seconds, Dima was sitting next to the bewildered man, Marfa next to Jacob, arms folded and a scowl on her face.

The man sniffed back a tear. "I have to be home in an hour. It's my daughter's birthday. She's turning five."

Jacob shook his head. "Not sure you'll make it. But you'll have a helluva story to tell the family later." He tapped the man on the shoulder. "Give me your phone."

"What?"

"Please, don't make me shoot you. I won't hesitate. And I'll take your wallet, too, thanks."

The man reached into his pocket and handed over both items. Jacob removed the SIM from the phone, snapped it between his fingers, and tossed the pieces out the window. He read the man's plastic vehicle registration certificate, memorized every detail, returned it to the wallet, and handed it back.

"Thanks, Grigory. Now can you get us to Ivangorod in a hurry?"

"Why did you destroy my SIM card?"

Jacob sighed. "So we can't be followed. You can always get a new one. Now answer the question. Do you know the fastest way to get to Ivangorod?"

He nodded at the dash display. "No, but I've got GPS."

"Excellent. How's the fuel situation?"

"Three-quarters of a tank."

"Perfect. Let's get going, shall we?"

As they exited the parking lot, three drones flew overhead, making for the site of the abandoned BMW.

"Grigory," said Jacob "What ETA does the GPS give?"

"Checkered flag in one hour 58 minutes." The man offered a weak smile although he was clearly terrified.

Jacob patted Grigory on the shoulder. "I have no intention of hurting you, *druzhok*. Please try and relax. Put on your favorite music, set the heating to how you like it. We'll shut up and let you get on with it. Fair?"

A nod. "Absolutely."

Jacob blew out his cheeks, then sent an encrypted message to Fletcher on the satellite phone.

Escaped drone attack by skin of teeth. Three of us OK, but shaken, esp. Petko. Have hijacked black RAV4 tags B564KT 78, heading toward Ivangorod. 4 in car incl. volunteer driver. Please advise nearest coords for safe crossing with Estonian welcoming committee on other side. Do whatever necessary.

THE FOREST on either side of the RAV4 thickened as they continued driving through the rural winter landscape. The sun, behind thick clouds, sank toward the horizon.

Jacob's satphone buzzed.

Fletcher.

About time. He checked his watch. 18:39.

Jacob. Sorry for the delay, but your request needed time. We've found you a gap. It's dangerous but it's the best option you're going to get.

The best crossing point (agreed by SKIA + CIA + State Dept. analysts + Estonian authorities) is a narrow (≈ 200 m) frozen stretch across the Narva river. Drive north-west from Ivangorod to the village of Popovka. From there, proceed along Gospitalnaya Street until the road forks right at 59.40518, 28.18677. From there you are on foot. Use your compass to guide you through the forest until you reach coordinates: 59.41394, 28.15885. This is where you cross.

We have isolated two active FSB border units in this area. Patrols are known to use thermal imaging. Kolodin will also have deployed his own forces to intercept you.

I know this is superfluous, but I have to say it. Exercise the utmost caution. Once you get on the ice, walk as fast as you can, run if possible. And don't look back.

On the Estonian side you will meet Officer Taavi Kurm of the Estonian Police and Border Guard Office.

He'll have a two-man escort team and a warm vehicle staged two hundred meters from the river. They have been instructed to wait for you until dawn, however if you don't get stopped you should be across by 21:00 max.

Protocol once across:

— Marfa Petko and Dmitry Sechkin will be taken directly to Tallinn for processing and debrief.

— You do NOT go with them.

Kurm will hand you straight to a US liaison team.

They have a chartered flight wheels-up for New York waiting at Ämari Air Base.

Get across. Keep your head down.

Time now: 18:40.

You've got roughly 7 minutes before full dark.

Godspeed.

Grant.

The plan sounded about as risky as anything Jacob had done in his life. But kudos to Fletcher; he had done well to cobble the rescue package together at such short notice. A spark of hope was better than no hope.

One aspect of the plan needed addressing from this end. Crossing on foot meant the salvaged cargo would not be carried across. Unless...

"I've got a huge favor to ask, Grigory," said Jacob.

"Yes?" came the timid reply.

"That stuff we tossed in the back of the car."

"Yes?"

"I need you to take it somewhere for me."

"Oh, shit. I...don't know."

"Yes, you do know, Grigory." Jacob hated himself for the next part. He recited the man's address as displayed on the pink vehicle registration card. "I'd really hate for anything to happen to that daughter of yours." He sighed. "Only five, hey?"

Grigory's head shrank into his shoulders. "You wouldn't..."

"To sweeten the deal, I'll pay you...let's see." He checked his cash reserves. "Ten thousand euros. How does that sound?"

A rapid nod. "That sounds...generous."

"Not at all, Grigory."

At Jacob's request, Marfa called Detective Mladenov and told him to expect a call from a Grigory Shlyapkin who would be delivering a load of goodies to the lockup address. Mladenov was instructed to wait for a call from another person who would pick it all up and pay Mladenov a storage fee. Jacob had yet to figure out who that pick-up agent would be. Maybe one of the sleepers on Vanya's list or perhaps an embassy employee from Moscow would make the drive up and collect. Details.

As the last light of day faded into black, the BMW rolled past a line of grim Soviet-era apartment blocks on the outskirts of the border town, their concrete panels dimming to a pale washed-out gray. Ahead, Ivangorod fortress's ancient limestone walls loomed over the Narva River. The ironically named Friendship Bridge—the bridge to freedom they could not cross—lay a tantalizing 250 meters away. At Jacob's instruction, Grigory swung right onto Gagarin Street.

"My heart is about to give out," said Marfa. "This place is crawling with FSB and soldiers, I can feel it."

"Stay strong," said Dima. "A nice walk in the woods, over the river, and we'll be safe."

"I need a cigarette."

Jacob leaned forward. "Can she smoke in your car, Grigory?"

"I'd prefer not. My wife will kill me."

"You heard the man. Put them away. You can have one once we're over the river."

Twelve minutes later, after a sedate drive through the middle of the tiny hamlet of Popovka, they had reached the fork in the road where it was time to get out and hoof it.

Jacob had one last word to Grigory. "Don't lose that gear. Remember what will happen if you do?"

"I remember."

He tapped twice on the roof of the RAV4. "Wish your kid a happy birthday from me."

They stared into the void, their breathing the only sound. No moon or stars on this overcast night. Cell phone flashlights lit up small circles of snow in front of them.

"It's 1.9 kilometers to the crossing," said Jacob. "Easy, as long as we concentrate on where we put our feet. Should take thirty minutes or so."

"Next time, remind me to wear proper hiking boots," said Marfa.

"I'll try and remember." He held the flashlight under his chin. "Keep talking to a minimum and avoid stepping on branches."

"Branches? They're all buried under a mile of fucking snow," said Marfa. "We will be too if we don't get a move on."

She was right. Light snow had begun to fall.

"OK. Let's go."

Jacob took the lead, following the GPS on the screen while the LED lit up the path at his feet. Marfa walked a meter behind him while Dima took the rear guard.

Going was tough and slow, the snow thick and uneven on the logging track. Marfa stumbled a couple of times, Dima quick to extend a hand and hoist her up again. She swore softly at regular intervals but not as much as Jacob would have expected from the feisty woman.

They reached a bottleneck—a fallen log lay across the path, waist-high and too big to shift by hand, impossible to go around. Jacob turned and whispered, "I'll help you over, Marfa." She extended her right hand, and he took it. "Only another four hundred meters and we're there."

Once she was on the other side, he handed her the Vityaz and scrambled up and over.

Dima passed his gun to Jacob, then leapfrogged over the log. The trio resumed the trek—slow and steady.

Six minutes later, Jacob stopped and turned around. In a hushed voice, he said, "GPS says we're parallel with the crossing point." He consulted the glowing screen, pointed into a thicket of birch. "No more paths. We weave our way through that, then we're on the edge of the river. After that, 200 meters. Easy." He held the phone up, light shining on their tired faces, and said, "Are we ready?"

Dima nodded once. Marfa bent at the waist and sucked in three deep breaths. She stood up straight and declared, "I'm ready."

No sooner were the words out of her mouth than a deafening crack echoed in the darkness, splinters flying off a tree branch.

"*Stoi! Kto idyot?* Stop! Who goes there?" commanded a deep male voice.

Jacob felt his heart climb into his throat, neck veins throbbing fit to burst.

Two bulky men stepped out from behind the trees. Their outlines were mostly swallowed by the darkness, but the faint green gleam of their night-vision scopes pulsed softly with each step closer. Five paces away, the guards halted, their silhouettes resolving. Heavy winter jackets, fur-rimmed hoods, rifles held low. Both men were baby-faced, barely in their twenties. Jacob squinted through the dark. Real FSB border guards—had to be. If they were Kolodin's men, the three of them would already be sprawled in the snow.

"Who goes there, I said, fuck your mother!" The man on the right shouldered his rifle, swinging it toward the weakest link. Marfa.

"My...dog...ran away and my...friends are...helping me...look for him," said Marfa, breathless with fear but still clever enough to improvise. "Are we somewhere we're not supposed to be?"

The second man, a lot taller and more solid, barked, "All of you. Hands in the air!"

Despite their words, Jacob's sixth sense detected a hesitancy in the tone, even in their stance. They didn't want this to escalate. They wanted these forest intruders to surrender like lambs.

But Jacob wasn't prepared to surrender.

He swung the Vityaz forward from where it had been hidden against his shoulder, the sling snapping free as he raised it. The tall guard dropped instantly. The short one managed half a turn as Jacob's bullet entered his chest, firing on reflex. His round caught Marfa high in the throat, just under the chin. She collapsed with a wet, choking gasp, blood gushing between her shaking fingers. Her eyes fluttered as the life force left her body.

Dima fell beside her, howling with anguish. Jacob somehow smothered his grief, grabbed Dima by the collar of his coat, and yanked him away from Marfa's still body.

"Come on! Run!"

"We can't leave her!" cried Dima. "She might be—"

"She's dead. Leave it. Other patrols will be here in minutes."

They ran blindly toward the river, crashing through the thicket, branches scratching their faces. Jacob's lungs burned as he sucked in the cold air. Their boots slipped on the frozen surface, but they kept their feet.

Jacob shed his weapon; it was only slowing him down. Dima dropped his, too. Speed was the only thing that mattered now.

With the image of Marfa's beautiful, dead face in his mind, Jacob ran like he had never run in his life.

Halfway across now, he saw a patch of light. Fifty meters to go, and it became clearer. Two cars in a parking lot. A man standing between them, waving his arms frantically.

Above them, but closer to the Russian side of the river, a helicopter hovered, beams of light sweeping left and right, garbled Russian coming through a loudspeaker. Angry, demanding words. Words into a vacuum.

Jacob blocked it all out, homing in on the man on the shore.

Dima never lost pace with him, and they scrambled up the embankment together, collapsing in a heap on icy asphalt.

THIRTY-SIX

Veteran Skia director Grant Fletcher had been hoping for an invitation to Washington to discuss what would happen next. He hadn't been to the Oval Office since the reign of the last president, Daniel Claxton, a man Fletcher had come to regard almost as a friend. McIvor was a shrewd operator—shrewder than her predecessor—able to formulate plans without the phalanx of advisors characteristic of so many past presidents.

"I can make the West 30th Street Heliport in under half an hour," he'd said, half joking, half serious. "Be in DC in ninety minutes if you send one of your HMX-1 choppers to fetch me."

"Sorry, Grant," she demurred. "If there was more time, then yes. But that's a luxury we don't have."

Instead, a hastily arranged video-link had been set up. At least it allowed Fletcher to attend in formal attire from the waist up only. Under the desk, he wore his favorite gray sweatpants.

"Your man, Hunter," said McIvor. "Wow."

Fletcher smiled. "That's a rather laconic description, Madam President."

"How many times have I told you, please call me Hannah."

He sucked air through his teeth. "Plenty. But it doesn't feel right."

"What if I said it was an order?"

"Then I'd have to reluctantly obey...Hannah."

"Just call me Madam President when there are other people around."

"Sounds like a fair compromise."

She flashed a toothy smile of almost regal benevolence. McIvor's thousand-watt smile had been a huge asset in her presidential campaign, appealing to the broadest range of demographics since polling began. "I've built a political career on the art of the compromise."

Someone out of camera shot handed her a piece of paper at the very moment an envelope icon flashed in the corner of Fletcher's screen.

"Fantastic. He's confirmed as onboard the charter flight." She put down the paper. "Hunter will arrive at Teterboro in about eight hours."

"Great news." He clicked the envelope. A message from Jacob confirmed the president's words. There was more in the email, but he'd wait till the president's call ended.

"Indeed." She cleared her throat. "I'd like to arrange a meeting with him in the next week. Once he's been debriefed by you and had time to rest."

In his lap and out of shot, Fletcher's fingers caressed a Cuban Montecristo No. 2 cigar. Outwardly he was circumspect; inside, he was jumping for joy. Jacob's escape was nothing short of miraculous. Once he'd finished talking with McIvor, he'd smoke the stogie and drink a Hennessy cognac to celebrate.

"I'd like to meet your other agent, too, if I may."

"I take it you're referring to Irene Frobisher?"

McIvor sipped sparkling water then said, "Yes. I want to express my enormous gratitude to her for getting the material we needed to expose the...oh, my, excuse me if I pronounce it wrong...Severnaya Volna plot."

"I'm pretty sure that's exactly how it's said." He had no idea. Russian sounded like barbaric, nasally nonsense to him.

"My people are preparing a press statement that I'll be reading out live in two hours. A similar statement will be read out by the president of the European Union." She paused to take a steadying breath. "There must be no mistake—accord with Russia or no accord, Estonia remains our ally, a vital member of NATO and the EU, and has been since 2004." She tapped a pencil on the desk in front of her. "Please, Grant. See if you can squeeze one last drop out of Ms. Frobisher. Those train tickets you told me about. If we can get proof they were government ordered or even government adjacent, it will give us enormous leverage over the Kremlin."

"I'll see what I can do...Hannah."

"Excellent. It's time to reveal the extent of the rot in the Russian establishment."

"Good luck," said Fletcher. "Although I know you won't need it."

With only his beloved tropical fish for company, cigar lit and cognac in hand, Fletcher stared at the giant aquarium as he pondered the president's last words. If she ever felt the need to expose the rot in the American establishment, he was sure Irene would have a field day. He sucked on his Montecristo, sending a trio of rings skyward.

He dialed Irene's cell and waited.

THIRTY-SEVEN

SHE WAS TALKING TO FLETCHER, HEARING THE NEWS she didn't want to hear—that *more* had to be done—when she heard the call-waiting beeps. She didn't have to look at the screen to know who it was.

"Yakov's calling me, Grant. Can I—"

"Of course." He disconnected.

She pressed the button to accept the call.

"I made it," he said.

"Like I knew you would."

A weird silence hung in the air for a moment.

"Marfa didn't make it."

The grief in his voice was raw, almost palpable.

"Don't blame yourself, *zaichik*."

"Only one of the four survived, Irochka. It's a fucking disaster."

She ran a hand over her face. How could she make him feel better? Validated?

"You aren't to blame for any of this." She stood and began pacing. "They all knew what they were getting involved in. I know what opposing that regime is like. Nobody takes the stand they took without accepting the possibility of your own death." She sat and twirled a pen on the desk. "And it's not a disaster. You're *preventing* a disaster."

He sighed deeply. She could hear the sound of jet engines winding up for take-off. "I'm sick of feeling like this." Shallow breathing joined the sounds of the aircraft. "I...can you..."

"I know what you're trying to say. Find the order. Get off the phone and let me do what I can, OK? Every second talking with you is a wasted second." She swallowed hard. That sounded like the biggest insult in the world, but it was the exact opposite.

"OK. I need to sleep now. Let's see what shape the world is in when I wake up."

"Better shape, Yakov. Much better."

BALTENERGOTORG'S BEEFED-UP defenses had stymied every effort she made to sneak into its inner sanctum. It was like trying to ram the castle gates with a toothpick.

Time to implement the idea she'd come up with nine hours ago. *Use the man who collected the tickets—Klitschko—to get to Izmailov.* If she was going to be totally honest with herself, her brain had been a whole lot fresher nine hours ago. This was a helluva long shot.

Klitschko stared back at her from the photo Fletcher had sent. Soft brown eyes with barely a hint of intellect behind them. Upturned button nose. Not ugly for an enforcer but not handsome either. The kind of unworldly patsy whose email a class hacker like Irina should be able to get hold of—if he'd left the gate open.

If only it were that simple.

She started with the obvious. Internet searches for the man's name. Google and LinkedIn revealed a piano teacher in Odessa. Photo of a bald retiree in Vladivostok. Not him.

Another younger man with the same name was a YouTube vlogger who lived in Texas. Scratch him.

The number-one Russian social media site, VKontakte, known widely as VK, a lookalike analogue of banned-in-Russia Facebook, had five members called Oleg Klitschko, three with photos obviously not of our guy. Two did have profile pictures, one in deep shadow: a deliberate—and successful—attempt to hide his face. The other was of a man who resembled our Klitschko, but the photo was at least ten years old. Had to be him.

Irina ran the VK photo through Skia face-recognition software, comparing it to the photo from Fletcher.

Positive match.

As her son, Vova, would say, *level one cleared*.

But the game wasn't over until the next locked room in the quest was opened. The email account.

Finding the address turned out to be a simple exercise. The profile's contact section listed one email: klitschko.olezhka@mail-net.ru. Irina shook her head. Most platforms today caution against listing your private email, but this wasn't always the case. VK had shown private information by default until 2018. Either Klitschko was blasé about his email being public, or, equally possible, he barely used the site and wasn't aware of the settings. The fact that a diminutive form of Oleg—Olezhka—appeared in the email likely meant it was primarily used for communicating with family and friends.

Back on our Klitschko's profile page. A trawl through old photos came up with plenty featuring a dark-haired little boy. Gap-toothed in front of a birthday cake; covered in mud, arms across his chest, one cleated boot resting on top of a soccer ball like he'd conquered his own air-filled Mount Everest; riding a bicycle in a park.

Perfect.

Let's look at the archive more thoroughly.

Images on his profile would have had the EXIF data stripped, so she couldn't see metadata indicating when a particular photo was taken. However, like on all social media sites, you *could* see time of upload. Which was extremely useful. All the photos of the little boy on Klitschko's page were at least five years old, as were the comments.

Irina figured the kid would be fifteen or sixteen now. One username kept popping up in the comments, filled with praise for the boy, heart emojis, typical cutesy stuff for a little kid: iggy_009. One long comment from Klitschko made it crystal clear that Iggy —Igor—was his son. Klitschko referred to the boy everywhere as Gosha, a standard diminutive form of Igor. Why did the kid pick Iggy for a handle? Probably because it sounded Western and cool. Gosha was surely the name for Irina to run with.

A click to access Gosha's profile. Posts by a stereotypical Russian teenage male: video games, combat sports and park workouts (lots of action photos of Igor and others his age), edgy rap acts like Morgenshtern and Skryptonite, school stresses.

Irina hated what was coming next, but setting Yakov free from his contract shackles was paramount.

She set up a burner VK account using Klitschko's photo and a username that was one character different from the real one. The kid wouldn't spot the difference in the handle. Irina immediately drafted a feeler to send out via VK Messenger. She reread it four times, each time thinking it was more and more ridiculous.

She drew a breath and sent the message.

Irina: Gosha, it's Papa. I know I haven't been on VK for a long time, but I need your help. I'm in trouble.

Irina sat back, exhaled, fingers interlocked behind her head, and waited. She wasn't hopeful. She checked the time. One hour left in the window before McIvor's press conference.

The boy answered within ten minutes: Long time no hear, old man. What's up?

Irina sighed with relief. She'd been anxious Gosha might ask why papa wasn't simply calling on the phone. She didn't rush her reply. The aim was to portray a halting, tech-illiterate father.

Irina: I need you to send me an email to my old address to test that it works.

Gosha: Why?

Irina: I'm at a branch of Sberbank in the city. They won't let me withdraw my own money unless I can prove the email is mine.

Gosha: Of course it's yours. What a bunch of dicks.

Irina: I know it and you know it.

An idea came to her that might spur the boy along.

Irina: I need the money to buy you a ticket to the MMA tournament in Moscow.

Gosha: You're kidding? The All-Stars Series next month at Luzhniki stadium?

Irina: Yes. We'll stay in the best hotel. But no money, no trip.

Gosha: Wouldn't you pay for all that stuff online?

Not an unexpected question.

Irina: I'm getting a cheap deal from a friend with connections. I pay him in cash, he takes a small cut and organizes it all on the Internet. You know I'm hopeless at that stuff.

Gosha: You got that right. What's this email address of yours?

Irina: klitschko.olezhka@mailnet.ru

Gosha: OK, I sent you a blank message, subject line 'test.'

Irina waited a minute, then: Thanks for sending the email, but I can't see it.

Gosha: Why not?

Irina: Because papa's a stupid idiot. I set up this bank account years ago, gave them an email address I don't use anymore. Which means I can't remember my password.

Gosha: Try hard to remember it, Papa. That tournament is the best!

She took a breath, waited a moment.

Irina: I'm drawing a total blank, son.

Gosha: It's got to be something simple. You're not the smartest man around...lol

Irina: Like my own birthday?

Gosha: Maybe. Or mine. Or mama's. I know she hates your guts now, but you two used to be in love. It was sickening sometimes [vomiting emoji].

This was bad. He couldn't possibly ask the kid for any of

those dates. Klitschko might be a simple-minded goon, but he would at least remember the birthdays of his ex and his son. A long shot.

Irina: Listen son, could you type them all out for me in the right format, and I can just kinda paste them in? The woman in the bank is starting to give me dirty looks.

Gosha: *Blin.* Damn, you are a numbskull. Here you go. You, mama, me = 07051987, 13121989, 21012009

Irina: *Molodets.* Attaboy. Give me a minute while I try them.

If these failed, she'd have to try and brute-force her way in, but the interface would lock her out after a certain number of unsuccessful attempts. She guessed that number would be small, probably no more than ten.

She stared at the open browser. The home page of mailnet.ru.

Klitschko's email address was already waiting patiently in the box, waiting for the perfect pairing with the password. The provider was one of the first to exist in Russia, offering a clunky, old-fashioned interface. Even so, it insisted on a minimum password comprising eight characters, including at least one capital letter and one symbol.

Irina opened a text document and copied across the dates Gosha had provided. She applied what her gut told her would be the most common pattern: add an initial capital of the name of the account owner and append a simple symbol—first !, then 1, then @, then #—since these were statistically the most popular non-letter additions.

Klitschko's name started with K, so she built a small matrix: K + date + symbol. That gave her a predictable, tidy list. She ordered them by what an unsophisticated user would have most likely chosen: first his own birthday, then his kid's, then the ex's, rotating through the common symbols.

The ten attempts formed themselves: K07051987!, K07051987@, K21012009!, K21012009@, K07051987#, K21012009#, K13121989!, K131219891, K13121989@, and K13121989#.

She copied them one by one into the login box, heart thumping. Each click of the mouse was met with predictable rejection. Until the ninth—K13121989@. Of course, the ex-wife! Gosha had said Klitschko used to be madly in love with the woman.

Oleg Klitschko's mailbox opened up obediently as Irina imagined the "Hallelujah Chorus" from Handel's Messiah playing in her mind.

What a mess. It looked to be about eighty percent spam, intermingled with a broad range of real content.

A search for BaltEnergoTorg brought up a dozen exchanges between Klitschko and Marat Izmailov. The second-most recent message made her heart gallop. Subject line: *Urgent pickup.* Text: *Oleg. Get your ass down to Finland Station and pick up two train tickets (goszakaz attached). Print it off and take it with you, just in case their computers aren't working properly. Deliver the tickets to the office of Colonel-General Denis Kolodin immediately. He needs to get them to our man traveling to Tallinn so he can bring back the Estonian after they mess with their border surveillance. Do not fuck up. Marat.*

Irina hovered over the attached PDF, right-clicked and downloaded it. Before even checking the contents, she forwarded the email to Fletcher, Jacob, and herself, saved the attachment locally, and uploaded it to the Skia cloud.

She called Fletcher. "Check your inbox. I'm literally shaking. I found the order for the train tickets."

"No way!"

"Yes. I'm done, Grant. Seriously done."

"Thank you, Irene. The president will be over the moon."

She wanted to say "whatever"; instead, she said, "I'm very glad."

A quick glance back at the VK page she still had open. Poor Gosha was getting antsy. Five unanswered lines. The last one was a row of pissed-off exclamation marks.

Irina: Sorry I took so long. I got the password right. Money's in my hand.

Gosha: You did? Wow. I can't wait to go to Moscow.

Irina: Gotta go. Chat soon.

She clicked the x in the corner of the tab, VK disappearing into the void like a light being switched off.

Ice gripped her stomach. Deceiving the innocent boy felt like the most evil thing she had ever done.

She wanted to crawl into bed more than anything. But not before satisfying her curiosity, which for Irina was almost as powerful an urge as hunger, thirst, breathing and sex.

She held her breath as she read the PDF.

State Order

Ministry of Defence of the Russian Federation

Department of Regional Operations

Order No. 47/11-RO

Date: 9 November

Subject: Procurement of Rail Travel Tickets

Pursuant to operational requirements authorized under Regional Operations Directive 148-Д, the Department of Regional Operations hereby instructs the procurement of the following:

– Two (2) passenger rail tickets

– Route: Ivangorod → Saint Petersburg

– Date of travel: 11 November

– Standard class or nearest available equivalent

This order is issued under the authority of Colonel-General Denis Kolodin, Ministry of Defence (Regional Operations). All participating offices and transport personnel are to facilitate immediate fulfillment without delay.

Payment for the above is to be rendered in cash and delivered directly into the hands of the bearer of this order.

Signature:

Colonel-General Denis Kolodin

Ministry of Defence, Regional Operations Division

THIRTY-EIGHT

Fletcher decided not to watch the press conference at home. He wanted noise, people, the pulse of a crowd, so he headed to The Chalkboard on Leonard Street—a sports-themed bar that had become a Tribeca favorite in all kinds of weather. He'd been twice in the last month to watch his Jets get blown out, and he didn't care; the beer was cold, the food excellent, and the atmosphere a welcome distraction.

With no warning, every big screen cut to black. The games vanished mid-play as if someone had yanked a power cord. A wave of boos rolled across the room, tapering only when several patrons called for silence. President Hannah McIvor appeared, her expression grave. Blond hair pulled into a tight bun, makeup minimal, she cleared her throat.

The bar fell still.

"My fellow Americans. Our security agencies have uncovered a plot by rogue elements within Russia to invade Estonia—tomorrow morning—and topple its democratically elected government."

Fletcher watched the crowd as much as he listened to the speech. A few cursed Russia outright—Putin was called a dog, a devil, an asshole. Others muttered darkly about false flags and government theatrics. The room vibrated with tension.

McIvor took a sip of water. "Thanks to the selfless efforts of our special agents overseas, the operation, code-named Severnaya Volna, or Northern Wave, has been crushed."

Cheers burst from every corner. Fletcher felt one rising in his own throat and barely suppressed it.

"I want to be clear," she continued, "that this plot was orchestrated by three high-level individuals: Colonel-General Denis Kolodin, Sergei Semak, the Deputy Governor of the Leningrad Region, and oligarch Marat Izmailov."

As each name was spoken, a face flashed across the screen.

"The fact that these men hold positions of power and influence is deeply troubling. I have spoken with President Putin"—boos, plus a scattering of ironic applause—"and he has assured me that all three will be taken into custody and put on trial."

She pressed on. "As I speak, the President of the European Union is addressing his citizens, confirming that the situation is under control and that the Estonian border—long a bulwark against Russian aggression—is secure. I've also spoken with Estonian President Karilaid, who has serious doubts about the future of the recent accord with Russia. He believes it may be irretrievable unless the Kremlin provides concrete assurances."

McIvor lifted a sheet of paper.

"This document is incontrovertible proof that an agent was sent to Tallinn with instructions to sabotage Estonia's border-security systems. The train tickets were purchased through the Ministry of Defense's regional office in Saint Petersburg. Additional evidence—including emails, video recordings, and internal correspondence—has also been recovered."

She let the silence sit before continuing.

"The conspirators may have assumed that NATO would sit by and watch Estonia fall. Make no mistake: NATO and the United States would have responded. Too many people have already died in the pursuit of this madness. I call on President Putin to do everything necessary to set this right."

She nodded once. "Thank you, and good night."

For a moment, the bar held its breath, then applause and cheers broke out again. Within a minute, the screens flicked back to sports, conversations resumed, and the whole room seemed to exhale.

Fletcher pulled on his hat and stepped into the freezing wind screaming off the Hudson. He paused, breath searing in the cold, and shook his head.

World War III had been avoided because Jacob and Irina had refused to blink.

THIRTY-NINE

Marat Izmailov needed only three minutes of the European president's press conference to understand that the game was over. With this much international attention focused on the plot, staying in Russia to face what came next was not an option.

He packed fast and without sentiment. One suitcase lay open on the bed of his luxury penthouse, filled with only the essentials: three changes of clothes, a toiletry bag, and his laptop. Anything else could be replaced. He slipped two thick envelopes of US dollars into an inside pocket of the suitcase and another into his carry-on. He had wiped his phone as thoroughly as he knew how and could only hope it would be enough. Before closing the bag, he patted his jacket three times to reassure himself the passport was still there.

God bless the UAE. One of the few places left where a Russian could arrive without arranging a visa in advance, where money still opened doors and extradition could take its time. A friend in Abu Dhabi had already agreed to put him up. After that, he would improvise.

A soft knock came on the front door.

Three evenly spaced taps.

Izmailov stopped moving. No one reached this floor without passing a security desk and a private elevator. Only people with the right authority—or the wrong kind—could be standing on the other side.

He slid open the bedside drawer and took hold of the Makarov. The pistol was pristine, unfired. He stared at it for a moment, then gave a quiet, humorless shake of his head. It would never be used. The FSB did not lose gunfights.

"Marat Ibragimovich Izmailov," a calm voice called through the door. He almost wished it were shouting instead. "Federal Security Service. Open the door."

He should never have pushed Ivan Beglov as far as he had.

Now look at the mess you've made.

He tossed the pistol under the bed.

The knock came again, firmer this time. "Don't make us break the door down."

Izmailov smoothed his hair, drew in a steadying breath, and walked to the door. He opened it.

Three men entered without ceremony. One wore a gray suit. The other two were black-clad and helmeted, faces unreadable. The man in the suit produced a warrant.

"You are under arrest for participation in an attempted conspiracy against the security of the Russian Federation."

"There must be some kind of misunderstanding." Izmailov exhaled, the breath trembling despite his effort to control it. "I was packing for a business trip."

"No misunderstanding," the man replied evenly. "No business trip."

Hands closed around Izmailov's arms—not roughly but with a certainty that made his legs feel hollow. Behind him, one of the helmeted men zipped the suitcase shut. Everything inside would become evidence. The apartment would be stripped, then his office. There would be nothing left untouched.

Semak had insisted they could deny their way through it. But there was too much proof now. Denials would amount to nothing more than noise.

As they marched him toward the elevator, Izmailov looked back at the apartment a lifetime of careful ambition had built and understood with sudden clarity that he would never see it again.

COLONEL-GENERAL DENIS KOLODIN was in good spirits. Severnaya Volna was on track, and dawn would see the beginning of a fabulous new era. He had just said goodnight to Anna and settled into his favorite armchair with a mug of cocoa and a dog-eared book on Estonian history when the front door exploded inward. The handle punched a neat hole in the drywall as three men surged into the apartment. Two wore Alpha Group black, helmets on, AK-105s already shouldered and steady.

Kolodin lurched to his feet. The blanket slid from his lap and pooled uselessly around his ankles.

"What in God's name is the meaning of this?" he thundered. Age had thinned him, but it had not softened his voice. Decades of command still lived in it.

The man in the gray suit stepped forward. "Denis Petrovich Kolodin, you are under arrest for treason—"

"Treason?" Kolodin bellowed, fists cutting the air. "You and whichever idiot ordered this will rot in Siberia. You wouldn't recognize treason if it bit you on the ass."

No one reacted. One operator moved past him and pulled the living room blinds closed. Another calmly lifted Kolodin's laptop from the desk and tucked it under his arm. Kolodin actually smiled. Solitaire was the only thing he used the damned machine for. If they were looking for secrets, they would need to dig deeper.

Kolodin straightened to his full height. His broad shoulders had not narrowed with age; even stooped, he filled the room. His face had gone red with fury, the veins at his temples standing out.

"You think you can talk to me like this?" he snapped. "You think you're better than me?"

"We're not here to debate," the officer said.

Kolodin jabbed a finger at him. "I've fought in countries whose names you couldn't pronounce." His voice cracked despite himself. "And now you drag me out like a common criminal—"

The officer nodded once.

A fist drove into Kolodin's stomach, folding him in half. The breath rushed out of him in a wet wheeze. He straightened slowly, saliva stringing from his lips, and fixed the men with a murderous stare.

"Keep your mouth shut," one of them said quietly, "or the next one's in the kidneys."

The third man stepped forward with cuffs. Kolodin slapped his hand away. The blow to his lower back came instantly. He screamed.

Anna appeared in the doorway, wrapped in a fluffy pink robe, her lined face already streaked with tears.

"What's happening?" she cried. "You can't do this to my husband!"

"Anna Mikhailovna," the lead officer said evenly, "your husband is a traitor to the Russian Federation."

Kolodin's head snapped up. "How the hell do you know my wife's patronymic?"

The officer smiled thinly. "You'd be surprised what we know. And I imagine we're about to learn quite a bit more."

They hauled him toward the door. Kolodin met Anna's eyes and forced his face into reassurance, trying to tell her it was all a mistake, that everything would be fine.

Her look back at him said: *fuck you*.

Deputy Governor Sergei Semak was exactly where the FSB expected to find him: a private room in a discreet but infamous brothel off Vladimirskiy Prospekt, buried under satin sheets with two women young enough to be his daughters.

The door blew inward before anyone had time to react.

Alpha Group commandos flooded the room, boots thudding, rifles up, voices barking clipped commands. They showed no interest in modesty or mercy, kicking aside discarded clothes, stepping over champagne bottles and glasses of half-drunk vodka, sweeping underwear from the floor with the casual flick of a rifle barrel.

Semak jerked upright, yanking the sheet to his chest. His eyes darted wildly as the women shrieked and bolted for the bathroom, naked bodies colliding in their panic, breasts bouncing.

"What the hell do you think you're doing?" he roared. "I'm the deputy governor of the Leningrad Oblast!"

A thickset operator seized him by a fistful of gray hair and dragged him out of the bed. Semak yelped like a whipped dog.

"I don't give a fuck who you are," the man said evenly. "Orders are orders."

Two others hauled Semak across the carpet, naked and scrambling, his protests tumbling over one another. Every name he dropped was met with silence. When he invoked President Putin, someone laughed.

They forced him face-down, a knee grinding into his spine, arms wrenched behind his back. Metal cuffs snapped shut. His cheek scraped against the carpet, skin burning.

"Cuffs off," the team leader said.

Semak turned his head, breath ragged. "You understand you've made a terrible mistake."

"Get dressed," the officer replied. "Pig."

Hands shaking uncontrollably, Semak fumbled into his clothes. The cuffs went back on the moment he finished.

As they dragged him through the brothel's dim corridors, lights blinked off one by one. Semak managed a thin, ironic smile. The patrons and girls must think it was a vice raid, scrambling to hide. Fools.

"You'll all be looking for new jobs tomorrow," he said hoarsely.

The officer behind him leaned in and twisted his ear until white-hot pain exploded through his head. Semak screamed.

"Keep talking," the man said softly, "and you'll be looking for your teeth on the floor."

Semak shut his mouth and focused on breathing.

He would deny everything. Lawyer up.

Yes.

That would have to be enough.

MAJOR ROBIN SAAR woke with a jolt, forehead plastered to the desk where he'd dozed off. A thin line of drool ran between his cheek and a folder. His uniform jacket hung stiffly over the back of the chair, untouched since midnight. He rubbed his eyes, muttering under his breath, and shuffled toward the coffee machine, desperate for anything to keep him upright before the next phase.

The cell phone on the desk buzzed, spinning slightly across the surface.

Andrejev.

Saar's stomach tightened.

He picked it up. "Sir?"

"Major..." Andrejev's voice was constricted. "Listen carefully. Delete the diagnostics script from the system. Every line. Then call in someone to take your place—anyone—and go home."

Saar straightened, incredulous. "Sir? Has the timeline changed?"

"Forget about timelines," Andrejev said, clipped and urgent. "Forget about everything. There was a speech tonight. The EU president exposed the plan to the whole world. The American president, too. Party's over. This ends now."

Saar's throat went dry. "You can't be serious."

"As serious as a heart attack," Andrejev replied quietly. "Names were named. Severnaya Volna has been blown wide open. They'll all be arrested."

"What about us?" Saar whispered.

Andrejev gave a humorless laugh. "I don't know. They might spill everything under interrogation. Prepare for the worst."

Silence stretched for a moment.

"Sir," Saar said finally, "what should I do?"

"Weren't you listening before? Go home, I said. Hold your wife. Pretend you never got involved. If you're lucky, you'll be overlooked."

Saar's chest tightened. The defeatism in the colonel's voice hit him harder than anything else could. Nothing ever rattled Andrejev. And yet—there was something in the tone that made Saar shiver. He imagined the colonel shoving a gun in his mouth.

"Colonel—please, don't do anything rash," he said.

A long exhale. "Goodbye, Major."

The line clicked dead.

Saar froze for a moment, staring at the screen. Then his fingers moved, deleting the script that had been meant to open the door to a new era. When he was sure everything had been erased, he called in another officer, told him he wasn't feeling well and needed relief. He shrugged his jacket back on, paced the office, and waited for the change of guard.

When the new officer arrived, Saar handed over the station and slipped out, the night air biting as he walked to his car.

He wanted only one thing now: to get home, crawl into bed next to Nora, and tell her he loved her and that everything would be all right.

FORTY

Jacob swirled the pint of beer, staring at the amber liquid he'd barely touched in twenty minutes. Flat, lifeless, uninspired. Pretty much how he felt. Fletcher, sitting opposite in the booth, had the flushed look of a man edging toward the upper limit of his drinking capacity.

The boss had drifted into a fatuous conversation with a passing fan in a Jets jersey. Irina took the opportunity to lean in and whisper, "You OK, *zaichik*?" She squeezed his hand beneath the table. "We can go home if you like. No point sticking around if your heart's not in it."

He blew out his cheeks, lifted the glass, and took a long sip. The taste disgusted him, but he tipped it back and finished it anyway. "I'm fine," he said. He nodded at her empty glass. "Looks like you could use a refill."

She started to protest, but he pulled his hand free and threaded his way toward the crowded bar. He bought another round and returned to the booth, Fletcher having wrapped up his conversation and now babbling to Irina about something or other.

Jacob set the three beers down, slid them across the table, and dropped into his seat. He caught himself slouching—shoulders rounded, spine at an insolent angle, legs jammed under the table like a sulky teenager—and forced himself upright.

"Jacob," Fletcher said. "I still can't get over the color of your eyes. I was so used to the baby blues. Honestly, the whole procedure's changed you more than I ever imagined possible."

Jacob reached up and rubbed the back of his head. "Couple more months of this monk's circle before it starts growing back."

"Lucky you're not a vain man, then," Fletcher said, friendly sarcasm dripping from every word.

"I'd love him no matter what he looked like," Irina said.

Ignoring the compliment, Jacob said, "Did you know they gave me fake fingerprints?"

"What?" Irina said, reaching for her drink. "You're kidding."

"Dead serious. Technically, they're biopolymer fingerprint overlays with artificial ridges. Bonded to my skin." He held up his hands, fingers spread.

Fletcher shook his head in disbelief. "I never asked about the details of your treatment. Sounds like they were thorough."

"They didn't miss much," Jacob said with a short laugh. "I could burgle half of Manhattan, and they'd never pin it on me if they had to rely on dabs."

Irina studied him. "Your real prints aren't on any database, are they?"

"Are you serious?" He gave her a sideways look. "The Russians have them. Plenty of other countries, too."

She sighed. "I meant here. In America."

"Yeah," Fletcher slurred. "We go to great lengths to make sure no agency in this country has your biometric data." He raised his glass. "So in theory, you can burgle to your heart's content, Hunter. And with the new face, I guarantee you'll never get caught." He burst out laughing.

Jacob took a sip of his beer. Zero alcohol this time. He'd ordered the same for all three.

Fletcher's expression shifted. "All jokes aside, Hunter, I've booked you in for a full mental health assessment."

Jacob dipped his head slightly. "Thank you." He felt Irina's fingers tighten around his. He looked up and gave them both a thin half-smile. "Once upon a time, even mentioning that would've made my blood boil. Not anymore."

After this last mission—nearly all his associates dead, by their own hand or someone else's—his brain felt fried. So did his soul. He could admit that to himself now, if not out loud. PTSD.

"I came within a whisker of being killed a couple of times," he said quietly. "Why I was spared and the others weren't, I'll never know. One thing I do know—I'm glad to be alive."

Irina stroked his fingers. "We're glad too. Every day's a gift now. For all of us."

Jacob shifted the conversation. "I still can't believe they're reducing Kolodin's charges."

Fletcher tilted his head. "I'm hearing whispers out of Moscow station he might walk altogether. Apparently ratting out the Estonian traitors helped his cause."

Jacob nodded. "That and his age. The man's over eighty. Can you believe an old fart like that thinking he's General Kutuzov?"

"Who the hell's that?" Fletcher said, scooping up a handful of peanuts.

Irina frowned. "Only the great man who defeated Napoleon."

Fletcher sniffed. "Oh. That Kutuzov."

They laughed. Jacob shook his head. "Before your time, Fletch?"

"Something like that." He drained more beer. "At least Izmailov and Semak won't wiggle out. Rumor is they're both headed for life inside the Arctic Circle."

"I doubt we'll see any more harebrained stunts like that while Putin's still in power," Jacob said.

Fletcher grinned. "You mean not for the next fifty years?"

"At the very least," Irina said, laughing loudly.

Ten minutes later, Jacob and Irina leaned into a cutting wind, making their slow way back to his apartment on Duane Street. It was too cold for conversation; mouths didn't work properly in weather like that. They walked in silence. Jacob's thoughts circled one thing only—President McIvor's refusal to release him from Article 7 of his contract.

At their two-hour meeting the day before, in her plush Inter-Continental suite, he'd wanted to scream, throw things, break things. Somehow, he'd kept it together.

He'd listened and nodded as she explained: *We need you, Mr. Hunter. No one else can do what you do. The country needs you. The world needs you.* She signed off on a substantial pay increase—for him and for Irina—and promised they'd only be called in for extreme circumstances. No more brushfire nonsense the CIA or NSA could handle themselves.

He pressed the elevator button. While they waited, he pulled Irina into a tight, silent embrace.

Inside the apartment, they made love fast and hard. Irina fell asleep within five minutes of finishing. Jacob took a freezing shower, sobbing quietly, muffling the sounds. Then he ran an ice-cold bath and sat in it until he couldn't feel anything at all.

In the kitchen, he drank cold water, loaded the glass into the dishwasher, and turned toward the bedroom. He stood beside the bed for a long moment, flipping the Skia psychiatrist's business card between his fingers. The appointment was tomorrow at noon.

He couldn't wait.

DON'T MISS ANYTHING!

If you want to stay up to date on all new releases in this series, with this author, or with any of our new deals, you can do so by joining our newsletters below.

In addition, you will immediately gain access to our entire *Right House VIP Library,* which includes many riveting Mystery and Thriller novels for your enjoyment. Including a prequel novella to this series!

righthouse.com/email

(Easy to unsubscribe. No spam. Ever.)

ALSO BY DAVID ARCHER

Up to date books can be found at:
www.righthouse.com/david-archer

ROGUE THRILLERS
Gates of Hell (Book 1)
Hell's Fury (Book 2)
Ice Burn (Book 3)
Judgement by Fire (Book 4)

JACOB HUNTER THRILLERS
The Kyiv File (Book 1)
The Bogota File (Book 2)
The Havana File (Book 3)
The Amsterdam File (Book 4)
The Saint Petersburg File (Book 5)

PETER BLACK THRILLERS
Burden of the Assassin (Book 1)
The Man Without A Face (Book 2)
Unpunished Deeds (Book 3)
Hunter Killer (Book 4)
Silent Shadows (Book 5)
The Last Run (Book 6)
Dark Corners (Book 7)
Ghost Operative (Book 8)
A Fire Burning (Book 9)
Dawnlight (Book 10)
Dead Ice (Book 11)
No Loose Ends (Book 12)

ALEX MASON THRILLERS

Odin (Book 1)
Ice Cold Spy (Book 2)
Mason's Law (Book 3)
Assets and Liabilities (Book 4)
Russian Roulette (Book 5)
Executive Order (Book 6)
Dead Man Talking (Book 7)
All The King's Men (Book 8)
Flashpoint (Book 9)
Brotherhood of the Goat (Book 10)
Dead Hot (Book 11)
Blood on Megiddo (Book 12)
Son of Hell (Book 13)
Merchant of Death (Book 14)
Extinction C-14 (Book 15)
A Vengeful God (Book 16)

NOAH WOLF THRILLERS

Code Name Camelot (Book 1)
Lone Wolf (Book 2)
In Sheep's Clothing (Book 3)
Hit for Hire (Book 4)
The Wolf's Bite (Book 5)
Black Sheep (Book 6)
Balance of Power (Book 7)
Time to Hunt (Book 8)
Red Square (Book 9)
Highest Order (Book 10)
Edge of Anarchy (Book 11)
Unknown Evil (Book 12)
Black Harvest (Book 13)
World Order (Book 14)
Caged Animal (Book 15)
Deep Allegiance (Book 16)

Pack Leader (Book 17)
High Treason (Book 18)
A Wolf Among Men (Book 19)
Rogue Intelligence (Book 20)
Alpha (Book 21)
Rogue Wolf (Book 22)
Shadows of Allegiance (Book 23)
In the Grip of Darkness (Book 24)
Wolves in the Dark (Book 25)
Olympus Must Fall (Book 26)
Children of the Empire (Book 27)
Wolf at the Gates (Book 28)

SAM PRICHARD MYSTERIES

The Grave Man (Book 1)
Death Sung Softly (Book 2)
Love and War (Book 3)
Framed (Book 4)
The Kill List (Book 5)
Drifter: Part One (Book 6)
Drifter: Part Two (Book 7)
Drifter: Part Three (Book 8)
The Last Song (Book 9)
Ghost (Book 10)
Hidden Agenda (Book 11)

SAM AND INDIE MYSTERIES

Aces and Eights (Book 1)
Fact or Fiction (Book 2)
Close to Home (Book 3)
Brave New World (Book 4)
Innocent Conspiracy (Book 5)
Unfinished Business (Book 6)
Live Bait (Book 7)
Alter Ego (Book 8)

More Than It Seems (Book 9)
Moving On (Book 10)
Worst Nightmare (Book 11)
Chasing Ghosts (Book 12)
Serial Superstition (Book 13)

CHANCE REDDICK THRILLERS
Innocent Injustice (Book 1)
Angel of Justice (Book 2)
High Stakes Hunting (Book 3)
Personal Asset (Book 4)

CASSIE MCGRAW MYSTERIES
What Lies Beneath (Book 1)
Can't Fight Fate (Book 2)
One Last Game (Book 3)
Never Really Gone (Book 4)

ABOUT US

Right House is an independent publisher created by authors for readers. We specialize in Action, Thriller, Mystery, and Crime novels.

If you enjoyed this novel, then there is a good chance you will like what else we have to offer! Please stay up to date by using any of the links below.

Join our mailing lists to stay up to date --> righthouse.com/email
Visit our website --> righthouse.com
Contact us --> contact@righthouse.com

facebook.com/righthousebooks
x.com/righthousebooks
instagram.com/righthousebooks

www.ingramcontent.com/pod-product-compliance
Lightning Source LLC
LaVergne TN
LVHW091111080826
845145LV00008B/1874

* 9 7 8 1 6 3 6 9 6 4 7 1 3 *